Saint Maggie

Saint Maggie

By

Janet R. Stafford

ISBN 978-0-615-45204-3

For Dan, Kristina, and Diane

1 Corinthians 13: 1-8a, 13

Though I speak with the tongues of men and of angels, and have not charity, I am become as sounding brass, or a tinkling cymbal.

And though I have the gift of prophecy, and understand all mysteries, and all knowledge; and though I have all faith, so that I could remove mountains, and have not charity, I am nothing.

And though I bestow all my goods to feed the poor, and though I give my body to be burned, and have not charity, it profiteth me nothing.

Charity suffereth long, and is kind; charity envieth not; charity vaunteth not itself, is not puffed up, doth not behave itself unseemly, seeketh not her own, is not easily provoked, thinketh no evil; rejoiceth not in iniquity, but rejoiceth in the truth; beareth all things, believeth all things, hopeth all things, endureth all things.

Charity never faileth . . .

And now abideth faith, hope, charity, these three; but the greatest of these is charity.

CHAPTER ONE

From Maggie's Journal, 16 April 1861

The changes that have occurred over the past year for my country and my family have been great. In the spring of 1860, I would not have been able, nor would have dared, to imagine that which has transpired.

I was so delighted when the Presiding Elder came to me and asked if my boarding house could find a room for the new minister. At last, I thought, perhaps the people of Blaineton will afford me and my establishment some respect. This past year has taught me some hard lessons, indeed.

****

It was a blue-skied, warm day on the 13th of April. Maggie would have liked to have had her house composed and organized. But she had been given a scant four days to prepare for their new boarder, and Grandpa O'Reilly had caught a cold and someone needed to care for him. Maggie had given this job to her eldest daughter, Lydia, so now she lacked an extra pair of hands. The eighteen-year old had just returned to the kitchen to report that Grandpa was feeling much better and that she was going to make a pot of tea for her patient.

In the confines of the kitchen, Lydia, Maggie, and Emily the cook danced deftly around one another: Lydia pouring steaming water into a teapot, Emily energetically mixing a bowl of butter, powdered sugar, and milk, Maggie mixing biscuits. The rhythm of their work was interrupted by a loud clomping on the stairs. The women braced themselves as Frankie, Maggie's youngest daughter burst into the kitchen, declaring, "I hate corsets and crinolines!"

Lydia calmly set the teapot on a tray. She turned, smiled indulgently and tugged the material around the fourteen-year-old's waist so that her dress hung straight. "Don't be such a silly goose," she gently scolded, tucking wisps of unruly red hair behind her sister's ear.

"You're fourteen. You're not a little girl anymore. This is what women wear. Besides, you want to look good for Mr. Madison, don't you?"

Frankie sniffed with no small amount of disdain.

Maggie looked up from kneading. "And, Frankie, what you want at this time is of no real importance. Mr. Madison is our new minister. He deserves our respect."

But Frankie continued to pout. "I don't know why he has to stay here. No one seems to like our place, anyway."

Maggie had to remind herself that her daughter was not yet an adult. She took a deep breath and prayed for patience. "What others think of us also is of no real importance." How she wished that were true! "We live as we do because it is right. Our boarders have nowhere else to go and have become our friends. I believe everyone is deserving of respect. As for Mr. Madison, the other rooming houses are full, so he too has nowhere else to go. I for one am pleased that our Presiding Elder has confidence that we will provide Mr. Madison with a pleasant and comfortable chamber."

Emily Johnson stopped mixing the icing and turned to fetch the molasses cake. "I just wish they'd given us more time. We only finished getting the room ready yesterday. I scrubbed myself last night 'til I was raw. Nate says I still have paint in my hair!"

Maggie laughed. "He was teasing you. Your hair is clean as usual."

"Mm, hm. And just as nappy."

"We are as God made us," Frankie said, doing her best imitation of her mother.

Maggie ignored her daughter and opened a cupboard to retrieve her best china plates. "I know we were asked at the last moment, Emily. But surely the African Methodist Episcopal Church does much the same thing." She passed the stack of plates to Frankie, who frowned, grunted, and galumphed out of the kitchen to set the dining table. "The Newark Annual Conference meets, new appointments are announced, and the ministers move. It all happens within the space of a few days."

"My church does the same," Emily responded. "But I still believe that it works only if you like surprises every couple of years. And I still don't know why they asked us to board your new minister. I'm sure your brother would've been only too happy to give Mr. Madison a room. His place is certainly big enough."

"And I'm sure Samuel would have liked that." Maggie felt the back of her neck tense up at the mention of her brother's name. "But he's a prominent member of the congregation. Perhaps the Presiding Elder is afraid that living in such close quarters would subject a minister to undue pressure and influence. Our little rooming house is neither powerful nor prominent. Thus," she added, with a wry smile, "all we have to give is a clean room and good food."

Frankie, who had returned to the kitchen, awkwardly arranged her hoops and plopped down on a chair. "Besides, we can use the money."

"Frankie!" the other women chorused.

She gave them a defiant look. "Well, we *could*."

Maggie could feel the exasperation rising again. "Yes, well, it isn't proper to talk about such things."

"Why not? It's the truth."

In their hearts both women knew that Frankie was right. She was completely improper, but right.

Frankie poked a finger into Emily's bowl of white frosting. "What do you think Mr. Madison will make of the boarders?"

Emily promptly slapped her on the wrist. "He's a minister. He's probably seen it all."

"Yes," Frankie said, licking her finger, "but has he lived with it?"

Once again, the girl was right. While Maggie ran what she considered to be a proper rooming house, it did have an eccentric collection of boarders. She knew all too well what people said about her. She took in strays. She opened her doors a bit too freely than was proper. She flew in the face of convention.

Maggie took a deep breath. "If I can see that each person is a child of God, then surely a minister can. I cannot turn someone away just because they aren't of my class or color."

"Mm," Emily commented thoughtfully, "I hope he can see past class and color."

The boarding house on Second Street was large. Located on Blaineton Square, it had originally been a two-story home built on the standard plan during the federal era – front and back parlor, kitchen and dining room separated by a hallway and stairs. The second floor accommodated four bedrooms. But somewhere in the 1840s, an expansion had been built to allow for six more bedrooms, obviously for children and servants. The newer wing was accessible through a door in the kitchen. Maggie and her girls had occupied the two large downstairs rooms. Emily and her husband Nate were ensconced on the second floor. Maggie provided Emily with free room and board, as well as with a small salary for doing the cooking and helping with other housekeeping chores. Nate ran a carpenter shop in the small community of black residents located on Water Street, but lent a hand when things needed to be repaired. At Maggie's insistence, Nate and Emily had two of the upstairs rooms, one for sleeping and one for sitting. This housing arrangement was convenient to all, and over the years the Johnson and Blaine families had become close friends.

"When the town finds out the girls have moved upstairs near our room, tongues will be wagging," Emily warned. "You know how people are."

"But where else should I put them?" Maggie countered. "I cannot fit the both of them in my room. And their old room in the front is pleasant and quiet – perfect for a clergyman. The move is practical. I don't care what the town thinks. And if our new pastor doesn't like you and Nate, well, then he can just leave." Personal experience had taught Maggie some hard lessons, the primary one being that people could be amazingly cruel to one another. Clergyman or not, the minister was sure to come with his own set of prejudices, and she was ready. "At any rate, I won't stand for bigotry. Not in my house."

Lydia chuckled, "Oh, now, that would certainly make us the talk of the town if Mr. Madison left our rooming house. We would then have to leave the *church*!"

"Good!" Frankie chirped. "Church is dull."

Maggie stared her younger girl down. "Dull or not, it's good for you."

"Just like medicine," she muttered. "Mama, why does medicine have to taste bad to do good? I should like to have a more lively religion. We could go to Emily and Nate's church!"

"And that would start the town talking, too!" Emily chuckled.

Frankie's hazel eyes widened. "Or we could just *not go*, like Mr. Smith!"

On cue, the door to the back porch creaked opened. As if he knew that he was about to become the next topic of conversation, Elijah Smith, owner and editor of the Blaineton *Gazette* ambled in.

"Mr. Smith!" Frankie cried. "Tell Mama that it's not necessary to go to church."

He laughed, brown eyes sparkling behind his wire-rim glasses. "No, thank you! Your mother and I have had plenty of spirited discussions about *that* already."

Maggie flashed a smile at Eli. His suit was rumpled, but he had made the attempt to dress for dinner and that pleased her. He had even taken the time to shave. Unlike many men, he bucked fashion and sported neither beard nor mustache.

Frankie got to her feet and examined his face. "You cut yourself," she commented, with a critical frown. "On the chin."

"Let's see *you* try shaving with a straight razor, my dear," he retorted.

"Besides which, you're being rude again, Frankie." Maggie turned to Eli. "You look quite nice, Mr. Smith."

He grinned and stuffed his hands into his pockets. "Yes, well, just wanted to get ready for the new minister."

Frankie rolled her eyes. "Argh! That's all we ever talk about!"

"Yes, and you'd just better remember your manners when he gets here," Emily warned.

The girl whirled about. "Of course, I will! I'm not a child." Once again, she moved to dip a finger into the bowl of frosting.

Quick as lightning, Emily's hand shot out and gave the girl another smack on the wrist. "If you want this cake, girl, then you'll keep your fingers out of my icing."

Eli chuckled. He was used to the family's feeble attempts to rein in Frankie's ill-mannered exuberance. He took a hearty – and appreciative – sniff of the kitchen's many aromas. "Mm. Is that beef stew?"

"Mm, hm," Emily replied.

"You, Mrs. Johnson, are a genius in the kitchen."

She smiled. "Thank you. But this is Maggie's doing. She made that stew."

"Well, then, I really *am* looking forward to the meal."

Maggie felt her cheeks flush.

Eli cleared his throat, and somewhat clumsily added, "You know, *you* look rather nice, too. In fact, you look most – becoming in green."

Maggie could almost feel the knowing smile spreading across Emily's face. Everyone seemed to know what was going on – she and Eli had been behaving as if they were moonstruck for too many months. And yet neither had addressed the issue with the other.

Maggie worked hard to sound casual. "By the way, thank you for offering to fetch the new minister at the station."

"Oh, it is nothing. My pleasure."

Lydia and Frankie watched the exchange with complete amusement, while Maggie desperately wished she could turn a color other than pink. It was all so unbecoming. A woman of nine and thirty should have better control of herself. The trouble was her composure of late had completely disappeared.

"Still," she managed to say, "you didn't have to rent the horse and carriage. I could have done it. You must allow me to pay you."

"Oh, no, I wouldn't think of it. Anyway, you're busy with the house. And I'm always happy to help out, Mrs. Blaine. You know that. And, well, I had the time."

Frankie smiled slyly. "Of course you did, Mr. Smith. These days, when it comes to Mama, you *always* have more than enough time."

Eli began to look like a rat caught in an awkward trap. Fortunately, Emily came to his rescue by raising her spatula and waving it at Frankie. "Scat, you little trouble maker!"

Chortling, Frankie danced out of the kitchen.

The room was suddenly very warm and Maggie's corset way too tight. "I apologize for her behavior, Mr. Smith."

"Oh, no," He stammered. "It's all right. Frankie's a young girl. And she's probably noticed that we're – um – friends."

"We've *all* noticed that you and Mama are – um – friends, Mr. Smith," Lydia teased. "Now, if you'll excuse me, I'll go see to Frankie and make sure she's civilized for the new minister."

As the eighteen-year-old left the room, Maggie heaved a sigh. "Again, I'm so sorry."

"No, no. Nothing to be sorry about." But Eli was still stammering. "I mean, they're young, aren't they? They say things." He took a breath, noticed Emily's cake on the table, and eagerly changed the subject. "Oh, hey, is that cake for tonight?"

No one could ever claim that Eli Smith disliked food. He was too portly for that. More friendly-looking than handsome, he had an easygoing manner that hid a deeper side – a seriousness and passion for justice. But right now he focused – more than a bit gratefully – on the cake.

Emily glared at him. "Yes. The cake is for tonight. *Tonight.* Understand?"

"Completely. Just curious." He glanced toward the hallway, and then lowered his voice. "Have our visitors left?"

"Mm, hm," Emily replied as her husband Nate, arms loaded with wood for the stove, came in the back door. "We sent them off to the next stop this morning,"

"Two brothers," Maggie added. "Do you know that one of them had his wife and children sold off? He doesn't even know where they are. It breaks my heart no matter how many times I hear stories like that. What's the world coming to?"

Eli sighed. "War, I'm afraid."

"There's got to be another way to resolve this."

"I don't think there is. The situation's too far gone. It's been too far gone for years. It's just a matter of time now. If Mr. Lincoln gets elected, it's clear the South will secede. And if the South secedes, there's going to be war."

Nate dusted his hands. "Well, if there's a war, I'm joining up. If they'll let me."

"Think that's a good idea?" Eli asked. "What if you end up getting taken prisoner? You could lose your freedom."

"I'd risk it." His black eyes were fierce. "Those folk down South are my brothers and sisters. My heart won't let me stay out of this fight."

Emily quietly kept her eyes on her work. Her hand moved deliberately from the bowl to the cake, methodically spreading the icing in circles, then going back for more. Maggie also was quiet, turning her attention to the stew.

****

From Maggie's Journal, 13 April 1860

Talk of secession and war is steadily increasing. The men bat the idea about with a strange and serious eagerness that is most unsettling. It is as if they cannot wait to get a rifle in their hands and commence killing one another.

They say the dispute is over states rights. The South claims it should be able to keep its traditions and practices, with no interference from Washington. But in my heart I know the truth. Slavery is wicked, and the very idea that this inhumane institution will spread if unchecked grieves me. So I am an abolitionist. I cannot help but be so. My dear friends are colored. I fear every time I hear there is a bounty hunter in the area. Emily was smuggled out of Maryland when she was an infant. She bears the imprint of the wickedness of slavery: her skin is lighter than Nate's, and her eyes are amber, rather than deep brown. I fear for her even now, should her former owner or his successors wish to send bounty hunters to reclaim her.

Shall I tell you a secret, dear Journal? I am breaking the law. Nate and Emily serve the Underground Railroad. When they shared this with Eli and me one night four months ago, we did the sensible thing – we joined them in their endeavor. When word comes through, Eli hangs a lantern by his print shop. Nate shepherds the escaped slaves through the darkness and into the shop. We have constructed a hiding place for them. We feed them, clothe them, and then send them on their way. With God's grace they will make it to Canada.

If our conspiracy is uncovered there will be serious repercussions. The Fugitive Slave Act demands a $1,000 fine, which none of us can pay, and six months imprisonment. There will be no trial, nor will we have any lawyers. There simply will be a sentence – and an unpleasant one, at that. But we do what we must. Even more importantly, we do what is right.

I do not mind fighting this battle. But all the talk about going to war, that is something else. No matter how noble and just one believes a war might be, every woman cringes at the thought of sending the men in her life into battle. I simply do not understand the male need to fight. Why must talking consistently disintegrate into arguing and arguing into violence? It seems the men actually *want* to fight.

****

"Would *you* go?" Nate asked Eli. "To war?"

Eli glanced down at his pot belly. "Look at me, Nate. Do I look like a soldier? Anyway, the Quaker in me won't permit it. So, no – no fighting for me. If I do anything, I'll cover the war as a correspondent. Folks need to know what's going on."

Nate's gaze did not waver. "War correspondents get killed, too."

"Yes, I know," Eli murmured.

Maggie found herself studying Emily's hand as she frosted the cake. She wondered why women felt as if they had to be silent when men spoke of war. She wondered why women listened to men talk of dying in battle. Why was war *their* business only? Women were the ones left behind and bereaved. Women were the ones who had to struggle on. Why, Maggie asked herself, do we keep silent?

After an uneasy pause, Eli took a deep breath. "Look, I'd better go to the station. The timetable said the train is due in from Morristown in fifteen minutes." He turned to leave.

Impulsively, Maggie called, "Mr. Smith!"

He looked over his shoulder.

She realized what she was doing. She did not want him to leave, not after all that talk of war and death. Feeling completely awkward, she blurted, "Thank you, once again."

"You're welcome, Mrs. Blaine."

Their clumsy exchanges complete, he left.

"Mm, hm," Emily said. "That's right, Maggie. Thank him. Nice man like that should settle down. And you know what I mean."

Maggie blushed, "Emily, please . . ." She hurried to the range and pretended to busy herself with the stew.

That did not stop Emily. "Mm, hm. That's the trouble with you white folks. You spend too much time being polite to each other. You've known Mr. Smith for years, and finally – *finally* the both of you have started paying attention to each other – about time, too, if you ask me. But what do you go and do? You stammer and stutter and dance around each other like you're afraid or something. Now, me – I saw a good, hard-working man and I got him. Reliable, strong, and handsome to boot. Ain't I a lucky gal?"

Nate plopped down in a chair. "I think so. And I'm a lucky man!"

"That's right. I'm the best woman you'll ever have. I just hope I'm teaching *her* a thing of two."

Nate made a move to say something to Maggie, but she stopped him with a stern look.

He held up his hands in self-defense. "Don't look at me. I just brought in the wood."

And Emily said, "Mm, hm."

Fortunately, Maggie remembered that she still had to dust the new minister's room one more time. Relieved, she hurried off to her task. A short while later, as she was tidying up the front parlor, Maggie heard a horse and carriage coming up Second Street. Looking quickly out the window, she saw Eli pulling up in front of the rooming house. A man in a black suit was seated on the bench next to him. Maggie hurried removed her apron and scurried to the kitchen to let Emily know that their new border had arrived.

****

From Maggie's Journal, 13 April 1860

I have seen a great many ministers in my time, but I did not expect this. The Reverend Mr. Jeremiah Madison is handsome. No. Not merely handsome. He is beautiful, but in the way that men are beautiful – young, tall and lithe, chestnut hair glittering in the late afternoon sun. His voice is a pleasant tenor. He has a strong, yet fine-featured face set off by a neat mustache and striking blue eyes. I must confess that his gaze is mesmerizing – but not nearly to the degree that Lydia and Frankie were mesmerized. They seemed to be struck immobile, gaping rather stupidly at our new boarder.

I briefly introduced myself to our new arrival. He smiled and he thrust out his hand toward me. Now that was a surprise. Genteel men usually bow to women, and genteel women usually curtsey back. But this man wanted to shake hands with me as if I were another man. It is contrary to all social convention. But, my dear journal, I liked it very much. We met as equals. His grip was firm and his palm warm and dry. I do believe that I will like Mr. Madison.

****

Jeremiah Madison stepped into the hallway. He was carrying a carpet bag in one hand and a larger case in the other. As Maggie introduced her two daughters – who had been rendered speechless by the minister's appearance – she heard a loud grunt from outside. Peering around Jeremiah, she spotted Eli lugging a large wooden box onto the porch. He paused, sweating profusely, and then looked up at her and wheezed, "Books."

Fortunately for Eli's back, Nate and Emily were coming down the hall and Nate immediately went to his aid.

Now came the moment, the test. Taking a deep breath, Maggie braced herself for the tension. The new minister had been unconventional enough to shake her hand, but how would he react to living in the same house with colored people? "Mr. Madison," she said, "may I also introduce Nathaniel and Emily Johnson? Nate owns a carpenter shop, and Emily works here as a cook. They live on the second floor."

Jeremiah could have stiffened, made a very bad excuse, and fled (never to return). But instead, he smiled. "I'm delighted to meet you and your husband, Mrs. Johnson." Once again he extended his hand.

Emily paused, and then – with an absolutely beautiful smile – took his hand in hers.

Once pleasantries had been exchanged, Emily escorted Jeremiah down the hall through the kitchen and into the "new" wing. Lydia and Frankie trailed hungrily behind. Maggie stayed, waiting as Nate and Eli wrestled the crate through the front door.

Eli was muttering, "This Madison fellow reads more than I do."

"Well, I've got a suggestion for him," Nate grunted. "Try the lending library."

"I've got a better suggestion. Start one."

With a sigh, Maggie scooted past their complaints and went on to the wing. The minister's room was freshly clean. Large and located in the front of the house, it afforded an excellent view of Second Street. Outside the window, trees were unfolding their new leaves. The curtains billowed in the warm, light breeze, and whispered of the promise of spring. Newly cut daffodils on the bureau added a splash of yellow to the large, light-filled room. A pleasant aroma of beeswax on wood permeated the air.

Jeremiah happily surveyed his new chamber. "How very pleasant this is, Mrs. Blaine!" he exclaimed. "I'm sure I shall be quite happy here!"

Maggie thanked him for his kindness. Her girls were still gaping at him as if they were complete ninnies. Oh, well, there was nothing she could do about that right now, so she pressed on. "The custom of our house is to have supper at six."

"Yes," Frankie said, lamely adding, "that's when we . . . eat."

Lydia kicked her sister's ankle.

"Ow!" Frankie squeaked. "Stop it!"

"You stop it," Lydia hissed out of the corner of her mouth.

Maggie made an effort to ignore them. The Reverend, however, was amused. Fortunately, the arrival of Nate, Eli and the crate of books made a ready distraction, and Maggie continued her speech, "I'm sure the other boarders will stop in to visit with you. But, regardless, we'll all get to know each other at table."

Mr. Madison grinned winningly. "Ah, yes! There's nothing like table fellowship!"

"Yes . . ." Frankie agreed. "It's so . . . fellowshippy."

Emily smiled graciously at Jeremiah, then took a girl with each hand and hauled them out of the room. Nate nodded at the new boarder and followed them out. That left Eli, who was mopping his brow with a handkerchief.

Social convention was not prominent in a house that opened its doors to the lost and lonely, as well as to people with some color to their skin. Maggie wondered what Jeremiah Madison was really thinking. She also knew that her daughters, particularly Frankie, were headstrong. She worried that Mr. Madison might consider them a pack of heathens and lodge a complaint with the church. If he did so, what then? Maggie had to struggle to push away the anxiety of battling even more gossip and scandal.

But Mr. Madison's smile was warm. "You have two lively – and completely delightful – daughters, Mrs. Blaine."

She tried not to look too relieved.

"If you don't mind my asking, are you by any chance connected to the founders of this community? I can't help but notice that you and the town share the same name."

The details were too long and tiresome to relate, so Maggie gave him the short story. "My late husband, John, was a Blaine. He was their only son. I'm a Beatty."

"Of the Beatty Carriage Manufactory?"

She nodded.

"Then you are also related to Samuel Beatty?"

Maggie braced herself and explained, "He's my brother, but the difficulty, indeed the tragedy, lies in the fact that when John Blaine and I decided to marry, both of our families did not take kindly to our decision. So you see, although I appear to have connections, I have been rather thoroughly un-connected."

"I'm terribly sorry."

Eli cleared his throat.

Maggie pretended not to hear. "Thank you, Mr. Madison. But I am not bereaved, really. I have found that life is infinitely better – and richer – with love. My husband meant the world to me. I don't regret a thing. And my beautiful daughters *are* the world to me. With their love and the love of God, what more do I need?"

Jeremiah nodded approvingly. "Indeed, what more?"

Eli cleared his throat again. "I think we ought to leave Mr. Madison so he may unpack." He closed his hand round Maggie's upper arm. "Nice meeting you, Reverend. See you in an hour." With that, he propelled Maggie out the door and into the hall. "What on earth is going on?" he hissed. "You, Lydia, and Frankie are acting like mooncalves!"

Maggie stopped in the middle of the hall and laughed. "Are you blind, Elijah Smith? The new minister is considerate, kind, and beautiful!"

"Huh," he grunted. "All *I* know is he owns a ton of books."

****

Maggie's rooming house had four boarders, not counting Jeremiah Madison. All four men occupied the rooms on the second floor of the old house. Edgar Lape, a young man of 22, was struggling to start his first law practice. He worked as a lawyer's assistant and spent most of his time at the county courthouse, which sat at one end of the Blaineton green opposite the Presbyterian Church. Earnest and determined, Edgar most often was found with his nose in a legal book. Despite this tendency, he and Lydia had managed to catch each other's eye, begun to court, and (Maggie hoped) would someday soon announce their engagement.

The home's resident writer was the white-haired, white-bearded, very dapper Chester Carson. He had sold a few novels in his youth, but now in his later years, he made what money he could from writing for magazines and newspapers, including Eli's *Gazette*. Lately, he had begun to experiment with photography and was taking portraits.

The oldest boarder was Jim O'Reilly, an Irishman who used to do odd jobs around town, but had been curtailed by arthritis. Unlike Chester Carson, Jim rarely had money enough to pay room and board. Maggie had no intention of turning him out, though. She had long decided that was no way to treat an elder. So over the past seven years, he had become Lydia and Frankie's "grandfather," and they all referred to him as "Grandpa O'Reilly."

Finally, there was Patrick McCoy. Only seventeen years of age, he worked as the undertaker's apprentice. Despite his grim occupation, Patrick was full of energy and life. He was a handsome boy – dark haired, green eyes framed by long dark lashes – yet he was shy around girls. He was also very kind-hearted. Maggie hoped that someday he would find a wife. He was the sort of decent, dependable young man who would make an excellent husband.

The members of Maggie's household gathered around the dining table at six. Conversations were almost always lively – sometimes a bit too lively when opinions clashed. But everyone managed to get along, nonetheless. The motto was "everyone has a right to his (or her) opinion."

As soon as the food was blessed and the plates were being filled, Grandpa O'Reilly, who was now feeling well enough to join the others at table, cleared his throat. "Tell me now, Father."

"No, please." Jeremiah corrected. "Mr. Madison will do."

"Yes. Now where have you come from?"

"The Warren Charge," the minister answered. "That is, I served three small congregations and more recently two congregations in the Morristown District. And before that, Mr. O'Reilly, I was a colporteur."

Frankie frowned. "A col . . ."

"Colporteur," Eli interjected. "That means Mr. Madison sold books for a living."

"Yes, exactly! When I first sensed my call, I worked selling Bibles and books of religion door to door."

"Yep," Eli muttered to Nate, just loud enough for Maggie to hear. "That explains the crate."

Lydia was impressed. "Door to door? You must be very brave, Mr. Madison! I'd never be able to speak to strange people day in and day out."

"Actually, the experience was quite interesting. I learned a great deal about people and their lives – so many fascinating details, but so much tragedy and sorrow, as well. My heart went out to them. Then, one night as I was praying for the people I had met that day, everything became clear. It was as if a voice said to me, 'Jeremiah, *you* help them. *You* preach my Word.' The feeling was so strong that I knew it had to be from our Lord. And that, to make a long story short, is how I came to the ministry."

Eli grunted, but Patrick exclaimed, "A voice from God! I'd sure like to hear that!"

The young minister grinned. "Perhaps you will. All you have to do is pray."

"I do. But I've never heard *God's* voice!"

Frankie frowned. "I don't think Mr. Madison means an actual voice from heaven, Patrick. I think he means a – a kind of feeling."

"Yes, Frances, that's right – it's a feeling, but more than that. It's something deep inside that you know is right and true. If you're attentive, God is always there."

Edgar Lape interjected, "Oh, I'd have to have more proof than that, if I were to be assured that the feeling was from God."

Jeremiah rested his fork and knife, and leaned toward the young lawyer. "May I ask you a question, sir? What made you choose to go into law?"

"I want to help people."

"And where did that desire come from?"

The young man shrugged. "I don't know, exactly."

"Allow me to suggest," Jeremiah said, "that it came from God, and that, even as you knew your calling was to law, so I knew mine was to ministry."

Eli grunted again.

"Indeed!" Mr. Carson interjected. "You simply must allow me to write your story down, Reverend. I have a keen interest in supernaturalism and collect stories of conversions and calls. I find that such subject matter makes fascinating reading. It has as much to say about people as it does about God."

The supper conversation was going very well and Maggie was extremely pleased. The only resistant element was Eli Smith, who did not seem to be taking to the new minister. The grunting was a dead give-away.

Jeremiah, fortunately, did not seem to notice Eli's dissent. "You know, Mr. Carson, in three months, there will be a district camp meeting. I intend to encourage as many from the Methodist congregation as will go. I hope you'll go, too, so you may write about what you see and experience." He paused and then added, "You know, my greatest desire would be to see a revival in this town."

Eli had grunted one time too many, and Maggie's annoyance finally spilled over. "Mr. Smith, do you have something to say?"

"Oh, no," he replied, brown eyes all innocence. "I was just clearing my throat." He harrumphed loudly to prove his point. "There. Much better. Would anyone like more potatoes?"

Maggie eyed him, but turned back to Jeremiah. "You were saying about revival?"

"It seems to me that with the help of the camp meeting, we have an excellent opportunity for the town to be revived spiritually. Not, of course, that I come to this pulpit with the predisposition that Blaineton is spiritually stagnated."

"Of course not," Eli commented, with an undertone of sarcasm.

"It's just that the first few months of a pastorate offer a fresh start for everyone. And I believe that all of us can do with reviving. A good revival never hinders, it can only help."

"Amen!" Emily concurred.

"Oh, yes!" Frankie gushed. "Amen!"

Eli rolled his eyes. "Amen. Please pass the biscuits."

****

After supper, the men retired to the back parlor to smoke their pipes. Emily, Lydia, and Frankie took care of cleaning the kitchen. Maggie meanwhile lit a lamp and went down the wooden stairs into the cellar. The thick stone walls of the foundation kept the area cool even during the warmest months. She was grateful for the change in temperature – she was flushed and still quite peeved at Eli. The chill quiet enveloped her like a welcome cloud.

One side of the cellar held shelves stacked with crocks of salted pork and beef as well as Mason jars filled with canned fruit and vegetables. The other side was lined with bins of potatoes, onions and other roots. Maggie picked a basket off a shelf, continued to the very back of the cellar, and paused in front of an old wardrobe. Reaching into the collar of her dress, she fished out a chain fastened around her neck. On the end was a key, and she used this to open the wardrobe's lock. Creaking, the door swung open. She lifted a small latch, barely discernable on the back wall of the wardrobe, and then pushed on the back wall, which proved to be a door. A dark, narrow corridor lay beyond.

Maggie entered the corridor and carefully pushed the door shut behind her. The passageway's ceiling and walls were made of brick. The floor was earth, like that of the cellar. It had taken Eli and Nate a good two months to dig the tunnel and create the little room situated between Eli's shop and the rooming house.

The corridor led to another door, which opened into that room. It was no more than twelve by ten feet. Its furnishings were spare – a table with two lamps and four stools, two narrow beds with rope springs and straw mattresses, four blankets, a chamber pot, and a few dishes.

Maggie set the basket on the table and began to stack the dirty dishes into it. Then she moved to the beds and started folding the blankets. She had just finished this task, when she heard the wardrobe door creak. Turning, she saw a lantern coming down the tunnel. She was not surprised when Eli finally stepped into the room. She was, however, terribly upset with him. Maggie had found his behavior to be unacceptable.

"You needn't have followed me. I do not require help down here," she said rather tartly.

But he stayed where he was. "I need to tell you something."

When she tried to push by him, he took hold of her arm. "I *apologize*, Mrs. Blaine. I'm sorry. I mean it."

But this only exasperated her all the more. "Why do you not like Mr. Madison?"

Eli looked down and scuffed a foot over the dirt floor. "I don't know. I don't care for the way Madison conducts himself. Just seems, well, a bit self-important."

"Self-important or not, Jeremiah Madison will be living in here for the next one or two years."

Eli shoved his hands into his pockets and heaved a large sigh. "I know. I guess I might as well admit that I'm a little jealous. You look at him as if he's the most interesting person you've ever met." And then he added something that took Maggie by complete surprise. "I guess your daughters, Emily and Nate, and nearly everyone we know are right."

She frowned. "Right? What do you mean by right?"

Eli threw his arms into the air. "Mrs. Blaine, you cannot tell me that you're blind to this!" And he began to tick examples off on his fingers. "One, we spend a great deal of time together. Two, we have more than a few things in common. Like abolition. And *this* – we help escaped slaves make it to Canada. And three, we talk all the time. And four, we have good discussions. No, we have *excellent* discussions!" He paused to take a long, deep breath. "*And*, seeing as how we've known each other for four years and seeing as how we get along . . ."

"Mr. Smith, precisely what are you trying to say?"

"I want to know, Mrs. Blaine, if it would be all right – that is, would you like it if we – if we – oh, blast!" He took a huge breath and finished all in a rush, "Would you like it if we kept company?"

Everything stopped for Maggie. She was stunned. "Are you saying you want to court me?"

"Yes!!" Eli straightened his shoulders and pushed his spectacles up his nose. "Yes, that's exactly what I'm saying. I know I'm not doing a good job of it. I haven't gone courting since Martha. That's been eleven years and . . ." He shoved his hands back into his pockets. "Oh, I just don't know how to say it."

The two of them had been skirting around their feelings for the past few months as if they were afraid to acknowledge the change. It was a relief to hear everything finally confirmed by Eli's own words, no matter how clumsily said. Maggie's heart began to flutter as if she were a schoolgirl. She had a suitor! Better yet, a suitor of whom she thought a great deal. "It's all right, Mr. Smith. You said it, and you said it just right."

His brown eyes grew round.

"That is, I'd be honored to have you court me, Mr. Smith."

"Oh." It took him awhile to comprehend what she had said. "Oh!"

They stood looking at each other for a long moment. Finally they began to laugh.

"Well," he chuckled, "I guess under the circumstances I should ask you to call me Eli."

"And you should call me Maggie."

There was another long, awkward pause, but this time they grinned at each other with no small degree of satisfaction. At length, Maggie cleared her throat and broke the silence. "I think I had better get these dishes upstairs – and you can join the men on the – "

"Maggie, wait."

****

From Maggie's Journal, 13 April 1860

I knew what he wanted. We needed to seal the agreement, so to speak. If I were a younger woman, I would have continued to leave. I would not wish to engage in any sort of behavior that might be considered unladylike. But I am no longer a young woman. And according to some people I am not much of a lady. No matter. I was happily married once upon a time. I know all about men and women. And I like dark-eyed, dark-haired Elijah Smith. I like him a great deal. So I turned around.

And then, dear Journal, we kissed.

The kiss was complete and passionate and tender. In fact, it fairly took my breath away. I must confess that when it was over, my knees were weak for it had been a very long time since I had been kissed like that. My cheeks were burning and my heart pounding. More could have followed – but, perhaps I am not that much of a rebel.

I picked up the basket and my lamp and made ready to go.

Mr. Smith, who is every inch the gentleman, made a half-hearted comment about joining the men on the porch.

I spoke of washing the dishes.

And so we went our separate ways.

But I am so very happy tonight! I did not expect that I would ever be this happy again. Thanks be to God, for I have been blessed indeed. I am surrounded by good people, two beautiful daughters, dear friends… and now Mr. Smith, my Eli.

CHAPTER TWO

Jeremiah Madison's first Sunday at Blaineton Methodist Episcopal Church dawned sunny and warm. The congregation gathered in their plain, small meeting house. Built of local stone, covered with white-washed plaster to keep the elements from seeping through, it possessed two front doors, one for men and the other for women. Wooden benches were arranged along a center aisle. A potbelly stove sat front right and a small organ, powered by pedals pumped by the organist, was front left.

The upper quarter of the church was divided from the lower three quarters by a wooden rail. This was split in the middle to allow the minister to walk out into the congregational area, should he so desire or need to. Within this Methodist-style "holy of holies," a table serving as an altar pressed against the center of the wall and was flanked by two large chairs. A simple wooden cross and vase of fresh flowers had been placed upon the table. One's eye, though, was drawn to the podium that sat about six feet from the altar. This was where the minister read scripture and delivered the Word.

Methodist founder John Wesley had stressed the importance of regular participation in the Lord's Supper; however the centrality of the sacrament was lost during the spread of Methodism in the United States. In the early days, circuit-riding Methodist preachers served numerous churches spread over a large area and thus were unable to consecrate the wine and bread for weekly communion. In fact, many small congregations were lucky if their minister worshipped with them once a month.

The act of preaching therefore had taken on sacramental significance, even if the one delivering the sermon was a lay person. Like many Methodists, the people of the Blaineton congregation believed that the Holy Spirit could flow through the preacher, seize sinful hearts, convince listeners that they were destined for perdition, and bring them to repentance and salvation. Today was a test to see if their new clergyman was a conduit for God's Spirit.

Mrs. Kendall played a meditative piece on the organ, while the parishioners prayed silently. A few people passed quiet whispers back and forth. The windows had been thrown open, allowing in the sound of bird songs and the occasional muffled clomping of hooves on the dirt track known as Main Street. The cobbled road did not begin until Main Street intersected with First Street a quarter mile away.

Outside the little building, horses with their buggies were hitched to posts. Their pungent animal smell added to the aroma of new grass and leaves and road dust. Some horses had been lodged in a long shed that had been constructed behind the meeting house to shield the animals from the elements.

The men of the congregation sat to the left facing the pulpit. Some, however, gathered near the door – for a quick exit should the sermon run too long or become boring. The need for a pipe and manly conversation could, at times, override the need to receive the Word. Many of those who sat in the pews assumed a "show me" attitude – sitting with arms crossed and legs firmly planted on the floor. One could almost hear their thoughts: Was the new pastor's theology sound? Did he have preaching gifts? Was he a "man's man" or would he be too "feminine," appealing only to the women?

The women, who were seated to the right, also were eager to learn about the new minister. As they jostled babies on their laps and shushed the young children sitting beside them, they prayed that the newcomer's words would touch their souls and move others to Christ. Not a few hoped that the new minister's preaching would convert their husbands. Dressed in their best frocks and wearing their best bonnets, the women held their collective breath in anticipation.

As for the young single women, they simply wanted to see this new, single man in town. Youthful, unattached clergymen were of great interest. If this Mr. Madison proved to be an inspiring speaker, a strong leader, and pleasing to the eye, then many a girl would plead with her mama to invite him to supper. A man possessed of powerful, spiritual connections was intensely attractive and desirable, even though most ministers lived in humble circumstances.

Maggie was relieved to see that Lydia had overcome her initial infatuation and was busy casting her eyes upon beau, Edgar Lape. The tall, blond twenty-year-old answered the girl with glances and blushes. In a few years he would have a secure enough living for him to propose, but for the present the two had an unspoken agreement to meet every Sunday after church. Edgar had received Maggie's permission to escort Lydia home, so the two usually took their time and only met up with the rest of the rooming house in time for Sunday dinner. Maggie was relieved that, despite the arrival of the new minister, nothing of real importance had changed for Lydia.

Frankie, on the other hand, was another story. She sat with a smug look upon her face, all too aware that the other girls knew Jeremiah Madison was lodging at Second Street. Having apparently forgotten the many biblical warnings against the sin of pride, her posture and expression crowed, "I know what the new minister is like." Maggie fretted about this new interest. Although schoolgirl crushes were perfectly acceptable, the fourteen-year-old's lack of reticence was liable to cause repercussions – not to mention immense embarrassment – for both herself and Jeremiah, whom Maggie judged to be about 25 years of age.

An insistent nudging against her arm broke Maggie out of her reverie. The culprit was Frankie, who grinned and whispered, "Look who's decided to join our little congregation." She nodded toward the meeting house entrance.

****

From Maggie's Journal, 14 April 1860

I was utterly amazed to see that Eli had entered our church. He was greeted by some of the men gathered at the back. These attend services only to please their wives, and their wives complain that they have not yet come to Jesus. I suppose I could say much the same of Eli. But he was raised as a Quaker, and things are different with them.

Eli must have felt my stare, for his eyes met mine and he smiled at me. He was dressed in his best but rumpled clothing, and held his hat awkwardly by the brim.

I smiled in return. Frankie commented that Mr. Smith seemed to have suddenly gotten religion. At this, I felt my cheeks grow hot.

Lydia whispered that, if such were the case, then we should expect Mr. Smith to throw himself upon the altar rail.

Dear Journal, their comments caused me to flip open my fan and wave it furiously in an effort to cool my burning face. In hushed tones, I informed both of my darling daughters that it was they who needed to pray, and that they needed to do so *now*. My girls are obedient, thank God. They both bowed their heads. Thus I was able to regain my composure once more.

****

It was a relief for Maggie when her brother Samuel stood and announced the first hymn. As Mrs. Kendall began to play the introduction, Maggie rose to her feet with the rest of the congregation. The piece chosen, written by John Wesley's prolific poet-brother Charles was familiar to all Methodists and was sung lustily to welcome the new minister.

O for a thousand tongues, to sing
my great Redeemer's praise;
the glories of my God and King,
the triumphs of his grace.

My gracious Master, and my God,
assist me to proclaim,—
to spread, through all the earth abroad,
the honours of thy Name.

Jesus!—the Name that charms our fears,
that bids our sorrows cease;
'tis music in the sinner's ears,
'tis life, and health, and peace.

He breaks the power of cancell'd sin,
he sets the prisoner free;
his blood can make the foulest clean;
his blood avail'd for me.

He speaks,—and, list'ning to his voice,
new life the dead receive;
the mournful, broken hearts rejoice;
the humble poor believe.

Hear him, ye deaf; his praise, ye dumb,
your loosen'd tongues employ;
ye blind, behold your Saviour come;
and leap, ye lame, for joy.

Following this the congregation continued with another two hymns. With each one their anticipation grew. Every note brought with it the growing presence of the Holy Spirit. By the time they had finished, their hearts were open and ready.

Samuel Beatty now stood and, carrying his Bible, walked solemnly to the podium. "Hear the Old Testament chapter for the day," he intoned. "It is from the First Book of Samuel, chapter three." He then read the story of how the boy Samuel was called by God to become a prophet. This reading was followed by scripture from the New Testament, chapter two of the Book of Acts. This described how the Holy Spirit came upon Jesus' followers at the festival of Pentecost and included a speech from the apostle Peter.

Maggie noticed that Frankie was starting to squirm. The girl was obviously anxious to hear Jeremiah Madison preach, and the hymns and readings were starting to lose appeal. But a hand placed gently on Frankie's wrist helped Maggie remind her daughter to practice patience and proper etiquette.

At last, a door in the wall to the right of the altar opened, and the Reverend Mr. Jeremiah Madison made his entrance. Wearing a simple black suit and carrying an old, worn Bible, he looked every bit the Man of God, despite his youth. Jeremiah took his place at the podium, reverently set the Bible upon it, and finally looked out at the faces of the forty-three people in the meeting house.

They waited his response.

A gracious smile spread over his face. "I wish to thank you for this most warm and deferential welcome." His voice was clear, his tone earnest. "The Lord truly has been gracious to me, and I hope, with God's help, together we will sow His Word until not a single weed remains in the town of Blaineton, and all here may be gathered up when the Lord comes."

The entire congregation leaned forward. Their last few clergymen had been lacking in passion and resolve. As a result, the small church had dwindled both spiritually and numerically. They now placed their hopes for renewal in this one man. They were panting for a cooling breeze from the Holy Spirit, and they sought anything to revive them. They hoped and prayed that Mr. Madison would be the one to channel God's blessing of renewal.

Jeremiah calmly opened his Bible and focused on his text for the day. "The Gospel of John, chapter 14, verse 12. 'Verily, verily, I say unto you, he that believeth on me, the works that I do shall he do also;

and greater works than these shall he do; because I go unto my Father.'"

He looked up now, directly meeting the eyes of his parishioners. "How difficult and uncomfortable it is for us to hear these words is it not? And yet they are in our scripture. We cannot remove them from the canon. They are the very words our Lord Jesus spoke before he entered into his Passion. He was imparting his last thoughts to those who followed him, and yet what do they mean for us, we who also are his followers?

"Jesus says that those who believe on him will be imbued with supernatural power, such power that they will be able to perform the same works as their Savior. That, my brethren, is a most astounding thing!

"But our Lord has yet something else to add – those that believe on him will also do *greater* works than their Savior. What, we cry, greater works than the Christ? How can this be? This makes no sense! We are rational men. Are we to return to notions of magic and superstition? Are we to expect that each of us will heal the sick with a touch, raise the dead with a word, and multiply a few loaves into several thousand?"

There was a pause. Then Jeremiah Madison leaned forward, gripping the pulpit with both hands. "In a word, my friends, yes. We are to *expect* miracles. And we are to *do* miracles."

****

From Maggie's Journal, 14 April 1860

Mr. Madison took us all by surprise. We have hoped and prayed for a good preacher, but we did not expect so gifted a man. He conveys an authority that our previous pastors have lacked. His prayers are heart-felt. His singing voice is angelic. His reading of Scripture so lucid that even the children understood the morning's lesson. But all that pales in comparison to his preaching.

To be plain, Mr. Madison is mesmerizing. He had no notes at all, and began his sermon simply, but built idea upon idea, emotion upon emotion, as if he wished to wring every single heart and soul in the church of earthly attachments. He told us that we are Christ's emissaries on earth, and that we are to be Christ to others.

He painted magnificent pictures of heaven, gave us warm words of the loving heart of Christ, and presented wondrous images of God's bounteous grace. He asked who among us would not wish to partake of this grace. Who among us would not wish to rest in the blessing and peace of our Lord?

Mr. Madison ended his sermon with a plea for all to come forward. It matters not if one has already been converted, he said. The communion rail is open equally to all believers – those who have newly accepted Christ and those who desire to re-commit their lives to Christ. He also pleaded with those in need of conversion to give up their pride and throw themselves upon the tender mercies of a Lord who would forgive their sins and present them spotless before God. Mr. Madison invited these people to come sit on the "anxious bench" to await the Holy Ghost's touch on their hearts.

Journal, I never saw so many move forward so quickly in all my years in Blaineton M.E.C. Lydia was weeping openly. Frankie fairly ran to the rail. Patrick McCoy and Edgar Lape threw themselves to their knees in prayer. I must admit that my own eyes filled with tears. The only one who seemed to resist Mr. Madison's preaching was Eli. He stood at the back with his arms crossed over his stomach, feet firmly planted on the floor. From the look in his eyes, I could see that something was going on in his mind – but it was not surrender to God

****

After the benediction, the exhausted congregation turned and shuffled toward the door, where Jeremiah was waiting outside in the surprisingly warm, sweet air to greet everyone. He took each person's hands in his, looked him or her directly in the eye, and said something to each one. As groups of people walked away, they were of one opinion: the Holy Spirit was once again present in their little congregation.

Miss Tryphena Moore, an aging maiden lady, and her slightly younger and equally maiden sister, Tryphosa were standing behind Maggie. "He is a blessing," Tryphena declared. "And it is about time."

"Amen, sister," agreed the younger.

"And," Tryphena added just loud enough to make sure Maggie could hear, "we will certainly need to build a parsonage. We want to get him out of that rooming house as soon as possible."

The comment stung, but fortunately, Frankie caught her mother's arm as they moved toward the door and offered a diversion, chattering ecstatically about Jeremiah's amazing gifts. "Did you see, Mama?

Even Patrick and Mr. Lape went forward. They *never* do that." She nodded in Eli's direction. "Too bad about him though."

Maggie wasn't sure whether to feel embarrassed or defensive. "Now, Frankie, you know it is not Christian to judge. We cannot know what goes on in another's heart." She decided that she needed to withhold her own judgment, as well, for Tryphena's comment had left a burning in the pit of her stomach.

Eli squeezed his way through the crowd and joined them. With a smile, Maggie asked, "What do you think of our new minister?"

"Interesting," was all he said.

As they reached the door, a flushed and beaming Jeremiah reached out and took Maggie's hands warmly in his. They had just begun to exchange pleasantries, when another voice called, "Mr. Madison!"

Maggie steeled herself. The voice belonged to her brother, Samuel. He was flanked by his wife Abigail, sons Robert and Joshua, and daughter Leah. Like most of the young girls, Leah was gazing starry-eyed upon Jeremiah Madison. The minister met her gaze and smiled back which, Maggie noticed, made Frankie bristle. Her youngest daughter was about to have her heart broken for the first time.

"Reverend," Samuel was saying, "Mrs. Beatty and I would be honored to have you come to dinner this afternoon. Would you be so kind as to say yes?"

Jeremiah glanced at Maggie. "Mrs. Blaine, have you made any plans to have me at table?"

She knew it would not be politic for the minister to refuse her brother's invitation, so she managed a smile and said, "I expected that you would not be joining us today, Mr. Madison. After all, you will have many families to visit. You are free to come and go as your duties dictate."

"But Mama . . ." Frankie began. Maggie gave her arm a gentle little tweak to silence her.

The minister turned to Samuel. "Very well, then, Mr. Beatty, I would be delighted to dine with you and your family."

And suddenly the Beattys were crowding in on the pastor, and Maggie– along with Frankie and Eli – quite abruptly found themselves pushed to the outside of the circle. She knew that it was useless to try to fight their way back in. She was not wanted. She was neither powerful nor important. Samuel had made that very clear to her, as had the Moore sisters. Resignedly, Maggie turned to Frankie. "Well, it's time to go home."

"But Mama," the girl objected.

"I said it's time to go home. Now, go run and catch up with Lydia and Edgar."

She acquiesced – although not without a pout – and scampered away. Maggie cast one more glance at what had once been her family. The Beatty clan was now involved in occupying every square inch of Jeremiah Madison. Fighting off a wave of anger, she turned and walked rapidly away from the knot of people on the church lawn.

Eli had to hurry to catch up with her. "What's going on?" he asked.

"It's of no importance."

"But you're acting as if it *is* of importance. I thought you and your brother were through."

Maggie sighed. "I doubt that 'through' will ever mean 'completely finished'."

"What's the problem, then?"

She sighed again. "Oh, Eli, you know the story. Do you need to ask?"

He did not mince words. "Well, it just seems to me that for people who had just done so much praying and praising, you two ought to be able to attempt a little forgiveness."

They had reached the road. It hadn't rained for several days and dust curled up around their feet as they walked. Maggie kept her mouth shut, and walked as fast as she could without appearing to hurry. The truth was that Sam still had the power to hurt her. She wondered when she would ever harden herself to his slights. Everything he did, every word he said, still stung sharply, but she had resolved that her personal pain would never be made public. The family break was well-known, of course, but it simply would not do to make a scene. As far as Maggie was concerned, displays of anger never produced anything of value. And, yet – she missed her brother deeply, and the coldness between them stung.

"Look," Eli pressed, "just because we're courting doesn't mean that I'm going to stop being plain with you. Why can't you and your brother forgive each other?"

"I *have* forgiven him, Eli. Or at least I keep trying – over and over and over. It's just I don't think he's forgiven *me*. In fact, I *know* he hasn't forgiven me."

"Forgiven you for what? For marrying the man you loved twenty years ago?"

"Nineteen years ago," she corrected as they passed First Street.

"Oh, forgive me, that one year makes all the difference in the world. Maggie!" He took her arm and spun her round to face him.

"Not here!" she protested. "People will –"

"I don't care about people. I care about you." He looked her straight in the eyes. "John's been dead for ten years. Why can't you and Samuel patch things up?"

Being vulnerable was not easy. The subject of family was too sore, and Maggie was loath to admit that Samuel had hurt her so deeply. Yet she knew that Eli wouldn't let her tell him anything but the truth. After a brief pause, she muttered, "I have tried. I wrote him five years ago, and then two years after, in an attempt to heal things properly. All I got in reply was a letter saying that I had offended my entire family by eloping with the son of our business rival. It made no difference to Samuel that most of John's family cut us off, too. In fact, if it hadn't been for John's Aunt Letty, we would have been homeless. She permitted us to live with her at Second Street."

Eli smiled slightly. "Aunt Letty Blaine. I like what I've heard about her. She did what she wanted and never mind what the rest of the town thought."

It had been Aunt Letty's idea to turn the old Second Street place into a rooming house when John died. Maggie needed a source of income and forever was grateful to the dear old woman. Unfortunately, Aunty Letty did not live to see her generosity come to fruition. She passed on a year after John, and willed her house to Maggie. While not wildly successful, the small rooming house provided income and offered a home for those in need. Maggie knew that Aunt Letty would have given her blessing to the eclectic collection of boarders, despite what others in the town thought.

Samuel, of course, was of a different opinion.

Maggie looked down at her hands and saw that she had balled them into fists. "Do you know, Eli, that in his letter Samuel told me he would have considered a reconciliation, had I come crawling back home after John died? He said that because I persisted in my independent ways by running the rooming house, I showed little regard for my own family. He said that a woman of my status degrades herself by entering the world of business and handling money, and by living with un-genteel people – not to mention Nate and Emily. He said that I was an embarrassment to the Beatty family, to my own blood. As far as Samuel is concerned, I am no longer a relation. And yet, on too many occasions, he feels perfectly free to lecture me about my behavior. It's all so terribly humiliating and hurtful, Eli. He makes me feel unworthy. He makes me feel unclean and unwomanly."

Eli's eyes flashed behind his wire spectacles. "Damn him, anyway!"

Maggie gasped. "Elijah Smith! And on a Sunday!"

"Well, then I'll damn him on a Monday!" He shook his head. "I can't believe it, treating you the way he does. I can't believe the complete and utter disrespect. Why, you're the bravest, most competent, most independent woman I've ever met. Don't ever let him make you think you aren't worthy of his family. He's not worthy of *you*, and that's the truth!" When she said nothing, he lost some of his certainty. "Why are you looking at me like that?"

Despite her best efforts, Maggie's eyes began to brim with tears.

"Oh, no," he said, softly. "Oh, no, Maggie. I didn't mean to make you cry. I'm sorry . . ." He fumbled a handkerchief out of his pocket and held it out.

Maggie gratefully grabbed the rumpled hankie and daubed at her wet eyes.

"I'm sorry I upset you."

She smiled amid her tears. "You didn't upset me. It's just . . ." An onslaught of sobs caught her by surprised and nearly robbed her of her voice. "It's just that I've worked so hard for ten years, raising the girls, keeping a roof over our heads, food on the table. No one's ever said nice things like that to me. I've always felt as if I were somehow wrong – wicked and wrong. No one's ever said I was worthy of anything before."

"I've always thought you were worthy of *everything*, Maggie. Always. Ever since I first met you. You're strong and smart and talented." She glanced down, but he wouldn't have it. "Hey, look at me. Come on, Maggie, look at me."

She brought her eyes up to meet his.

"I think you're beautiful."

"I'm not beautiful," she demurred. "I'm really quite plain."

"Wrong, wrong, wrong," he said. "You're beautiful. Absolutely beautiful."

She leaned forward, impulsively kissing him on the cheek. "You're a dear soul, Elijah Smith. I love you."

"And I love you, too, Maggie Blaine." A playful smile spread across his face. "And now the entire town knows it, because we're standing in front of the Widow Greeley's house and I can see her peeking out the curtains."

Maggie laughed, sniffing back the rest of her tears. "Good! Let's go home."

Eli offered his arm. "Come on. Let's make Aunty Letty proud." Maggie happily linked her arm through his, and the two marched triumphantly down Main Street.

****

From Maggie's Journal, 14 April 1860

I am not a strict Sabbatarian. I believe that God meant for us to enjoy the Sabbath, but I am not so strict that our Sunday meal must be limited to cold foods. To me, part of the joy of Sunday is to have a good, hot dinner with friends and family. The cooking and the washing up afterwards are a blessing because Emily, Frankie, Lydia, and I work together and always with great cheer. All is accomplished with less bother than one might suspect. Today we killed an old hen that had ceased to lay. Emily prepared fricasseed chicken with dumplings. As is customary, we returned to church after dinner for the evening service. I was not the least surprised that Eli did not come with us this time. I suspect that he has experienced more than his fill of religion for one day.

Although the evening service is less formal, Jeremiah Madison is no less compelling. The congregation's final consensus is that God has smiled upon our little flock. Now they are visited with visions of glory and growth. Their prayers are that the Bishop will leave Mr. Madison in place for two or three years. If he stays, miracles might indeed happen in our little town. I would be satisfied with a modest revival and reduction of gossip. But perhaps I am satisfied with too little. Perhaps, as Mr. Madison says, we are to be Christ to our town. Perhaps we are to expect miracles.

Eli rejoined us once we returned home. Emily and I served a light meal, and then all turned to various activities. Some of the boarders took walks or engaged in conversation on the porch. Others read. Frankie, Lydia, and Edgar gathered round the piano and sang hymns for awhile. Then the trio called us in to enjoy a dramatic presentation based on the book of Esther. Edgar took the part of the villain Haman, Lydia played the heroine, and Frankie took the roles of the King and Mordecai. I am not sure how much Mr. Madison will approve of this activity, but it is all innocent fun and on Sundays we have stories from the Bible. Dramatics, as long as they are confined to the parlor and of wholesome content, are perfectly permissible to my mind. After all, God intended the Sabbath to be a lazy and refreshing day, a change of pace. To amuse ourselves thusly is part of the process of renewal.

****

Later, since the evening was fine, Maggie threw on a shawl and settled comfortably into her favorite rocking chair on the corner of the porch. She welcomed Eli as he took the chair beside hers. Smiling, he told her that he had a gift and then passed her a small book.

Maggie read the cover. *Woman in the Nineteenth Century and Kindred Papers Relating to the Sphere, Condition and Duties, of Woman.*

The author was Margaret Fuller Ossoli. Maggie opened the book and noticed that it had been reprinted in 1855. As she turned a page, she saw that Horace Greeley had written the introduction. This mildly surprised her – that so many had read a book by a woman and that a famous publisher had deigned to take notice of her.

"Besides sharing a first name," Eli said, "you and Margaret Ossoli also share an independent spirit. Unfortunately, she died in a shipwreck in '49."

"Oh, how sad."

"Yes. I guess you'll just have to carry on for her."

Maggie chuckled at this. "I'm hardly a radical, Eli. Tell me, where did you find this book?"

He sat back in his chair. "My sister Becky."

Eli had five sisters and a brother. He was located somewhere in the middle of the group. Maggie knew that Becky, his eldest sister, lived in New York City. She was unmarried and made her living by writing. Maggie had always been fascinated by Becky and hoped to have a chance to talk with her one day.

"Becky's very keen on the woman question," Eli was saying.

Maggie turned the book over in her hands. "I wasn't aware that there *was* a question about us."

"Oh, yes. It's called the emancipation of woman. Becky's been telling me all about it and sending me books and papers to read. Do you know, twenty years ago, she tried to address a group at an abolition meeting and got booed off the stage! They told her it wasn't proper for a woman to speak to a group made up of both men and women. Women, yes. But men? Outrage and horror!"

Maggie knew all about restrictions. She had heard stern-faced men silence women who dared to exhort a bit too much at mixed prayer meetings. Too much exhortation was considered preaching, and preaching was reserved for men. But, Maggie wondered, what if a woman believed that the Holy Ghost compelled her to speak? She believed that such a thing was possible, but knew that most men and many women believed it to be impossible, if not outright evil. "Why is women speaking in public is so wrong?" she mused aloud.

"I don't know. But that little set-to did something to Becky. It made her realize something. You see, when she tried to get involved in freeing slaves, she discovered that *she* wasn't free, either. She says women may not be held captive by iron chains, but they're certainly held captive by laws and customs."

Maggie rocked back and forth, thinking about Eli's comments. The chair creaked comfortably. She could hear the murmur of Lydia, Edgar, and Frankie's voices at the other end of the porch. A slight breeze stirred and whispered past her. It was nice to sit and talk. In fact, it was heaven to have someone with whom she could share ideas and feelings.

Eli sat back in his chair and rocked, too. "I agree with Becky. I think women ought to be free to pursue their lives as they see fit. I think all people ought to be free, regardless of color or sex."

That made Maggie smile. "*You* are a radical thinker, Elijah Smith."

"And proud of it." He watched her intently. "So tell me. What do *you* think?" His tone was serious. He really wanted to know.

What did she think? Maggie realized that she seldom had been asked that question. She stopped rocking. "Well . . ." she ventured, wondering what to say and how Eli would respond. "I think it's good for a woman to have a skill and it is good for her to use her talents. Why not? Did not God give these things to us? Using our skills and talents may even be a matter of survival. Life is uncertain, after all. For instance, when John died and then Aunt Letty, I had nothing but this home and two little girls. All I could do was start a rooming house. Had I been able to find another sort of employment, had I been able to find someone to help me with Lydia and Frankie . . ." The thought hovered in front of her, shimmering, beautiful, and at the same time unattainable. She felt a twinge of sadness, a pang of regret. "Anyway, it irks me that Samuel and others in this town feel I've degraded myself by running this rooming house. Especially since I don't feel in the least bit degraded – at least not until someone tells me that I ought to feel that way."

"If you hadn't started the rooming house," Eli asked, "what would you have liked to have done?"

She blushed and stared down at her hands. Maggie was glad that it was growing dark and Eli couldn't see her color.

"You're blushing."

She looked up in surprise, suddenly feeling exposed, as if he could see through her clothing.

"Are you embarrassed?" He laid a hand on the arm of her rocking chair and teased, "Maggie Blaine, you didn't want to do something *shameful*, did you?"

"No," she murmured. "Of course not. It's nothing. Never mind."

"No, I will mind because it's quite obviously something. Tell me. I won't laugh. I promise I won't even be shocked."

Maggie took a deep breath. "All right. I should have liked to have been a writer. I've kept a journal for years. Writing is different. My work each day is rather repetitive." She laughed tiredly. "No, make that boring and back breaking. Being able to write gives me relief. It helps me think things through. And I find joy and satisfaction in it, too. I could have written stories, had I the time. I might even have been a journalist for a newspaper." She smiled wryly. "Except no one would have hired me. I'm afraid that, like your sister, I am handicapped by my sex."

Eli snorted. "Nonsense! Did you ever try to get a job?"

"Well, no."

"Then how do you know that no one would've hired you?"

He had thrown down a challenge. Maggie stared steadily into his eyes. "All right, Elijah Smith. Would *you* have hired me?"

He hesitated. It was obvious that he had never considered hiring a woman. Not even Maggie. After a few seconds, though, he said, slowly, "Hire you, eh? Write me a story first, and then we'll talk."

That broke the tension. They both began to laugh. "Anyway," Maggie said as she stared into the dark street, "it's too late for me. But I believe that *Frankie* could have a career. She's very intelligent. She could teach. She could support herself and contribute something important to society. She wouldn't need to . . .." At this, she trailed off, a bit embarrassed at what she had almost said, for what she was thinking would strike at the heart of the social order.

But Eli finished the sentence for her. "Get married?"

Maggie took a breath. "Does that sound awful? I don't want her to stay single forever, but Frankie is so independent-minded. I just can't see her tending hearth and home, the way I can with Lydia."

"I agree. I think Frankie's just like her mother."

She felt her cheeks redden again. "Maybe. But I strongly feel that a woman should marry only if she wants to marry, not because she has no other choice."

"There! See? You *are* a radical. And I love you." Grinning, Eli leaned in, but Maggie put a hand to his chest to stop the on-coming kiss, whispering, "No. Not here."

"Come on, you're a free-thinker and you know it." Eli leaned into her hand, which made her giggle like a schoolgirl and try to push him away.

He was still trying to get a kiss and Maggie was still laughing when the sound of hooves and carriage wheels on cobbles broke them out of their fit of merriment. Both sat up attentively as the vehicle, lanterns lit beside the driver's seat, moved down Second Street. Maggie, the daughter of a carriage maker, immediately knew the vehicle was top of the line and just as quickly knew that it belonged to Samuel. As the driver pulled the horse up in front of the house, Jeremiah Madison alighted and bade the man goodnight. In another second, the carriage was off, horse hooves clopping on the cobblestones and fading away.

Like three moths chasing a flame, Frankie, Lydia, and Edgar followed the new minister as he strode across the porch to Maggie and Eli. Maggie asked how his visit went with the Beatty family. To tell the truth, she had not seen her family home in nearly two decades and couldn't help but be curious. Jeremiah was only too happy to provide then with full details about the graciousness of the Beatty home and the warm welcome he had received. He had taken two meals there – both of which had been excellent. He spoke of the family's great piety, and how they had invited him to join them in evening devotions after supper. The three Beatty children had been very polite and well-spoken. The youngest had recited Bible verses for him. And Leah had sung "Rejoice, the Lord is King," while her mother accompanied her on the piano.

"I can sing that!" Frankie announced and launched into a wobbly, "Rejoice the Lord is King; Your Lord and King adore; Mortals, give thanks and sing, and triumph—"

Maggie cut her off. "Thank you, Frankie. Some other time, perhaps." She turned back to Jeremiah. "I am glad you enjoyed the music, Mr. Madison."

"Yes, indeed. Lydia sings quite beautifully and comports herself with great modesty. I felt honored to have her sing for me."

Frankie – red hair refusing to be tamed and dress in an untidy tangle – frowned, turned on her heel, and stomped into the house. Sadly for her, Jeremiah did not notice the display of disappointment and temper. But Maggie did.

Lydia sighed. "Yes, well, it sounds as if they have a wonderful life. It must be lovely to have money."

"Money isn't everything," the minister corrected. "Remember, the *love* of money is the root of all evil."

Lydia considered this, and then replied, "All right, I will not love it. But I'd like to *have* it. Just once."

The group laughed. Jeremiah added that the Beatty family had invited him to dine again next week, and he had accepted.

Maggie was more than certain Samuel would see to it that he dined frequently with them, but worried the Beatty family would monopolize the new minister. "I'm sure there are many families who wish to spend time with you."

"Oh, yes!" Jeremiah averred. "And I intend to start my visitation this week. I wish to learn about our families to determine if they need help or if they can be of help to someone else."

Eli had been quietly listening; but he suddenly spoke up. "You made quite an impression today, Mr. Madison. I'm sure you'll be in great demand. People like to have the minister visit. Makes them feel good. Better yet, makes them feel important."

Jeremiah Madison considered his comment. "I take your meaning, but I must say that such a thought makes me rather uneasy."

Eli's brown eyes grew wide behind his wire-rim glasses. He had intense eyes – a reporter's eyes – and they held steady on the young minister. "Really?"

"That is, to preach is to presume to speak for God," he clarified, "which I find a rather daunting task – particularly if people make the mistake of thinking that God's Spirit has taken up permanent residence in the pastor's soul."

"A risk every minister takes, I'm sure," Eli noted. "Leadership is a tricky business – especially in the church. Someone with your gifts can't help but encounter a great deal of admiration."

"Yes, but don't forget that there may be a great deal of criticism, as well, should one not live up to expectations." An expression – one that was hard to read – crossed Jeremiah Madison's handsome face. "Or should one slip and fall."

Eli leaned forward. He was intrigued and Maggie knew that he had many more questions. But before he could say anything further, Jeremiah exclaimed, "Well! It's late. So, if you will excuse me, I think I shall retire."

"One more minute, Reverend," Eli said quickly. "If you don't mind, I'd like to interview you." When the pastor looked uncertain, he smiled easily. "I do this every time a new minister arrives. The *Gazette's* a very respectable penny weekly, and I try to keep people abreast of the doings in Blaineton, and let's be honest, people are curious about you. Perhaps you could talk about your hopes for the church and the town, where you served last, that sort of thing. I don't expect a big story." He grinned. "Just a small one."

Jeremiah smiled back, but there was a bit of discomfort in it. "Of course, Mr. Smith."

As he left, Maggie realized that it was time for her to retire, as well. The next day was Wash Day, which meant that she, Emily, and Lydia had the back-breaking task of scrubbing stains from the white clothes and sheets, sorting colors and types of fabric, washing each batch in a tub of steaming, soapy water, rinsing each in another tub of equally steaming water, plunging the whites into a tub of blueing, wringing the clothes out, and finally hanging all the things up to dry. It was no surprise that Monday was her least favorite day of the week. Over time she had become convinced that God had created a weekly Sabbath just so she could have the energy and peace of mind to tackle Wash Day.

Maggie informed Lydia that she could spend another ten minutes on the porch with Edgar but then needed to say goodnight, close up the house, and turn out any lamps.

She and Eli then walked through the quiet, darkened house to the kitchen. Usually, Eli went out the back door and cut through the yard to get to his chambers above the *Gazette*. The arrangement now gave the couple an excuse to get away from the other people in the building. As they stepped outside, Eli casually checked the back porch. No one was there. When he turned, Maggie slipped into his arms – as close as her crinoline cage would permit – and they shared a very gentle kiss. He pulled Maggie a bit too close and her cage shifted upwards in the back. "Eli," she whispered. "My hoops."

"Blasted things. Blasted corset, too."

"Ah," she nuzzled his face, "then it is a good thing they're there."

He nuzzled back. "You're going to read that book, aren't you?"

She nodded.

"Good. I think you'll like it."

"I'm sure I will."

He paused to kiss her. "That Madison fellow said some interesting things tonight."

Maggie chuckled. "Ah, ha! You've finally fallen under his spell. Just like the rest of us."

"Me? Not a chance. But he's got a history." He brushed his lips over her cheek. "And I wonder what that history is." Over her mouth. "Maybe I'll see where he was last." Over her ear. "You know, ask around." His lips began to work his way down her neck.

Now Maggie was the one who was beginning to rue her crinoline and corset. "Eli, I think you had better stop."

He looked up. "What? Don't you like this?"

She sighed and placed a hand on his chest. "I do like it. Entirely too much. That's the trouble."

They stood staring into each other's eyes for quite awhile.

"Got to go," he finally said, but didn't break the gaze.

She smiled.

"Tomorrow?"

"Tomorrow." Putting a hand to his face, she kissed him once more. "Good night, Eli."

"'Night, Maggie."

She watched him cross the yard and disappear into the print shop. Once he was out of sight, Maggie returned to the kitchen, shut the door and entered the addition where her girls, the Johnsons, and now Jeremiah had their rooms. She climbed the stairs to the second floor in order to check on Frankie – she never missed giving her girls a goodnight kiss. As she entered the hall, she heard someone sobbing. Maggie hesitated, and then knocked on the door to the room that Frankie and Lydia shared, and entered.

Her youngest daughter's dress, petticoats and hoop skirts were strewn all over the floor. Clad only in her corset and under things, the girl was sprawled across her bed and sobbing into a pillow. Maggie suppressed the urge to tidy the room, but went directly to the bed and sat down beside Frankie.

It always amazed her that Frankie could cry as heart-wrenchingly as a disconsolate child. Maggie was further amazed that her own response was exactly the same as when Frankie had been a tot – she gently rubbed the girl's back to soothe her. "You poor moppet. What's got you so upset?"

Quite abruptly, Frankie sat upright and, with unrestrained hatred, snarled, "Leah Beatty! Who else? She has everything! Money, clothes, boys! And now she's after Mr. Madison!"

"Oh, moppet, come here, please." Maggie gathered her unresisting daughter into her arms and gave her a kiss on the head. "Life isn't fair, is it? But I think perhaps you got your hopes up a bit too high."

"Why?" Frankie snuffled. "Because we're poor?"

"We're not poor. We just have to work hard. What I mean, Frankie, is that you're only fourteen years old."

She pulled away. "That's old enough to have a beau!"

"Yes, but not old enough for Mr. Madison. Leah's older. She's eighteen. That's closer to Mr. Madison's age. Plus, Leah is out of school."

The girl pouted. "And Leah's an awful flirt. Everyone knows that. Modest, my foot!"

"Frances, that's gossip. You know how I feel about that."

"If I weren't a schoolgirl, do you think he would like me?"

"I don't know. All I know is that everything happens in its own time. It did for me. And it will for you. It's just not your time yet."

"Well, my time is taking forever." Frankie wiped her nose on the back of her hand.

Maggie produced a handkerchief from her sleeve. Frankie took the hankie and vigorously mopped her face.

"I really do like him, Mama," she said between swipes. "I fancied we'd get married and I'd help him in his ministry. We'd be partners. I'd go visit the sick with him, and teach, and preach."

Maggie lifted an eyebrow. "Preach? Do you mean that you would do it, too?"

She sniffed. "Yes."

The idea put a strange feeling in the pit of Maggie's stomach – something akin to both fear and excitement.

"I should have known my dreams were wrong," Frankie muttered.

"Oh, no!" Maggie quickly replied. "Maybe what you were dreaming of is to be a *preacher*, and not merely a preacher's wife." She couldn't believe that she was saying those words. But in her heart Maggie knew that Frankie was born to do something great – provided she received the right training and learned a little self-restraint. "If God is indeed calling you to preach, then you needn't marry a clergyman to answer that call. You could preach as your own person."

"I could?" Her eyes were wide with potential.

The strange feeling grew in Maggie's stomach. "Yes, but you'd encounter a great deal of resistance. Women preachers aren't by any means common. And some people believe that women *shouldn't* preach. They believe that God does not wish it. The Methodist Episcopal Church does not permit the ordination of women, so you'd have to be very strong and very brave, and trust God with all your heart." The idea made the room feel as if it were throbbing. Promise was alive and tangible. Hope was present. Maggie took a deep breath and changed the subject, for she did not know what else to do. "Ah, well, that is for the future, isn't it? Stand up now and I'll help unlace your corset."

Frankie hopped to her feet. "Oh, I do so hate corsets!"

****

From Maggie's Journal, 14 April 1860

Has my daughter been called to preach? In my heart, I believe that it is unusual, but not wrong. If God is all-powerful, as He is, then can He not do anything? Can He not call a female to spread His Word? What does the Holy Ghost care for male and female? Are not all souls the same? Perhaps Frankie is being called by God to do this. If so, then I will support her.

I will reveal this to you, Journal. I believe that women are fitted to do many things – many more than men will let us do. I know that there are women who are smarter than men. I know that some women have done remarkable feats. Why then can we not speak to mixed groups in public? Ephesians says that women must be subject to their husbands. We hear that all the time. But Ephesians also tells men to love their wives as Christ loved the church and gave himself up for her. And it says that men should love their wives as they love their own bodies. I do not know many men who do all that – especially those who love to quote the former part of Ephesians. They go on about wives submitting to husbands, and conveniently forget what Ephesians has to say to husbands.

If God truly is calling my daughter, what then? She would have to leave our church, for the M.E.C. will not ordain women. But who among the churches *will* ordain a woman? To which church would she go? She would be a laughing stock, reviled, or both. My God, could I stand by and watch that, even if You called her? But Your Son had to endure that and much more. And I know this, my Frankie is strong – and Your Holy Ghost will make her even stronger.

****

Maggie sighed, closed her journal, picked up the lamp, and stood up from her *escritoire*. She walked to her bed, set the lamp on her nightstand, and then climbed wearily onto the mattress. For a few moments, she sat with her eyes closed. Finally, she opened her eyes and picked *Woman in the Nineteenth Century* off the nightstand. She stared at the front page for quite awhile, and then opened the book and began to read.

CHAPTER THREE

Maggie's Journal, 13 August 1860

It is hard to believe that Mr. Madison has been with us for only four months, yet in that time his preaching and warm manner have brought at least ten more people into our little church. He is, I daresay, extremely popular and well-loved. We await his sermons with an eagerness that we have not had in a very long time – he encourages us to be Christ-like in our daily lives, he gives us hope, and he inspires us. I have seen him play with the children, speak earnestly with the young people, and comfort the aged and infirm. We all feel exceedingly blessed.

I only wish Eli felt that way, too. He seems to reserve his judgment. Ah, but perhaps that will change once he goes to camp meeting! The district leaders have asked Mr. Madison to preach – and I know that he will light a fire of God's love there, too. God willing, Eli will be one of those touched.

****

The district camp meeting would begin Monday, August 20. Every member of the Blaineton Methodist congregation was stirred up and eager to go. Maggie was eagerly looking forward to going away for a week. Every August, the gathering of Methodist Episcopal churches met in a field donated by a farmer. Prior to the congregation's departure, the women checked and repaired the seams and canvas on their church's society tent. They also saw to the tents for their own families. Maggie, Emily, Frankie, and Lydia took care of three tents: one for Maggie and her girls, one for Nate and Emily (the African Methodist Episcopal church districts would be meeting a week later), and one for Patrick, Chester Carson, and Edgar Lape. Eli was coming with a small tent for himself.

At long last, very early on the appointed Monday morning, Nate and Emily helped Maggie load the hired wagon she and Eli would be taking to the camp grounds. "I wish Grandpa O'Reilly would go," Maggie sighed. "But he shows no interest at all. There's no Catholic church in town and he has not attended his peoples' services in years. I used to hope that he would join us at the chapel, but he staunchly refuses."

Emily smiled. "We all have our own ways, I suppose."

"But no church at all?"

"We'll just pray that God takes care of him."

Maggie passed the last bedroll to Nate, who secured it on the wagon. She then turned to Emily and warmly took her friend's hands. "You're right. God has taken care of him thus far. And you, Emily. You've been such a blessing these past eight years."

"As you are to us," Emily replied and kissed Maggie on the cheek. "See you Saturday." But when they turned to go back into the house, a grin spread slowly over Emily's face. "I won't be able to watch after you at camp meeting. So you behave yourself with your Mr. Smith."

As Nate chuckled, Maggie blushed and followed them inside.

A short while later, after she had finished packing her own trunk and was busying herself by tidying up the front parlor, the sound of hooves and wheels on cobblestones called her to the window. Peering out, Maggie saw a well-appointed coach, and knew that it belonged to Samuel. A moment later, a young girl hopped down from beside the driver and scurried onto the porch. She was perhaps seventeen or eighteen years old, thin and clad in the plain clothing of a servant; but even the drab color of her dress could not dampen the fact that she was very pretty. Her shining blond hair was tucked neatly under her bonnet. Maggie hurried to the front door. As she swung it open, she met a pair of green almond-shaped eyes. A lazy smile graced the young woman's face. "Mrs. Blaine?" she inquired. Her voice had a dusky quality. "My name is Carrie Hillsborough. I'm one of the maids at the Samuel Beatty residence. Paul – the driver – and I were sent to pick up Mr. Madison's effects for the camp meeting."

Maggie offered a welcoming smile, despite the fact that she was feeling a pang of annoyance. Sam had been insinuating himself and his family rather thoroughly into Jeremiah Madison's life and she found it irksome. Promptly reminding herself not to be judgmental, she silently confessed to her Maker that she was in fact a bit jealous. Sam did what he wanted as if it were perfectly natural and right. No one ever questioned him or his motives. However, he felt quite free to question

Maggie and the things she did – all because she was a woman and his sister. Maggie was all too aware that she did things differently from most other people – but she presented a danger to no one. She didn't cheat or steal. She worked hard to steer clear of gossip. Thus, she simply could not understand why Sam couldn't find something else to occupy his time. And then a dark thought occurred to her. Perhaps he *had* found something else – in the form of Jeremiah. Madison.

This thought was quite disturbing, because Maggie knew all too well that after awhile the glow would come off even that relationship, spiritual though it may be, and Samuel would begin to criticize the minister. She had seen him do the same with many other pastors. And that was where she stopped herself. You're being sinful, she thought. You must give up this anger – completely. Let it go. It's doing you no good. Anger only eats you from the inside out.

With her attitude re-ordered, Maggie smiled broadly at Carrie and invited her to come with her to the new wing, where they found that Jeremiah's door was open. Maggie paused nonetheless and rapped on one of the panels.

The young minister, who was reading the Bible and taking notes at his desk, looked up.

"Good morning, Reverend. May we interrupt?"

He smiled welcomingly at her, but when his eyes rested upon the maid, his face lit up. "Ah, Carrie!" He rose to his feet. "So, you and Paul are here already!"

She curtsied. "Yes, sir. Are you ready, sir?"

"Yes, yes!" He closed his Bible, gathered it and his notes, and carefully placed the items into his carpet bag. After shutting and securing the clasp, Jeremiah picked the bag up and walked briskly to the door. Maggie watched him pass by her and stop at Carrie's side.

"How are you feeling, Carrie?" he asked. "When I saw you last, you had a cold."

The two proceeded to walk down the hall. Carrie was saying that she had recovered and was most well, thank you very much, and now looking forward to the camp meeting.

Jeremiah responded that he, too, was looking forward to many sweet hours of prayer and good preaching – and then he laid his hand lightly on her back.

Now, Maggie knew that Jeremiah communicated easily with young people of all classes. He had a gentle almost intimate way of speaking that quickly drew them in. They seemed to feel as if he understood their very thoughts and emotions. Clearly he had a gift, and under his leadership and inspired preaching, the church had been thriving and growing. Jeremiah Madison was a blessing.

Yet, that touch to Carrie's back somehow bothered Maggie. There was something about it that was a bit too familiar.

Oh, she knew what Eli would tell her. He did not trust most pastors, which he blamed on his Quaker upbringing. In his church, everyone had the right to speak, provided they had Light and were properly moved by the Spirit. Quakers had no use for "hireling clergy." He claimed that the adulation many ministers received had a deleterious effect on them. "Some of them start believing that they're holier than their parishioners," he had told her, "just because someone put a hand on their head and ordained them. And the parishioners believe it, too – and if the man has some preaching skills, they begin to think that he can do no wrong."

Maggie sighed. If this were true, then Eli's assessment did not bode well for Jeremiah, for the young pastor seemed unable to do anything *but* court adulation. He was a kindly visitor to the sick, had a thorough knowledge of scripture, delivered extempore prayers that brought tears to the eye, and was a captivating preacher. He was more than competent and, as a result, good things were constantly laid at his feet. All of which made Maggie pray that their young minister would be able to rise above the demands and flattery of popularity.

Her practical side abruptly interrupted her musings. Why worry about such nonsense, it asked. There are no indications that Mr. Madison is anything but a good, Christian man. There is no reason to worry. Besides, before you leave, the floors need scrubbing, so you had better get to it.

****

Maggie and Eli had saved a little money, enough to rent two wagons and two teams of horses. They rode with the equipment in one wagon, and Frankie, Lydia, Patrick, Mr. Carson, and Edgar rode in the other. As they bounced along dirt roads, they were joined by wagons filled with people from other churches in the district. The wagons groaned and rattled over the ruts in the road, jostling their riders and contents and kicking up trails of dust. It was not the most comfortable ride in the world, but everyone was happy. They were off to camp meeting, off to rest and pray and visit. Voices singing a hymn abruptly rose from one wagon. And, one by one, each group joined in, until the air was filled with four-part harmonies praising God.

After several hours, they turned down the road to the campgrounds. Everyone was familiar with the routine of life at camp meeting and was eager to return to the familiar and beloved location.

The grounds were arranged in a circle. At the center was the tabernacle. This served as an outdoor church. A wooden stand or speakers' platform had been built at one end of it. The platform was actually a small building with a stage on the second floor. Three walls surrounded the place where the speakers stood. This upper story was actually divided in two by a wall. The speaker commanded the open front half where all could see him, but the enclosed room located directly behind him served as a place for private prayer as well as occasional housing for special speakers. The bottom floor of the stand was completely enclosed, and this room too was used for private prayer and lodging.

In front of the speaker's stand stood a large area called the altar. Twenty-eight feet in width, it contained seats with a center aisle and an entrance near the speakers' platform. This was where mourners sat as they prepared to surrender their souls to Christ. It was a holy place of intense prayer.

Then there was the space for the congregation, who sat on benches made of planks. As was the custom, men and women at the camp meeting sat on opposite sides of this space – the men on the left and the women on the right.

The tabernacle was surrounded by tents. Maggie and her family pitched theirs in a spot somewhat removed from the center, as the grounds were crowded and the best places had already been taken. Everyone knew that the tents and little cabins of the most faithful and powerful in the District were situated immediately around the tabernacle. Among them, of course, was the Beatty family tent.

Maggie and Eli were among the common folk and regular church attendees, a fact that did not displease Maggie in the least. She knew their place in society. Moreover, she always found those folks good-hearted and pious. The truth was she knew what it had been like to be in the inner circle and was much happier keeping her distance.

Going out, in concentric circles from the tabernacle were ever-decreasing levels of religiosity. The trick was to know one's place and to refrain from locating too close to the outer ring.

Near the entrance to the camp grounds one could find tradesmen selling meat, fruits and vegetables to the campers. The District had hired watchmen to keep the campground clear of rowdies, who liked to congregate near the entrance and were known to drink, carouse, and generally hoot and cat-call at the faithful going to and fro.

But it was camp meeting and that meant that everyone was there, from the pious to the rowdy. This was the place to be in the summer. There was always plenty of socializing and excitement to be had, no matter one's place and no matter how religious one was or was perceived to be.

As Maggie helped set up their family tents, she wondered how Jeremiah would fare. He was not nearly old enough in the ministry to be a featured preacher, so he would be assigned to preach at the lesser services. But he spoke with such fire and brilliance that she was certain the camp meeting association would quickly move him forward. In fact, she was sure that in perhaps as little as a year he would occupy the speakers' stand at one of the main services.

As Maggie emerged from her tent, she saw that Eli had finished putting his own up, and he and the other men had just raised the tent that the boarding house men would be using. Eli stood back, surveying their work with satisfaction. "Not bad, eh?" He chuckled and patted his stomach. "Especially for a rather portly newspaperman."

Maggie smiled. "I don't think weight has anything to do with raising a tent, but you certainly seem to know what you are doing. I didn't know Quakers had camp meetings."

"Actually," he replied, "I learned my camping skills out west. I'm not really all that enthusiastic about the idea of camp meetings. In fact, this is my first one. I figure at the very least, the fresh air will do me good. And I'm sure I'll find a story here for the *Gazette*. I mean, there's always a story at these things, isn't there?"

"From the twinkle in your eyes, I suspect you're hoping to find a scandal."

"Oh, no – not a scandal." But his thoroughly naughty grin said otherwise. "That is, not unless one happens."

A short while later, Eli, Patrick, and Mr. Carson ambled off to investigate the activity on the grounds, while Maggie set out to look for Lydia, Edgar, and Frankie. The trio had met some friends and told her that they wanted to see who else was at the meeting. Maggie wanted to remind them that supper in the District boarding tent would be at six p.m. The thought made her smile with pleasure. The boarding tent was a wondrous thing. Campers had to pay for the convenience of three meals a day, but it meant that she and many other women had at least one week out of the year in which they did not have to cook and endure the tedium of scrubbing piles of pots, pans, and dishes.

As she walked, Maggie noticed that not a few of the tents had impromptu prayer meetings within, while others held folks singing hymns. This sort of informal exhorting, singing, and praying went on nearly continuously, sometimes lasting well into the night. The activity was approved by the District because it supported the work done at the tabernacle. Emotions were stirred, conversions occurred, and the Holy Spirit moved like a sweet breeze through the grounds. Maggie could not help but enjoy the excitement and spiritual beauty she found every year. It made her wonder how and if Eli would be affected.

As she drew closer to the Blaineton church tent, her ears caught the familiar voice of Jeremiah Madison. She peeked inside as unobtrusively as she could. She found Jeremiah, rapt in prayer, loudly entreating the Lord for all he was worth. He was surrounded by a group of young men and women, among them, Lydia, Edgar, and Frankie. Maggie saw that Leah Beatty was on the other side of the tent. She had to admit the eighteen-year-old was truly beautiful. Her skin was smooth and flawlessly clear, set off by wide dark eyes and waves of blond hair. Her figure was healthy and rounded. The girl was pleasing to look at, to be sure, but – despite Jeremiah's glowing opinion of her – Maggie knew better. Leah was actually a demanding and difficult young woman, no doubt thanks to her pampered life as a child of Samuel Beatty.

****

From Maggie's Journal, 20 August 1860

Like the others in the tent, Leah was deep in prayer. Her hands were clenched tightly together and her head bowed. It was such a touching sight, and I had a mind to join them – that is, until Leah suddenly opened her eyes and gazed upon Mr. Madison. The expression in her eyes was one of utter adoration. Then a perfectly angelic smile lit her face and, with a glow that must have rivaled Moses' face after seeing God on Mount Sinai, Leah looked heavenward and closed her eyes once more.

The subject of her rapt prayer was all too clear.

Across from Leah, Carrie Hillsborough also knelt and likewise appeared to be immersed in prayer. But then I saw her eyes open, too. This girl gazed intently upon Mr. Madison with a fire that made me blush – and the slowest, the slyest, the most calculating of smiles crept across her face.

Dear Journal, seeing all this made me feel most ill at ease. It was not something that I should have seen, nor would I wish to see. I was struck by the realization that although the scene appeared quite innocent on the surface, something most unwholesome was lurking just below. I truly believe nearly all the girls were gathered in the tent not to draw closer to God, but to get nearer to Mr. Madison. Did they desire to impress him with their piety, and once he is impressed, do they hope to make him their own? If so this is most disturbing, for Mr. Madison is no longer a spiritual leader, but a prize to be won.

****

Maggie nervously turned and hurried away – past the tents of people, past the praying, past the singing. She could not bear to see any more, and so she retreated into her tent and prayed.

By evening, the shock had subsided, but Maggie was now on her guard. She desperately wanted to shake away that feeling and so after evening tea, she, her girls, Edgar, and Mr. Carson went to the evening worship service. Good skeptic that he was, Eli lurked on the edge of the worshipers, joining their group only after the service was over. The little boarding house family returned to their place in the circle to sit about the fire, where they talked and sang until it was time to retire.

It would have been a happy thing had Maggie fallen asleep immediately. After all, she had had plenty of exercise and fresh air. Instead she lay most unhappily awake, feeling every lump in the bedding of her cot and every minor discomfort in her body. Her mind continued to see Leah, Carrie, and Jeremiah. Her heart fretted about the young minister's vulnerability. After squirming and shifting for half an hour, she had finally had enough. Maggie got out of bed, pulled her clothes back on and slipped out into the night air, while her daughters slept, breathing softly, on their cots.

As she looked around, she found Eli sitting by the dying embers of the fire. He smiled at her and whispered, "Can't sleep, huh?"

She shook her head.

"Got just the thing." He stood up and held a hand out to her. "Come on."

Maggie put her hand in his, feeling his fingers close securely around hers, and let him pull her into the woods, away from the camp sites, the low fires, and the softly sung hymns. The heavy smell of greenery hung in the damp air. After awhile, she detected a rushing sound, which grew steadily louder. At length, they came out of the woods to a place where a stream cut through the back fields of the farmer who permitted the District to use his grove.

The moon overhead was bright and pure, lighting the area nearly as brightly as day. The silvery brightness allowed rocks and trees to cast shadows as the creek sparkled and sang its meandering way through the field. Maggie's breath caught at the mysterious beauty before her.

Eli indicated the grass. "Would you care for a seat, Madam?"

She laughed as the two of them sat down.

"Now," he said, "*here* . . . here is where *I* meet God."

Maggie drew her knees to her chest and stared up at the sky.

"They look like diamonds scattered over black velvet, don't they? And this creek – it makes music. Music you can smell." Eli sniffed the air appreciably. "This is what it's all about. This is good. On nights like this I feel lucky just to be part of it all."

"A blessing," Maggie concurred, soothed by her peaceful surroundings. "I think sometimes that camp meetings are a bit too emotional."

"What makes you say that?"

She paused a moment. "What I am about to say must be held in confidence."

"You don't have to worry about me. You should know that by now."

"I do." At first Maggie wondered how much she should reveal, but something made her decide to trust him, and trust him completely. "I saw something today. I happened upon a group of young people in prayer with Mr. Madison. That was fine, and to be expected. What I did not expect was that two of the girls had something on their minds other than God. One, I'm sure, was praying to marry our minister. And the other was – well, let me just say that I believe her feelings were less than modest."

Eli chuckled. "What a naughty girl. Doesn't she know that she's expected to maintain purity of mind at all times?"

"Eli!"

"Oh, Maggie, she's young. Young people have those feelings." He threw a sly smile in her direction. "And those of us who are older have them, too."

Maggie let his comment pass. "I just mean that there's a time and a place for everything, and that was neither. Worse yet, their feelings are directed at a clergyman. It's clear that they are not pursuing him only because he is a gifted minister."

"He is a man, too," Eli reminded her.

"Of course, but he also has tremendous influence. That makes him extremely attractive, especially to women and particularly to young girls. And so he becomes the target of all sorts of silly romantic fantasies."

"And what can *you* do?" he teased. "He's talented and popular. You cannot protect him from unwanted advances. He's a grown man, and he's been a pastor for awhile. I'm sure he has encountered this sort of thing. Girls probably fall in love with him all the time."

Maggie stared at the water as it skimmed over the rocks in the creek bed. "What I saw is not proper at a camp meeting, Eli."

"Of course, it isn't. But it happens. The power of God is still power. And power, my dear woman, is always seductive."

"But what attracts the girls is not the power of God. So what is it then, the power of lust?"

"Possible," he replied. "From what I've heard, emotions run high at camp meetings. You know what they say: more souls are made than saved at camp meetings.'"

Maggie hugged her knees to her chest. "I hope it doesn't come to that. I wish I could do something."

"Well, you can't, nor should you." Eli looked up at the sky, and then added a bit wearily, "Maybe that's the problem with all you good church people."

"Eli!"

"Now, don't get upset. It's just how *I* see it. Church folk do all sorts of things to learn about God and to talk to God. They exhort and cry and sing and do all manner of exercises. But everyone seems to forget one thing. They forget that God is also in the silence. They don't know how to *listen*, Maggie. They're a people who have forgotten how. They're too busy doing and talking. If everyone listened for a change, then maybe everyone would have a bit more discernment."

She let this sink in for a moment. Although she wanted to argue with him, Maggie realized that there was truth in his criticism. "Are all you Quakers this blunt?"

He guffawed. "I'm not a Quaker. Well, not in the sense of belonging to a meeting. But I guess my mother managed to give me a few Quaker values."

"More than a few, Elijah Smith."

Her comment made them both laugh.

Once their chuckles had subsided, the two sat quietly, letting the river and stars speak. The stream made the air around it cool, and Maggie had forgotten her shawl. With a little shiver, she snuggled close to Eli. He put an arm around her and hugged her. After another few seconds, something dawned on them. They were alone for the first time. A bit surprised, each looked into the other's face and, smiling, they shared a kiss. More kisses eventually pulled them down into the grass, where they lay in each other's arms.

"You know," Eli said, brushing his mouth over her cheek, "something's bound to happen if a man and a woman are left alone in a field on a night like this, at a camp meeting."

"You're right," Maggie whispered.

He grinned widely. "Madam, I do believe you're compromising me."

"Oh, hush up, and be compromised."

"Why, Maggie, I am shocked! Shocked!"

She giggled. "No, you aren't, Elijah Smith. Now, hush up and kiss me."

Lying together in the grass was bliss. Maggie forgot about the rooming house, her daughters, her brother, and the young people in the tent. Her attention was on the man she loved.

But Eli abruptly stopped everything and sat up. "Damn!" his hissed.

Maggie blinked at him. "What?"

"I can't."

She laughed. "It seems to me that you *can*."

"That's not what I mean." He gently pulled her up so that she was sitting beside him. "What I mean is, maybe we *shouldn't* be doing this."

Maggie's conscience awoke with a start and she was embarrassed at her behavior. She wanted things with him that a proper, unmarried Christian woman shouldn't want, at least not before their wedding. What must he think of me, she wondered.

Eli heaved a sigh. "Maybe my mother taught me better than I realize. I just remembered her telling me about the Apostle Paul's advice to courting couples. 'If they cannot contain, let them marry; for it is better to marry than to burn.'"

Speechless, she stared at him.

He took a deep breath and continued, "Look, it's pretty obvious that I'm having trouble containing. And so are you. I mean, it's really quite simple, when you think about it. Rather than letting the both of us suffer or, worse yet, ruin your reputation we, you know – we just ought to get married. I mean, if we keep on like this, we might end up, you know, maybe making a little soul of our own. I know we haven't talked about it yet, but we both know that we're going to get married eventually. So why wait?"

"Eli," she finally said. "You quoted Scripture."

He might have blushed. She couldn't be sure because of the shadows, but his voice held a trace of pink as he said, "Look, just because a man doesn't care to go to church doesn't mean he doesn't believe and know something!" He took a breath and added, "But I also know this. I love you Maggie Blaine and I'd even become Methodist for you. Say you'll marry me."

"Do you mean it?"

"Yes. Proposals of marriage don't tumble out of my mouth every day." He paused. "I'm not so sure about becoming Methodist, though."

That made her smile. "I love you, too, Elijah Smith."

"And so?"

Now Maggie laughed out right. "And so, yes, Elijah Smith, I will marry you!"

****

From Maggie's Journal, 21 August 1860

And so, dear Journal, we walked hand in hand back toward the campgrounds. But when we were still in the woods, we heard the sound of voices. We two stopped walking and listened. One of the voices was male and the other female.

Eli made a joke about more souls being made at camp meetings, and I had to shush him, for fear that we might be discovered.

We could hear the woman giggle in response to something the man had murmured. Their tones sounded very familiar. As we drew back into the shadows, the couple came to a patch of dusky moonlight. The man was tall but it was difficult to see more, as he was closer to the shadows. The light, however, graced the girl's blond hair and curvy figure. In another second, the couple disappeared as they continued their progress toward the field. Finally, their voices faded.

I realized that I had been holding my breath the entire time and slowly let it out. The girl was Leah. There was no doubt about that. But I also knew who than man was, despite his being in the shadows, for his voice was all too familiar. It was Mr. Madison.

"Maybe there is some trouble brewing," Eli said.

Ah, if it would only be that small! For there would be more than "some" trouble, if what we saw indicated that the couple had developed an affection for one another. What Eli did not know was that my brother had great plans for Leah – plans that did not include a penniless preacher. Now I was left to wonder how Mr. Madison behaved with other the girls in our congregation. My mind was so busy by the time I returned to the tent, that once again I was unable to fall asleep. So I prayed. I prayed with all my heart that scandal and trouble would not come my church's way.

****

Wednesday was full of prayers and hymns and sermons. Jeremiah Madison preached in the tabernacle early that evening. Despite the early hour, he still managed to gather quite a crowd.

He began his sermon by saying that he would not be preaching on Christian joy or justification, nor would he preach on sanctification or mission work. Instead, he wished to preach on the kingdom of heaven. "Do you know," he told the congregation, "that Christ spoke often of the kingdom of heaven? So is this not worth some of our time this day? What is this kingdom? What is it like? My brothers and sisters, Christ gives us many examples. The kingdom of heaven is like a pearl of great price, like a coin lost by a woman, like a mustard seed, like yeast mixed into dough, like a feast with God, like a net, and much, much more. And, my friends, do you know that the kingdom of heaven is not just where we may go after we die, but is something that can be among us now, at this very moment? It can! And it is!"

The young preacher's voice twisted its way round the souls of his listeners. His handsome features pleaded for their attention. His tall, lean body – arms outstretched – reached imploringly to each and every one, as if Jesus himself were there inviting them to come into the embrace of his loving Father.

"And when the scribe asked Jesus which of the commandments were the greatest, Jesus told him, 'Hear, O Israel; The Lord our God is one Lord: And thou shalt love the Lord thy God with all thy heart, and with all thy soul, and with all thy mind, and with all thy strength: this is the first commandment. And the second is like, namely this, Thou shalt love thy neighbor as thyself. There is none other commandment greater than these.' And do you know how that scribe replied?"

The congregation waited, although many knew the answer.

"He told Jesus that he had spoken the truth, 'for there is one God; and there is none other but he: And to love him with all the heart, and with all the understanding, and with all the soul, and with all the strength, and to love his neighbor as himself, is more than all whole burnt offerings and sacrifices.' And to that Jesus responded, 'Thou art not far from the kingdom of God.' Yes! That scribe was not far from the kingdom of God! For that scribe *understood* God's greatest commandments. How much closer would he have been to the Kingdom had he also been *practicing* the commandments? Friends, when we believe with our hearts, know with our minds, and do with our hands, with our lives – yes, my friends, *then*, and *only* then is the Kingdom of Heaven among us! Oh, do you not want that? Do you not want that now?"

The response was amazing. People fell weeping to their knees. Every soul there was moved – all except Elijah Smith, who narrowed his brown eyes, tightened his lips, and squinted thoughtfully at the figure in the pulpit.

Maggie, meanwhile, found herself struggling with the power of Jeremiah's message, his obvious attractiveness to young women, and possibly his attraction to them. She wanted desperately to enter into the spirit of the preaching and to feel her soul moved. But she could not let go. She would not let go of the things she had seen the other day.

She was so absorbed in her own thoughts that she was thrown completely off balance when Frankie suddenly got to her feet and announced, "I have a word to share."

All eyes focused on the girl. Maggie stifled an urge to reach out, grab her daughter's dress, and pull her back down onto the bench. Heart pounding, she asked herself if a fourteen-year-old girl was qualified to exhort. Exhorting, of course, was permissible for a woman, but Frankie was not a woman – girls her age rarely spoke to an assembly.

Maggie flashed a silent plea in Eli's direction, but he was watching her daughter both in amazement and with something akin to paternal pride.

Frankie swallowed hard, and then began to speak in a small voice. "I know that I'm young. But the Apostle Paul told Timothy not to let anyone despise his youth. So, I have a word." She swallowed again. "It's just this. We've all been praying and singing and worshiping together these past days, we're all filled with brotherly love. We have just heard Mr. Madison tell us how loving God and loving neighbor brings us into the Kingdom of Heaven. I daresay some of us have felt very near to the Kingdom. But I just wonder, well, will we be able to *keep* that Spirit of love when we go back home? I was reading the First Letter of John this morning." She opened her Bible to the page marked by a blade of grass. Maggie could see that she had several blades stuck in the book. "In the third chapter, 'And this is his commandment, that we should believe on the name of his Son Jesus Christ, and love one another, as he gave us commandment.' And it also says in the second chapter, 'He that saith he is in the light, and hateth his brother, is in darkness even until now. He that loveth his brother abideth in the light, and there is none occasion of stumbling in him.' So what I need to say is that we must abide in the light *all* the time. We must love one another *everyday* and not just on Sundays or at camp meeting. And ..." She turned to another page marked by a blade of grass. "The third chapter says, 'My little children, let us not love in word, neither in tongue; but in deed *and* in truth.' So we have to love not just with what we say but with what we do." With that, she closed the Bible and looked up at the congregation. She was preaching. Maggie knew it. Everyone knew it. But Maggie knew she would tell everyone that Frankie had merely been exhorting. "And so I pray that we take the Spirit that God has so graciously given us this week and take it back to our towns, back to our families, and back to our churches. May we dare to love one another in word *and* deed, for the sake of our dear Lord." Frankie looked nervously at those listening to her. "Um . . . thank you," she murmured and promptly sat down.

Waves of "amen's" swept through the gathering, but so did busy whisperings from people such as the Moore sisters, Mrs. Mendenhall, and others.

****

From Maggie's Journal, 22 August 1860

The Spirit spoke through my daughter this afternoon. I heard it loud and clear. We may sing and pray and listen, but what do our actions say about how we love? I knew then what I had to do.

After the service, I sought out Mr. Madison. It was difficult to broach the subject. I did not wish to appear as a meddler, but neither could I remain silent. "Your sermon was most inspiring," I told him. "When you preach tomorrow for the last time at camp meeting, I am sure that you will be speaking before a very full crowd." He smiled generously and thanked me. "It does seem," I added, wishing that I had a talent for words, "that the young people like you very much. In only a short while you have become a great influence in their lives." Once again, that handsome smile and melodious voice answered me, "If I influence them in the way that your daughter was influenced this evening then I have done God's work."

I decided that now was the time to move into what troubled me. "Have you thought that influence through, Mr. Madison?"

He asked what I meant.

"I just notice that more than a few girls have taken a fancy to you."

He laughed outright at this, and told me that this had happened to him before. He was quick to assure me that the girls were experiencing childish affection and attraction – and nothing more. Such things as these would go away with time.

"Yet, they do come to you for counsel," I pressed.

He agreed, but reminded me that this was precisely why he was their minister: to inspire, to counsel, and to shepherd.

I could not argue with that, dear Journal. And so I was reduced to saying, "Just the same, it would be good for you to take care not to get overly close."

He graciously told me that he was aware of the dangers, but again added that I was not to worry.

How shall I do that, after what I have seen?

****

After a good supper of vegetable stew and bread in the boarding tent and the final preaching service for the day, Maggie's family returned to their camp area and sat, perched on fallen logs as seats, while they watched the fire. After awhile, Mr. Carson, Patrick, and

Edgar decided to go to a hymn sing in a nearby tent. Eli, Maggie, and the girls were left, alternately singing and chatting by the fire.

At one point, Frankie commented, "I do believe that Leah Beatty has set her cap for Mr. Madison."

"Nonsense," Lydia replied. "In no way would Uncle Samuel permit that. I daresay he has a better alliance in mind for Leah."

Frankie laughed. "What better alliance could there be than a minister like Mr. Madison?"

"Ministers are poor, Frankie. Uncle will not permit his daughter to be poor."

Maggie intervened at this point. "It is best we do not gossip about others, especially our family."

"He doesn't like us anyway," Frankie sniffed. "I don't see what difference it makes. And, no matter what Uncle Sam may think, Leah fancies Mr. Madison!"

"She and all the other girls," Lydia responded, then taunted, "Yourself included. The lot of you flutter round him like moths to a flame!"

"That will be enough," Maggie said, more firmly this time. "And, Frankie, I will remind you of what you said about love earlier. Practicing love brings us closer to the Kingdom of Heaven. Gossip does not." But she was fully aware of the mischief that girls and boys could get into. She knew how close she and Eli had come the night before. What if they had been young and inexperienced? It was worrying that her daughters were talking about Jeremiah and Leah. That meant other folk probably were doing the same thing, and idle talk could be devastating to a young clergyman's vocation.

Maggie's musings were broken when Eli cleared his throat. He gave her a pointed look, and then poked at the fire with a stick. The two had agreed to tell the girls about their plans. It was time. Maggie knew that Eli expected her to be the first to speak. She took a deep breath. "Anyway, to change the topic, I have something to tell you. That is, *Mr. Smith* and I have something to tell you."

The girls sat up expectantly. Maggie glanced nervously at Eli. When he gave her a reassuring wink, she plunged in. "Last night, Mr. Smith proposed to me." She took another deep breath for composure. "And I accepted."

Lydia gave a little squeal of delight. Frankie burst forth with a war whoop of magnificent proportions and flew to her feet. The folks at the other campsites looked curiously in her direction.

"Frankie, sit down," Maggie murmured. "You're causing a scene."

"I don't care!" she hooted, then turned and announced to the neighbors, "Good news should be celebrated, don't you think? Of course, you do!" She dashed over to Eli and hugged his neck with the kind of recklessness that only Frankie could pull off. "You're going to be our papa!"

"Papa?" Eli chuckled. "Does this mean you approve?"

Lydia got up, went to Eli's side, and sat beside him. "Of course, we approve. We've been hoping you would marry Mama for some time. The two of you make a good team." With that, she kissed him on the cheek.

Frankie plopped down on the other side of her soon-to-be stepfather. "When will you marry?"

"Soon," Maggie replied.

"Do it in two weeks, Mama!"

"Two weeks?? Why?"

Frankie smiled slyly. "Neither of you are getting any younger, you know. Why waste time?"

Eli guffawed and nearly rolled off the log.

After a few more congratulations, the two girls hurried away to spread the news to their friends. Eli glanced at Maggie. "So what do you think? *Shall* we get married in two weeks?"

The fire snapped and popped. Maggie didn't know quite what to say. Stalling for time, she looked down at her hands. She didn't know of anyone who had married within two weeks' time – not unless there was a reason. And they had no reason. She certainly was not with child. "Two weeks? Oh, no. That's too soon. People would surely talk. We need to do this properly. Six months is the acceptable – "

"Six months??" he nearly shouted. "Maggie, in six months' time I'll be dead of containment!"

Maggie fidgeted on the log, twisting her hands on her lap. Eli was right. She had grave doubts that even she could withstand a six-month wait without a grievous lapse of social convention. And if that happened, then they actually just might have to marry in a hurry. "Three," she finally offered. "Three months. Any less than that wouldn't be proper."

Eli's expression said he was disappointed, but he replied, "All right. Three months – if we must be proper."

Maggie watched the fire for a moment. "We've never discussed this," she said at length, "but do you expect me to give up the rooming house after we marry?"

Now it was his turn to let the fire talk. Finally, he said, "I don't know. I haven't thought about it."

"Well, *I* don't want to give up the rooming house," she replied in a rush. "Where would our people go? What would happen to Grandpa O'Reilly?"

"But you're always saying that the work is so hard."

"Yes, it *is* hard. And I know I complain some, but I also like it. And I care a great deal about the men in the house. It wouldn't be right."

Eli smiled. "I understand."

"Are you sure? Many men would insist that their wives simply keep house."

He laughed. "Maggie, you *are* keeping house! It just happens to be for a very large family with no blood ties." His eyes lit up with mock inspiration. "Hey! Know what I think? I think we're starting a family empire. You own the rooming house and I own the newspaper. We've got some good possibilities here. What should we take over next? The dry goods store?"

"If Madame Louisa would give it up," Maggie said, with a wry smile. "Perhaps we should consider the Beatty Carriage Manufactory?"

Eli was looking at her with outright admiration. "With you by my side, Maggie, we could do it. We can do anything we set out to do"

Blushing, she glanced down at her hands. "There's one other thing."

"There always is with women."

"Eli!"

"Sorry. Go on."

"Where shall we live? The rooming house? The rooms upstairs at the *Gazette* aren't big enough for us and the girls. But I don't want you to feel strange about moving in with us."

He shrugged. "Truth is I don't care where I live, Maggie, so long as it's with you. Staying at Second Street is a fine idea. But there's one other thing."

She grinned. "There usually is with men."

He laughed. "I don't think we ought to rent out the living quarters above the *Gazette*. At least, not just yet." With a wink, he added, "We're going to need a lot of privacy."

"Elijah Smith!" Maggie felt her face go bright red.

"Oh, now, Maggie, you're acting shocked, but I know you. In another few seconds you would've been thinking the same thing." He reached for her hand and pulled her over to his log. "You know," he said, eying her appraisingly, "I bet you really *were* just like Frankie, once upon a time."

"Maybe."

"There's no 'maybe' about it. She favors you." He touched her hair. She could tell he was resisting the impulse to take the pins out. "You've got the same red hair, the same big, hazel eyes. In fact, your eyes both have the same sparkle." He leaned toward her. "But as far as I'm concerned, there's nothing like the original." He gave her a kiss. "Mm. Want to go to for a walk in the woods?"

"Contain, Eli," she teased. "Contain."

****

Maggie was never one to believe overmuch in a Devil with mighty powers. But she knew there was something that broke readily into people's happiness, contentment, and peace. There was something that delighted in provoking discord and anger. And she knew for certain that something was at work Thursday afternoon when Carrie Hillsborough brought word that Samuel wanted to speak with her. Maggie did not want to go to him – she never did – but custom and manners dictated that she follow through. She had a strong suspicion as to what the topic of conversation would be.

Samuel was waiting by his tent when she entered the inner circle. Upon seeing her, his mouth became a tight, narrow line. Maggie was familiar with that face. As she drew near, he held open the tent flap. "In here, please, Margaret." She did as he requested.

The dwelling was a large one, with board walls and canvas for the ends and roof. The inside was fitted with cots, camp chairs, and chests. Despite the impressive interior, the place still smelled of damp canvas, just like Maggie's tent and the tents of all the other people beyond the inner circle. That gave her a little jab of satisfaction.

The second the flap fell shut behind him, though, Samuel began to berate her. "I simply cannot believe what I have been hearing about you, Margaret, and about your daughter Frances."

Margaret Fuller Ossoli crossed her mind – and this gave Maggie strength. She kept her face composed and looked mildly into his eyes. "Oh?" she asked. "What did you hear?"

"First of all, your daughter dared to stand and preach before a crowd of people."

"No, she did not," Maggie replied. "She exhorted. There is a difference. And it was an excellent exhortation."

"Honestly, have you no control whatsoever over that child? Everyone is talking."

"Samuel, I do *not* understand the concern. It's quite common for women to exhort at camp meetings. It isn't as if Frankie preached a sermon." Maggie knew she was fibbing. The girl *had* preached. She knew a sermon when she heard one, however short it was. "What's the problem with exhorting, so long as she is moved by God to do so? God does not check credentials or social standing. God only cares about the interior person, the soul."

"Frances is a girl," he retorted. "She can have nothing to say to anyone yet."

Maggie smiled. "As it turns out, she had quite a bit to say. And may I remind you that the Apostle Paul told Timothy not to let anyone despise *him* because he was young?"

Samuel frowned. "That was written for Timothy – a young *man*. The point is your daughter needs minding. Think of what that kind of behavior does to our family reputation. As if that weren't enough, news has come that you are betrothed to that newspaperman."

Maggie folded her arms. "Ah, yes. Elijah Smith. What of him? He is a wonderful man."

At this, Samuel's eyes snapped and his face reddened. "One would think you should have learned your lesson by now, Margaret. First you defy your family by marrying John Blaine, and then you run a rooming house filled with all manner of strange men. For heaven's sake, you have an old *Irishman* living with you!"

"That old Irishman," she interrupted, "is the only grandfather my daughters have ever known. Mr. O'Reilly is kind and gentle with them. And he is present when they need him – unlike their uncle."

He didn't seem to hear her. "And what of those two Negroes? How can you, as a mother, permit a Negro man to live under the same roof, on the very floor with your young daughters? Do you not fear for their purity, for their very safety?"

At this, Maggie's temper spiked. "No, I don't fear for them. Nate is a good man. Yes, he and Emily are colored. So what? They're Christians, too. And, as the Apostle says, 'there is neither Jew nor Greek, there is neither bond nor free, there is neither male nor female.' They are just one more brother and sister in Christ to me."

It was now Samuel's turn to flush crimson. "You use Scripture quite handily to make excuses for your unconventional behavior, Margaret. But may I remind you that even the Devil is able to quote Scripture. In fact, I'm tempted to say that Satan has been the one behind all of your conduct. You insist on flying in the face of good, Christian custom. What's more, the way you live your life is most unladylike. The idea of marrying that newspaperman . . . it's completely unacceptable. Why, he rarely sets foot in church! And I have heard rumors that he is a free thinker. To judge from those editorials of his, he is obviously a raving abolitionist. I understand they burned his printing press back in Ohio in '55! If I were a betting man, I'd wager Smith even approves of that horrible raid on Harper's Ferry last October! He is sure to side with those who believe that John Brown is a martyr."

Maggie laughed in his face. "Oh, honestly, Sam! Mr. Smith is a pacifist. He finds violence deplorable and unacceptable. Yes, he was run out of town by a pro-slavery opposition because of his radical views on abolition. But there is no shame in having those views. This is a free nation. People are allowed to say what they think."

"But there is a limit – and he's gone far beyond it on any number of occasions. Why, just look at his views on the so-called rights of woman. He promotes female suffrage! Who ever heard of such a thing? Could you imagine what would happen if women started running about acting like men? Smith even says that women should be able to have careers other than wife and mother. What would happen to our families if they that did that? It is utterly scandalous!"

"May I remind you that *this* woman has done all right caring for her family *and* running a boarding house? And please tell me what is so scandalous about treating a woman simply as another soul, just as you would treat another man?" Maggie was quite angry. "*I* have a soul, Samuel. And, indeed, I have a mind. And Mr. Smith recognizes that."

Samuel smiled condescendingly. "Oh, Margaret, I'm afraid that you've been completely ensnared by this man. All right, then. If you cannot conceive that Smith is a dangerous radical then at least consider the fact that he is in no way near you socially. He is coarse, outspoken, and common. Horribly common. In fact, he is far, far below your station!"

"Below my – !" A fire roared from the soles of her feet to the crown of her head. She took a step toward her brother and wagged a finger in his face. "Now, you listen to me, Samuel Beatty. So what if Eli is a free thinker? So what if he is an abolitionist? Abolition is a wonderful cause! Colored people – men, women, and little children – are in chains, Samuel! Literal chains! So are women, for that matter! *All* women! Not chains you can see, but chains of custom and legalities. And as for whether or not Mr. Smith is below my station, let me remind you that, thanks to your efforts, I *have* no station! What's more, Eli Smith is *far* above you in terms of character and decency! That's right. A humble newspaperman is *better* than the man who owns the big carriage manufactory. And may I remind you that you acquired half of that business when John's father died? It was because John was cut out of the will that you were able to buy the Blaine Manufactory when his father died. The factory rightfully should have gone to John. It was that sinful feud you had with the Blaine family that made *your* station possible to begin with!"

Samuel's face was ashen. "That is quite enough, Margaret. I always thought you tended to behave in a questionable manner, but now – now you have become *most unwomanly*. I regret the fact that Father never remarried after Mother died. If he had, his new wife would have taught you how to comport yourself properly."

"Indeed? Well, then I say, 'Thank God, Father never remarried!'"

Samuel gaped at her. "I simply cannot comprehend this defiance."

"No? Well, you had better comprehend it, Sam Beatty, because I simply will not take any more of this."

"What has come over you?"

"Knowledge, Sam. But I'm sure *you* think it is Satan – since I am refusing meekly to stand by and let you bully me."

"How dare you speak to me that way?"

"Because I am an *adult*, not a child!" She wanted to throttle him, but kept her hands clenched tightly at her sides. "In this republic, sir, all are created equal – even an industrialist and a humble rooming house owner. And *this* humble rooming house owner happens to love the owner and editor of the *Gazette*. Furthermore, if this humble rooming house owner wants to fill her establishment to the eaves with oddballs and humbugs, then she is free to do just that. And she is free to befriend and share her home with the Irish and the Negro alike! Hear me, Samuel Beatty – I am a *woman*, not a child! I will no longer allow you to berate and humiliate me any further!" Maggie started for the tent flap but, thinking better of it, turned back around. "Sam, you once told me that you no longer considered me a relation. Well, if that's the case, then whom I marry should be of no concern to you. But if that is not the case – if you do still consider me a relation – then I suggest that you cease judging me. The trouble with judging others is that sooner or later *you* will be judged by the same standards!" With that, she threw the flap open and marched away from him.

Blood was pounding in Maggie's ears and she imagined that the heaviness of her steps could send shudders through the canvas of every tent she passed. Before she knew it, she had entered the woods and was headed toward the farmer's field. She marched through the field and then flopped down on the bank of the little stream. Wrapping her arms around her knees, she drew them to her chest and buried her face in her arms.

She hated being angry. She also hated her brother and that broke her heart. She wanted so to love him and to have him love her. But it was just impossible. He would not permit it, and so she found herself sucked into hateful words and actions nearly every time they spoke.

Desperate, she threw a prayer heavenward: Have mercy on this sinner, Almighty Father. I'm so angry with Samuel. So very angry. I have killed him a hundred times over in my heart these past few minutes alone. Forgive *me*, and help me forgive *him*.

And then another part of her wrenched itself loose. It began to wail with fury and shake its fist at the very heavens.

Why, Lord, her heart howled. Why are Samuel and so many others in Blaineton so quick to find fault with me? What is it that I do that offends everyone? Why can I not behave in a normal, womanly fashion? What is wrong with me?? Why can I not be like everyone else?

A sob welled up before she could stop it – then another, and another. All she wanted was peace of mind and soul. Why couldn't she find it?

Because you won't accept it, something said.

Abruptly, Maggie stopped her weeping. The words did not come from outside but from within. Yet, they were not her thoughts, not her words.

And now she could hear people singing. The wind must have been coming from the direction of the camp, carrying the sound of worship with it. The melody and voices were faint, but she recognized the hymn nonetheless – "And Can It Be That I Should Gain" by Charles Wesley. Suddenly the words were clear and bright as angels' wings.

> Long my imprison'd spirit lay,
> Fast bound in sin and nature's night:
> Thine eye diffused a quick'ning ray;
> I woke, the dungeon flamed with light:
> My chains fell off, my heart was free,--
> I rose, went forth, and follow'd thee.

She heard only that one verse, which was odd. Odder still was that the words and the beautiful voices disappeared as quickly as they had come. Had the wind changed so abruptly?

And then Maggie understood. The verse had been a gift. She had been told that she was free – had been so ever since she had accepted Christ as her savior. She was, in essence, being asked, *whom will you follow?*

Two Bible verses rose up in her mind. One was from Galatians: "Stand fast therefore in the liberty wherewith Christ hath made us free, and *be not entangled again* with the yoke of bondage." The other verse was from I Corinthians: "Though I speak with the tongues of men and of angels, and *have not charity*, I am become as sounding brass, or a tinkling cymbal."

Her bruised heart lifted and began to soar. She *always* had been free in the Lord. The difficulty came when she allowed other people to place their yokes on her back. God's only rule was love and so long as she acted out of charity – out of love – she was doing what Christ wanted. Granted, sometimes what Christ desired was far different from what social custom demanded, but she did not need to take on the burden of other people's criticism. She could stand up as a free woman with Christ's yoke – light and easy – on her neck.

****

From Maggie's Journal, 23 August 1860

That moment changed everything, dear Journal. My reading about the rights of woman, my struggles with Samuel and the opinions of others – it all came together in that moment. I knew in my *heart* –

and not merely in my head – that I was free and that the only one to whom I was accountable was God. I resolved then and there to live a life of love without regret, and never mind what anyone said. If I choose to extend love to Grandpa O'Reilly, then I am doing God's will. If I choose to live with Nate and Emily as with a brother and sister, then that also is doing God's will. All the men in my rooming house are family to me. That is doing God's will. And if I am in love with a man who stands for love and against oppression – then that also is within God's will.

And then there is my dear, elfin Frankie – she whose red hair escapes her braids, whose dress is untidy, whose voice is always too loud. God called *her* to exhort. No, Journal, I will be plain. God called my dear daughter to *preach*. Perhaps God is calling her to become a minister. I must admit that I do not know how that could happen, but I will make this resolution: never will I quench her spirit. I vow here and now also to do all within my power to prevent others from quenching Frankie's spirit until she is old enough to stand free.

****

Maggie took out a hankie and mopped her face. She didn't know how long she had sat by the stream, but a rustling in the woods caught her attention. There was movement just within her field of vision and the Reverend Jeremiah Madison emerged from the trees and began walking along the edge of the field. Carrie Hillsborough was with him this time. Unaware of Maggie's presence they strolled along, Jeremiah talking animatedly, gesturing with his hands at the heavens, at the stream, at the woods. Carrie, walking sedately beside him, stared up at him in rapt adoration. The young minister seemed unaware that he – and not the Lord – was the object of her worship. But then, as Maggie watched, he tenderly took Carrie's arm in his. Within seconds, they were gone from sight.

She sighed and lifted her face to the sky, praying that God would protect Jeremiah Madison, and that he would be kept safe from error or misunderstanding. From personal experience, she knew only too well how the purest and most innocent of intentions could be misconstrued. In his case, flattery and adoration were very seductive and could lead to terrible complications – complications that no one would want to consider. She hoped that Mr. Madison would be able to exercise his God-given wisdom with all the adoring young women who surrounded him.

At length, Maggie rose and walked back through the heavy-smelling greenery to her campsite. As she drew near the tents, she found Eli sitting on a log and scribbling in his notebook. Suddenly, the point to his pencil snapped. He lifted the writing utensil and looked at the broken tip in consternation. As he did so, she was filled with both deep affection and physical hunger.

She wanted Elijah Smith – in every way possible. Three months? She must have been mad to have insisted on waiting that long. What did it matter what anyone else said or thought? They loved each other. That was enough.

And so she made one final resolution: she would wait no longer. Before Eli could reach for his pocket knife to sharpen the tip of his pencil, she was upon him. Maggie seized the front of his shirt and made to pull him to his feet, which was impossible because he simply out-weighed her. Her effort caused Eli, glasses on the end of his nose, to look up at her in surprise. Still gripping his shirt, she leaned down and kissed him as hard and as full as she could. He nearly fell over, but managed to catch his balance with a hand to the ground.

When she broke the kiss, she announced, "Two weeks, Elijah Smith. *Two weeks!*"

He blinked at her, searching for a response. His mouth opened, but for once nothing came out. He looked a bit like a stunned fish.

"Neither of us is getting any younger, you know." And with that, Maggie stalked off.

CHAPTER FOUR

Maggie and Lydia walked to the dry goods store across the town square to look for lace and fabric with which to embellish one of Maggie's dresses for the wedding. It was a fine day and the door to the shop was open. The second they entered, they were hit with the smell of cloth and wood polish. Parasols and umbrellas hung suspended from the ceiling. A long wooden counter ran along each side of the store. Chairs were placed along the counters for the customer's convenience.

Lydia's eyes lit up as she spotted a display case filled with spools of brightly colored ribbon. "Oh, Mama, look! Just the thing we need."

But Maggie's eyes were on the bolts of fabric stored on the shelves lining the walls. "Oh, there is so much to look at. I haven't been here in ages."

Madame Louisa, the shop's proprietor, now swept over. "Welcome, Madame Blaine, Mademoiselle Blaine. Please be seated."

Mother and daughter did so.

Before Maggie could open her mouth, Madame Louisa was saying, "You are here to find fabric for your wedding dress, no?"

News was traveling faster than Maggie had anticipated. "Yes," she said, trying not to stammer. "I shall be marrying Mr. Smith in two weeks' time."

Madame scurried along the line of shelves, pulling bolts of material into her arms. "Such a short time to do so much!"

Maggie was at a loss for words. She had already encountered the knowing glances of the older women in her congregation – the pursed lips, the hushed comments. "Yes, well, we have been courting for awhile…" she stammered.

Lydia came to her rescue. "And, as Frankie says, they are not getting any younger. No need for propriety when it comes to a second marriage."

Madame returned with a mountain of material. "*Oui*! My sentiments *exactement*. I personally will help you find what you need so you will have a wedding dress *exemplaire*." She read Maggie's somewhat uncomfortable expression and smiled kindly. "You know, in France, we care not for this so-called propriety. If one is in love and wishes to marry *tout de suite,* everyone is happy. Love is what is important, no?"

At this Maggie laughed. It was as if God were speaking to her through the flamboyant Frenchwoman. "Yes! Yes, love *is* what matters."

"And now… tell me what you would like to do for this wedding dress."

Maggie leaned across the counter toward Madame. "Well, I have a good dress of sky-blue linen, but it is quite plain. I would like to modify it to make it more appropriate for the occasion."

"Oh, *non, non, non,* Madame Blaine. We will start with satin, I think. Emerald green, no?" Madame pulled a bolt of said cloth from the tottering pile on the counter and held it before them.

Maggie and Lydia simultaneously reached out to stroke the fabric. It was exquisite – and both knew that it would cost much more than Maggie could afford.

Madame noted their expressions. "Lovely, is it not? A bit costly, I know. But…" She gave mother and daughter a conspiratorial smile. "It is for love, no? I will cut the price in half – a wedding gift from me to you."

That changed everything. Maggie and Lydia's eyes grew wide and they threw themselves into the thrill of the moment. Madame, completely in her element, was more than prepared to help them find not only suitable materials, but also a suitable style from *Godey's Lady's Book.*

****

From Maggie's Journal, 27 August 1860

Madame Louisa was more than generous with us and did not appear affected by the rumors that have been spreading, none of which, of course, are true. Many townsfolk will be terribly disappointed when my waistline refuses to expand in the next month. They will be even more disappointed when no baby arrives after six. Naturally the gossips will comfort themselves by believing that the child has been lost – and that such a great sadness is only God's judgment on us for our sin of fornication.

It is too bad none of that is true. If it were, I know that my Eli would be happier man. I've never seen him so tense. But the good folk of Blaineton cannot tell whether Elijah is relaxed or frustrated. They may only guess at what goes on between us – and they are guessing wrongly. Thus, we live in the midst of a maelstrom of chatter. Never mind. Let the winds of rumor howl about me. I am joyful in mind and spirit, for I am to be married again! Eli is a wonderful man. And, oh, how lovely it is to fuss over my wedding dress like any other bride. I scarcely can believe that I will be clothed in emerald green satin. Journal, I am to have double skirts, one of which is looped up with large bows of creamy silk ribbon. The corsage is to be draped with short sleeves that bell at the bottom and the neckline will be trimmed with cream lace. I fear I am becoming quite spoiled! And, I must confess that I love it.

****

Two days before the wedding found Emily in Maggie's room helping her with the final fitting for the dress. Every evening, the two, along with Madame Louisa and Lydia, had feverishly cut and stitched the pieces together. Now the dress was nearly complete. Maggie loved everything about it – everything but the neckline. Each time she pulled the offending bodice up, Emily promptly yanked it back down.

"No," she protested. "It shows too much bosom."

Emily took the pins out from between her lips and fixed her brown eyes on Maggie. "Honey, you want to show some bosom. You're giving Eli a foretaste of what's to come."

"Yes, but I don't want to show everyone else while I'm at it." Maggie frowned at her reflection in the mirror. "And if we show Eli too much bosom, he's liable to carry me off before the wedding starts." She tried to pull the bodice up once more.

Emily yanked it back down again. "The fashions in *Godey's Ladies' Book* show a lot more than this. As Madame Louisa says, it is `*a la mode*. Now, stand still."

With a sigh, Maggie did as ordered.

The window was open. A cool, rain-kissed breeze was slipping in and with it the hint of autumn. Maggie was surprised to find herself suddenly thinking of John Blaine. He and little Gideon had been ripped from her and the girls by rheumatic fever. She still missed John and yearned to know how Gideon would have grown up. He was a good boy, and he probably would have become a good man.

And then she was thinking of Eli and how different he and John were. She wondered what she was doing. Would she be as happy with Eli as she had been with John? Even though she was excited to be marrying Eli, she still wondered what their marriage would actually be like.

When Emily finally had everything pinned to her liking, she helped Maggie unbutton and remove the bodice. Dressed in petticoats and corset, Maggie sank down onto her bed. "Emily . . . I was thinking. What if tomorrow night . . . what if things aren't the same?"

Emily laid the corsage aside and took a seat beside her. "Maggie, things *won't* be the same. You're not marrying John, you're marrying Eli."

"Maybe I don't mean the same. Maybe I mean, what if things aren't . . . good? John was so tall and almost too thin. And Eli, well, he's not very tall and he's rather . . ." Despite her best efforts, an involuntary giggle rose up. "He's rather round."

Emily smiled. "Yes, I guess you could say that man *does* have a bit to spare stomach-wise. But that's not bad." She chuckled. "He'll be nice and warm come winter!"

The two sat giggling like schoolgirls for a moment. At length, Emily put her arm around Maggie and gave her a loving hug. "Now, Maggie, don't you be silly so close to your wedding day."

"I'm afraid I *am* being silly. Silly about the wedding *night*."

Emily laughed. "Good Lord, girl! You know what to expect!"

"With John, yes. But not with Eli."

Her friend heaved a weary sigh. "All right, let's go over this in a reasonable manner. You've been kissing on Eli. I know because I caught you at it once or twice."

Maggie blushed and looked down at her hands.

"And from what I saw, you two are in sore need of privacy. Am I right?"

She was blushing scarlet. "Emily . . ."

"Come on. We're women. We can talk about this. We all know *he* wants more – men always do – but do *you*?"

Maggie took a deep breath and confessed, "Yes." Her voice was huskier than she would have wished, but her feelings were beyond her control. "Oh, my goodness, yes."

At this, Emily burst into a loud laugh. "Well, from the sound of it, you've got nothing to worry about."

"But what if . . . he doesn't like *me*?"

"Oh, Maggie!" She was now fully exasperated. "The man's been trying to get at you for months. Trust me. He *likes* you!" She patted her friend's knee. "Anyway, as long as you love each other and you're patient with each other, the both of you will be just fine, believe me."

****

Later that day, Maggie was in the kitchen. She had just finished putting together a basket of food to take down to two boys who had arrived via the Underground Railroad. They had come in rather suddenly in the night, and had been smuggled through Eli's print shop. Maggie wanted to make sure they had enough food to last them through the evening, when they would be smuggled out once more and sent up the Delaware River to their next stop.

Maggie stared out the window at the damp garden and grounds that lay between the rooming house and the *Gazette*. She could hear the dripping of the light rain, and under that the sounds of the printing press. Eli had his workshop windows open. It was comforting to know that he was over there, getting on with business, as usual. Maggie was glad to have something to do, too, for Emily, Lydia, and Frankie had refused to let her do any work around the boarding house. In reality, she would have preferred to have been busy.

As she placed bread, butter, jam, apples, and roast chicken in the basket, she caught sight of Jeremiah Madison coming up the lane. He had a hat and slicker on, and kept his head down to avoid soaking his face. The mud from the lane splashed over his shoes and trousers – but he didn't seem to notice. She watched him walk up the steps to the back porch, and then clean his shoes on the mud scraper. She saw that his skin was quite pale and his expression worn.

"Mr. Madison," she said as he opened the door, "are you well?"

He did not reply – because he was looking over her shoulder toward the door to the cellar.

Maggie turned her head, and then stifled a gasp. The older of the slave boys, the one who was about fourteen years old, was standing in the doorway.

"Sorry, missus," he said, "but my brother... he's doing poorly. I need help."

Maggie grabbed the basket and hurried to the boy's side. "Go back downstairs, Pompey." She pushed the food into his arms. "Take this with you. I will be there to look in on Tom as soon as I can."

"Yes, ma'am." The boy disappeared down the stairs.

She turned to face Mr. Madison. What she had feared had happened.

"A new tenant?" he asked.

"One might say that."

He glanced at the dark cellar doorway. "He's dressed in rags."

"Yes. That is how they come to us. We have some new clothes for them down stairs."

"I thought *Mr. Smith* was the abolitionist."

Maggie smiled faintly. "We all are, sir, every last one of us, including Grandpa O'Reilly."

"Harboring runaway slaves is illegal, you know."

"I know. But if we are all God's children, then slavery is wrong. And sometimes one must break the law to force the hand of justice and mercy."

Jeremiah nodded and quoted, "...what doth the Lord require of thee, but to do justly, and to love mercy, and to walk humbly with thy God?"

"Then you understand this is what I must do."

There was long pause, and then Jeremiah said. "How may I help? The boy is concerned for his brother."

"You may come along with me," she replied.

Maggie led him into the cellar and to the secret room located between the boarding house and Eli's print shop. She went directly to Tom, a boy of about twelve years. She sat on the cot beside him and laid a hand across his forehead. "No fever." She looked into the boy's eyes. "Tell me what is wrong, Tom."

"My belly hurts."

She smiled reassuringly. "You ate breakfast well enough."

"He ate a lot of breakfast, ma'am," Pompey said. "Half of mine, too."

"Oh," Maggie replied. "And when did you eat last before this morning's breakfast?"

Pompey bit his lip and thought. "I reckon we've been traveling two days."

"Mm," Jeremiah said, "and your brother ate his breakfast and half of yours. It just may be that Tom has eaten more than his stomach can hold."

Maggie's heart nearly broke, but she forced a comforting smile. "That often happens when one has not eaten for a day or so. You must take care to eat a little at a time." She gently stroked the side of Tom's face. "Even if you are very, very hungry." As she got to her feet, she added, "I'll ask Lydia to come down and sit with you, Tom. She is a very good nurse."

Pompey still looked worried, but Maggie took his hand in hers. "Don't fret, my dear. Your little brother will be fine. In the meantime, we have some clothing in that trunk over there. Why don't you see if you can find some things that will fit you and Tom? Lydia will see to it that you are well-clothed before you leave."

Once Maggie had located Lydia and sent her to care for the boys, she and Jeremiah retired to the rocking chairs on the front porch. They sat in silence for a bit, looking out at the light drizzle and listening to its sound.

At length, she said, "This is *our* secret, Mr. Madison. You must never tell anyone what you have seen."

"You have my word," Jeremiah assured her. He stared out at the street. "And since you have been so forthcoming with me, I feel that I must share something with you. However, the matter is of an exceedingly delicate nature and . . ." The young minister hesitated and for a moment looked like a lost little boy. "And I find myself embarrassed to speak of this. Still, I need a sympathetic ear. But it must also be a discreet ear – very discreet."

"I'll keep your secret, Mr. Madison. After all, you are keeping mine."

He heaved a troubled sigh. "I do so hate to unburden myself to you so close to your happy day. What I have to say may very well change your mind about me. You may wish to engage another minister for your nuptials."

Maggie stopped rocking, reached out, and laid her hand over his. "Why don't you tell me what is wrong?"

"I fear, Mrs. Blaine, that I have conducted myself in a manner that is most . . . unchristian." His blue eyes – always mesmerizing – met hers. "You see, I began keeping company with Leah Beatty shortly after I arrived here three months ago."

That certainly came as no real surprise. Maggie had seen the way Leah had been looking at the pastor. The girl obviously saw Jeremiah as a prestigious catch.

"Early on," Jeremiah continued, "Mr. Beatty saw that we liked one another and discouraged me from further pursuit."

Maggie was not surprised at this, either.

He shifted uncomfortably on his chair. "I am afraid that Leah and I have been together – without a chaperone – and that perhaps I have made promises to her that I am not ready to fulfill. She now says that I have committed breach of promise and compromised her reputation."

At this point, Maggie was struck by a strong sense of irony. She was reputedly the town's fallen woman, but meanwhile her brother's daughter actually may have been playing that role. If it were true, then word would surely escape sooner or later, and Leah and Jeremiah would be the subject of interest for the clucking hens of Blaineton. Were Samuel's judgmental attitudes coming back around to bite him? She had to admit that part of her enjoyed the idea, as Samuel might finally know what it was like to be judged unfairly. But another part of her felt a deep pity. Gossip and scandal were difficult yokes to bear, and Samuel's family was liable to collapse under their weight.

"So you did promise to marry Leah," she said.

Jeremiah nodded.

"You must be honest with me, Mr. Madison. Has Leah said that she is going to have a baby?"

Jeremiah shook his head. "It's still too early. But there are . . . indications."

Maggie swallowed her desire to lecture him. "Well, then do you *wish* to marry the girl?"

"I have no choice!" he cried in sudden and complete frustration. "Whether she's carrying my child or not is immaterial. She is no longer a maiden. Once her father knows, I must make amends. We *must* marry."

"Now, listen to me, Jeremiah Madison." She found herself using her best maternal voice. "If there is no child, then Leah is most likely no worse off than half the young women in this town. Such behavior – while not commendable – still occurs and is more common than most people wish. Passion is very powerful." As she said this, she remembered the passion she felt for Eli. "Very powerful, indeed. It's all too easy to forget about the consequences."

"Yes, but a minister must not forget himself with a parishioner."

"'Must not,'" Maggie replied, "is far different from 'cannot.' And I suspect that it too is more common than anyone will admit."

Jeremiah focused on the house across the square. "Still, that does not diminish the seriousness of the sin. Of *my* sin."

"Indeed it does not. So you have two choices: marry the girl or ask to be reappointed."

"If I ask to be reappointed," he moaned, "Samuel Beatty will discover the situation and report my behavior to the Bishop, and then I will be defrocked. So, you see, I really have no choice if I wish to keep my vocation. And, despite my actions with Leah, please believe me when I say that I wish to remain a minister. Whether I have sinned or not, it is still my calling."

His situation brought the story of King David to mind. His sin had been far worse than a mere dalliance with Bathsheba, for he had gone so far as to murder her husband, Uriah. And yet, once David had repented and taken the consequences of his sin, he was still acceptable to God and came to be the greatest of the kings of Israel. Therefore, Jeremiah Madison was not so far beyond the pale that he was completely lost. As far as Maggie knew, no one was ever completely lost, so long as they were willing to accept that they had behaved sinfully, ask for forgiveness, and change their ways. "At one time or another we are all less than what God would have of us. But forgiveness *is* possible."

"Yes, it is. So long as I marry the girl. There is no other choice." He paused a moment, and then whispered, "Mrs. Blaine, I must confess something further. I am afraid that I have a fondness for women – a fondness that is also a weakness – and in turn they have a fondness for me. This has plagued me in each church I have served. Although," he added somewhat hastily, "it has never got to this extent."

Maggie now dropped all formality. "Jeremiah, are you truly sorry for your actions?"

He nodded.

"As a clergyman, you must surely understand that true repentance involves turning away from the things that got you into trouble in the first place. You know that you must turn instead toward God."

He nodded again.

"Then if you *marry* Leah, you must also remain *faithful* to Leah, weakness or no weakness." Maggie stared steadily into his face, searching for truth in his response. "Will you do that?"

He grasped her hands in his. "God help me, I will." His expression was one of genuine sorrow and willingness to change.

Maggie smiled gently. "Then, my dear friend and pastor, I would be *honored* to have you as our minister tomorrow. And I will pray that you and Leah do the right thing." She promised herself that she would pray for *Samuel*, too: that he would open his heart and not place a stumbling block before the young couple.

****

From Maggie's Journal, 6 September 1860

My heart hurts for Jeremiah Madison as acutely as if he were my own son. Such indiscretions happen every day among the laity. There is a bit of talk, a hasty marriage or a departure from town and that is that. Not so with a clergyman. He is expected to carry high the banner of moral standards – thus, the sin of fornication is a vocational death sentence. God, of course, is sure to forgive a penitent sinner, even if that sinner is a minister. And a true Christian will quickly pardon a wayward pastor. But sadly, the Church hierarchy and the more judgmental in our congregations and towns are less likely to do so. Whether they cannot or will not, I cannot say. All I know is that Jeremiah is right. He needs to marry Leah, and as soon as possible.

As for me, I must side with the God who so graciously forgives me when I fail. Thus, I will forgive my young friend.

****

Saturday, September 8 was Maggie's wedding day. That morning she was sitting on a chair in her room and submitting to Lydia's insistent pinching of her cheeks, which her daughter claimed would give her color. In her heart, Maggie suspected that she was more than likely to end up black and blue, rather than pink. Meanwhile, Frankie was exhorting her to bite on her lips to redden them.

All of it made Maggie want to laugh. There she was, a considerable portion of her bosom exposed to the air not to mention everyone's eyes, her waist strapped tightly into a corset, her hips burdened with hoops and petticoats, her cheeks pinched, and her lips bitten. It was all so terribly unnatural. And yet, Frankie declared that she was beautiful. To be truthful, not only was she suffering the discomfort of this "beauty," but Maggie also thought that she looked rather tired. Dark circles had crept under her eyes. The night before she had tossed and turned alternately thinking of the wedding day, the wedding night, and Jeremiah Madison's situation.

But none of that mattered now. She was to be married shortly. She was in her dress and, once Emily yanked the corsage down one more time, ready to begin a new chapter of her life.

Before Maggie could think further, they all left the room and swept through the kitchen and down the hall to the front parlor. At the door, Grandpa O'Reilly took Maggie's arm and led her into the room, which was festooned with September flowers and filled with boarding house family, Madame Louisa, and colored friends from Water Street. Maggie and her escort stopped in front of Jeremiah, who also looked as if he had not slept well. Under normal circumstances, he should have been wreathed in triumphant smiles, for not only was he presiding at a wedding, but the groom had actually promised to attend church. The townspeople would certainly be amazed to discover Elijah Smith planted in a pew (or more likely near the door) every Sunday – and they no doubt would attribute the miracle to Jeremiah. The reality, of course, was that Eli believed it was important for husband and wife to worship together, and had chosen to sacrifice his personal comfort in favor of family solidarity. Still, to have a lapsed Quaker go Methodist was quite impressive. Jeremiah, by rights, should have been glowing all over.

Grandpa O'Reilly stepped aside. Eli came forward to take Maggie's arm. As he did so, he gave her a reassuring grin, but she could see that he was in need of reassurance himself. She offered him a warm smile, and this seemed to assure him.

Then Jeremiah began the vows. Both she and Eli struggled to keep their voices even. However, when Eli slipped the ring on her finger, she thought he might cry: his face clearly was working quite hard to keep that from happening. Touched, tears welled up in Maggie's own eyes, and she was besieged by an avalanche of emotions. She remembered marrying John Blaine and seeing his face as he put the ring on her finger. Her heart stung again with grief. John had been gone ten years. Time had passed so quickly. Too fast.

Maggie glanced at Eli. She did love him. She loved him intensely. How could that be? How could she love two such different men? Was she being disloyal to John? No, she decided. John had said that he would pray for her happiness. And his prayers had been answered. She *was* happy. She was marrying Eli. She was *marrying* Elijah Smith.

This realization brought with it a dizzying sense of disorientation. Her identity was changing, and changing abruptly. She had been

Margaret Blaine for so many years. She had given herself very little time to think about being Margaret Smith. But in the space of seconds, she would have a new name, a new identity. She had been someone's daughter, then someone's wife, then someone's widow, and now someone's wife again. There was a certain injustice to all that. After all, once the deed was done, Elijah Smith would remain essentially Elijah Smith. Women, on the other hand, were forced to change their very essence when they entered the state of matrimony. They were even denied an essence during their single years. A woman was always someone's daughter, someone's wife, or someone's widow. Will we never be permitted to be simply ourselves? Maggie wondered.

These were very odd thoughts to have on her wedding day. She could only hope that Eli would see her as herself.

And, as she looked into his eyes, she saw that he did, and she loved him all the more for it.

Jeremiah blessed their union, Maggie and Eli shared a rather chaste kiss, and the disturbing thoughts flew away. Suddenly, the family was all about them with wishes and kisses and blessings, and the party began. There was an excellent meal of a fine smoked ham, fried chicken, giblet soup, stewed tomatoes, boiled spinach, salad with dressing, a large cake (Mrs. H's Raised Wedding Cake, taken from *Miss Beecher's Domestic Receipt Book*), and, despite the presence of brandy and wine in the cake, a temperance punch made of oranges, sugar, water and a little lemon. There were presents and laughter – great bushels of laughter.

After dinner, Mr. Carson brought his camera into the room. He sat the enormous wooden box up on its three legs, threw a black cloth over his head, and had Eli and Maggie pose for a photograph. Eli was very interested in the camera, claiming that photographs of exciting or news-worthy events would someday appear in the papers. "I might like to learn how to use a camera," he commented and glanced at Maggie. "What about you? Would you like to learn to make photographs?"

She smiled. "Perhaps, but I'd much rather write."

"You will. You have talent." With that, he gave her a kiss, and Maggie felt serene confidence in the future – her future, his future, their future – for the first time.

Two of the men from the Water Street community began to play a tune on their fiddles, and the dancing began. There were dizzying reels and exuberant galops and even a graceful waltz or two.

As the evening wore on, a few of the men slipped away. Maggie sitting with her female family in the kitchen missed Eli and craned her neck to see where he had gone. Emily put a hand on her arm. "He'll be back."

"Where did he go?"

She smirked. "Oh, out to the shed – with Grandpa O'Reilly, Nate, Ike, Edgar, and Patrick."

Maggie's eyes grew round. "Oh, no. Tell me that they aren't . . ."

"I'm afraid that they *are*."

She felt her face flush. "He can't! Eli knows I'm temperance!"

"Honey," Emily reminded her, "you're temperance, not tee-total. I've seen you sip a little dandelion wine and such. And we had alcohol in the cake."

"But that cooks off," Maggie protested.

"Makes no never mind. Besides, let them be men. A little whiskey isn't going to hurt them. You know they don't do this regular. This is a wedding party. They've got to get together and do some back-slapping, that's all. You know they've just got to make their jokes about the wedding night."

Lydia giggled. "I wonder what they're saying."

Maggie chuckled. "Whatever it is, you can be sure it's rude!"

Emily nudged her friend. "Well, at least we know what they're *doing*."

"Yes," she answered with a grimace. "Getting drunk."

"More than that. Your man's in need of a little liquid courage and they're just helping him out."

"Eli? In need of wedding night courage?" Maggie laughed. "Hardly!"

Lydia snickered, even as Frankie took it all in with utter confusion.

"I'm telling the truth, girl," Emily said with a straight face. "Don't you know the reputation of all mankind sits upon the head of each new groom?"

And suddenly Maggie couldn't help herself. She blurted, "Tell me, Emily, which head might that *be*?" The women exploded into the most unladylike of guffaws. All, that is, except poor Frankie.

She frowned. "What's so funny?"

Emily chuckled heartily and threw her arms around the girl. "When are you going to talk to this child, Maggie?"

"Not now," Maggie answered, brushing tears of mirth from her eyes. "Not now."

The men came back a short while later, looking very pleased with themselves. Actually, Ike, Edgar, and Patrick lay down on the back porch and began to sing drinking songs with Grandpa O'Reilly, whom they had deposited in a rocking chair.

Nate was still slapping Eli on the back as the two of them burst into the kitchen. When they saw the women, they immediately stopped. Eli cleared his throat, straightened his waistcoat, and tried to look more sober than he was. "Well, Maggie . . . I guess it's time to say goodnight."

With that Nate hooted and pounded Eli on the back once more. "Take her home, my man! Take her *home*!"

Emily feigned a threatening glare at her husband. "Nate, if you don't quiet down I'm going to soak your head under the pump."

Nate immediately sobered up. "Then I guess it's goodnight, Eli."

"Indeed it is," his friend replied and offered an arm to his bride.

The two left the boarding house, picked their way over the songsters on the back porch, and strolled through the yard to his home. Some people take their honeymoons in exotic, far-off climes. Theirs would be spent above the *Gazette*.

The little house was dark. Eli lit a lamp, took Maggie's hand and led the way upstairs. As they entered his room, they could hear the sound of questionable lyrics drifting through the open window.

"Egad," Eli said, "I hope they don't keep singing all night." He set the lamp on the stand beside the bed, and peeked out the window. "All that racket isn't exactly conducive to . . . well . . . a wedding night. Plus, it'll annoy the neighbors." He shut the window, cutting off what was passing for music on the back porch. He drew the curtains, doing the same to the other window. Turning, he nervously stuck his hands in his pockets. "Well . . . um . . . I guess this is it. Welcome home, Maggie."

He looked awfully nervous and not entirely sober. Maggie's nerves immediately vanished. Although she did not approve of the daily consumption of liquor, her temperance beliefs had not removed her sense of humor. She realized that drink had rendered Eli at her mercy.

Maggie strode across the room and gave him a very full kiss. She had never tasted whiskey before, but was familiar enough with the smell to know that Eli tasted just like it. He knew he did, too. Abruptly pulling away, he walked over to the bed post and nervously cleared his throat. "All right. All right. I might as well confess. I've been drinking. But I guess you know that."

"Indeed I do."

He looked quite uncomfortable. "Grandpa O'Reilly insisted on toasting me." With a wince, he added, "Five or six times."

It was very amusing, but Maggie folded her arms and tried to look stern. "And how much did *you* drink, Elijah Smith?"

"Umm . . . not as much as O'Reilly?"

"But you are drunk."

"No, no!" he said quickly. "I mean, look at me. I didn't stumble coming up the stairs. I didn't drop the lamp. I'm not drunk. Really."

She eyed him. "Are you sure?"

"Absolutely sure."

"We'll see," she replied, and began to unbutton the corsage to her dress. "Because I've heard it said that too much drink inhibits a man in a particular way." She removed the bodice and tossed it in his direction. "Hang this up, would you, please?"

Eli caught the top, stared at it in utter bewilderment for a second, and then draped it over the bed post.

He watched as Maggie undid the hooks to the skirt, and then untied the three petticoats. She was being quite the coquette. One at a time, each of the petticoats fell to the floor. Next, she untied the tabs to her crinoline cage. The hoops collapsed as they, too, dropped to the wood floor. She stepped over the yards and yards of stuff, saying, "What a relief to be rid of *that*."

Then she trailed a hand along his shoulder and back. "I believe that *you* need to relax, sir. Let's remove your dress-coat." She slipped it off his unresisting body. Reaching around his neck, she found his cravat, which was tied in a bow-knot, and loosened it. She had a bit more trouble getting around to his waistcoat – impossible with both arms, as his girth was a just bit too wide – but found that she could, with one hand, unbutton the article. "Let's remove this, as well," she suggested. When that was done, she walked around and positioned herself with her back to him. "Would you mind seeing to my stays? Emily laced me up rather tightly."

Maggie felt him fumbling about with the strings and fighting with the knot. She smiled. "Why, Mr. Smith . . . are your hands trembling? Have you never unlaced a woman's corset before?"

"It's this knot . . ." he muttered. But she could feel that he was indeed trembling a bit.

In another second, he freed the knot and loosened the laces. Being released from the corset's restriction was heavenly. She couldn't help but sigh with relief. "Oh, thank you." Suddenly, Eli was pulling the pins out of her hair, putting his arms around her, and kissing her shoulder, her neck, her ear – all in one frenzy of activity.

"Oh, no!" Maggie teased, wriggling away from his hands. "First things first!"

"Oh, yeah?" He grinned and started to unbutton his shirt. "What first things are those?"

She unhooked the front of her corset, removed it, and jauntily threw the wretched thing aside.

"I see. We're playing a game." In response, he tossed off his shirt.

"No game, Elijah Smith," Maggie replied. "Merely the proper sequence of things." Sitting down on the bed, she slowly unlaced one shoe, took it off and, with a naughty smile, dropped it to the floor.

Smirking, Eli pulled his suspenders off his shoulders.

Maggie removed the other shoe, dropped it, and then slowly peeled her stockings off – which caused Eli to sigh in admiration.

Dressed only in her chemise and drawers, she scooted up to the head of the bed.

Eli unbuttoned his trousers and, with a flourish, let them fall.

Now, a man in his undershirt and drawers is a ridiculous thing. Maggie always thought John looked silly, and it was no different with Eli. She collapsed into giggles.

"Oh," he teased, "so now I'm funny, am I?"

"Yes. You've still got your shoes and stockings on!" She nearly had to hold her side, she was laughing so hard.

"Mrs. Smith, *you* are a rude woman." Eli pulled his shoes and stockings off, set his eyeglasses on the table, and blew out the lamp. "And, oh, I do so love a rude woman." The bed sank as he climbed in. "Now . . ." he murmured. "I'm going to show you just what kind of effect drink has on *this* man."

****

Any concerns Maggie had about compatibility with Eli vanished in those first moments together. She had never had any complaints about John Blaine, but Eli was skilled in ways that she had never experienced. Furthermore, he was curious to know what *she* enjoyed. It had been her opinion that most men did not care about such matters. Furthermore, all the best books said that women were not supposed to have physical passions. It surprised her then that Eli so blatantly set out to please her. What surprised her even more were her own responses.

The next morning, Maggie awoke as contented as a cat. Indeed, had she been able, she would have purred. The music of the bird songs, the clop of horse hooves and rattle of carriage wheels on the street, the sunlight playfully sneaking in around the curtains – she could not have been happier had she been in heaven.

As she stretched, she glanced over at her husband. He was sleeping soundly – looking like a rather large boy, but sounding more like a hibernating bear. However, even the snoring was fine. She had missed those sorts of sounds over the past ten years. It was nice to feel his warmth, to know that she was not alone in the bed.

Looking around the room, Maggie saw that the place was a shambles – clothes strewn all over, bedding hopelessly twisted. She realized that she was lying on something, and fished Eli's drawers out from under her back. There was something intensely freeing about losing all pretense and fear – and, yes, even one's modesty. Snuggling up to her husband, she kissed the tip of his nose. He breathed a little sigh, and nestled in. Finally, he opened his eyes and yawned, "Morning."

"Good morning," she replied and gave him a kiss. She couldn't help but grin. "We had quite a night. Everything is a wreck."

He lifted his head and squinted at their surroundings. "Is it?"

"Mm. I didn't expect some of our . . . activities last night. Tell me, where did you learn those things?"

Smiling, Eli pressed his lips warmly to hers. "Tell me, where did you learn to be that *eager*?"

Maggie laughed. "I am so glad that my rooming house has told me that it will run itself these next few days." As she said those words, she smiled. "And I am so glad it's still mine."

Eli raised an eyebrow. "Really?"

"Yes. The rooming house remains my property. Legally, what I bring into a marriage in terms of property remains mine. I am grateful New Jersey has that law."

He laughed. "Thank goodness! I don't need another business. I have enough trouble with the *Gazette*. Besides, even if the law were different, I would never want to take away something that is rightfully yours."

Maggie kissed him on the mouth. "You're not only the most handsome of men, Elijah Smith, but you're the *best* among men."

"Only because," he replied, "I've found the best among *women*."

****

They spent five days more or less on their own, and then returned to the work-a-day world. Energized and extremely content, Maggie threw herself into the fall cleaning. Rugs had to be brought out and beaten, then laid down to keep feet warm on icy days. Everything needed deep cleaning from floor to ceiling. Normally, it was a tedious, back-breaking job. But this year, Maggie didn't mind the work at all. As she was on the porch vigorously washing the front parlor windows, she heard someone come up the steps. Turning, she found Carrie Hillsborough on the top step. Maggie pushed escaping strands of red hair back from her face. "May I help you?"

"I have a letter to give to Mr. Madison," the girl replied in her husky voice.

"A letter?" Jeremiah said as he strode toward the doorway. He obviously had seen the young girl's approach and hurried over from his room.

Carrie curtseyed and held the missive out to him. He stepped onto the porch, took the letter, opened it and began to read while Carrie watched him with her almond-shaped eyes. Maggie saw the young man's face cloud. Realizing that she was intruding on his feelings, she dipped her cleaning rag into the bucket and began to wash the window panes once more.

"Will there be any reply, sir?" Carrie asked.

"No," he said, quietly. "No reply today."

The girl curtseyed once more and scampered off the porch. Maggie realized that she had come in the Beatty carriage with another servant. This was the day that the Beatty household usually purchased supplies in Blaineton.

Jeremiah heaved a sigh. "I beg your pardon, Mrs. Smith, but have you a moment?"

Maggie nodded and dropped her rag in the bucket. "Shall we speak privately?"

When he nodded, they retreated to the secret room, lit the lamps, and sat down at the little table. Without a word, he passed the letter to Maggie. She unfolded the paper and began to read.

Wednesday, September 12, 1860

Mr. J. Madison –

Sir: I have just received your latest letter this morning. I do not know how to respond, and I can scarcely hold the pen, I am so distressed. My dear Jeremiah, these are harsh words – not the words of a suitor. I barely know what to think. You had words sweet enough for me when we were alone. Under the present circumstances, one would expect you to be particularly tender. Hence, I am most troubled. You say now that my father knows he is forcing your hand in this matter. I cannot believe that a minister leading a congregation could be so cruel. From the sound of it, you would be happier if we did not marry and I – as you yourself suggested earlier – go over to the church in Frenchtown. To what avail, I ask you? Talk will only follow me there. We will not be able to escape it. In addition, my father's anger will not permit such a simple solution.

What then should I do, sir? Please believe me when I say that I have only the deepest of feelings for you. In truth, when I contemplate life without your presence, I no longer wish to go on. And if I should take my life, what horrors await me? For my head will bear a double sin for taking double lives. And, yet, when I think on your cold words – O, how can such sentiment lay the foundation for happy matrimony?

Sir, you loved me well enough, and not so very long ago. Please do not leave my heart thus abandoned. I fear that I will not be able to bear it. I remain yours always,

L.M. Beatty

"Leah sounds as if she is suffering a great deal," Maggie said as she glanced up at the young minister.

"Perhaps," he replied. "But she is also highly emotional."

"Judging from this letter, it seems as if you've been rather harsh with her. Can you not be more tender towards Leah? Women need tenderness, especially young women with romantic notions. Why did you tell her to go to the church in Frenchtown?"

"We were arguing," he confessed. "I was angry. The words just slipped out."

That did not bode well for the marriage. Maggie knew that arguments were normal. Couples were bound to disagree. Perfect harmony and contentment was not possible. Therefore, husband and wife had to learn the art of arguing and reconciling. But these two were arguing bitterly and very early in their lives together. "You are the more mature party," she told him flatly. "Therefore, you must try to be patient with her. You must guide her in this."

"I'm afraid that is very difficult to do. Leah demands much. And she takes my words and twists them in a most disagreeable manner. No matter what I say or do these days displeases her . . . and her family, as well. Under other circumstances, we would have broken off our courtship. But these circumstances make it impossible."

"I see." Maggie softened her tone of voice. "So what she says is true. Leah *is* with child."

With a resigned sigh, Jeremiah nodded and looked down at the worn wood of the tabletop. "We were alone together several times. One time, we – well, like it or not, this is the girl that I *must marry* and within the next few weeks. We are just going to have to make the best of a bad situation."

Maggie laid a hand over his, but said nothing. Leah and her baby were a bad situation to him. She felt enormous pity for everyone concerned, including the baby. Things just were not right. Jeremiah's flaw – his love of flattery and female adoration – obviously had led him nowhere but to trouble. And would things get even worse once he married Leah? She shuddered inwardly and tried to push those thoughts out of her mind.

****

Over the next weeks letters flew back and forth between the two residences. A wedding date of Saturday, October 6 was set and plans hastily made. The quick wedding created talk, of course – but somewhat less talk than the whirlwind which had enveloped Maggie's nuptials. Perhaps it was because to gossip about a minister seemed like spreading rumors about God. At the same time, perhaps there was less talk because folks believed that a minister ought to be married. A married man usually meant a stable man. Oh, they might count the months between wedding and baby, but that just became so much titillating speculation. And Leah would no doubt claim that the child had arrived early. Aside from her immediate family and Maggie, who would really know the truth?

Naturally, Maggie had not been invited to the wedding. The ceremony would be held at the Presbyterian Church in Blaineton, the only building big enough to hold all the guests. Even Samuel's home could not accommodate everyone. Jeremiah's presiding elder would officiate at the service. There was sure to be much pomp and circumstance, and a great deal of celebration.

And yet she felt so sorry for Jeremiah. The letters from Leah were often angry or pouting. She frequently accused him of encouraging other women. It was not the type of correspondence one would expect between lovers.

And Jeremiah was beside himself. He told Maggie that he tried to placate Leah, but she usually managed to goad him into saying harsh words. Rather than billing and cooing, they were spitting and hissing. The more Maggie learned about his situation, the more she came to understand that the minister was a man who had been felled by his own passions.

On bath night Maggie went over to Eli's house. They still desired their privacy, seeking it out whenever possible. As she lounged in the tub set by the little kitchen stove, she reflected on the difference between her own marriage and Jeremiah's impending marriage. His just was so very sad. It was awful not to experience the joy, the adventure, the discovery of being newly-wed. To have a love, to be married, to revel in each other – that was how it should be. Maggie's early months with John Blaine and the first weeks with Eli had been delightful. She had forgotten how glorious it was to have a lover wash her hair, scrub her back, and even soap her toes. All was intimacy and discovery. It was absolutely glorious.

"Hey, don't sit there forever," Eli said, as he fetched the kettle from the stove. "Remember I need to get in next." He knelt down, put one hand in the bath, and poured hot water from the kettle into the tub with the other hand. When he sensed that the bath water had warmed up enough, he set the kettle down. "Perfect," he said, but kept his hand in the water and smiled broadly at her.

Maggie smiled back. "Sir, you're obviously in search of something. Are you looking for the soap?"

"Nope."

They laughed and shared a very pleased kiss.

"I can't wait for my turn to bathe you," she whispered. "I know exactly what I'll wash first."

Eli thought for a moment, and then gave her a quick kiss. "Know what?"

"What?"

"I'm getting in there with you. There's room enough."

She held the washrag to her chest. "Why, sir, I'm sure I don't know what you mean."

He nuzzled her face. "I'm sure you do know what I mean."

Maggie exhaled with delight. "Oh, Eli, why isn't *everyone* happy like us?"

"Because everyone *isn't* us." He kissed her again.

"That's very true. Mr. Madison is getting married tomorrow and the poor soul is absolutely miserable."

Eli gave her a quizzical look. "I don't recall inviting *him* to take a bath with us."

"Eli . . ."

"I just mean, why do you have to bring him up now?"

"The situation is so very sad, that's all. With all the gossip and the difficulty he and Leah are having, that poor man is one person who *won't* have much in the way of happiness."

Her husband grunted irritably and stood up. "Yeah, poor, poor Jeremiah Madison." He retrieved a towel from the table and held it up. "All right, Maggie. Come on. Time to dry off."

That took her aback. "But what about –"

"Forget it. I'm not in the mood to play anymore."

She stood, wrapped the towel about her and stepped out of the large metal tub. "What's the matter?"

"Nothing," he muttered. "I just want to take a bath and go to bed. To *sleep*."

It dawned on her what was wrong. "Elijah Smith! Are you jealous?"

He snorted. "Jealous? Me? Of Madison? Just because he's tall and thin and good-looking, and makes the women swoon? No. Not a bit." He began unbuttoning his shirt. "Why should I be jealous of that silly humbug?"

"Eli!"

He frowned peevishly at his wife. "Oh, honestly, Maggie. You know what your trouble is? You're just too damned trusting!"

"Eli! Don't swear."

"Don't *swear*??" he fired back. "Listen, Maggie, this is *my* house! I can say anything I want here. So damn, damn, damn, and *damn*!"

Momentarily silenced, all Maggie could do was clutch the towel and stare. He was genuinely angry.

"I mean, good Lord, Maggie, you're acting as if Madison is some poor, misunderstood soul." Eli took his eyeglasses off and put them on the kitchen table. "Well, maybe he's not. Ever think you may have misjudged him? Ever?" He took his shirt off. "No, of course, you haven't. You have no reason to."

"All right," she said with frustration. "I'm breaking a confidence, but you're my husband and it's important that I have *your* trust. So here's what I know. Mr. Madison is being forced into this marriage because of an indiscretion with Leah. And, yes, the rumors are true. She's with child. But he's really quite broken-hearted and repentant over his behavior. And the worst part of it is that they do not get along at all. She is demanding of him, and he's cool toward her. This is a very difficult situation and things aren't quite the way they appear."

"No, Maggie, they *aren't* quite the way they appear." Eli stalked over and looked her dead in the eyes. "Because you know what? I happen know some things, too! A friend of mine over in Morris County told me that Madison left his first appointment under a cloud. It seems he got a little too friendly with a couple of the girls there. One of them was sent to live with an aunt in Newark."

"What!?" she gasped. "Oh, no, that can't be right. Eli, it must be a rumor."

"Hardly. My source is unimpeachable. He happened to be the presiding elder in Madison's old district."

She frowned. "If Mr. Madison did all that, then why did the Bishop continue to appoint him to other churches?"

"Who knows why leaders do anything? Maybe he thought it was a youthful indiscretion. But apparently, it's more than that."

Maggie struggled with this new information. "But Mr. Madison told me that he had not been indiscreet with any other girls." And then, with another little gasp, she blurted, "He lied to me! Oh, Eli, he looked me in the eyes and lied to me!"

"I'm not surprised," was her husband's response.

"But how could he do that? To *me*?? We are friends! At least that is what I thought." She felt her eyes tear up. "Oh, I'm such a fool!"

"No, you're not, sweetheart. Madison's a smooth-talker and he's handsome and he appears to be the perfect pastor. But that's all on the surface. He's really only slightly better than a confidence man."

Maggie wrestled with a profound sense of betrayal and anger. Not only had Jeremiah let her down, but perhaps more importantly, her own ability to discern had failed her, too. "How could I have been so wrong?"

Eli abandoned his anger. "I'm sorry."

She clumsily used the towel to wipe at the tears in her eyes.

He quickly put his hand over hers. "Maggie, you're a dear, good-hearted woman. I wish Mr. Madison was who we hoped he would be, but the hard, cold truth is that not everyone in this world is sincere." He lifted her hand to his lips and kissed it. "I'm truly sorry. I didn't want to tell you. I wanted to make sure before . . ." He abruptly gave up trying to explain and heaved a large sigh. "Oh, I don't know. Maybe I *am* jealous. Small wonder, huh? I mean, look at me. I'm pudgy. I'm not handsome. I'm educated, but not polished. And when a man like Madison takes your attention, I can't help it. I feel nervous."

She managed a wan smile. "You big, silly bear, it's *you* I love. You should know that by now."

"Yes, well, sometimes my mouth runs ahead of my brain. Please don't be upset with me."

"I'm not upset with you." The truth was that Maggie was upset with herself. She was angry that she – in her eagerness to live out God's rule of love – had permitted herself to be fooled. She had believed that Jeremiah was the victim of a momentary lapse of judgment. To find that she could have been taken in by a habitual ladies' man was both shocking and painful. She took a deep breath. "You know, Eli, I really do want to be outside that church tomorrow. I need to see for myself."

Eager to please, he said, "Sure, sweetheart. Anything you want." He pulled her close. "Come here. I hate arguing with you."

She put her arms around him, comforted by his solid warmth.

****

From Maggie's Journal, 6 October 1860

The morning dawned rainy and cold. If I were prone to superstition, I would take the weather as a bad omen. The wealthy and the genteel arrived for Jeremiah Madison's wedding in carriages and fine dress, whereupon they flowed into the old Presbyterian Church. Eli and I walked from the rooming house through the puddles that had accumulated on Second Street. A sloppy walk, to be sure, but a stroll through the green would have been much soggier and muddier.

Our destination was the crowd of curiosity-seekers that – like wet dogs – huddled close against the elements and waited outside the church.

Blaineton Presbyterian Church has survived flood and wind, and somehow managed to remain untouched by the fires that often befall other churches. It is a lovely old thing, and very sensible in design. No stained glass for such common-sense folk as founded the congregation. The church's panes are primly clear and how fortunate for us, for we on the outside were afforded an excellent view of the proceedings within. My love and I drew near, strolling along the length of the building until we found a spot from which we could see the altar. Eli, rain dripping off the brim of his hat, stood beside me.

I had wrapped myself in a warm shawl, and held an umbrella over my head. My hands, of course, quickly got cold. The damp began to seep in through my shoes. Autumn weather has arrived. It would have been far more sensible for the two of us to have stayed home – both Eli and I shall probably catch cold – but I would not go home. Something inside me needed to watch our minister and Leah Beatty exchange vows. I do not know what I expected to see – an expression on Mr. Madison's face, perhaps. I do not know. But I was driven to watch.

Eli's excuse for coming along was that he was planning to write a report on the nuptials for the *Gazette*. Dear Eli. There was no need for him to be there. Mr. Carson (who is friends with the church organist) was already neatly secured in the balcony and jotting wedding details into his notebook. Eli will merely edit Mr. Carson's article. So the plain truth is that my gallant husband did not want me to go to the church alone. I fancy that he wished to protect me. But I cannot be protected. The damage has already been done. My trust has been betrayed.

And so we watched. The bride and groom began to exchange vows. I strained to see Jeremiah Madison's face. What I saw shocked me nearly more than Eli's news of the previous evening. In all my discussions with Mr. Madison prior to this moment, our minister had appeared distressed – even agonized – about marrying Leah. He clearly did not wish this wedding to take place, but felt that he must marry the girl for propriety's sake. Or so I thought. But at the ceremony, Mr. Madison showed not one trace of hesitation, no hint of the slightest unease. Instead, he gazed lovingly into Leah's eyes as he pledged his troth. And she! For all the haranguing and pleading and pouting in her letters, now she gazed back. Her beautiful face was smiling, trusting, adoring. Perhaps Mr. Madison really does love Leah and she him. Perhaps his dalliances with other women will cease. Or perhaps he is, indeed, a sincere man burdened with a weak will. I do not know, and this distresses me. All I can say is what troubles me the most is why – if he truly does love the girl – did he indicate otherwise to me? What could he hope to gain from that?

Regardless, he has not been forthright with me. I think I see him more clearly now than ever, and I must say that I do not like the view.

As the couple turned and marched down the aisle – and as some in the crowd outside let forth with a mighty cheer – I could not help but feel that it was all terribly wrong.

****

"Well, that's over and done with," Tryphena Moore said dryly to Madame Louisa.

"Perhaps everything will settle down now," Tryphosa Moore offered.

"*Non,*" Madame Louisa sighed. "I think not. It is *trés* sad. Even though her dress is beautiful, it is really a sad occasion, *non?*"

Mrs. Mendenhall arched an eyebrow. "They are only doing what must be done, considering the circumstances."

"*Oui.* I see their smiles, but I also see that there is no love."

Tryphosa was confused at this. "They are marrying, nonetheless, so they must love each other even a little, mustn't they?"

"Yes, dear," Tryphena answered, voice as dry as tinder. "Of course." She glanced once at Maggie and then said pointedly, "Not surprising, though, when you think about it, considering where he lodges. One can't help but be influenced."

Maggie refused to let the comment penetrate. Instead, she turned to her husband and said, "I have heard and seen enough. Let's go home."

CHAPTER FIVE

The newly-married couple went on a two-week honeymoon, courtesy of Samuel Beatty. While they were gone, all of Blaineton whispered about a baby and would be counting off the months once Leah publically announced that she was expecting.

But for Maggie, October found her wrestling with other questions. Eli's news that Jeremiah had had dalliances with other young women, one of whom had mysteriously moved to another town, had shaken her trust in the minister. She was baffled as to how a man of the cloth could repeatedly fall prey to his own desires.

****

From Maggie's Journal, 8 October 1860

Psalm 24 says he "that hath clean hands, and a pure heart; who hath not lifted up his soul unto vanity, nor sworn deceitfully" may enter the house of the Lord. I fear that my Mr. Madison has neither clean hands nor a clean heart. Does he not understand that he is displeasing God? Does he not see that he is cutting himself off from our Lord? And, if all that is so, then how dare he stand before our congregation each Sunday and deign speak to us of spiritual matters? How can he pretend to lead us? He has fallen so grievously far himself – and makes so little effort to repent.

And yet, when I consider it, is he really so different than the rest of us? Do we not all have demons? We are every one of us fallible and easily tempted. And repentance, when we do not lean on the Lord for strength, is so very hard, if not impossible.

Yet, Mr. Madison is our spiritual leader. Should not more be expected of him?

Journal, I am utterly mired in confusion.

****

Late one night, as Eli snored blissfully in bed and Maggie sat reading the Gospel of Luke by a low lamp, she happened upon a verse that spoke to her. It was quite blunt, but cut directly through to her heart. "Judge not, and ye shall not be judged; condemn not, and ye shall not be condemned: forgive, and ye shall be forgiven."

Ah, she thought. That is it! I am judging and condemning Mr. Madison. It is not my place to censure, regardless of what I know. Judgment is God's business, not mine.

And then she remembered how God had spoken to her at the camp meeting and how she had thrown off the chains that had held her fast and pledged to follow Christ's way of love. Judgments and condemnation were chains, she realized. They held her back from loving Jeremiah Madison as Christ would love him, as a man suffering from the burden of sin and in need of release and redemption. Maggie realized that if she had truly left her chains behind, then she needed to forgive Mr. Madison and withhold her own judgment – a difficult path, but one that she had promised to follow.

Decision made, she shut the Bible, blew out the lamp, and returned to the warmth of her husband in bed.

****

The situation in the United States was volatile: pro-slavery forces were on one side, abolitionists on the other and many more people were confused and in the middle. Eli devoured newspapers from New York and Philadelphia so he could inform readers of his weekly paper about political circumstances. He read all he could about the growing crisis and talked endless politics with Nate and the boarders. The election was a little more than two weeks away, and the names of the four candidates – Abraham Lincoln, Stephen Douglas, John C. Breckinridge, and John Bell – were now as familiar in the little boarding house as the names of its family.

The continuous discussion of secession and war was beginning to weary Maggie. What is it about war, she wondered, that men find so intriguing? Even her decidedly pacifist husband was absorbed by the fervent speculation.

****

From Maggie's Journal, 17 October 1860

This is precisely why women are not allowed to vote. We wouldn't stand for all this saber-rattling, and we would surely ruin all excitement. After all, we women are told over and over that we have greater morality, purer motives, and more tender hearts than men could ever hope to have. Yet men are the ones set loose upon the world, while women are told to tend the sacred fires of the hearth and raise up pious, civic-minded youth. Then we women are expected to turn our carefully nurtured and educated young men over to the world so that they may add to the extant war, hatred, and discord. At the same time, we force our daughters to stay demurely within the home so as to concentrate on rearing the next generation. Something is very wrong. But that "something very wrong" is championed as the right way. Small wonder I am teary and aggravated these days – the world has become a place of madness.

****

The boarders had finished their breakfast, and the immediate family was finally sitting down to their own meal. Nate had eaten quickly and rushed off to his carpentry shop on Water Street. Frankie was wolfing her breakfast in a most unladylike fashion.

As Maggie and Lydia finally joined the table, the back door swung open and Eli, who had gone to the *Gazette* early to set type, wandered in. He fell into a chair, unfolded *The New-York Times* and, as he had done so many mornings of late, began to read.

Emily was by the range, dishing up eggs, fried potatoes, and biscuits. As a plate was placed before each person, he or she tucked happily into the meal – all except Maggie. She hadn't had much of an appetite, and soon realized that she was spending more time pushing food around her plate than actually ingesting what was set before her.

"More bad news, Eli?" Emily asked as she buttered a biscuit.

He nodded.

"Don't know why you read all those papers," she muttered. "Nothing good ever seems to happen."

Frankie happily slammed her fork down. "Well, *I've* got something good to say! I would like to go to college."

Maggie lifted an eyebrow.

"I will turn fifteen soon and next year, when I become sixteen, I will be finished with school. I could teach for two years and then go to college."

Maggie glanced at her husband. "Eli, do you hear that? Frankie wants to go to college."

Eli nodded. "Mm, hm."

He was paying only peripheral attention, but Maggie knew his views on the issue, so she had no trouble speaking for the both of them. "Well, Frankie, why not? It is good for a young woman to be well-educated. Which places permit females?"

"The normal school near Trenton trains teachers. So does Mount Holyoke Female Seminary in Massachusetts. But," she lowered her voice, "I would really like to study religion. It is so interesting! Mr. Madison loaned me some texts on theology. So, I just might consider Oberlin in Ohio."

Visions of her-daughter-the-preacher assailed Maggie yet again. "And what would you do, having studied religion?"

"Why, Mama, I'm shocked. Religion is the foundation of life. If I become a teacher, I could be a great help to my students. But I could even teach *and* exhort – with authority!"

"I see."

Frankie stuffed a biscuit loaded with butter and jam into her mouth. "What do you think?"

Maggie tried to sound rational. "Well, I've heard of all of those schools and they sound very good. But two of them are so far away." Frankie was only a child, and so she found herself fighting off an awful sense of impending loss. "Let's see if Eli has family near Oberlin. Perhaps you could board with them. And if not, well, I'm sure we would be able to make appropriate arrangements."

Grinning, Frankie hopped to her feet, cleared her plate and cup, and was off to school – leaving Maggie to realize that her daughter would be gone forever from her house in as equally a quick manner. She wanted to cry, but the breakfast table was not the place for a show of emotion.

A moment of silence passed, and then Lydia looked up from her plate. "Well, since we're on the subject of news, Mama, I need to speak with you and Eli. You, see, Edgar and I were talking last night, and – well, we'd like to get married right away."

Maggie nearly dropped her fork.

Lydia held her mother's gaze. "It's just that things are so uncertain these days. And if there's a war – oh, Mama, you understand, don't you?"

What could she say? She had had a two-week engagement. Her daughter hardly had a conventional model for her life. But Lydia wanted to get *married*! Must I lose both girls in one day, Maggie cried to God in desperation. Not knowing what else to do, she turned to her husband. "Eli, did you hear that? Lydia's asking if she may marry Edgar."

"Mm, hm," he said around a mouthful of eggs, his head still buried in the paper.

Men, Maggie thought with not a little exasperation. She would need to discuss the matter with him later. She turned to Lydia. "Where would you live?"

"With you?" she suggested in a meek voice.

That was more comforting news. Maggie thought of the chambers on the second floor of the new wing. Lydia currently shared a room with Frankie. Nate and Emily had two rooms: one for sleeping and the other for sitting. There was one other room of good size, which was used for storage. It would be an acceptable chamber for newlyweds. Edgar's room in the old part of the house could then be freed up for another boarder. But what would she do with the items in storage? Maggie thought for a moment. Perhaps she could move those things to the rooms above the *Gazette*. And when Lydia and Edgar began having children, what then? Maybe after Frankie went to college they might be able to create a nursery from her old room.

Maggie stopped her churning thoughts. She decided that she had better not think too far into the future. Adjustments would and could be made as necessary as life dictated.

She studied her eldest daughter's face. "Do you two really wish to marry this soon?"

The girl was glowing. She needed nothing more for confirmation.

Maggie smiled in reply. "Well, then, if your heart tells you to get married, who am I to object?"

Lydia leapt up, gave her mother a quick kiss on the cheek, and hurried out of the kitchen.

Eli pointed his fork at the biscuit on Maggie's plate. "Don't you want that?"

"No." She sighed. "Take it."

"Thanks. Pass the jam, please."

She pushed the jar of strawberry jam in his direction and smiled tiredly at Emily, who asked, "Not very hungry these days, are you?"

She shook her head.

"Wish I could say the same. I can't seem to get filled up." As Emily's brown eyes met Maggie's, she grinned broadly. "But that's because I'm eating for two now."

Maggie's mouth fell open.

Scooting her chair back, Emily patted her stomach, which Maggie could see was well-rounded. The two women immediately fell to laughing.

"How wonderful!" Maggie cried. "I never thought – I never noticed – how far along are you?"

"Oh, nearly five months. Nate and I didn't want to say anything because, well, you know, we've lost so many." She ran a hand lovingly over the small bulge under her dress. "But this one stayed put."

Maggie turned to her husband. "Eli, did you hear? Emily's going to have a baby."

"Mm, hm," he replied once again, head still in the paper.

Emily narrowed her eyes. "Men and their politics! Why're they dragging it on like this? Why don't they just start the shooting and get it over with?"

"Please God that will never happen." The thought of war made Maggie dizzy, and as she looked down at her plate, her stomach began to churn at the mound of potatoes and eggs. Swallowing hard, she shoved her breakfast in Eli's direction.

"For me?" he said. "Thanks!"

Emily frowned. "If you don't start eating, Maggie, you and he are going to look like the Jack Sprat rhyme – only in reverse."

"I just can't eat these days. Every time I look at food, I feel sick. In fact, half the time I feel sick simply smelling . . ." She stopped rather abruptly.

The two women stared at each other for a long moment.

"Simply smelling food," Maggie finally finished.

"Mm, hm," Emily said. "You late?"

"What do you mean?"

"You know what I mean. Are you late?"

"Should we be talking about this in front of . . ." Maggie indicated Eli.

"Does he look like he's listening? Anyway, he knows about women. So answer my question. Are you late?"

Maggie sighed. "Yes."

"How many months?"

"Two. Just."

Emily stood up and began clearing the plates from the table. "When were you going to tell him?"

Maggie did not know what to say. She had considered waiting another month just to be sure.

Now, the ways of men can be most peculiar. Eli could read through the loudest of discussions and the most raucous of laughter. But when silence descended upon the table that morning, he immediately looked up from the newspaper. "What's going on?"

Smirking, Emily set the plates down near the dish tub. "I think I'll let your wife explain that to you."

Baffled, Eli watched her walk out of the kitchen. "Maggie?" he asked.

His wife reached over and put her hand on his. "We need to talk." He blinked. "Oh?"

"Something may be happening."

A frown creased his forehead. "To who? Our girls?"

"No," Maggie replied. "To me."

"To you? Is something wrong? Aren't you well?"

"No, I'm well – in a way. You see, I've been feeling sick to my stomach and I've been tired a great deal." She found herself having trouble putting the situation into words. "Well, Eli, there are some other indications – for instance, my monthly has been or rather *hasn't* been – so maybe this just might be . . . ."

He frowned in confusion and concern. "Just might be what?"

"Well, something *else*, something that's not illness."

"Oh." It took half a second. Suddenly, Eli's eyes got quite round. "Oh!" And he said nothing further.

Maggie was not prepared to have a child, and was sure that her husband was even less so. But they had not given a moment's thought to withholding anything from each other and thereby preventing a child. "Eli?" She knew that this might not be exactly good news for him.

"Yeah." He wiped his mouth off with the napkin. "Something else, huh?" He exhaled nervously. "All right. Something else." Leaning over, he kissed Maggie on the lips. "Um . . . need to go, sweetheart. 'Bye." With that, he got up and hurried out the door.

Before Maggie could do or say anything further, Lydia breezed back into the kitchen. "Mama, Mr. Madison and Leah have just arrived!"

She lifted her eyes heavenward and silently asked, "Will it never end?" Within the space of breaths, she had learned that her youngest daughter wished to go away to college and study theology, her eldest wanted to marry, her closest friend was having a baby, and she had just told her husband that she probably was with child. Now, Jeremiah Madison was home with his new bride. The last thing Maggie needed that morning was precisely what she got – another change.

She paused, took a breath, said a little prayer, and reminded herself of Jesus' commandments regarding love and good will. She shook off the chains of judgment and condemnation. Jeremiah Madison did not know that she had sensitive information about his previous life. And it would not do to attempt to broach the subject in Leah's presence. Maggie knew that she must appear welcoming and must help Leah adjust to living in the boarding house. And that would indeed be a great adjustment for girl, for she was used to a large house and a staff. At Second Street she would be confined to one room (albeit a comfortable one) and would be bereft servants.

Composing herself, Maggie stood and then strode to the front parlor. Jeremiah was still outside but Leah was waiting in the room. Maggie smiled warmly. "My dear niece, welcome!"

The young girl turned. Her face was angelic, beautifully framed by a bonnet of deep blue. "Thank you, Aunt," she said, but her voice was quite stiff. "Of course, you must know that I do not intend to live here long. I am afraid the room will be much too small for my needs. Mr. Madison and I require a house, and so we shall move."

"I understand," Maggie replied as sweetly as she could, "but right now you're living in the rooming house. And you're welcome as long as you stay."

"Indeed, my dear," another voice said. They both turned as Jeremiah, carrying two carpet bags, entered the parlor. "You must learn to be thankful no matter where you are. As a minister's wife, you no doubt will live in diverse residences."

"My father will help us," she answered, cooly. "We won't need to be subject to the whims of the congregation."

Jeremiah ignored her comments and smiled at Maggie. "My dear Mrs. Smith." The handsome young man held out his hands.

Despite her best efforts, she still struggled with conflicting feelings. Part of her wanted to reach out to him in the old manner – as both her pastor and her young spiritual friend. But the other part was still hesitant and suspicious. This disjuncture between his life as a man called by God and his dalliances with young women, including her niece, was jarring. Why had he told her that his weakness was not a problem? His behavior indicated that it was very much a problem. And now Maggie found herself wondering whether he would be able to devote himself entirely to Leah or whether he would still desire the attention of other women.

Jesus rules all, Maggie reminded herself, and so love must rule me. With a mighty effort, she pushed the nagging questions aside, placed her hands in Jeremiah's, and allowed him to kiss her cheek in Christian friendship. "I am pleased that you've returned safely," she said.

"Yes, and quite ready to set up housekeeping under new circumstances." The young minister turned his bride. "Would you like to see our quarters, Leah?"

The girl gave Maggie a very cool look. "I believe I know where we will be staying – for the present." With that, she brushed past her aunt and marched down the hall, through the kitchen, and into the new wing.

Jeremiah heaved a weary sigh. "I'm afraid that my wife is being most uncooperative."

"Being married is a big adjustment."

"Just the same, I apologize for her behavior, Mrs. Smith." His tone was sincere. As he looked in the direction of the kitchen, his voice softened and saddened. "Perhaps this is my penance."

That caught Maggie's attention.

But the mood immediately lifted from him as quickly as someone would remove a dust sheet from a piece of furniture, and he smiled reassuringly at her. "I'm sorry. The trip was tiring and my nerves are rather strained, as are my wife's. If you don't mind, I think I will retire to my chambers for a rest."

She frowned as he walked away. For that fleeting second, Jeremiah had sounded so full of regret and pain.

****

From Maggie's Journal, 19 October 1860

All is change, dear Journal, most for the good, but not all. In fact, I fear that some of it bodes ill. Leah is clearly unhappy with her living arrangements and Jeremiah is certainly not the picture of the happy groom. But perhaps things seem that way because of my condition and the emotion it brings with it.

****

Eli avoided Maggie all that day and evening. He was quite clever, finding opportunities to have other people around so the couple was never alone and never able to speak privately. However, Maggie did not allow his evasion bother her over much. She knew that there was one place where he would have to face her.

By the time she had seen to the settling of the house, as well as to her daughters' settling into bed, Eli also was abed and, for all appearances, fast asleep. Maggie, of course, knew better. She blew out the lamp and climbed in beside him. He had his back to her – and his back could be a large, effective wall. But Maggie had gained no little skill at scaling that particular barrier. She took the polite approach first, whispering, "Eli?"

There was no answer.

"Eli!" She gently shook his shoulder.

Still there was no answer.

But she was not easily dissuaded. The evening was chill, as mid-October evenings often were – and so were her hands. Snuggling up to Eli's broad back, she snaked an arm around him and up into his nightshirt.

"Maggie!" he nearly shrieked.

"Ah! I knew you were awake."

"And your hands are like ice!" He rolled over and faced her now. "That is not fair!"

"Neither is playing possum."

It was dark, but enough moonlight was coming in the window for Maggie to see his expression. He looked sheepish, obviously not ready to hear what she had to say. But there was no sense in mincing words. She took a breath. "I think I am pregnant."

He averted his eyes. "I know, but I thought maybe . . ."

"Eli, surely you didn't think that nothing would come of our –"

"Look, it's all right. These things happen when a man and a woman are together. It's just – I didn't think – I mean, so soon. You know? It's just too soon."

"I know it seems so," she replied. "But we can't do anything about this. A child's on the way and I cannot stop it. I am sorry if you don't want a baby."

"No, no, no," he whispered quickly. "A baby is fine. It's just . . ." He swallowed and muttered, "Look, Maggie, this is hard for me to say."

"Please say it, anyway. I want to know why you're acting like this."

"All right, all right. I'm acting like this because," he breathed in, as if to brace himself, "my wife, Martha, died in childbirth." After clearing his throat, he continued in a quiet voice. "See, the trouble is I lost first my son and then my wife all within the space of a few hours. The midwife wouldn't even let me in. Men aren't supposed to be around. That's normal, I suppose, but the baby was a stillbirth and Martha, well, she was gone before they could get me. What should have been a happy day became the worst day of my life." He paused a moment before continuing. "You know, I had a great job with the *Times* in New York, but I'm sorry to say I quit. And I started drinking some. No. I started drinking *a lot*. And I did other things I'm not real proud of. I suppose I went a little mad, but I'd lost everything, see. I just didn't know what to do. No one ever tells you what to do when these things happen."

Maggie waited.

At last, he looked her in the eyes again. "So, it's not the baby. It's you. Do you understand? I couldn't take it if – I won't stand for it, not again."

"Oh, no," she said in a rush. "No, no. I'll be fine, Eli. And if you want to stay with me when the baby comes, you may. You'll see. I'm quite strong. I've given birth to three children with no problems at all."

"*Three* children?"

Now it was her turn to confess. "I had a boy three years after Frankie. Rheumatic fever took John *and* our son Gideon. I also had a pregnancy between Lydia and Frankie, but miscarried. So I too know what it feels like to be drowning in grief. If it hadn't been for my children, the rooming house, and Aunt Letty, *I* might have gone a bit mad, too. Grief is a kind of madness, isn't it? But sadly it is a madness that we all must go through one time or another." She wondered why men didn't have close friends to uphold them through the trials of life. She also wondered how Eli could have survived even one day of heart-crushing grief without someone in whom he could confide. Maggie caressed his face, and loved him for his sorrow. "But there's no grief now. Now we just may have some joy. God gave us this baby, Eli. Think of it as good, not sorrow."

He said nothing, but began to kiss her. The emotional pain was still too great for him to want to talk further. Touching and holding comforted him. The two were kissing quietly, when a loud thumping and the sound of angry, raised voices interrupted them. They tried to ignore it, but when it did not abate, both heaved a simultaneous sigh, sat up and stared at the door. The racket was coming from Madison's chambers. After a few seconds, Eli threw the covers off. "All right, let's go before they get the entire place stirred up."

They lit a candle and threw on their dressing gowns. As they hurried into the hall, Maggie heard Lydia call, "Mama?" She was standing at the top of the stairs to the second floor.

"It's all right, dear," Maggie said. "We are going to discover what is going on."

She and Eli paused before the door to the Madison chamber. They exchanged a glance and then Maggie knocked rather firmly.

Jeremiah Madison opened the door. Beyond him, Maggie could see Leah sitting on a chair. She was weeping into her hands.

"Sorry, Reverend," Eli said, "but your argument is carrying a bit too well."

"Yes, I know," he replied, eyes downcast. "I'm so sorry."

Leah lifted her head and sobbed, "I want to go home!"

Jeremiah rolled his eyes heavenward. "For the last time, *this* is your home, Leah!"

"I will not stay here. *I will not!*"

Eli put his hands up. "All right, all right, everybody calm down." He and Maggie slipped into the room and shut the door behind them. "We're going to discuss this quietly or not at all."

Maggie went to the girl's side. "Niece, you must have known that you would live here after the wedding."

She dabbed at her face with a lace handkerchief. "But what kind of a life is it for me in a poky little room like this?"

Laying a hand on her shoulder, Jeremiah gently said, "As a minister's wife, Leah, you must learn to adapt."

"Why?" She began to cry anew. "Why, when Father can pay for a house of our own?"

"Because *I* am your husband!" he nearly shouted.

She leapt to her feet. "And you're entirely too proud!"

"I? I am anything but proud! I'm a clergyman. I am obliged to live humbly. And, as my wife, you are, too."

And this, Maggie thought, is the result of a genteel upbringing. Leah was unaccustomed to anything but the most protected of lives. She wished to do pointless hours of needlework and visiting, hoped to raise children through a nurse and a governess, and desired to manage her household through servants. She was unprepared for life beyond her father's home. The prestige and power of this up-and-coming minister had clouded her conception of reality. She did not know that if and until Jeremiah rose sufficiently within the ranks of Methodism, she would be living in small rooms and drafty, ill-repaired parsonages. Maggie thanked God that she had sense enough and little income enough to seek only her daughters' happiness – and nothing more.

The utter stupidity of the Madisons' situation suddenly irked her. It was late. Everyone should be in bed and asleep. Her husband was in need of reassurance and love. And she, she was wrestling with the full realization that she was pregnant, not to mention fighting off mild nausea. The newlywed couple's petty bickering and inability to communicate was an annoying, unnecessary interruption. "Well, it's obvious that nothing can be solved this evening," Maggie said tersely. "Leah, you must be reasonable. There is no way that we can move you out of here tonight. And there is no reason for you and Mr. Madison to be arguing so violently, especially at this hour."

The girl pouted. "I shall complain about your tone to my father."

"That is unlikely to change his opinion, since he already thinks so little of me," was Maggie's tart reply.

"I apologize, Mrs. Smith," Jeremiah said. "My wife and I should have been more considerate. We will conduct ourselves henceforth in a more rational manner."

"Thank you. I expect that we will have no further disturbances tonight."

Leah merely sniffed, and refused to look at her aunt.

Maggie motioned to Eli. No sooner had they returned to their room and shut the door, than her husband began to sputter. "Incredible! Can't they solve their problems on their own? I mean, he's a minister, for pity's sake! All this nonsense is not improving my opinion of him." He fluffed up his pillow and hopped into bed. "They act as if they don't have a lick of sense between them. All right, granted, Leah's young, but she's behaving like a spoiled child." Maggie blew out the candle and climbed into bed as he raved on.

"I'll tell you this much, Samuel should have turned Leah over his knee long ago and given her a good spanking. Mark my words, Maggie; if we have a girl, she is not going to turn out like Leah Madison! No, sir, she'll be strong and sure of herself. She won't be some wheedling, whiny, little . . ." He noticed that his wife was just barely suppressing a grin. "What's so funny?"

"You."

His forehead wrinkled in confusion.

"A few minutes ago you were claiming that you didn't want children right away. Now, all of a sudden, you've changed your mind. Moreover, you've decided on the baby's sex and how she'll be raised."

He grinned and snuggled up. "You're right. Guess I'm starting to like the idea of a baby. Think I'll make a good father?"

Giggling like a schoolgirl, Maggie said, "Yes, Papa," and gave him a playful kiss. "And, you know, we might have a boy."

"A boy?" He put his hand on her stomach. "That would be splendid, too." He caressed her through the quilts. "You know, Maggie, I think you're getting round already."

"Not yet!" she protested. "It's too soon. You're feeling the covers."

Eli slid down and pressed his face to her abdomen. "Nope. Feels like a baby's in there." He kissed her belly, and then addressed it. "Hello, baby, it's your papa. And I'm warning you, don't kick me when I do this."

"I don't think it'll pay attention to that particular command. They never do."

"So when do you think it'll be born?"

"Oh, by my reckoning, early June."

Impressed, he whistled. "We really *didn't* waste any time, did we?"

Maggie laughed. "No, we didn't. I must admit I'm surprised. After all, I'm not young anymore."

Eli scooted back up and gave her a kiss on the lips. "Evidently you're still young *enough*."

****

From Maggie's Journal, 25 October 1860

Letters once again have been flying back and forth between Blaineton and my brother's house. Leah wishes to return home. Mr. Madison refuses to let her do so. Samuel has offered to purchase a house, but our minister has declined the offer, claiming that come spring the church will begin construction on our parsonage. Mr. Madison is quite firm that until such time as a parsonage is available, Leah will have to learn to be content at the rooming house. But, alas, she is not learning contentment. She pouts and cries and storms about like cross child. I would like very much to turn her over my knee, Journal. Married woman or not, she is in bad need of a spanking.

****

A few days later, Maggie was dusting the back parlor, when she was interrupted by the sound of raised voices in the front parlor. Hurrying in, she found Leah and Frankie engaged in a shouting match.

"Admit it!" Leah was snapping.

Frankie's lower lip jutted out. "Admit what? You're imagining things!" She whirled around to face Maggie. "Tell her, Mama. Tell her that we're not abolitionists." There was an edge to Frankie's voice – fear and desperation.

Leah met Maggie's eyes and produced a nasty little smile. "I know what's down in your cellar."

Maggie kept her face impassive. "Is that so?"

"I know about the secret door and the tunnel and the room!" Her face was almost gleeful.

"You're not supposed to be snooping around!" Frankie blurted. "None of our boarders go into the cellar."

The other girl smirked and adjusted her skirts over her hoop cage. "Well, I wouldn't have done so had I not seen something a few nights ago."

By now, Emily and Nate were peering in the doorway.

"I couldn't sleep so I decided to go to the back porch for a breath of fresh air." Her eyes were glowing. "I saw them," she nodded at the Johnsons. "And they were not alone. They had some others with them and they looked all raggedy. They were slaves. So now I know what you are. You're abolitionists. You're nigger lovers."

"I think that girl needs to be taught some manners," Nate growled, eyes flashing. He took a step forward.

Emily put a restraining hand on her husband's arm. "Nate, don't."

Leah folded her arms over her chest. "My, my, have I said something amiss?"

"What's wrong?" Eli asked, as he joined the growing throng at the door. Behind him, Maggie caught a glimpse of Grandpa O'Reilly and Mr. Carson.

Nate gestured angrily in Leah's direction. "Her language, for one thing."

Meanwhile, Frankie was hissing, "How dare you, Leah? How dare you use that word?"

"Everybody uses that word!" Leah taunted. "I wonder what happens up on the second floor at night – you and your sister and that darkie."

Indignant, Frankie straightened her posture. "Nothing happens because Nate Johnson is a fine, well-bred *gentleman.*"

"A gentleman, you say? As if you would know what one of *those* looked like."

There was the briefest of pauses, and then Frankie said, "That's really quite funny, Leah,"

"It is?"

"Yes. I may not know what a gentlemen looks like, but I do know what ladies *aren't.* And they aren't usually with child *before* their wedding day."

Leah gasped, stepped forward, and slapped Frankie hard across the face.

There was another pause – just enough time for Eli to push past Maggie and get to Frankie before the girl lunged at her cousin. Wrapping his arms around her waist, Eli swung Frankie around and away, as she clawed and kicked at the air like an angry cat. "Maggie," he grunted, "are you *sure* this girl doesn't know the facts of life?"

By this time, Maggie was moving, too. "That will be enough, all of you!" She advanced upon Leah. "I will not have such language and such a display in my house, *do you understand?*"

Leah sneered at her. "And I deserve better accommodations – unless you would like the world to know your little secret!"

"What's all this?" It was Jeremiah's voice.

All eyes turned to him, and then suddenly it seemed as everyone in the room was speaking all at once.

"Do you know what your wife just said??? Nate was sputtering.

"Leah's not a lady!" Frankie shouted. "And she is saying horrible things!"

"Hey, Madison," Eli added, still struggling to hold onto the girl. "Maybe you *ought* to let Sam Beatty build you that house,"

A baffled Jeremiah glanced at Maggie, who heaved a tired sigh. "Leah has just accused us of being abolitionists and of harboring slaves."

Astounded, the minster turned to his wife. "Leah! How could you?"

"How could I? Don't be so foolish! You know the truth, too!" The young woman angrily tossed her head. "I have had enough. I am telling my father about this and you all will be arrested!" With that, she marched toward the door. The group of onlookers there parted as neatly as if they were the Red Sea parting for Moses. And then she was out the front door and gone.

"Leah!" Jeremiah barked. "Come back here!" He ran out after her.

There was a brief pause, and then Mr. Carson calmly lit his pipe. "Rather ill-behaved child, isn't she?"

"Needs a trip to the woodshed, is what she needs," Grandpa O'Reilly agreed.

Eli finally released Frankie. The girl brushed escaped strands of red hair behind her ear and sniffed petulantly. When she met her mother's narrowed eyes, she grumbled, "She started it."

"I expect better of you," Maggie replied. "And *you're* not too old for the woodshed."

"Mama, you have never spanked me!"

"I just might start," she answered. She turned to Nate and Emily. "I am so sorry. Leah had no right."

"They never do," Emily responded.

"And they never change," Nate added. "Damn it! They never change!" Furious, he stormed out of the room. Emily sighed tiredly and followed him.

The excitement was over for the time being. The others began to drift away. Maggie pursed her lips as she worked out what to do next. Meanwhile, Eli banished Frankie to her room, saying, "We'll be up to talk to you in a few minutes." The girl did as she was told. When she was gone, Eli folded his arms across his chest and addressed Maggie. "Well? What now?"

"I'm writing to Samuel," she replied. "This has got to stop."

****

From Maggie's Journal, 29 October 1960

Leah is becoming most dangerous and disruptive. Mr. Madison managed to bring her back to the rooming house and has all but locked her in their chambers. I wrote immediately, telling Samuel about Leah's many outbursts. Journal, what shall I do? I cannot tell him the truth about our abolitionist activities, for he does not believe in the cause. Should I do so, he might go to the authorities. I am thus quite torn. We cannot stop rescuing enslaved people, for we believe this is our moral duty. At the same time, I find it repugnant to lie to my brother. But how ever shall we keep Leah quiet? He is sure to find out.

****

The next day Samuel Beatty turned up on the rooming house's front porch. Maggie was stunned to see that his haughty attitude had been replaced by a weary expression and drooping posture.

She had been sweeping and dusting, but invited him to enter and asked if he would care for some tea. When Sam replied in the affirmative, Maggie showed him to the front parlor with its formal furniture, and hurried to the kitchen. The kettle was already hot so it took only a few minutes to pour the water into a pot of tea leaves and lay some of Emily's tasty molasses cookies on a plate. The time away also gave Maggie the opportunity to roll down her sleeves and tidy her hair, although she suspected that she still looked like a mess and she knew that her complexion was pale because she was not feeling well. When she returned to the parlor, she poured a cup for Samuel and added sugar, remembering that he had always liked his tea sweet, with two lumps.

And that was when a powerful memory flitted through her mind: the two of them as children sitting at their table in the nursery. Maggie could almost smell the strawberry jam they had spread on their pieces of bread. She remembered the scent and crackle of the wood fire. They were having tea. The beverage was mostly milk, but to their young minds, they were having tea. She played the lady and gave Sam his cup – always with two lumps. She recalled the governess, Miss Stewart, sitting on the bench by the window and nodding in approval as Maggie mastered her etiquette. They were so young, and playing at being adults. In those days, Maggie never imagined that tension would build between them. A wave of deep regret swept over her.

As she passed a cup and saucer to her brother, she said, "So what shall we do, Sam?" She took a sip from her own cup. The tea tasted good. It slid comfortingly down her throat, warming her stomach and easing the nausea of which she never seemed to be completely rid.

Samuel stirred his tea for a moment. "I don't know," he finally said. "My family has been in a great uproar these several months."

"Mine, as well."

"To put it simply, I'm desperate for peace. My daughter wishes to move home. But that's out of the question. Yet Madison won't acquiesce to a different living arrangement. They must remain here, he says. I feel constrained to appease my daughter. Whenever we see her, which is quite often, all she does is cry. At the same time, I feel also constrained to accept her husband's dictates. After all, he *is* her husband."

"And there is more, Sam," Maggie said quietly. "She believes that we are hiding escaped slaves."

"What?" He almost laughed.

"It seems she thinks that she saw Nate and Emily bringing slaves to our establishment." Maggie took a deep breath and for the first time in her adult life began to lie. "They were merely friends of theirs from Water Street in need of provisions. As you know, it would not do for them to bring their colored friends here by the light of day. Furthermore, Leah believes that we have a door in the cellar that leads to a tunnel and a secret room. This, I suspect, is the result of a rather vivid dream." She prayed that God would forgive her for the fabrications.

"But why would she have such a dream?"

Maggie managed a slight smile. "I don't know. But come see for yourself." She placed the cup and saucer down and stood up. "Let's go to the cellar."

She led her brother by the light of an oil lamp down the narrow, wooden stairs and onto the dirt floor of the cellar. Maggie walked directly to the old wardrobe and opened the doors. "She claimed it was in here, but as you can see, there is no door."

Samuel took the lamp from her. He looked inside the wardrobe, pushing on its back wall and tugging at the pegs. Nothing moved. All was solid. "I will have a word with my daughter now," was all he said.

****

From Maggie's Journal, 30 October 1860

Our dear Lord once said, "Behold, I send you forth as sheep in the midst of wolves: be ye therefore wise as serpents, and harmless as doves." Is this what he means? Are the wolves those who wish to perpetuate the institution of slavery? Are the abolitionists the sheep in the story? Or is it the reverse? Have we learned to be the wolves, too? And have we now become more serpent than dove?

We have saved many lives and kept ourselves out of jail, but are we not harming Leah in the process? We have willingly allowed the word of my niece to be questioned – indeed, perhaps allowed her very sanity to be questioned.

We all of us are complicit. Grandpa O'Reilly, Eli, and Edgar are excellent masons. And Patrick, who can now build a coffin in his sleep, rendered seamless repairs to the wardrobe. The tunnel from Eli's print shop to the secret room remains open. It will be more difficult to get provisions and other necessities to our guests, but since our marriage, no one will question my coming to and going from the *Gazette*.

But I wonder: in our anxiety to save the lives of many, have we not hurt one person? And is that not also a grievous thing in your sight, O God? It seems to me that we have no good answer. There will be pain no matter what we do.

****

Samuel had left Leah weeping hysterically in her room. As he entered the front parlor, he heaved a weary sigh. "I shall take her home for a few days. Perhaps she will come to her senses."

Maggie nodded, trying not to pay heed to the sobs that could be heard even in the parlor.

After a moment's thought, Samuel added, "Sister, when Leah returns – and she will – it might be easier by far for her if she were to have a friendly face here."

Maggie wanted to suggest that her own face could have been friendly enough, had Sam not cut her off so coldly. She truly would have enjoyed contact with her niece and nephews. But she held her tongue and waited for him to go on.

It was all too obvious that Samuel was trying to maintain his dignity even as he found himself reduced to asking his sister for a favor. "If I sent our maid, Carrie Hillsborough, to live here and assist my daughter, perhaps then Leah will settle more easily into her new life."

Maggie remembered the maid's green, almond-shaped eyes and the sly curve of her smile as the girl watched Jeremiah pray at camp meeting. She also remembered how she had seen Jeremiah and Carrie walking together by the edge of the woods and how he had taken her arm.

"I'll pay you," Samuel was saying. "I'll pay for her room and board. In addition, you may ask Carrie to help out here as you see fit."

Maggie feared that the maid might discover their secret, too, despite the fact that the main reception area had shifted to Eli's print shop. She tried to voice an excuse, "Samuel, I do not have enough rooms for Carrie to have her own accommodations on the new wing's second floor. And to bring in a new person, a stranger –"

"You have those two Negroes living there already."

Maggie bit her tongue once again. Samuel would never be able to understand that she regarded Nate and Emily as brother and sister. The notion was too radical for him. But she had to attempt an explanation, so she said, "They are my closest friends and not strangers to me, colored or not. At any rate, I was planning to give the spare room over to my daughter, Lydia. She and her beau, Edgar, plan to be married very soon."

Her brother set his cup down. "Must I beg, Margaret? Something wants doing and soon!"

"I know." Despite all that had happened between them, Maggie found herself reconsidering her answer. The situation with his daughter had disturbed him as much as it had disturbed the rooming house family. Despite Leah's spoiled-child antics, Maggie knew that Samuel dearly loved the girl. She was his sole daughter, a treasure, something to be protected and cherished. He needed to set his mind at rest, and if Maggie was the only one who could help him do it, then so be it. He was still her brother, and her heart yearned to recover the tender feelings of family. Having a maid might make Leah feel more at home and keep her mind off other things. "All right, Sam," she finally said. "But Carrie will have to share with Lydia and Frankie until Lydia gets married. I will make up a pallet on the floor for her."

Samuel looked utterly relieved. "That would be most kind and Christian."

His words took her aback. "Kind and Christian? Samuel, you're my brother! It's only right to help family. Mind you, I am not completely convinced that Carrie's presence will solve Leah's difficulties, nor am I certain that Carrie will be a suitable roommate for Frankie. But I am willing to try – for *your* peace of mind." And for ours, too, she thought. "You see, Samuel, I really *do* love you, even though we have our differences."

His eyes pooled with tears. He quickly looked down to retrieve his cup and saucer. "I've been over-harsh with you, I know."

Maggie almost laughed at the understatement. "Yes, Samuel, you have." She took a sip of her tea, and then said more gently, "Please understand, we've disagreed on how I should live my life, but that's the past. Can we not leave it behind?"

"Do you think we will ever be able to do that?" He seemed so sad. It made Maggie want to gather him up in her arms and comfort him, but she knew he would not permit it.

"I know that *I* can do it, Sam. All I ask of you is that you see me as I am – a woman who is happy with her life. Can you do *that*?"

"Perhaps – at least, I will try." He stood up. "I must go, Margaret. Will it be all right if I take Leah with me now? I have a letter for Mr. Madison explaining everything."

Maggie nodded. "I do hope you will be able to calm Leah down."

"Thank you. With any luck, she should be back here in a few days." An expression crossed his face. Was it regret, or wistfulness, perhaps? Maggie thought she even saw a bit of sorrow and repentance.

Yearning to help him, she rose, went to his side, and, taking his arm, kissed his cheek. "Don't worry, Sam. We'll do our best to help."

Then, to her surprise, he laid his hand over hers. "Thank you, sister."

CHAPTER SIX

True to his word, Samuel returned a much calmer Leah to the boarding house within four days. With her came the little maid, Carrie Hillsborough.

Carrie's presence seemed to ease Leah's homesickness, although the young bride continued to be critical of her lodgings. Fortunately, she was spending most of her time in her room or visiting friends and family. As a result, Maggie and the rest of the boarding house were spared her complaints and could breathe easy, knowing that the girl was not snooping around the house. When Leah joined them at mealtimes, most of them learned to turn a deaf ear on the occasions when she uttered disparaging remarks.

Carrie, on the other hand, turned out to be a great blessing. Despite Maggie's earlier qualms about her, the maid proved to be a conscientious worker. Since Emily's now-obvious condition was slowing her down, Carrie came to her aid the very day she arrived by assisting with the cooking. Moreover, the girl fell happily to scrubbing floors and dusting whenever Maggie needed help. And Carrie was a godsend during the steaming drudgery of Monday Wash Day. The maid even ironed and mended without being asked. Most amazing of all was the fact that she maintained good cheer throughout each job and each day. Maggie took particular relief in the fact that Carrie treated Jeremiah as one of her betters – and she no longer gave the minister yearning looks.

The boarders all took an instant liking to Carrie, Patrick in particular. In return, she was friendly, but did not offer him any encouragement. That disappointed Maggie. She was beginning to think that Carrie would be a good match for Patrick. The eighteen-year-old was learning to be an undertaker, which as Eli liked to joke, meant he'd never be at a loss for customers. With Carrie's industriousness and Patrick's skill at a trade, Maggie thought the two could have a very comfortable life together. But, she reminded herself, what they did with their lives was their own affair.

Four days after Leah's return to the boarding house, Election Day was upon them. The men trooped out to vote and joined the crowd of males that gathered in the square during elections. In addition, there were parades sponsored by political parties, shouting, and the obligatory firing of rifles.

In contrast, most of the boarding house women sat mending and sewing in the back parlor – all but Frankie. Original-minded, independent of action, and not the least bit inclined to pick up a needle, she chose to lean on the front porch railing and gawk at the festivities in the square and around the courthouse. On her infrequent visits to the back parlor, Frankie complained of how unjust it was that women were not permitted to vote. Maggie agreed with her, but also was thankful that she did not have to be exposed to the madness in the streets. The sheer noise and physicality of it all was disturbing. It caused her to wonder if Election Day would be any different if women indeed had the vote. Would things be more sedate? Perhaps it would be a more sober time, as people contemplated how their votes would direct the fate of the country. Maggie could not imagine that women would be so foolish as to succumb to male behavior – racing about, shouting, and drinking.

In the blessed quiet of the back parlor, she found time to open the chest that she usually kept in storage. All items not in use were being shifted to Emily and Nate's sitting room. The couple had generously given that room so that the former storage room, which was larger, could be made ready for Lydia and Edgar. Emily was adamant that they wanted the baby in their room and added that she and Nate rarely used their sitting room. So as boxes and old furniture were being moved over, Maggie requested that the men carry the little chest that held her daughters' old baby clothes down to the back parlor.

As she lifted up a tiny white linen dress, she sighed. "It's hard to imagine that you and Frankie were once this small, Lydia."

Her eldest daughter grinned. "I can't believe that I'm going to have a new brother or sister, at my age!"

"Let alone at my age," Maggie joked as she checked the garment to see if it needed mending.

"Why, Mrs. Smith!" Carrie set down the stocking she was darning. "Don't tell me you're expecting, too?"

Maggie nodded, feeling rather pleased with herself.

"I don't know why everyone gets so happy about it," Leah complained. "It's a miserable state to be in." She stood up and wandered restlessly to the window. "I have been feeling ill for the last few weeks."

Emily paused in her knitting. "The first few months are the most difficult. It's not unusual to feel sick to your stomach."

Lydia only sniffed a reply.

Carrie smiled. "Well, I think it's wonderful that this house will have *three babies* soon."

Maggie chuckled. "Our men boarders have no idea what's going to befall them. They think they have a bastion of male peace and quiet here. They are in for quite a surprise."

With that the front door banged and an ungainly and very loud clomping made its way down the hall. Frankie was first to burst into the back parlor, followed by Nate, Jeremiah, Eli, Edgar, Mr. Carson, and Patrick. The men were every bit as flushed and excited as Frankie. Hooting with laughter, they spilled noisily into the room.

"Well, so much for your theories about male peace," Emily muttered. "They make a bigger ruckus than fifteen babies."

Undeterred, the men launched into a booming discussion about the candidates and who might win the election. Green eyes shining, Carrie paused in her work to ask, "Who do *you* think will win, Mr. Madison?"

The young minister scratched his head. "Well, actually, I'm not sure. I've done a great deal of reading about this election. You know, Mr. Lincoln isn't even on the ballots in the South, so I don't see how he can possibly win."

"Of course, he'll win," Eli argued. "He's a moderate. The North'll go for him. You see, Mr. Douglas's platform – popular sovereignty – is nonsense to most Northerners and objectionable to Southerners. And Northerners will never go for Mr. Breckinridge. He wants to protect people and personal property in the Territories. That's just fancy talk for letting slavery spread all over the place. And Mr. Bell says he'll preserve the Constitution. But no one's going to vote for that. I mean, what does that mean exactly? It's just too doggoned vague."

"Yes, but I still don't see how a winner can be determined. From what you're saying, the South will back Breckinridge and the North will back Lincoln."

"Ah, but you're forgetting about the Electoral College," Eli replied. "The Northern states have the greater population, hence the most electoral votes."

"And so the election will go to Mr. Lincoln," Nate concluded. "Simple."

"Simple as mud," Emily commented. "And every bit as messy."

He sighed. "Yeah, but I still wish I could vote. It's important, especially this election."

Maggie sighed in sympathy. The election campaigning had been vicious, replete with deplorable mud-slinging, but Nate was right. It was an important election. It grieved her that Nate, because of his color, could not vote. She did not understand why New Jersey maintained such a law, nor did she understand why so many people in her town looked askance at Nate, Emily, and the handful of families on Water Street. They are people, she thought, just people. Why do others persist in seeing them as inferior?

Her thoughts made her angry and she began to mend with a vigor that bordered on the vengeful.

"Personally, I don't care who wins," Leah was grousing. "I'm tired. I think I'll go to my room."

"Good night, my dear," Jeremiah said as she passed him.

"Good night," she replied without any warmth whatsoever.

Carrie's enthusiasm was undeterred. "Well, *I* think this is all very exciting!"

"In more ways than one," Jeremiah told her. Suddenly he became quite somber. "Sadly, the outcome will most likely lead to dis-union."

"Perhaps you're mistaken. Perhaps those elected will exercise good sense."

"You're a dear girl, Carrie. And you have great faith in mankind, but mankind possesses a sinful nature. I'm afraid common sense will not prevail in this case. Whatever the voters decide will cause rancor on one side or the other. The sad truth of it is everyone is anxious for a fight."

Eli agreed. "Things are too far gone. Too much hatred and misunderstanding has piled up for too long."

Mr. Carson lit his pipe. "Too true. The South hates us, and we do not exactly like them, either."

"So the South will to secede from the Union," Patrick deduced. "Bet it'll happen within the week."

The older man smiled fondly at the boy. "No, no, my dear lad, it'll take a *bit* longer than that, I should think."

"But they'll still *secede*. And then we'll have war."

"Oh, yes. War. No doubt about that." He picked up one of the New York newspapers, sat down, and opened it. The pages crackled loudly. "No doubt at all."

Eli noticed that Maggie was overly-focusing on her mending. He put a reassuring hand on her shoulder. "Hey, baby clothes!" he declared and, picking one of the items up, he whistled. "Will you look at the size of this? I've got some news for you, Maggie. No baby of *mine* will ever be able to fit into such a teeny thing."

"Elijah Smith, I guarantee you that when our baby arrives it will be baby-size."

He laughed.

At that moment, a loud crack echoed outside. It was followed by a long volley of rifle fire. Maggie flinched.

Eli squatted beside her. "It's all right, sweetheart. It's just some of the neighbors." With a wink, he added, "Neighbors full of whiskey and armed with loaded weapons."

"Somehow, my love, drunken men with guns is not a comforting idea."

The men all guffawed.

"Oh, don't worry," Nate joked. "They're just getting a little practice in."

"They're going to need it," Edgar declared. "Pick up your rifles, men! Answer the call of your country!"

Patrick snapped to attention and saluted. "I'm ready to give my life for dear old New Jersey!"

"Fools," Emily grunted. "You're a bunch of doggoned fools."

Eli sighed, "Guess this just is a time for fools. The Union's going to hell in a hand-bucket."

"Eli!" Maggie hissed.

He was instantly contrite. "Sorry."

Nate elbowed Mr. Carson. "Looks to me like someone's already henpecked."

The men guffawed once again and Mr. Carson replied, "Not to worry. A turn in the army will take care of that. It will make him a man again."

"All right!" Emily threw down her knitting and stood up. "You can just stop this nonsense right now. Your jokes aren't funny and neither is all this talk of war. If there's fighting, some of you will join our state's militia and just might not come back. I don't want to hear anymore of this foolishness!"

Nate's expression softened. "Em, honey, I wish I could make it go away. Just like I wish I could make slavery go away. But I can't."

She placed her hands protectively over her stomach. "Well, then, God help us. The world's gone mad."

****

The election of November 6 elected Abraham Lincoln as President of the United States. And, as predicted, the political tension immediately escalated. It rose dramatically in the boarding house, as well. The women felt a sense of fear that until now they had been able to put aside. And, despite their bravado on Election Day, many of the men suddenly grew introspective.

Lydia, meanwhile, was planning her wedding with a grim determination, as Emily's waistline continued to expand with new life and Carrie continued to be helpful. Leah, on the other hand, was now complaining of stomach aches.

As for Maggie, she was irritable and jumpy, and it was becoming more and more difficult to blame her mood solely on her condition. Work therefore became her only solace. Scrubbing and washing took her mind off the dark clouds forming over the nation.

Weeks went by. No war was declared. But on the morning of December 4, Maggie was still cleaning like a charwoman. She began by lugging a bucket of water out to the entry way in order to scrub the floors. Dirt was the bane of her existence. No matter how hard she tried the filth outside always found its way into the house. Eli told her that she should give up and learn to live with it, but Maggie was not so easily convinced.

Realizing that she had left one of her rags behind, she hurried back down the hall. As she stepped into the kitchen doorway, she froze. Carrie and Jeremiah Madison stood near the door to the back porch. They were in a close embrace – body against body.

Maggie instantly stepped back and slid into the hall. As she did, she heard Carrie's throaty laugh. Daring not to breathe and wondering if they had seen her, Maggie let a few seconds pass. Finally, she felt assured that her presence had gone undetected. Had she disturbed them, they would have followed her with abundant explanations and apologies. But she had been left to lean against the wall and wonder what she had seen.

What to do next? Should she march back in there and demand an explanation? That would be embarrassing for all, including her.

Should she just ignore what her eyes had seen? Perhaps that would be best. At any rate, she needed to think.

Wiping her hands on her apron, Maggie decided that she could do without the extra rag and returned to the front entry. Her mind was churning by the time she knelt by the pail, fished out a rag, and furiously began scrubbing the floor.

Jeremiah had been holding Carrie. How could a man of God betray his wife that way? Granted, Leah had all the essential hallmarks of a nag, but she was still his wife. Jeremiah had taken vows – vows he had made before God.

Maggie's stomach roiled and she scrubbed harder to chase the nausea away, but she was overwhelmed by disturbing thought after disturbing thought. A man of God – a man of God, someone who morally and spiritually led her congregation – was keeping a wife and carrying on with a maid at the same time – and it was all happening under her roof.

What should I do? Maggie asked herself. She needed to speak to Jeremiah, but then what? Ought she to demand that he leave the ministry? Should she report him to his supervising elder? What would either man say in response? Would she be accused of being a busy-body?

Maggie knew that even if she said nothing to anyone, she would still feel uncomfortable. The truth was that sitting through worship would be impossible for her. In her mind and heart and soul, Jeremiah Madison had lost his authority. Horrified, she realized that his entire position had become a sham.

And what should she do about Carrie? The girl obviously needed to return to Samuel Beatty's house. But how would she explain that to Samuel? And what would she tell Leah?

Maggie prayed desperately for peace and clarity, but none came. By the time she was done with her cleaning, she had all but scrubbed the wood from the floor. Weary, she stood up and hefted her pail back to the kitchen.

Not surprisingly there was no trace of the illicit couple. Relieved, Maggie lugged the bucket out the back door. With a grunt, she heaved the dirty water onto the yard.

When she returned to the kitchen, she spotted the kettle sitting on the back of the stove. Steam was issuing from its spout. Setting the pail down, Maggie gingerly touched the pot, which proved to be nice and warm. She smiled. Yes, a good cup of tea was exactly what she needed. Soon she was spooning loose tea into the little china pot that sat on the table. Fetching a cup and saucer from the cupboard, she set them on the table too and then, wrapping her apron around her hand, grasped the kettle's handle. After pouring the hot water into the teapot, she returned the kettle to the range and finally, gratefully sat down. When the tea had steeped, she poured the steaming amber liquid into her cup and added to it a lump of sugar from the sugar bowl and a little milk from the jug on the table.

Her condition was already starting to sap her energy and her swelling stomach was beginning to get in the way. How would she manage six more months of this? Both she and Emily were going to have increasingly limited efficiency. Who would scrub the floors? Do the laundry? And what would happen after the babies came? Two suckling infants would continue to curb their ability to do necessary work. Maggie abruptly stopped her thoughts from whirling any further. She needed to handle one problem at a time. First, she would speak to Eli about Jeremiah and Carrie's embrace. Eli was sensible. He would help her sort things out, and then the two of them could go to Madison. As for Carrie, there was no question in her mind that the maid would have to leave.

Once that problem was settled and her tea consumed, Maggie turned her attention to the next project. She set two irons to heat on the stove, set up the board, and pulled over the clothes piled in a wicker basket. For perhaps thirty or forty-five minutes she worked her way through shirts, skirts, waists, petticoats, trousers, and baby clothes.

As she pressed a pretty little gown, she couldn't help but wonder who the baby would favor. Would it have Eli's brown eyes? She liked that idea, because Eli's eyes were a kind, friendly brown.

What about hair? Would the baby have red hair like hers or dark brown like Eli's? And would it be a big baby, as Eli suggested? That thought made Maggie smile. She hoped for her sake that the child would not be all that big. She ran her hand over the small bump in her belly. Like John before him, Eli was fascinated by the changes in her body. He seemed proud, especially as Maggie's condition became more noticeable. In fact, his reaction was rather territorial and just a bit amusing. This was *his* child after all and he was happy to let everyone know.

"So," Maggie said to the baby, "are you a boy or a girl?"

No sooner than she said this than a fearful pain – sharp and savage – tore through her stomach. Gasping, Maggie dropped the iron.

It crashed to the floor as she clutched at her middle. The pain was followed almost immediately by a fierce wave of nausea. She barely had time to seize the nearby wash bucket before vomiting violently into it. She had just recovered when another wave gripped her and she threw up again. The pain that followed was severe – so severe that it knocked her to her knees.

"Maggie?" Emily's voice came down the hall. "Did you scrub that floor all by your—" The woman's sentence died as she entered the kitchen and found her friend doubled over in pain. She ran to Maggie's side and put her arms around her. Looking over her shoulder, Emily shouted, "Lydia! Come quick!"

Within minutes, the two women had pulled Maggie to her feet, moved her to the bedroom, and laid her on the bed. Frankie was sent to fetch Eli, who arrived in a panic. By this time, Maggie was cold and clammy, feeling very faint, and heaving even when there was nothing left to heave.

In short order, Grandpa O'Reilly was sent to get Dr. Lightner, the town physician. By the time he arrived, Maggie's condition had worsened. Now she was suffering from both vomiting and diarrhea. Soon something else was evident – she was losing the baby.

The rest of the day blurred into a haze of unrelenting agony and horror. It occurred to Maggie that she might not live. She could hear people praying around her, especially Frankie, whose voice was lifted in fervent pleas. Good girl, she thought, as her mind detached itself from her body. Use the gifts God gave you.

She knew that Eli was holding her hand, that Emily bathing her face and arms, and that Lydia sitting beside her. She could see their grim expressions and their tears. She could hear their miserable, watching silences.

I am dying, Maggie finally decided, and with surprising ease began to let go. Her life no longer mattered. But she wanted – desperately wanted – Eli to have comfort and asked God to keep him safe. She prayed that her girls, and Emily and Nate would be kept safe. Most of all, Maggie wanted them all to know that she would be safe with her Lord. Then she surrendered her soul to the Almighty.

Suddenly, it was as if she was lifted up and taken to another place. A wonderful, warm, peaceful light was all around. Before she had time to marvel at what was happening, someone came out of that light and walked toward her. Unafraid, Maggie waited, and was delighted when she saw that the figure was John Blaine. Her husband smiled at her – he always had a lovely smile, lopsided and slightly amused. He held out his hands. Happily, she grasped them in hers.

"My Maggie," he said.

She didn't know what to say. There he was, standing right before her.

"You can see how I am," he continued. "I am fine. And Gideon's fine, too. And the unnamed babies are fine, as well."

"May I see them?" she asked.

He smiled again. "Of course – but not yet. You need to care for our girls first, and for Eli. I'm glad you found him. You had been so lonely and he's a good man. But he needs you, and so do our girls, so we must say goodbye – for a little awhile, anyway."

Maggie was not ready to go. She hadn't seen John in so long. She wanted to talk. She had a thousand questions.

"There are troubles, Maggie," he said. "Things are wrong. But with the good Lord's help, you will persevere. You will make things right."

****

She opened her eyes a crack, then immediately shut them against the light from the lamp. Carefully, gradually, Maggie opened her eyes again. As things came into focus, she could see Lydia sitting beside her.

Her daughter leaned forward and smiled. "Hello, Mama. Don't worry. You're going to be fine."

She managed a faint smile in return and fell asleep once more.

By the end of the second day, the pains had almost ebbed away. The fog was lifting too and Maggie was becoming more aware of her surroundings. As she woke up, she realized that she was weak and extremely thirsty. Turning her head, she saw that Lydia was still sitting on the chair beside the bed. Her daughter saw that she had come round and caressed her mother's forehead. "How do you feel?"

Maggie's mouth was so dry. "Thirsty," she managed to rasp.

Lydia turned to the bedside table to pour water from a pitcher into a glass. Then she slipped a hand under Maggie's head and put the glass to her lips. The water was cold – an absolute blessing. Maggie wanted to gulp the whole glassful, but Lydia took it away. "Not too much at first, Mama. Take a little at a time."

Maggie let her daughter put her head back onto the pillow. "You're a good nurse, Lydia."

"I had a good teacher."

She noticed that Emily was in the room, too. Her friend came over and sat down on the edge of the bed. "What do you remember?"

Maggie licked her lips. "Not much. You thought I was going to die."

"Frankie prayed you out of that," Lydia said with no small pride. "She led us all, even Mr. Madison."

"My rebel minister girl."

"Dr. Lightner said you had a severe attack of gastric fever." Emily put a hand on her friend's arm and gave it a warm squeeze. "But, honey, I'm so sorry. I need to tell you some bad news." She took a breath. "Maggie, your baby's gone."

She looked away.

"Did you hear what I said? You had a miscarriage."

She managed to nod, anything to make Emily stop saying those words. She wanted to cry but didn't have the energy.

"The doctor thinks the gastric fever was just too much for the baby."

Gone. All that hope was gone. What was it John Blaine had said about the unnamed babies? Were they all really all right?

Emily was still speaking. "Eli's worried about you. You want to see him now?"

"Yes," she managed to say.

Maggie shut her eyes and listened to the sound of Emily's shoes on the wood floor and the creak of the door as it opened and shut. There were muffled voices for a few minutes. She thought she could hear Emily lecturing Eli not to upset her. That was just like her friend. Bossy come what may. Then the door creaked again. Heavier footsteps drew near. Maggie opened her eyes. Lydia was gone and Eli was now standing by the bedside. He looked wan and exhausted. There were deep circles under his eyes.

He cleared his throat and asked, "How are you?"

"Better," she said.

He sank down onto the chair beside the bed. Picking up her left hand, the one with the wedding band, he held it between his. "We – we thought we were going to lose you." His eyes were teary. "Don't ever do that again, Maggie, because," he managed to get control of his voice and finish, "because I just wouldn't like it very much."

He clumsily stuck a finger under his spectacles to wipe the tears from his eyes. "Oh, God, Maggie. I prayed so hard."

"The baby . . ."

He scooped her up in his arms. "I know. I was with you. I didn't leave you. But I couldn't help. All I could do was pray."

And then the two of them clung together and wept until they were exhausted.

****

Early the next morning, Maggie awoke. She did not know how long she had been sleeping, but she slowly became aware that there were voices outside in the hall. She wasn't quite sure if she were awake or asleep because everything was a patchwork – confused snatches of sentences drifting past her consciousness. Finally she realized that she recognized one voice. It belonged to Jeremiah.

He was talking, but she only caught snippets of what he was saying.

"Thank God everything's all right . . . sleeping now . . . getting better . . ."

Another voice beyond the door murmured in response, but it was too soft for Maggie to hear the words. Jeremiah responded, "Regardless . . . how could you?"

How could you. What does that mean? Maggie wondered.

Disturbed, she struggled toward the sound. When she finally came fully awake, she realized that she was on her feet and clinging to the foot post of the bed. Legs shaky as a newborn colt's, Maggie leaned against the bed and hung on to the post as she tried to sort things out. Why did she get up? Were the voices a dream?

Abruptly, the door to the room swung open and Eli entered. His mouth dropped open. "Maggie!" he gasped as he hurried to her side. "What do you think you're doing? You're not strong enough to get up yet."

Before she could answer, he picked her up – as easily as if she had been a rag doll – and deposited her back in bed. As he tucked her in, Maggie managed to say, "Did you see Mr. Madison in the hall?"

"No."

"He was right outside our room. I heard him talking to someone."

"Maybe you dreamt it," her husband gently said, then changed the subject, "Emily's bringing some beef tea up for you. Would you like that?"

"Yes." But Maggie was confused.

Eli kissed her on the cheek. "It's going to take awhile for you to recover, sweetheart. Don't rush things. Do you understand?"

She swallowed dryly. "May I have some water?"

"Sure." He poured a glass from the pitcher on the bed table and held it to her lips. Maggie wanted to take it from him, but her hands were shaking very badly. She felt weak and washed out. "Better?" he asked when she stopped drinking.

She nodded. But something was bothering her and she needed to tell him. "John said there are troubles."

Eli gave her a strange look. "But Maggie . . ."

"I know he is dead, but I saw him. He spoke to me. He said there are troubles and that things are wrong. Eli, I saw Mr. Madison and Carrie. They were embracing."

"Sweetheart, you've had a serious illness. It's only natural that you're going to be a little confused and imagine things."

"*No*," she protested. "It's true. I saw it. And I saw John."

"Maggie, it was the fever."

"I saw Mr. Madison and Carrie *before* I took ill."

Eli pulled his hand away and looked steadily into her eyes. "You're really starting to worry me. I think you dreamt about John, and I want you to forget Madison and Carrie. You need to *rest*."

"But something's not right. I saw John Blaine. He said there are troubles. I don't think I dreamt it. I think it was real. Eli, I saw heaven."

Heaving a sigh, Eli looked down for a moment. After a bit of thought, he looked up and said, "I'll be right back." Maggie watched him walk out of the room. Less than a quarter hour later, he returned with Jeremiah Madison. He cleared his throat. "Mr. Madison, as I explained to you on the way, we don't wish to accuse you of anything or make you uncomfortable. But my wife needs to be reassured of something." Folding his arms over his chest, Eli met his wife's eyes. "Maggie?"

Maggie hesitated, but Eli nodded at her. She quickly found her voice. "Mr. Madison, before I took ill, I saw something that has been troubling me. I came into the kitchen and found you and Carrie in each other's arms."

After only the briefest of pauses, Jeremiah smiled easily. "Yes, I can see how that would cause you some concern. But the explanation is really quite simple. Carrie had been the recipient of a particularly harsh scolding from my wife. The poor girl was distraught and needed comfort. It was a friendly hug and no more. A pastoral hug, if you will. She has no one, you know."

Maggie's memory of the scene did not match his explanation. What she had encountered was intimate. She and Eli held each other that way. She would never think to hug another man that closely. Their bodies had been pressed together. She remembered Carrie's laugh –it was deep and sensual – not the laugh of a hurt girl being comforted, but the laugh of a lover.

"So you see," Jeremiah was saying, "It was all quite innocent."

Eli leapt in now. "Hear that, Maggie? He was just comforting the girl." He turned to Jeremiah and gestured toward the door. As they walked out of the room, she heard him say, "Thank you for your help, Reverend. You've been most understanding."

Exhausted, Maggie sank back into the pillows.

She could hear Eli's words fading away. "I apologize for the topic of conversation, but I hope it eased Maggie's mind. She's not quite herself right now."

"Oh, yes," Jeremiah agreed. "She has suffered a dreadful illness."

****

They gave Maggie beef broth, which she was able to keep down. By the time night fell, she was feeling stronger. Eli crawled into bed with her saying how relieved he was to be sleeping with her again. Maggie thought perhaps he was being a little over-dramatic. He had not been away all that long. But when he put his arms around her, she was grateful – the night was cool and he felt nice and warm. She fell into a sound sleep.

But then she had the dreams – confusing and disturbing dreams about Jeremiah, Carrie, John Blaine, and secrets. The dreams shifted. Now someone had taken her baby. He was a boy, a beautiful, healthy boy. But he was missing. She searched frantically for him. People kept telling her where the child was, but every time she arrived at each place, he was already gone. She could hear him crying but she couldn't find him. Her baby needed her, and she ran from point to point, always just missing him, always hearing his cry.

****

Maggie woke with a start. She was in a cold sweat. Baffled, she wiped tears from her eyes.

Eli laid a hand on her arm. "What's wrong? You jumped a mile."

"I – I heard a baby cry." She was still unsure of where she was.

"It was a bad dream."

"There was a baby crying." She listened. "There it is again! Hear it?"

Eli paused. "Oh, that," he finally said. "That's Leah. Carrie said the grand Mrs. Madison hasn't been feeling very well the past few days." He gathered Maggie in his arms and rested his cheek on the top of her head. "Leah's crying. That's what the sound is."

"So there's no baby," Maggie said after a long silence.

"No, sweetheart, no baby." He kissed her hair and hugged her tighter.

"It was a boy."

He swallowed hard, but said nothing.

****

The morning of the third day after Maggie had become ill, she was only too happy to be waited on and lie abed. Amid the light meals, tea, and visits, Frankie reported that Leah was still unwell. Once her family had left her alone to rest, Maggie prayed for the girl down the hall, lest she lose her child, too. Whether she liked Leah or not was no longer of consequence. Maggie was a bereaved mother and wouldn't wish a miscarriage on anyone. She hoped Leah would have the happiness that she had lost. She also prayed for Emily, fearing that she might catch gastric fever next.

By December 8, the fourth day since she had taken ill, Maggie was ready to get up. There were things to do. She realized that she had no idea how the house was being tended. She knew that Emily, Carrie, and her girls were no doubt doing a fine job, but she needed to check to reassure herself. She also wanted to see Leah. She was beginning to get annoyed with being an invalid. Unfortunately, Maggie had also discovered that no one would allow her to do anything. She was repeatedly told to rest – and told this in the most paternalistic manner imaginable.

As if they understand the condition of my body, Maggie thought in frustration. This is *my* body. I know how I feel. I am a bit weak, but I need to get up and do something.

However, everyone – Emily and Eli in particular – told her to stay in bed – and so there she sat, feeling rather petulant.

At that point, Lydia breezed in, bearing morning tea on a tray. "How are you feeling, Mama?"

"Better," she said. "I'd like to get up."

"Not yet. You've not recovered."

Maggie sighed. "I knew you would say that."

Lydia chuckled, settled into the chair beside the bed, and passed a cup and saucer to her mother. "If you want news, I can provide you with it."

"Yes. News is exactly what I want. How is the house? Is all in order?"

"Of course, Mama." Lydia smiled. "Everything is smooth as silk. But that does not mean that we do not miss you."

Maggie was enjoying the tea. It was hot and good. "And Leah? How is she doing?"

Lydia became somber at this point. "I'm afraid that she is quite unwell this morning. She is getting worse rather than better. Mr. Madison is very worried."

Maggie stopped the teacup half-way to her lips. "Has he sent for the doctor?"

"He shall this noontime if there's no improvement."

"But she could have gastric fever," Maggie sputtered. "If it's as severe as my case . . ."

Lydia patted her hand. "Don't worry about Leah, Mama. You just need to get well. Besides, Carrie is helping to tend her. She has plenty of good care."

Maggie said nothing further because it was no use to argue. But enforced bed rest gave her little to do but think – and think she did.

Perhaps Leah had caught her illness. If she had, then the doctor needed to come right away, not at noon. He might be able to give her niece a tincture to ease the effects. If they did not address the illness, then she could very well lose the baby. Maggie was determined that no one else in the house suffer the pain that she had suffered.

The thoughts ate away at her until she could stand it no further. She had to do something. If what John Blaine had said was true, that there were troubles, then she could not simply sit in her room. It was wrong to do nothing, especially if the thing that was wrong was some sort of contagion in the rooming house.

By the time Lydia took the tray downstairs, Maggie had made up her mind. She got out of bed and washed and dressed, pausing now and then to rest. It was surprising how much energy such a small thing took, but finally she was presentable. She carefully opened the door and peeked into the hall. None of her family was about. Feeling more secure, she walked slowly to the minister's door and knocked.

When there was no answer, she knocked again.

There still was no answer, so she became bold. Taking a deep breath – and asking God to forgive her intrusion upon the Madison family chambers – she opened the door.

What she saw stopped her in her tracks. Leah was lying on the bed and Jeremiah was kneeling on the floor beside her, his hands clasped in prayer. Tears were flowing down his face.

Not believing her own eyes, Maggie hovered on the threshold to the room. There was indeed trouble. Leah was lying very still. Her face was flaccid, her skin jaundiced. As Maggie gathered the courage to draw near, she saw how dull the young woman's hair had become – indeed, within the space of a few short days it had lost nearly all its sheen.

And then she realized that things were worse, much worse.

Leah was not breathing.

At the sound of her footstep on the floor, Jeremiah looked up. "Mrs. Smith," he sobbed. "She's gone."

Maggie walked to his side.

"Oh, sweet Jesus, forgive me."

Speechless at what she was seeing, she laid a hand on his shoulder.

The young man began to weep helplessly.

At long last, she found her voice. "Why didn't you call for the doctor?"

He buried his face in a hand. "What could he have done?"

That perhaps was true. Dr. Lightner had merely named Maggie's ailment but had been helpless to treat her. But what if they had caught Leah's difficulty early? Perhaps something could have been done.

However, none of that mattered now. Jeremiah's wife was gone, and so was his child. "You poor boy," Maggie murmured, kneeling beside him. She bowed her head and prayed, once for Leah and once for Jeremiah. And then she rose to her feet and hurried to fetch Emily and Eli.

****

From Maggie's Journal, 7 December 1860

Patrick McCoy and the undertaker have laid Leah out in the front parlor. She lies, wearing her best silk dress of rose, as if she were asleep. But she is not lying in bed. She is lying on a cooling board with ice below.

According to custom, our family has gathered to sit and mourn. Samuel, Abigail, and their two sons have been weeping sedately and properly before the coffin, but I know that beneath the propriety their hearts have been torn to shreds. Jeremiah Madison, too, prays and weeps softly. But beneath his veneer, I know that he also is housing an utterly broken heart. He does love Leah. It is obvious to my eyes now. How could I have doubted his devotion to her? There is nothing left inside him. That is so clear. I find myself struggling with memories of how it had been when John and Gideon died – the empty shock, the complete loss of mooring for my soul. And now I have a dead, empty hole within me from my miscarriage. Why does death leave such hollowness, such nothingness, such aloneness? No words, no actions, nothing can touch the aching solitude.

There is little I can do for my brother and his family and for Mr. Madison but to sit, watch, and pray. I feel weary and battered in spirit.

I have found some comfort, though. The Bible says that the Holy Ghost will intercede when we cannot find words, and, oh, how I cling to that promise and rest in the hope that the Spirit is at work when I am unable to do a blessed thing!

****

That evening, as Maggie sat in the front parlor, keeping watch with the rest of the family, she noticed that Patrick, who was sitting beside her, kept looking from her to Leah and back again. Finally, she asked, "Is something wrong?"

"Well," he began, "it's just I noticed that you and Mrs. Madison are jaundiced, and your hair has lost its sheen."

That made her smile. "I am not about to die, Patrick."

"Oh, I am not worried about that, Mrs. Smith. I can see that you are on the mend."

"Then what? Mrs. Madison and I both had the same disease."

Patrick nodded. "Yes. Perhaps that is it."

Their *sotto voce* conversation was cut short by the arrival of Frankie, who plopped down on a chair on the other side of Maggie. The girl's eyes were red from crying. She laid her head on her mother's shoulder. "I said such awful things to Leah." Her lower lip was quivering. "I was really hateful. I didn't know this would happen. If I knew, I wouldn't have said a word."

"We all do things that hurt other people," Maggie gently told her. "We all can be quite sinful at times."

Frankie swiped her nose with a crumpled handkerchief. "I just wish I could take everything back."

"I know. I do, too." Maggie gave her daughter a hug. "Death can come quite suddenly. That is why we should try to be kind and loving to one another. It's also why we should strive to forgive one another. We never know when things will change." She placed a soft kiss on Frankie's cheek. "I think you have stayed in here long enough. Why don't you go into the kitchen and help Lydia and Emily with the food?"

The girl nodded, got up, and hurried out of the parlor.

Patrick watched her go and then said, "It's just I was thinking..."

Maggie looked at him.

"Would you mind if I had a sample of your hair? There's a test I'd like to do."

"You?" she asked in surprise.

"Yes. I have all the materials and equipment I need."

She did not understand what he wanted. "You can diagnose disease by looking at a hair?"

Patrick cleared his throat. "Yes. That is, some things can be discerned. For instance, there was something I read in one of Dr. Lightner's books." He stopped and added rather hurriedly, "Strange as it may sound I think doctors and undertakers can help each other."

"Oh." But Maggie still did not understand what he was looking for. "Well, I brushed my hair this morning but did not clean the brush. I can give you some strands."

"That would be sufficient. As I said, there was something in one of Dr. Lightner's books that bears a similarity to your illness." He blushed and looked away.

This baffled Maggie even more, but before she could say anything further, Eli plopped into the chair vacated by Frankie. Expression tight, he took Maggie's hand in his. After a bit, he muttered, "You know, I shouldn't have said what I did about Leah – all that nonsense about her being spoiled. If I knew –"

"But you didn't know," Maggie assured him. "None of us ever knows. I just told Frankie the same thing. And I've been lecturing myself, as well."

"Yes, well, I just learned that the hard way. I need to hold my tongue."

She sighed and leaned against his shoulder. He bore her weight without shifting. He was solid – physically, but also emotionally. She loved that about him. "I shouldn't have accused Mr. Madison of being improper with Carrie. I need to repent, too."

Eli was silent a moment. "Maggie," he finally whispered, "when I think about what happened to Leah . . . that could have been you."

"But it wasn't."

He drew a ragged breath. "Still, she died from the gastric fever." He stared down at their hands clasped together on his knee. "I know how Madison feels. When I lost Martha, it was terrible. And then I almost lost you. I shouldn't have been so critical of him. God forgive me."

His wife didn't reply. She couldn't. She was as guilty as he.

"I have a proposal. Let's let all our suspicions go. Madison's suffered enough. He may have done wrong, but it doesn't matter anymore."

Maggie smiled faintly and agreed. Regardless of what she had seen in the kitchen the day she took ill, Jeremiah was grieving– and that grief deserved her respect.

There was one more thing she needed to do now. Excusing herself from Eli, she stood and walked to the coffin. Her brother was there, staring down into Leah's face. "Samuel," she said softly.

He turned. His eyes were red-rimmed.

Without another word, Maggie held her arms out. His face crumpled and, with a small cry, he slid into her embrace. "I'm so sorry," she whispered into his ear. "Can we not make up?"

"Oh, Maggie," he sobbed. "Sister . . ."

That was all she needed. She knew that they had finally taken the first step onto the path of healing.

****

From Maggie's Journal, 9 December 1860

Leah Beatty Madison was buried at the cemetery behind the Methodist Church this shivery, cloudy day. We sent invitations –

funerals are private affairs for mourners only and not for curiosity-seekers – and family and close friends came to hear the Presbyterian minister's prayers and sermon. Everyone was in black, as is proper. As for me, I will wear black for the next three months. Leah was my niece, and I must go into mourning for her.

The procession was slow and solemn, as the four black-plumed horses drew the hearse toward the cemetery. We all followed quietly on foot. Our eyes were downcast and tear-filled. Eli, Nate, Edgar, Robert Beatty, and Joshua Beatty served as pall bearers. The rest of us stood, braced against a cold, sharp wind, as they shifted the coffin from the hearse and carried it to the grave. The bleakness of the weather matched the bleakness of our spirits: a fitting setting for the loss of a life so young and another life unborn.

When the family tossed clods of dirt on the coffin, the finality of the act echoed through us all. I know that in the future we will be comforted by the knowledge that Leah is with her Savior in heaven and that we shall all see her again someday. But now, at this moment, there is only death and cold and damp.

I wear black. Only weeks ago I told Eli that we were to have joy, not sorrow. But a war is building like thunderclouds overhead. I nearly lost my life. Our baby is gone. And poor, pretty, pampered Leah is dead. Why has all this happened at once? Have we committed some sin? Is God punishing us? What has gone wrong that our household should suffer so much anxiety and grief?

John Blaine told me – for it *was* John, I know it and not some fever-induced dream – there are troubles. But *what* troubles? How can I put things aright when I don't know exactly what *is* wrong? I pray to God hourly for discernment, but get none. God is silent. What an awful thing. I feel so alone and confounded and deserted.

CHAPTER SEVEN

The morning of December 10, Eli had hidden himself in the *Gazette* office to print the weekly issue. He usually worked through the day on the project, and it was Emily's custom to send his meals over on a tray. That particular afternoon the weather was dark and rainy, and the gloom of it crept into every corner of the house. For Maggie, wrestling with grief, everywhere she looked reminded her of Leah's death and of her own miscarriage. She slept poorly at night, waking about every hour for no reason, and was always tired come morning. Sometimes she was haunted by dreams of a crying baby or a weeping Leah. And she could scarcely stand her inner sadness. Looking for anything that would give her a change of environment, she volunteered to take the dinner tray to Eli.

As she came in the door, she found Eli wrapped in his printer's apron and covered with ink, as usual. The sight made her smile faintly. Come what may, Eli was her rock – a pudgy rock, to be sure – but solid and strong, nonetheless.

He looked up from the proof sheet, and with one finger pushed his eyeglasses back up his nose. "You have to read this, Maggie. The obit about Leah is beautiful. Mr. Carson wrote an excellent tribute. I think he's my best reporter."

"He's your *only* reporter," she teased, as she set the tray on his kitchen table. Looking about the small quarters brought back happy memories of their wedding night. Maggie momentarily felt a glow of pleasure. Yes, those were very good days. No doubt the baby had been conceived in Eli's house, perhaps even on their first night together. But with that thought, the melancholy began to prick again. Deflated, she realized that there was no place to which she could escape. Grief was going to hold her tight until its claws grew dull.

"May I see the obituary?" she asked, trying to chase her sadness away.

Eli passed her the proof page.

Maggie read in silence.

Mrs. Leah Madison died this morning, after an illness of a few weeks. She had only in October married the Rev. Jeremiah Madison, minister of the Blaineton Methodist Episcopal Church. The couple was looking forward to a long life together, and happily anticipating the birth of their first child. Mrs. Madison, formerly Leah Beatty, was the only daughter of Samuel and Abigail Beatty and sister to Samuel and Robert. Her father is the owner of the well-known Beatty Carriage Manufactory.

Mrs. Beatty recalled that her daughter was an accomplished pianist, who delighted in favoring her family with beautiful pieces of music, including hymns. The young woman was also known to have had a lovely voice. Oak Grove, the family home, was filled with many happy hours, thanks to the young woman's musical gifts. Her brothers, their eyes wet with tears, remembered that she was always ladylike in manner, and as a child enjoyed setting out and serving tea for them. Her father, though, was so overcome with grief that he was unable to relate stories of his beloved daughter.

Mrs. Madison first showed signs of illness in mid-November, complaining of stomach pains. Within a few weeks, she was unable to take anything but a cup of tea. The day of her death, she was bedridden, suffering from violent spasms accompanied by bouts of vomiting. Her alarmed husband thought to call in Dr. Lightner, who had previously seen Mrs. Smith, the owner of the rooming house within which the couple lived. However, Mrs. Madison's symptoms suddenly seemed to abate and thinking that perhaps she had made a turn for the better, Mr. Madison knelt by her bed and prayed for her deliverance. When he looked up, he was alarmed to find that his wife was no longer breathing. It was then that Mrs. Smith entered the room, discovered that life had ebbed from Mrs. Madison's body, and knelt beside the distraught husband. The two then prayed for the newly released soul. Dr. Lightner was called in shortly thereafter and declared the cause of death to be gastric fever, the same pernicious disease that had nearly taken Mrs. Smith's life a few days earlier.

Maggie looked up. She could not read any further. She wondered if she somehow had been responsible for Leah's death. Had she unknowingly spread a dangerous contagion to the newlywed? She held the proof sheet out to Eli. "Thank you. It is a touching memorial."

Keeping his eyes on hers, Eli received the sheet. "Are you all right?"

She shrugged. "I suppose so – well enough for one who grieves." She cleared her throat of the lump that threatened to take her voice. "Here is your lunch, Eli. Emily has made chicken and dumplings, your favorite." She noticed a black smudge of ink on his cheek. Instinctively, she took a handkerchief from her sleeve, wet it with her tongue, and began to clean the dirt from his face.

Eli smiled. "Thanks, Ma." His voice was warm, filled with affection.

She managed a small smile. "You're welcome."

"I love you, Maggie." He kissed her gently on the lips. "I'm a lucky man."

"And I am a lucky woman." She meant it. He was being wondrously patient with her. Deciding that it was time to change the subject, and perhaps her frame of mind, she said, "Patrick spoke to me this morning. At the funeral, he had requested a strand of my hair."

"Ah," Eli teased, "is that because he's secretly in love with you?"

"Silly," she said and this time her smile was genuine.

The house was cold. Maggie realized that her husband must have let the fire in the kitchen nearly go out. Rubbing her hands together for warmth, she turned to the pot belly stove. As she picked pieces of wood out of the box by the range, she continued, "He reminded me that he would like to do a test on a strand of my hair."

Eli lifted an eyebrow. "A test? Why?"

She opened the stove's grate. Luckily she saw that there was still a glow inside. She laid on the new pieces of wood and stirred the ashes with a poker to encourage the flames. "It's freezing in here, love. You will die of frostbite if you're not careful."

"I got busy. I forgot. Maggie, what sort of test?"

"He didn't say." The wood was finally starting to catch. She wiped her hands on her apron and shut the door to the grate. As she straightened up, she saw that he was frowning. "What's the matter?"

"Well, he must have said something."

She thought back. "Just that he had read about something in one of Dr. Lightner's books that bore a resemblance to my case of gastric fever. And that Leah and I both looked jaundiced and our hair had grown dull."

"Hmph." Eli turned away and lifted the cloth that covered his lunch. The delicious aroma of chicken and dumplings seeped enticingly into the room. To Maggie's surprise, he abruptly put the cloth down and turned back around. "You know, when I was at *The Times*, I covered a fair number of trails. Some of them were murder trials."

"How horrid!"

"Maybe, but people just seem to love a good murder story. Shocking. Titillating. That sort of thing. Do you know what the most common means of murder is, Maggie?"

She shook her head.

"Arsenic poisoning. Do you know what the symptoms are?"

An uneasy feeling lodged itself in the pit of her stomach.

Eli gently touched her face. "Jaundice color to the skin." His fingers brushed her hair. "Dull appearance to the hair. Intense pain in the stomach. Vomiting. Diarrhea."

She shook her head. "No, that can't be."

Without another word, Eli grabbed her hand and pulled her out of the *Gazette.*

****

Stunned, Maggie let Eli drag her all the way to the undertaker's shop. As they came in, they found Patrick sitting by the window. He had been reading a book in the sunlight. The undertaker, George Meany, had gone upstairs to his rooms to have lunch.

Seeing that he had company, Patrick stumbled clumsily to his feet.

"You want to do the Marsh Test?" Eli asked.

The boy blushed. "Yes, sir. I mean, if Mrs. Smith will consent to my having a strand of her hair."

"Do you realize what you are implying by asking to do that test?"

Patrick nodded.

"That's pretty serious. No, it's damned serious."

Maggie found her voice. "Eli!"

"Not now, Maggie," he said.

"You see," Patrick stammered, "I had recently finished reading one of Dr. Lightner's books on poisons and I thought the symptoms –

both Mrs. Smith and Mrs. Madison had the same symptoms – it seemed it all indicated something other than gastric fever."

Eli's eyes lit up behind his glasses. "You, son, ought to be a Pinkerton!"

"Well, actually, I'd really like to be a physician, but I don't have the money to go to school."

"I'll pay for you to go to college if you're right about this!" was Eli's impulsive reply. "Where do you want to do the test?"

Minutes later, they found themselves in a small room at the back of the building. Maggie gaped at the equipment: two tables with burners, and shelves on the walls that held bottles filled with liquids and powders, flasks, tubes, pipes, and mortars and pestles.

She winced as she pulled a strand of hair from her head. Passing it to Patrick, she asked, "But why do you use hair? How can you tell anything from that?"

The boy gently placed her offering on the table, and then energetically began to fetch things and place them beside it: a flask, a drying tube, a small burner, a ceramic bowl, and two bottles. "Traces of arsenic may be found in hair, other tissue, or body fluids," he explained as he worked. "Simply put, the Marsh Test works this way – first I put your hair sample into a glass flask. Then I will add arsenic-free zinc and sulfuric acid to it. The zinc and acid will produce arsine gas, which passes through a drying tube into a glass tube. Next, I will heat the gas mixture. This oxidizes arsine into arsenic and water vapor, which will then be deposited onto the cold ceramic bowl that I will hold over the flame. The bowl will reveal a stain, a deposit of arsenic, which is silvery-black in color." He looked up at her, his face flushed with excitement. "Do you know that I can even discover how much arsenic you may have been given?"

"I hope that it shows nothing," Maggie responded. "The very thought that someone may have poisoned me –" She frowned. "Wait. How could that be? I became ill quite suddenly, while my niece was ill for several weeks before she died."

Patrick nodded, as he arranged his materials on the table. "I know, but that can be explained. You must have been given a large dose, while hers was smaller, but cumulative. Arsenic is used both ways, but it is just as deadly."

Maggie looked imploringly at Eli, who shrugged and said, "The boy is right. Slow poisoning is the preferred method, though."

"Which means that perhaps the murderer was impatient," Patrick added. "Shall we begin? Everything is in readiness."

Eli crossed his arms over his chest. "Patrick, by any chance do you also enjoy Poe's stories about detective C. Auguste Dupin?"

The boy blushed. "Yes, actually. I borrow the books from Frankie."

"I knew it!" he chuckled.

A short time later, Patrick had the results.

Eli muttered, "Well, I'll be damned."

"Me, too," was his wife's reply.

"Maggie!"

"I did not swear," she retorted. "I merely agreed with you."

Eli heaved a sigh and sank onto a nearby chair. "This changes everything."

Maggie took a seat on the chair beside his. "What now?" she asked stunned that someone had poisoned her.

Eli thought a moment. "Well, let's look back at when you first took ill. The effects of a large dose of arsenic may be felt as soon as a half hour to one hour after it is consumed. What did you have to eat right before the pains began?"

Maggie frowned. "Nothing to eat, I'm sure of it." Suddenly her eyes widened. "Oh! Tea. I had a cup of tea. Someone had left a hot kettle on the stove and I made myself a cup." No sooner had she said this, than she went pale and covered her mouth with her hands. "Oh, no!"

"You couldn't have known," Eli said softly. "Arsenic is tasteless. That's why it is such an effective poison."

"Oh!" she cried again. "But who? Who could have done such a thing to me? And why?"

There was an uncomfortable silence. The sun was moving toward the west and the little room was growing dusky.

Patrick said, "Perhaps it wasn't meant for you. Perhaps it was meant for Mrs. Madison."

"But who would kill *her*?" Maggie blurted. "This makes no sense!"

There was another long silence. At length, Eli cleared his throat. "I hesitate to bring this up, but I must. Right now we only know *one* thing. We know that you, Maggie, were poisoned by arsenic."

Patrick's mouth dropped open and he exclaimed, "Oh!"

Maggie looked from one to the other. "What?"

Eli put his hand over hers. "We have to prove that Leah was poisoned. We'll need to see the judge and get an order for a coroner's inquest. Once we get that, we're going to have to exhume her body and have her liver and the contents of her stomach analyzed."

Upon seeing look of horror on his wife's face, Eli softened his next words. "It's the only way."

****

From Maggie's Journal, 10 December 1860

John Blaine said there were troubles, but I had no idea that they would be this terrible. Someone put arsenic in the tea that I drank and it is likely that the same person poisoned Leah. I feel sick at heart. Who would do such a thing? Eli, Patrick, Edgar, and Mr. Norton, the senior lawyer in Edgar's office, have gone to convince Judge Talbot that Leah's body must be exhumed.

But we shall have to tell Mr. Madison, as well as Samuel and Abigail about this. Mr. Madison, in his grief, has gone to visit his brother for a few days, and Sam and Abigail live miles away. My fear is that the exhumation will occur before we can tell them all.

And how shall I broach the subject with all three? Our actions will surely horrify them and then break their hearts all over again.

Oh, John, can you not come back to me just once more and tell me what needs to be done to make things right again? Alas, I know that will not happen. The curtain between earth and heaven separated just once and I fear it will not open again 'til I am ready to meet my Savior.

****

Maggie had not been in Oak Grove, the Beatty home, for twenty years. The lane leading to the house was long and tree-lined. Although leaves were gone from branches, the approach was impressive nonetheless. As Eli pulled the hired horse and carriage before the old three-story building, Maggie found herself inundated by wave after wave of memories. She remembered how it felt when she was ten years old and her mother died. The terrible loneliness and fear of that time returned with all its intensity. But she also recalled that she had been happy playing games with Samuel and receiving the attention of a beloved governess. Yes, there had been joy at Oak Grove, just never enough after her mother died.

"Odd," she commented to Eli as they contemplated the polished wood and brass of the double front doors. "I lived here so many years ago, but I still remember things so strong and clear. Memory is an odd thing, isn't it? It only takes a sight or a sound or a smell to pull the past so powerfully into the present."

"Will you be all right?" His brown eyes were concerned.

She nodded. "Let's go in."

Their visit did not entirely follow proper etiquette. It was afternoon – the time during which women saw one another – but Maggie did not possess calling cards. Having slid down the social ladder, she no longer had need of them. Females of her current status simply poked their heads into their friends' kitchen doorways and asked if they were busy. Furthermore, had Maggie still possessed a card, she no longer could remember which corner to fold to indicate that she had come visiting for personal or family reasons. Hence, when the butler opened the door, her only resort was to explain very politely, but very firmly who she and Eli were and whom they wished to see.

So many things have changed, Maggie thought as her brother's servant gave her a cool, slightly superior gaze. Yet she did not really miss being part of the upper crust, not one bit. Calling card or not, she was confident that Samuel would not turn them away. The wall of ice that had built up over the years was melting. However one thing was making her anxious and that was what she had to tell him.

The butler led the couple into the parlor and asked them to take a seat. Once he disappeared, Maggie took the opportunity to look around the room. It was much as she remembered: heavy furniture, burgundy draperies gracefully dragging along the floor, and dark portraits of grim-faced ancestors. But all the heaviness was punctuated by a grace note of windows – many windows that allowed a bath of light and provided beautiful views of the property.

Maggie smiled. "The windows were my mother's idea. She disliked dark, ponderous rooms."

Eli was taking it all in. "Hard to believe this was once your childhood home."

She nodded and fidgeted with the black cotton gloves on her hands.

He fixed his gaze upon her. "Yeah," he said thoughtfully. "You really do belong in a place like this. You've got the polish. Look at the way you're sitting and the way you carry yourself. You know what to

do. You shouldn't be wearing yourself out running a rooming house."
Somewhat ruefully, he added, "And you especially shouldn't be
married to a newspaperman."

"Elijah Smith! Don't you dare say that. I am *not* living in this
house precisely because I've made my *own* choices. Elements like this
place create the simpering, useless women you so dislike. And, by the
way, I happen to agree with your assessment of such women. What is
so right and fine about someone who has been bred to be nothing more
than an ornament, who has been taught to be useless, who has been
safely shut off behind domestic doors?"

That brought a smile to his lips. "You really have to meet my
sister Becky. The two of you could start a revolution."

"I married you because you don't stand for hypocrisy and
because you are sincere. This," she waved at the opulent room, "this,
however, can be full of insincerity – layer upon layer of it.
Unfortunately, people prefer to call it 'gentility and propriety.'"

At that moment, the door opened and Samuel, dressed in the dull
black of full mourning, entered. Eli rose while Maggie remained
seated. Sam crossed the thick oriental carpet and took his sister's
hands. To her surprise, he leaned forward and gently kissed her on the
cheek. "Margaret."

"Hello, Sam."

"I apologize that Abigail cannot join us. She is feeling unwell
today and is resting in her room." After shaking Eli's hand, he
indicated that the newspaperman take his seat once more. "Would you
care for some tea?"

"No, thank you," Maggie replied. She was not sure that she
would ever drink tea again.

"How is Carrie Hillsborough faring?"

"As well as can be expected. She is quite distraught at Leah's
passing. But I believe that allowing her to stay on with us is helping
heal her grief. She is a great help to Emily, and even rises before all of
us to stoke the stove. But," Maggie glanced down at her gloved hands,
"I am afraid that we're here on rather unpleasant business. In fact, I do
not know how well you will receive what I have to tell you. But you
must promise to hear it all the way through."

His brows knit together, but he said, "As you wish."

She took a deep breath. "First of all, please understand that we
had no intention of withholding anything from you. We needed to

verify some information before we said anything to anyone. I am sorry to say that the verification is rather shocking."

Her brother's countenance was somber. "What is it?"

There was no fire in the room – company was not expected, hence the air was quite cold. Despite her cloak, Maggie had to work hard not to shiver. She forced her mind away from her discomfort, knowing that she needed to choose her words carefully and considerately. "Patrick McCoy, the young undertaker's apprentice, noticed something quite distressing. He realized that Leah and I both had severe stomach pain and related symptoms, but also that our skin had become jaundiced and our hair dull. He realized that these symptoms when put together could indicate that we had been poisoned."

Her brother's face went pale.

"He believed that we did not become ill due to gastric fever, but due to arsenic poisoning."

"That cannot be," Samuel murmured.

Maggie forged on. "He asked if I would submit a strand of hair for a test that would reveal whether or not I had taken arsenic. The test, Samuel, was positive. I had been given a large dose." She leaned forward in her chair, toward her brother. "I remembered that someone had left a kettle on the stove and that I drank a cup of tea with that water. The arsenic had to be in the tea or the water."

Samuel sat straight, frozen for a moment, able only to say, "Dear God!"

"If," she said, now acutely aware that her words had to be chosen carefully, "we are to confirm that Leah also was poisoned, Patrick and Dr. Lightner will need to test something from Leah, as well. When the information was presented to Judge Talbot, he felt that there was sufficient evidence to call a coroner's inquest to investigate possible foul play and gave permission for Leah to be –."

"No!" Sam nearly shouted. His eyes were fierce. "No one's to touch her! Just let her rest in peace!"

Maggie rose, walked to his chair, and sank onto her knees imploringly before him as she took his balled fists into her hands. "Sam, if Leah was murdered, don't you think she deserves justice? We cannot start an investigation without evidence."

"But Leah *could have* succumbed to gastric fever," he argued. "It may not have been poison."

Eli sighed and stepped in. "They had the same symptoms. What are the odds on two people having the same symptoms and being deathly ill, but from different causes?"

Sam had no answer for this.

"Look, you lost Leah and your grandchild. I lost my child and nearly lost Maggie. We cannot let whoever did this get away with it!"

Samuel turned to Maggie. "Dear sister, please tell me this will not happen."

A tear slipped from her eye. He had not addressed her as "dear sister" in twenty years.

"This is so distasteful, so dreadful," he whispered, eyes brimming. "My poor baby."

Maggie wiped the tear from her cheek. "But it's necessary if we are to uncover the truth."

"Oh, my poor, dear Leah!" He buried his face in his hands.

She grasped his arms. "Justice needs to be done, brother. We must give Leah justice."

****

From Maggie's Journal, 12 December 1860

Journal, it breaks my heart to report this. A small group of us descended upon the Methodist cemetery. Ironically, we had fine weather for such a sad task. The sky was bright blue and a light wind was pushing a few cottony clouds westward. The sun shone benevolently upon the backs of the grave diggers as they thrust their shovels time after time into the loose dirt of the plot. When the coffin finally was exhumed, it was placed on a dray and covered out of respect for the dead. Two sturdy horses pulled the cart to the undertaker's shop. Dr. Lightner had arranged to meet us there to do the work necessary to ascertain the cause of the poor girl's death. Naturally, while we made our way to the undertaker's, word quickly spread throughout Blaineton. I could see and feel eyes peering out from behind curtains as our sad procession passed by. People on the street averted their gaze out of courtesy, but more than once I found town folk sneaking glimpses as we passed.

Once Leah's coffin was safely in the undertaker's keeping, we were free to leave. Eli returned to the *Gazette* to finish printing the next day's edition, and I went back to the rooming house. What happened next, dear Journal, baffles and frightens me.

****

As Maggie entered the kitchen, Emily instantly stopped stirring a pot of split pea soup. "Good heavens, girl! What's all this talk of folk opening up Leah's grave?"

Maggie sighed tiredly. "Bad news travels fast."

"The whole town saw you!"

"I know. We think there is an irregularity regarding Leah's death." She lowered herself onto one of the kitchen chairs. The room was toasty and smelled of freshly baked bread and split pea. It was good to be in a warm and welcoming place for a change.

Emily turned to the soup and gave it a taste. "What do you mean, an irregularity regarding Leah's death? I don't understand."

"She might not have died of gastric fever. There's a chance that she may have been poisoned."

Emily wheeled around. "*What*?"

Before Maggie could reply, the back door banged open and Jeremiah burst upon them. His chestnut-colored hair was as wild as his eyes, which darted about the room until they found Maggie. "What's all this about Leah?" he barked.

Maggie began to wish that Eli had not gone back to the *Gazette*. She felt vulnerable there in the kitchen. They had never consulted Jeremiah, but he had been away. Gripping her hands together on her lap – for she was afraid that she might tremble – she said calmly, "There seems to be some question regarding the cause of Leah's death. The doctor is doing an autopsy."

"Are you mad?" the minister sputtered. "Leah was *my wife*. No one asked *my* permission. *No one!* Have I no say in such a matter? Perhaps I don't wish my beloved wife to be dug up like an old bone and treated as if she were no better than a slaughtered animal."

She softened her voice. "I'm sorry, but Judge Talbot feels that it is necessary. And so do I, for that matter."

"You???" he spat. "She's nothing to you! You and she barely spoke!"

A flash of anger lit Maggie's face. She straightened her shoulders and looked directly into his half-mad eyes. "Regardless, Leah was my niece."

"And *I was her husband*! I shan't permit all of you to act as if that fact has no meaning! It was wrong for you to dig her up without consulting me! You've no idea what you've done, have you? No idea!"

Furious, Maggie stood now. "Oh, I know very well what we have done. I was ill, Leah was ill, we had the same symptoms, and I have arsenic in my hair! Something is very wrong!"

"Damn it, woman!" Jeremiah suddenly grabbed her shoulders and shook her. "Don't you understand? You've opened a Pandora's Box!!" He shook her again. "A *Pandora's Box*!!"

Emily dropped her spoon. "Stop it!" In the next second she was across the room and trying to wrest his arms away.

The kitchen door opened and, rubbing his hands from the chill air outside, Nate entered. He quickly took in Maggie's pale face, the fear in Emily's eyes, and Jeremiah's grip on Maggie's upper arms. In calm, casual voice, he said, "Good afternoon, all. Is there a problem here?"

Immediately, the fierceness fled from Jeremiah's face. "There is no problem," he replied with an eerie calm and released Maggie, but his piercing blue eyes stayed locked with hers. "We shall talk later," he told her and stalked from the room.

Trembling, Maggie sank onto the chair behind her. Emily roused herself, hurried to the sink and began vigorously to work the pump. She had a cup of water in front of Maggie before she could think further. "Drink it," she ordered.

Maggie had to use both shaking hands to bring the cup to her lips.

"Is someone going to tell me what's going on?" Nate demanded. "Or am I supposed to know?"

"He's a crazy man," Emily hissed, fussing over her friend like a mother hen. "He shook Maggie. Hard. And I just sat there like a bump on a log!"

"Why would Madison do something like that?"

Emily whirled around, sputtering, "He's not very happy with her, that's why. The sheriff gave an order to dig up Leah Madison's grave. He thinks someone poisoned her."

"Dang!" said Nate.

Maggie struggled to keep her voice even. "Patrick suspected that Leah and I may not have had gastric fever. He thought, from his readings, that perhaps we had been poisoned, and he asked me for a strand of hair. He did a test with it and it revealed traces of arsenic."

Nate stared open-mouthed at her.

"I took ill very soon after drinking a cup of tea. We believe that the hot water or the tea leaves may have been poisoned."

"Good God!" Emily dropped onto a chair. "You mean someone in this house?"

"*Dang!*" Nate said again. "What kind of devil is running around loose here?"

****

Just before supper, a knock upon the door brought Sheriff Miller and Samuel into the boarding house. The sheriff asked Maggie to gather the family in the front parlor. After sending her daughters to tell the others, Maggie walked to the parlor and lit lamps to brighten the room. She knew it would be useless to build a fire to dispel the cold. They would not be there but for a few minutes. It was better therefore to be frugal and endure a little chill.

Unfortunately, the icy air only augmented her growing sense of evil. She did not dare so much as to steal a glance at Jeremiah Madison. The notion of meeting his eyes made her feel colder than the room. It was then she realized that she had become afraid of him. Amazed, she wondered how that could have happened so quickly. He had been her pastor and her friend, and now she feared him.

Where he had gripped her arms began to throb in response. Wrapping her arms around herself, Maggie stared at the floor and tried to calm her pulse and breath. This will never do, she thought. I cannot live like this.

Once everyone had arrived, Eli shut the door to the parlor and they all stood about silently for a minute. The stark formality and cold air of the room made it impossible to feel any sense of comfort. Everyone knew that the news was not good.

Sheriff Miller, a big, no-nonsense sort of man, cleared his throat. "Now, folks, I've called you here to inform you of the results of the tests done on Leah Madison's remains by Dr. Lightner. To be blunt, he found arsenic in the contents of her stomach. That, ladies and gentlemen, means that Mrs. Madison's death is of a suspicious nature. Now, she could have taken her own life, but she also could have been murdered." He paused to let the words sink in.

As a murmur swept around the room, Maggie saw how pale Carrie had turned.

"Mrs. Smith," the sheriff continued, "I understand that you were seriously ill during the time of Mrs. Madison's passing and that young McCoy here determined that you too had ingested poison. In short, I don't see how that could make you a suspect. However, everyone else in this house must be considered a suspect, including you, Mr. Smith."

Eli opened his mouth to protest, but thought better of it and stayed quiet.

"In order to determine whether or not the death is a suicide, we need to know all we can about Mrs. Madison's emotional state prior to her passing." The sheriff scratched at his bushy, black beard. "And in order to determine whether or not it is murder, the investigation must then start with access to the victim and with a motive. To be blunt, many of you boarders had access to Mrs. Madison. Some of you may even have had a motive. It goes without saying that the people closest to Mrs. Madison are the most likely to have the greatest motive to kill her. I mean no disrespect to the memory of the deceased, but that's just the way things usually work out. So, in particular, I'd like you, Mr. Madison, to stay put. But no out of town trips for *any* of you, you hear?"

They all nodded. Maggie saw that the color had also drained from Jeremiah Madison's face and that Carrie was watching him with great trepidation. Maggie wondered again about the embrace she had seen them share in the kitchen. She wondered if Carrie had been so foolish as to have fallen in love with Mr. Madison – which surely she must have done in order to involve herself with a married man. It was no small wonder then that the girl was alarmed at this latest bit of news. How terrifying it must have been for her to entertain the notion that the wife of her lover had been poisoned.

And that was when it hit Maggie.

Was it Jeremiah? The relationship between the minister and the maid created quite a credible motive. As Sheriff Miller said, murder took access and motive. Jeremiah had both. Could he have poisoned Leah? Had the kettle in the kitchen been intended for her, rather than Maggie? And was Jeremiah angry over the exhumation of Leah's body or was he angry about something else? What was it he had said about a Pandora's Box?

Horrified, Maggie did not know whether to say anything to the sheriff, for fear the embrace she had seen was not actually as passionate as she remembered and for fear that the two were not really having an illicit affair.

"Well," Sheriff Miller was saying, "That's all for tonight. I'll be back first thing in the morning to begin the interrogations. Now, remember, no one goes anywhere."

****

From Maggie's journal, 12 December 1860

I shall receive little sleep tonight, dear Journal. I am alternately afraid of Jeremiah Madison and afraid of what we have unleashed on the rooming house and, by extension, on the town. What if, by some strange chance, we are wrong? For instance, what if Leah had committed suicide? It is not impossible. She had been upset, even melancholic before she took ill. Could she have left poisoned tea in the kitchen by mistake? But proof of a suicide would be an embarrassment to the family and a disgrace to Leah's memory.

On the other hand, what *if* Jeremiah Madison had murdered her? This is possible, too. Men have murdered for much less, and if truth be told, Leah had indeed made his life difficult, if not unbearable. But how can we prove that he killed her? He could have disposed of all traces of the arsenic by now. It is reasonable to think that no one witnessed him poisoning Leah's food or drink. Without the proper evidence, a murderer could end up being a free man. That would be another unacceptable situation, for the town would scarred by scandal and a murderer would be free to kill again.

I do not know which outcome to hope for. All outcomes are distressing and unsatisfying.

****

After writing her heart out in the journal, Maggie stood up from her little *escritoire* and turned the wooden chair around. Using the chair as a *prie-dieu*, she knelt and bowed her head.

Dearest Father, she prayed, if Jeremiah has done wrong, then he must be brought to justice. But more than that, he must confess and seek repentance for the sake of his soul. And, my Lord, give me the strength to withstand the scandal that will surely fall upon all of us. Protect my family, my friends, and help me.

She drifted into silence and waited for God to speak, but no words came from on High.

"Maggie?"

She lifted her head. The moonlight coming through the window helped her see that Eli had propped himself up on an elbow as he lay in bed.

"How long have you been up?" he asked.

"I don't know."

He observed her for a moment, then heaved a sigh and got out of bed, too. "Well," he said, as he pulled on his dressing gown, "whatever it is that's got you on your knees at this hour has to be pretty serious." He knelt beside her. "Subject?"

"This dreadful situation."

"Thought as much." He folded his hands on the seat of the chair. "I might as well warn you. I don't pray extemporaneously. But I can and will pray silently for some light to be shed. That sound fair?"

She smiled. "Yes, Eli. Thank you."

"All right," he replied, "let's pray so we can go back to bed before the both of us freeze." And with that they bowed their heads.

Although the room was getting icy, having the two of them praying was more powerful than a single voice. Maggie hoped they would receive an answer; but she was struggling even to feel God's presence. There will be no answer, the part of her that doubted hissed in her heart. She shooed the doubt back into the dark corner where it had been hiding and told herself that God would answer their prayer, that God would shed some light, and that God always heard.

The trouble was she did not fully expect the kind of light that God deigned to shed. For, when Sheriff Miller arrived the next morning to question the members of her household, Jeremiah Madison was nowhere to be found.

CHAPTER EIGHT

Sheriff Miller was sitting in Maggie's kitchen. A mug of steaming coffee was lodged in his huge fist. Surrounding him at the large table were Eli, Nate, Emily, Edgar, and Maggie. The Sheriff took a long draw from his cup and sat quietly for a moment while the others waited for him to speak. At long last, he mused, "You know, there's something peculiar about a man who disappears right before he's questioned about his wife's death."

Eli snorted. "I think we call that something peculiar 'guilt'."

"Can't say that yet. I can only say it's peculiar."

That did little to soothe Eli. "I don't understand you, Sheriff. Why didn't you take precautions?"

"Because you've got to give a man the benefit of the doubt."

"Benefit of the doubt? Of all the addle-pated – you should've arrested him on the spot!"

"We can't do that, Mr. Smith," Edgar interjected in a reasonable tone. "We can't make an arrest before we have evidence."

"So why didn't you look for evidence?" Eli sputtered.

"It was late," Sheriff Miller drawled. "Hard to do a search in the dark."

The deputy abruptly walked into the kitchen from the new wing. "Uh . . . Sheriff?"

The big man looked up.

"We found this in Madison's writing desk." The young man held up a small bottle.

"Oh, hey, what do you know? Evidence!" Eli glowered at the two of keepers of the peace. "Know what? This is incompetence, pure and simple. Well, don't expect me to be silent. No, sir. *I* have some power in this town, too. And you'd better believe that I'll have plenty to say in the *Gazette*!"

"Do what you need to do, Mr. Smith, and I'll do what I need to do." The sheriff moved heavily to his feet. "Meantime, I'll telegraph the other sheriffs and constables. See if they've seen Madison." He glanced at the deputy, adding, "Have the contents of that bottle analyzed."

Afraid that she might have valuable information after all, Maggie blurted, "Sheriff, I think you need to know, an hour or so before I took ill, I saw Mr. Madison and Miss Hillsborough embracing in this very room."

His bushy black eyebrows shot up. "Really?"

"I realize that a hug is not necessarily improper, but this one was intimate. They were very close. Like man and wife. Like lovers. That may be the motive you're looking for."

"Hmm . . . Now, *that* makes things a bit more interesting." Sheriff Miller sank back down onto his chair. The wood groaned under his weight. "Guess I'll have to talk to the girl next. See if she'll corroborate your story. Of course, you realize chances are she won't. Folks usually want to keep that sort of stuff quiet, if you know what I mean."

"Not anymore, sir," a soft voice chimed in.

The group all looked in the direction of the speaker. Carrie Hillsborough was standing in the kitchen doorway. "What Mrs. Smith said is true, I'm sorry to say." She offered up a small, weak smile. "I was always attracted to Mr. Madison. But when he became so unhappy in his marriage . . ." She glanced down at her hands in embarrassment. "'Well, I just wanted to comfort him. And so we became paramours. He told me that I was special, that I rightly should be his wife. But," she sighed, "the fact of the matter is that my conscience began to bother me. The Bible says that adultery is a sin. I needed to repent, and in order to repent, I needed to stop the adultery. However, when I told him that I no longer wished to be with him . . ." She hesitated, blushed, and then glanced up. "Well, he was very upset. He told me that he would do anything to win me back and that he could fix things so that we could be together."

A moment of clumsy silence passed.

Finally, Sheriff Miller took a deep breath. "Now *that* is interesting."

Eli hissed, "It's more than interesting. It's downright incriminating."

"I would have said something to someone," Carrie murmured, green eyes brimming with tears, "but I was so ashamed. And I never thought . . ."

"It's all right, honey," Emily said in a comforting tone. "None of us did."

Maggie nodded. "He fooled us all."

"All but me, apparently," was Eli's grumbled response.

The girl heaved a sigh. "I need to tell you one more thing. I saw Mr. Madison leave this morning. He had a satchel. He came out of the house and went toward the railroad station."

"Oh, that's just great!" Eli groused. "He could be on a train to who-knows-where by now!"

"Mr. Smith, let *us* handle the investigation, if you don't mind." Sheriff Miller rose and went to Carrie's side. "Thank you, young lady. Your information has been most valuable. Why don't we continue our talk in the front parlor, where we'll have some privacy? That is," he glanced at Maggie, "if you don't mind, ma'am."

"I don't mind at all. Please feel free."

The Sheriff nodded at her, "Ma'am," and escorted Carrie out of the room.

The mood had been broken at last. There would be no further discussion for the time being. Within the space of seconds, Edgar dashed off to the courthouse, Nate to his carpentry shop, and Emily to the back parlor to do some mending. That left Maggie sitting across the table from Eli, who looked far from happy.

"I'll have something to say in the *Gazette*," he was muttering half to himself. "Oh, that'll do a lot of good. Know what, Maggie? I'm a damned fool. What am I supposed to do? Write a strongly-worded editorial? Boy, that'll tell Madison, won't it? That would have the same effect on him as if I stood and wagged my finger in his pasty Methodist face." To illustrate the point, Eli waggled his finger at an imaginary opponent. "Naughty boy! Bad minister! It's wrong to poison people. Bad, bad, bad! Egad!"

Maggie leaned across the worn-smooth surface of the table. "They'll find him."

But her words did little to comfort her husband. Rather, they only made his dark eyes snap. Without warning, he brought his fist down hard onto the table, rattling the cups as if they had been startled. "Damn it, Maggie! That's not the point! This isn't about finding Madison. It's about – it's about –" Slamming the palms of both his hands onto the table, Eli leapt to his feet. "Damn it! It's about me! It's about my position as head of this family. How the hell am I supposed to keep you safe around here? How am I supposed to keep our girls safe? That's my *job*, Maggie! Keeping you safe, protecting you. I have *failed* at my job!" As he wheeled around, he kicked the chair back. It crashed to the floor as he stomped into the middle of the kitchen. "I can't believe I let this happen. Madison dances into our home, insinuates himself into your confidence, and then poisons you. *And I couldn't do a thing to stop it.* I stood there and watched you lose our baby. Then I watched *you* nearly die, and I couldn't do a thing. I just stood there, like some blasted ninny hammer!" His jaw tightened. "My God, I love you so much and along comes Madison and . . ." He clumsily shoved his glasses up to his brows and with a finger wiped tears of frustration from his eyes.

Maggie realized that her rock was crumbling before her. "Eli . . ."

"Ah, don't try to comfort me, Maggie. It's humiliating. All I can do to fight back is write a lousy editorial. Talk about losing your manhood." He pushed his eyeglasses back into place and sniffed himself under control. "But that's not the worst of it. You want to know how I really feel about Madison?" Maggie could see exactly how he felt simply by looking into his eyes – and it frightened her. "I want to kill him." He paced aimlessly about the room. "You know, I've never wanted to kill anyone before. That would be murder, and murder is wrong. Nonviolence was always the way to go. Good old Eli, the pacifist. Eli, the Quaker boy. And in the space of a day – a lousy, stinking *day*, Maggie – I'd happily take a gun and blow Madison's handsome head to kingdom come. I'd cheerfully abandon my beliefs and principles all because of him. Well, God save me, that's all I'll say!"

Maggie took a step toward him, but Eli waved her off.

"Save it. I'm not who you think I am. *I* don't even recognize myself." With that, he turned and marched to the back door. He threw it open and was gone.

She sat back down, admitting to herself that even rocks get worn by the elements. Let him get away for a bit, she thought. He needs time.

The truth was that there was nothing she could do to help her husband right now anyway, and she had other duties to which to attend. The women had put the laundry off since Monday and there was no getting around it any longer. Maggie needed to tackle that dreaded task right away. Pushing her husband's tantrum to the back of her mind, she went to fetch the others.

****

While Lydia, Emily, and Carrie gathered and changed the sheets on the beds, Maggie checked the heavily soiled items that required soaking and then saw to the water heating in two huge pots on the stove. By the time the three other women returned, the water was getting hot.

Spots were addressed first by the application of soap and vigorous scrubbing on washboards in cool water. Then Lydia and Carrie wrestled one pot of hot water to the laundry tub and dumped it in, careful not to scald themselves with either water or steam. Finally, Emily soaped the hot water and they all began the general wash.

As they worked, Maggie glanced gratefully at Carrie. The girl's presence meant that Frankie could go to school on Wash Day, rather than having to stay home and help. It was a further blessing that Samuel had been good enough to leave the maid with them until Emily's baby was born. Emily was having difficulty undertaking the more strenuous tasks of household management and Carrie happily took these things over for her. Despite her dalliance with Mr. Madison, Carrie appeared to be a good girl at heart. Maggie admired her courage. It was a brave thing to risk censure by admitting to an adulterous affair, and yet the girl had put doing right before her reputation. That was commendable.

As she pushed some damp, clinging hairs from her eyes, Maggie said to Carrie, "Mr. Madison didn't say anything to you when he left, did he?"

"How do you mean, ma'am?"

"Well," she was stirring a batch of sheets in the wash tub, "did he make any comments? Any hint of where he might have been going?"

Carrie shook her head. "Oh, no, ma'am. We didn't speak. I was watching out my bedroom window."

Maggie stopped in mid-stir and met the girl's eyes. "But your room looks out the back."

Carrie placidly returned to scrubbing a stain out of a blouse. "So it does, ma'am. He went out the back door."

"But you said he went toward the railroad station."

The girl paused for a moment, then smiled sweetly and met Maggie's eyes. "Yes, ma'am. He went through the backyard to the *Gazette* and then turned left onto Main Street."

Maggie accepted her answer, even though Jeremiah's actions sounded unusual. A much more direct route to the train station was to go four blocks directly down Second Street. But, she reminded herself, they were not speaking of usual circumstances. If Jeremiah had desired to be stealthy, then an indirect route would indeed make more sense. But why go around the house?

They were ready by now to begin rinsing the first batch of laundry, so Maggie had to put her thoughts aside to ask Lydia for help emptying the tub of dirty wash water.

****

Eli did not return for noon dinner. The washing had been completed by early afternoon, so Maggie went to her room, washed herself in the basin on her bureau, put on clean, dry clothing, and returned to the kitchen. Emily had heated the remains of dinner and put Eli's plate on a tray. Maggie knew exactly where he was hiding and quickly walked the tray through the backyard to the *Gazette*. She found him standing, hands stuffed in his pockets, between the parlor (which housed his printing press) and the little kitchen.

"I thought you might like dinner," she said.

Eli looked down to avoid meeting her eyes. "Thanks."

She could see that his ire had cooled and that he was embarrassed at his outburst. She set the tray on the table. "Do you feel better?"

He scuffed a foot over the wood floor. "A little."

"You know, Eli, no matter how much you wish it were otherwise, you won't always be able to protect me, the girls, or any other children we might have. Sometimes forces intervene that are beyond our control."

"I know."

"And," she gently reminded him, "I have taken care of myself for more than a few years."

"I know, but I'm *supposed* to protect –"

"Yes," she interrupted. "I know."

"He tried to kill you."

"Yes, he did, and so it's perfectly natural for you to be angry with Jeremiah Madison."

He heaved a large sigh. "But it's not natural to want to kill him. I don't like that feeling."

"But you can let go of the anger, Eli. Both of us can. We don't need to dwell on it."

"Not dwell on almost losing you? Oh, Maggie, I'm not sure I'm capable of that." He rested his hand on the back of one of the kitchen chairs. Like a penitent boy, he peeked up at her. "I'm sorry, sweetheart. I acted like a mad bull."

"Apology accepted."

"Good ol' Saint Maggie," he replied with a smile.

"I'm not a saint, Elijah Smith." She went to him, caressed the side of his face, and kissed him. "I am wrestling with my own disappointment, grief, and anger."

He put his arms around her and they held each other for quite some time. His big, warm, sturdy body was comforting. They hadn't been together since Maggie took ill. Right then and there she wanted him. Seeking his mouth, she gave him a warm, full kiss, and then murmured, "Let's go upstairs."

He hesitated. "Tonight, Maggie. I've got a deadline to meet right now."

"And you're the editor who set that deadline." She kissed him again. "And what has been set can be unset."

"No. I'm afraid I've just got too much on my mind. I don't think I could get in the mood."

She smiled slowly at him. "Ah, but you forget. I can *get* you in the mood."

****

Sometime later, up in Eli's bedroom, Maggie was awakened from a very pleasant dream. She thought she had heard footsteps on the floor below. Lifting herself up on an elbow, she listened closer, not sure whether she actually had heard the noises or dreamt them.

Her movement awakened Eli. Smiling sleepily, he pulled her close.

"Why, sir," she teased, "twice, and so soon?" She was very, very happy that he had extended the deadline. All her troubles, worries, and sadness stepped aside when she was in his arms.

****

After a pleasant afternoon together, Maggie dressed, fixed her hair and went downstairs. To her dismay, she saw that she had left Eli's dinner on the kitchen table. Lifting the cover from the plate, she found that the food was ice cold. She was still staring at it when Eli bounded down the stairs – causing the whole house to thunder – and danced into the kitchen. Sweeping her up into his arms, he twirled the two of them around. For a big man, he had a great deal of grace.

"Eli!" she squealed. "You're making me dizzy."

He stopped, but still held her tight. "You make *me* dizzy, Saint Maggie!"

She chuckled. "I don't think what we have done qualifies either one of us for sainthood. But if this is what it does to you, then we need to do it more often."

"You'll hear no complaints from me, madam."

"Well, here's something you *can* complain about – your dinner's gone cold." Deciding to heat the plate for him, she turned to the stove. As she did, her gaze lit on the entrance to the cellar. She frowned. "Did you leave that door open?"

"No."

"Maybe I *did* hear someone walking around down here."

He immediately was on alert. "What?? Why didn't you say something?"

She chuckled. "I tried, but you distracted me."

"Humbug. I can't be *that* good." He walked to the door, peeked down the stairs, and this time he was the one who frowned. "I don't like this." Retrieving the poker that sat beside the stove, he added, "I think I'll check it out."

"I'm going with you."

He gazed at his wife over the top of his spectacles. "Maggie, it might be dangerous."

"And it also might be runaway slaves. The last thing they'll need to see is a nervous white man brandishing a poker."

He sighed. "You win. But let me go first."

Maggie laid a hand on his arm. "Eli . . ."

Once again, he glanced at her over the rim of his glasses.

"You *are* that good."

He grinned and pushed his spectacles back up his nose.

The two of them made their way down the steep cellar steps – Eli clutching the poker in one hand and carrying a lantern in the other; Maggie hitching her skirts so as not to trip on the way down. Quietly crossing the dirt floor, they approached the wooden shelves at one end of the cellar. The piece of furniture, which had small wheels hidden on its bottom, had been pushed slightly to one side so that the entry to the tunnel was visible.

Eli turned to her. "I don't think runaway slaves are down there. Nate and any of the Water Street conductors always make sure everything's back in place. And it's broad daylight. Who could it be?"

Her stomach went cold. "Jeremiah Madison. When he was so upset about marrying Leah, I took him to the secret room so we could talk in private."

"What??" he sputtered. "You took him to the Underground Railroad room so you could talk in *private*?"

She sighed in exasperation. "Oh, Eli, please do not be jealous! It's unbecoming."

"Maggie, whether I'm jealous or not, the point is that this place is secret for a reason."

"I know that!" She was quite annoyed. "He said he was an abolitionist. He promised he'd keep the room secret."

Eli rolled his eyes. "He promised. Well, you know what? He also *promised* Leah that he would love her! Why is it I think he doesn't know the meaning of the word 'promise'?"

"At that time I had no way of knowing he wasn't trustworthy," she retorted rather stiffly, and said nothing further. Lips pursed, arms folded, she refused to look at her husband.

At length, Eli cleared his throat. "I'm sorry. I'm getting upset over nothing. Let's stop bickering." He peered into the dark of the tunnel. "I just don't like Madison. Haven't since the day I met him."

"That, my dear, is something that I have *known* since the day you met him."

"Look," he said, "if Madison's in there, we certainly don't want to alert him. I'll put the lantern out once we get inside."

They stepped through the opening. The tunnel was damp, musty and earthy, and – once Eli put the light out – pitch black. He felt his way with one hand on the brick-lined wall and one hand before him. Maggie grasped the back of his shirt and prayed that he wouldn't trip, fall, and take her with him. They would have enough trouble with whoever was in the hiding place and wouldn't need to give their approach away. In a bit, they could see light seeping out from under the door at the end of the tunnel. They drew near. Eli put his hand on the door's latch. She heard him take a breath, and then felt him push forward with great force.

In seconds, the two of them were standing in the secret room.

Jeremiah had leapt from a chair by the table and was backing away, staring wild-eyed at them. His face was rough with a growing beard. Edgy as a cornered animal, he looked first one way, then the other.

"Don't move," warned Eli. "Just stay put."

Nonetheless, the young minister made a feint toward the door that led to Maggie's cellar.

"You won't be able to get out that way," she called. "We blocked it up."

Trapped, Jeremiah looked around one more time. Suddenly, he tensed as if he were going to try to rush Eli.

"Go ahead," the other man growled, raising the poker above his head. "Try to get by me, Madison. I'd love it."

Those words caused Jeremiah's shoulders to sag, and he slumped down into a chair. He did not so much have the aura of evil and murder as he did that of a frightened, lost little boy. It gave Maggie a confusing, unexpected rush of pity.

Eli, on the other hand, was feeling something else. "I can't believe you came back here. Do you have any idea how much trouble you're in? Do you even have any idea what you've *done*?"

"I – I didn't think."

"Oh, you sure as hell didn't think!" Eli's face flushed red. "You poisoned two people. That's the act of a madman!"

Maggie pushed past her husband and placed herself between the two men. "Name calling won't solve anything, Eli. Neither will violence. Put the poker down. Please." She turned to Jeremiah and said more softly, "You need to give yourself up."

"I know," he said in a hoarse voice. "I tried to run away. I thought that I would go to New York City, and then take a train west as far as I could go. But I only got to Morristown. Something stopped me. Something wouldn't let me go further. I walked through the town to think. I went to the green, watched people. But no matter where I went, I felt as if every person saw the sin in me. It was if every eye that met mine knew what I had done, as if my soul had been stripped bare, as if all the people, every one of them, were accusing me of my crime. So I wandered, and then I saw the Methodist Church at the corner of the square. I went in for solace. No one was in there, but I did not dare approach the altar. So I knelt in the back and prayed. And that was when it happened. God spoke to me. God told me that I needed to come back and confess." His looked distraught and close to tears. "Perhaps you're right, Mr. Smith. Perhaps I am a madman, but I'm one who has at long last come to his senses enough to know that he *is* mad."

Maggie wondered if he were telling the truth. To take a life was an act of insanity brought on by sin. All the fine airs, all the preaching skills, all the physical beauty – none of it meant anything if the heart was corrupted and the mind unstable.

But Eli was having none of it. "Listen to me, Madison. Your stupidity nearly killed my wife and made her lose our baby. Accident or not, what you did was unforgivable. Do you hear me? Unforgivable! And let's not even talk about what you did to Leah. You're a pathetic excuse for a human being and I ought to . . ."

Maggie quickly placed a hand on his chest to restrain him, knowing full well that it would be physically impossible for her to hold him back and that she had to rely on love to keep him in check. By the grace of God, love carried the day – Eli stayed in place.

"I am so sorry, Mr. Smith. You have every right to loathe me," Jeremiah mourned. "But you must understand – what happened to your wife was an accident, a dreadful accident. She's kind and giving, and a good Christian woman. She's not wicked. Not soul-less. Not like . . ." He blanched and buried his face in his hands. "Oh, my Lord, what have I unleashed?"

Maggie's heart was unaccountably overcome with pity again. She hurried to his side and, putting an arm round his shoulders, was amazed that the touch did not revolt her. She only felt overwhelming sorrow for this lost soul. "Come, Jeremiah. We'll take you to Sheriff Miller. It's time to give yourself up."

****

From Maggie Blaine Johnson's Journal, 13 December 1860

Horror and shock has overwhelmed this town in a great wave. People struggle to understand how someone with the kind of blackness of heart that leads to murder could preach Christ's love on Sundays, visit the sick, baptize children and adults, and dine with us in our homes. We all wonder how a monster could live among us and we not know it.

Everyone feels betrayed on the deepest, most personal level. It is right that Mr. Madison should be in jail and accused of murder, we say. And it will be right when he is found guilty at his trial and sentenced to death.

The mercy that I had felt for him in the secret room has fled. I am angry to the pit of my soul, and not merely angry at Mr. Madison, but angry at my Creator. How could God permit this man to serve Him? How could we not see Mr. Madison's defective character? Eli shakes his head at all this. "We are deceived," he tells me. "I imagine you have never gone to the theater, but if you had, you would have seen how one may assume a character and become a very different person."

But two questions gnaw at me, dear Journal. If we cannot trust our ministers, who are reputedly men of God, then whom can we trust? And, again, why did God permit this outrage to happen?

And my heart breaks because I get no answer to either question, no matter how hard I pray. I feel alone, deserted by my Creator.

****

On December 16, the good people of Blaineton Methodist Episcopal Church gathered for worship as usual, but their hearts were not in it. The Presiding Elder, with determination befitting a bull dog, led the little congregation through scripture readings, prayers, and hymns. He preached a fervent sermon on hope, as if by preaching he forcibly could instill that hope into the hearts of the dazed, angry, and bereaved group before him.

It did not work.

After the service had concluded with the benediction, people stood in little knots and tried to make sense of what had happened. Maggie and her daughters were working their way to the door as quietly as possible, but found themselves abruptly surrounded by three of the church's ladies.

Mrs. Kendall, the wren of a woman who played the organ, wrung her hands. "It is all so horrible," she kept repeating. "And in our town!"

The two maiden Moore sisters looked as if they had just smelled something unpleasant. "It is a disgrace, if you ask me," Tryphena declared.

"He is a monster!" added Tryphosa. "What else can he be?"

Maggie, whose own emotions were exhausted, said nothing. Lydia also said nothing. But Frankie made to open her mouth. A surreptitious tug on her skirts by her mother, though, forced her bite her lower lip instead.

Meanwhile, Tryphena was adjusting the fingers of the kid gloves on her left hand. "Well, he's in jail now and I hope he rots there!"

"Oh, it's all so horrible," mourned Mrs. Kendall.

"They should hang him by the neck immediately," Tryphosa added.

Frankie's eyes flashed. "Doesn't Mr. Madison deserve a fair trial?"

"What on earth for?" Tryphosa replied.

Tryphena was now working on the fingers to the glove on her right hand. "I don't recall as he gave his *wife* a fair trial. He killed her."

"And in our town!" Mrs. Kendall moaned. "I never in all my born days!"

"He'll get what's coming to him," Tryphena concluded. "Mark my words. Justice will be done."

"But our Constitution says that he deserves a fair trial." Frankie straightened her back and ignored her mother's insistent tugs on her skirts. "And . . . and we should be merciful to him. After all, aren't we *all* sinners?"

Tryphena's expression grew steely. "*I* never killed anyone."

"No, but you might."

"Well!" The older of the maiden ladies glared at Maggie. "You had better teach this young pup some manners!"

Maggie knew that Frankie was right, and she did not like these clucking old hens picking at her daughter. "I apologize, Miss Moore," she replied rather tartly, "but I am afraid that I agree with my daughter. If we are all sinners, then cannot *we* be taken over by our emotions, too? Can't Satan whisper in *our* ears, too?"

All three ladies were aghast.

"Satan has no truck with me," Tryphosa snapped. "I pray regularly!"

"And read the Good Book," said Tryphena.

"And we all go to church," added Mrs. Kendall. "Imagine such a thing coming out of a child's mouth!"

"I'm not a—" Frankie began, but Maggie cut her off with, "That is enough, Frances."

All three church ladies appeared to be in high dudgeon, and Maggie was tired of anger and controversy. "If you will excuse us, we must leave," she murmured, looping her arm through Frankie's and pulling the girl toward the door. Lydia stifled a satisfied little grin and followed them.

"Mama," Frankie protested as they exited the church and began the walk home, "they are wrong! Christ tells us to love others."

Suddenly Maggie was very weary. "Mr. Madison committed a terrible crime, Frankie."

"He killed our cousin. He poisoned Mama," Lydia interjected. "Or did you forget?"

Frankie stopped dead in her tracks and glared at her sister. "I did not forget! I am upset. I cry every night. Just ask Carrie. But I also feel sad that Mr. Madison committed murder. He's lost. Are we supposed to stop caring if the lost one is a murderer? What about the parables of the lost sheep and the lost coin, and the parable of the prodigal son? Are they just nice stories?"

A long silence followed, broken only by the sound of their footsteps. The quiet encouraged Maggie's emotions to gnaw at her, so much so that she wished she could leave them in the dead weeds by the roadside. Truth be told, Jeremiah's crime had changed the way that she viewed him. She used to think of him as an attractive, gifted young minister, but now she saw evil in him one minute, a confused sinner the next, and an animal the minute after that. It was as if his positive qualities had been devoured by his act of murder. Furthermore, she disliked what it all was doing to her. She felt that her own soul had been tarnished by her feelings of suspicion, fear, anger, and revulsion. Yet she was so overwhelmed, she could not sort things out.

At length, Frankie took a deep breath. "Mama, I have made a decision."

Maggie and Lydia both looked at the young girl, whose hazel eyes had suddenly gone quite serious. They stopped walking and waited for her to speak.

Frankie lifted her chin defiantly. "I feel called to visit Mr. Madison."

Neither her mother nor her sister said a thing.

"He needs comfort and prayer now that he's in jail. It's biblical. Are we not supposed to visit the imprisoned? That means, even people who have done very bad things are still a soul, and souls need comfort and prayer. It's part of our Christian duty."

The first thought that occurred to Maggie was: I have taught her too well.

The second thing was: Perhaps God is using my daughter. Maybe I should listen to her.

"Please let me pray about your request," she finally replied. "I will give you my answer within a few days."

****

From Maggie's Journal, 16 December 1860

How can I in good conscience permit my daughter to see Jeremiah Madison unless I am willing to do it myself? Am I able to visit him in Christian love? Am I able to leave my anger, pity, fear, and hatred behind and do what Christ has commanded me?

I must protect my daughters, even though they are becoming young women. I must be assured that Mr. Madison will not get up to anymore wickedness – even behind bars. But how can I be assured of that, when he has betrayed me before?

May God forgive me for this, but the very thought of Jeremiah Madison sickens me. Is this what Satan is like? Not the very visage of evil, not reeking of putrescence and death, but pleasing to the eye, soothing of voice, and speaking words of love and hope? Is this true evil, that which masquerades as goodness, that which masquerades as Your ambassador? I tremble at the thought, O God, for if that is true, then we are all doomed.

****

The next day, Eli recruited Maggie to help proof the *Gazette*. As she stared at the sheet in her hand, she clearly saw that her husband also was feeling less than charitable. In fact, he was harboring more than a little hatred for Jeremiah and it was surfacing in his weekly editorial.

One looming question remains, and that is how such a moral monster could masquerade among us as a man of God. Why could not the authorities within the Methodist Episcopal Church detect the rotten core under the smooth, sweet exterior? Nearly everyone who came into contact with Mr. Madison was mesmerized by his charm. Indeed, mesmerized is an appropriate word, for his outer appearance blinded us to his inner nature, the true man. It is said that the serpent is the most subtle of all creatures. That is the plain truth of the matter, for the serpent dwelt among the good people of Blaineton and we never noticed until it was too late.

Maggie's heart suddenly sank at his words. Eli was always so logical, but he had allowed his anger to infiltrate his words, his actions, and perhaps his life. He and she too, had become vengeful, wrapped in their own ire and hatred. She cleared her throat to get his attention.

He looked up from laying the type and leading for page two.

"Very moving, but must you be so harsh?"

He frowned. "Maggie, the man's a murderer. Justice has to be done."

"I agree. Justice can and should be done, but must we do it without compassion?"

He stopped what he was doing and walked to where she sat at the little kitchen table. "Sweetheart, he nearly killed you. How do you expect me to feel? I'm *happy* he's locked up. Prison is where he belongs. And, if justice is done, the gallows are where he'll end."

"I understand that, but –"

Eli rolled his eyes. "Go ahead. Say it."

"I think we need to forgive him."

His response to this was a large sigh. "I'm not so sure I can do that."

"I'm not so sure I can, either," she responded. "I am deeply angry with him. But here's the trouble. We both say we're Christians. But as Christians, we're *required* to forgive. When we pray, we say the words, 'forgive us our trespasses as we forgive those who trespass against us.' We're asking God to forgive us *only* as we're able to forgive others. If we do not forgive, then we are hypocrites. Shall we withhold forgiveness in this one case? Don't we care whether or not God forgives *us*?"

Eli put his hands on his hips and looked down.

"If we expect God to forgive us, then we need to forgive others."

"I don't think I can forget what Madison has done."

"Nor do I, but perhaps forgetting is not forgiveness. Perhaps forgiveness is the letting go of anger. Look at what it is doing to us. We fuss and we fume and we seethe. Our souls are all stirred up like a thunderstorm. Maybe we need to let the Spirit blow the noise and the lightning away, Eli."

"I'm so not sure the Spirit is working around here these days," he told her.

Maggie hesitated a moment, then confessed, "Me, too. The God who was once as close as my very breath is nowhere to be found."

"I'm sorry."

"Thank you," she said, "but I do not want sympathy. Whether I feel God or not, I know what I must do in this case."

"You're going to quote scripture now, aren't you?" he teased.

She blushed.

"Allow me to do it for you. 'Love your enemies, bless them that curse you, do good to them that hate you, and pray for them which despitefully use you, and persecute you.'"

Her eyes widened in delight. "That's part of the Beatitudes!"

He grinned.

"You are so full of surprises, Elijah Smith. What troubles me is that I know Jesus would not have said that had he not expected us to follow his words and his example."

He winced. "So what you are saying is that you really *do* expect us to live what we profess."

"Yes."

"Damn," he sighed.

"Elijah . . ." she began.

"It's *my house!*" And with that, he laughed and kissed the end of her nose.

****

The next day, carrying a hamper packed with sandwiches, apples, cookies, and a tin of coffee, the couple walked into the courthouse, entered the jail, and waited as the guard unlocked Jeremiah Madison's cell. The room was small, chill, and rough. He had only a bed with a meager blanket, a table and two chairs, and a bucket for a chamber pot. Obviously stunned, the young man stumbled to his feet as Maggie and Eli entered.

Maggie set the hamper on the small table, then turned and looked directly into his eyes. "Jeremiah, I came because I want you to know that I bear you no ill will. I am struggling with feelings of anger and betrayal, but I wish you no ill."

A wisp of a smile crossed his haggard face. "I deserve no such kindness."

It took everything she had to fight back a tart response. This was more difficult than she imagined. "Nonsense, if God treated any of us as we deserved, not a single soul would ever reach heaven. The plain truth of it is I can't show you any less love than God shows me. This has nothing to do with deserving, and everything to do with God's love."

He blushed, but nodded in agreement, and watched as she began to unpack the basket. "Yet, what happened to you," he admitted quietly, "*is* my fault and I am so sorry."

Maggie wanted to turn and scream: And what of Leah? Are you sorry for what you did to her? But she held her tongue and merely nodded. "I accept your apology."

He glanced at Eli. "And I apologize to you, Mr. Smith, for all the heartache and worry. Please forgive me."

Eli pursed his lips for a moment. Maggie could tell he was wrestling with his response. At length, however, he said, "I have to be honest with you, Madison. It won't be easy for me. But," his eyes shifted momentarily in his wife's direction, "Maggie's convinced me that I need to let go of the anger. So I guess the place to start is here." He thrust out his hand.

Jeremiah gratefully took Eli's hand in his. "God bless you both. People have been so kind to me. Brother and Sister Purdy and Sister Effie Carter came to pray with me yesterday."

The news lightened Maggie's heart. Jeremiah's three visitors were part of her M.E.C. congregation. Effie was Emmeline Purdy's maiden sister. All three lived about one mile out of town, where they had a small farm. They were quiet people, seldom daring to put themselves forward as leaders, but always present when others or the church needed help.

"Who else from our church has come?" Maggie asked, hoping for more signs of mercy and compassion.

"None others," he replied simply, and at this she felt both annoyance and dismay. Were no others even attempting to do their duty? "But," Jeremiah added, "the Reverend Mr. Arthur from the African Methodist Episcopal Church has visited, as have Mr. and Mrs. Johnson."

That took Maggie by surprise – but it was a pleasant one. "*Our* Mr. and Mrs. Johnson? Nate and Emily?"

Jeremiah nodded.

"Huh," Eli mused. "Don't that beat all? They never said a word to us."

But that was typical of Nate and Emily. Like the Carters and Effie Purdy, they went about doing good works but did it quietly. The information restored Maggie's trust in her fellow Christians and she felt a warm rush of love for them as she invited Jeremiah to eat. To her surprise, he refused, saying that he wouldn't do so unless they joined him. And so the trio sat down on the rough wooden chairs and shared table fellowship in that cold, damp cell.

Jeremiah was delighted to have a hot cup of coffee and home cooking. Watching him gratefully eat and drink gave Maggie a sense of everyday activity and brought back memories she had of the old Jeremiah. Despite their grim surroundings, she found that she could chat amiably with him about things of inconsequence for quite awhile.

But, even munching on an egg sandwich, Eli was ever the reporter. A thoughtful look soon crossed his face and he said, "I hear you confessed to Leah's murder."

"Yes, I did. I must take the consequences for her death. Someone must."

Eli raised an eyebrow. "Even if it means the gallows?"

Jeremiah was silent a moment, contemplating the apple he held. "I don't wish to die. Understand that. But sooner or later one's sins catch up, don't they?"

Eli hesitated, and then replied, "So folks say."

"I have no doubt that I will hang," Jeremiah went on in a quiet tone. "I'm not a brave man by any means, but the penalty must be paid, and I'm making peace with it."

****

Maggie and Eli walked back home in the fading afternoon light. The sun was going down earlier and earlier each day. The tree branches had been stripped bare and shivered in the breeze. Soon snow would begin to fall. Maggie thought of Jeremiah in his cold cell and shivered.

"Did you notice something peculiar when we were talking to Madison?" Eli asked, as they crunched through the brown leaves that littered the square.

"Not really, except that he seemed almost relieved to be in jail."

The air was sharp. Their breath made little grey puffs as they spoke. The light wind had a bite as it pushed at their backs. Yes, Maggie decided, snow would mostly likely fall early this year.

"It's just I noticed something after he said he must take the consequences for Leah's death, he added 'Someone must.' That's kind of peculiar, don't you think?"

Maggie slowed her pace as she recalled the minister's words.

"I mean, he committed the murder, right? So if he committed the murder and confessed to it, then of course he should take the consequences. But, 'someone must' sounds as if there's a question about who murdered Leah."

She was trying to work it out in her head. "Couldn't it just be a slip of the tongue?"

"Maybe," he admitted, with a frown. "But something just doesn't sound right."

"Oh, Eli," she sighed. "Must you constantly look for a story?" But suddenly John Blaine's words echoed in her ears. There were troubles. Things were wrong. But how could that be now? Leah's was murderer behind bars and facing trial. Everything should be all right. Shouldn't it?

If so, then why did she keep thinking about John's words? Maggie shivered again and said to Eli, "Let's hurry, my love. I am cold. I expect it will snow tonight."

****

The pace of life, however, did not give her much time to reflect on John's warning. On December 22nd, her daughter Lydia and Edgar Lape were going to get married. There were far too many things to do, finishing the dress being chief among them.

It took days of communal sewing, but Lydia's dress was ready in good time. It was a plainer copy of a much grander gown found in *Godey's*, but the very simplicity of it made the silk frock exquisite. The corsage and under skirt were robin's egg blue. A second skirt, split in the middle, was made of a nearly transparent white silk patterned with small crimson roses. The corsage was sleeveless with a tasteful bodice.

Because it was almost Christmas, Emily had decided to bake a rich, hearty fruitcake dense with nuts and dried fruit – and with a generous splash of rum, much to Maggie's consternation. For the supper, they decided on ham, escalloped potatoes, carrots, and turnips.

When the day of the wedding arrived, Maggie felt her throat constrict as she finished helping her daughter dress. The girl's waist was small and her hoop skirts fell gracefully to the floor. Her shoulders were smooth and pale, her neck long. Her brown eyes sparkled with excitement and her dark hair shone. She was the very image of a happy, young bride. Maggie prayed that she and Edgar could enjoy a few months of happiness, despite the upcoming trial and the threat of war. No sooner had she thought this, than she was assailed by an image: Edgar in soldier's uniform. And she just as quickly, and stubbornly, forced the image from her mind.

When Lydia, face aglow, turned and smiled at her mother, Maggie had to wipe a tear from her eye. Her daughter was grown up now and ready to take on responsibilities of her own. This was the point at which Maggie was supposed to dispense motherly advice. It took a moment, but when she finally found her voice, she told Lydia how proud her father, John Blaine, would have been of her, and how proud Eli was. "And there's something else," she said. "Something important."

Lydia looked expectantly at her.

"You know about men and women."

The young woman blushed. "Mama! You told me some years ago."

Maggie smiled faintly and took the girl's hands. "I know. But I want you to understand something. Marriage is a wonderful institution, and God made it so that men and women should enjoy each other in every way."

Lydia glanced down.

"What I mean is that it's all right. You shouldn't feel guilty if you like the physical expression of love. It's part of God's plan. Books may tell you otherwise, but the books are wrong. Don't listen to them!"

Her daughter giggled and said slyly, "Why, Mama, you must be very, very happy with Eli."

Maggie chuckled in reply and gave her a kiss. "Indeed I am! And I pray that you will be as happy with Edgar. Now, let's go downstairs. I hear a wedding is about to happen."

Minutes later, Eli was escorting Lydia to Edgar's side, and the Reverend Mr. J.B. Arthur wed them. All of a sudden, life changed again for Maggie. Her oldest girl was a married woman. At this, she automatically cast a wistful eye upon Frankie. In the space of a couple of years, she might be going away to college. A strange kind of hole opened up inside Maggie's heart. She had been caring for her girls forever it seemed – watching them, guiding their steps, mothering the best way she knew how. And as they grew, they had become excellent, dear friends. But now they were women who did not need motherly oversight. That meant Maggie was left only with . . . what? Worry, she thought with some horror. I am left with worry!

But in the next instance, she strengthened her resolve. I will *not* worry, she told herself. Christ has bid us not to worry. I have seen what it does to others – it eats away at the heart just as surely as anger eats away at it. I will have none of that. Instead, I will send love to my daughters and pray that the Spirit strengthens and guides them.

The sound of the fiddler turning his instrument caught her attention.

Smiling broadly, Eli walked to her side. "Well, Mama, your daughter is married."

"And she is a beautiful bride."

"Perhaps we'll have a little one to look after soon," he joked.

Maggie gave him an impish grin. "Do you mean a grandchild or a child?"

The fiddler began playing a reel. People were lining up to dance, so Maggie stepped back to the wall. She was still in mourning and had to refrain. It was scandalous enough that she not only was allowing her daughter to get married, but also was hosting the wedding party.

As the music and stomping filled the room, she vowed never to be the type of mother who fretted endlessly over her daughters. She would trust God to care for them. Of course, she fully expected some worry to come her way – that would only be natural – but she decided to trust the whole of their lives – and her own future – to the One who was more powerful – even if that One had been so mysteriously silent for the past few months.

A voice was calling her name. Leaving her musings, Maggie found Samuel at her side. She smiled, but his expression remained somber, shades of their former relationship. "Is what I hear true?" he asked. "Are you really visiting Jeremiah Madison in jail?"

Laying a hand on his arm, she said gently, "I mean no disrespect to you or to Leah's memory. But, yes, I am."

"How can you, after what he did to you and to my poor Leah?"

She took Sam's hand in hers and led him outside while the wedding party continued inside. She knew that he would have to leave soon, anyway. Custom dictated that he refrain from gaiety for at least six months during his mourning period.

As they stepped onto the porch, a bath of surprisingly warm air surrounded them. The day had been relatively mild for a change. Maggie took a deep breath and felt it relax her. As she stared up into the expanse of black and sparking stars overhead, she said, "I began to visit Mr. Madison not because I felt any deep affection for him. Indeed, I actually felt rather afraid and angry. But Frankie pointed out that his soul needs comfort, too. She said she wanted to visit him. Before I would let her do that, I had to go myself. That changed me, Sam. I feel pity for Mr. Madison now, not anger. He's lost, so very lost. I pray that he finds forgiveness for his soul's sake."

Samuel was considering her words. Maggie braced herself for an argument – or at least criticism. She was stunned therefore when he said, "You're so much stronger than I, Margaret."

The words were flattering, but she knew the truth. She looped her arm through his. "My own strength did not get me there. In all honesty, I didn't *want* to go to the jail and visit."

Samuel was silent, as they both stared at the shadows of the bare trees and tired vegetable garden behind the rooming house. "Tell me," he said quietly. "Has he repented?"

"I believe he has. And, remember, he *did* give himself up. He could have run away."

A wan smile touched the corners of Samuel's mouth. "Yes. That much is true." He looked up at the night sky. "Perhaps someday *I'll* be moved to forgive him. But right now . . ."

"In God's time, Sam," she answered and kissed him warmly on the cheek.

Then he, to her great happiness, responded by kissing her cheek as well. "I pray so."

****

From Maggie's Journal, 22 December 1860

It is late, dear Journal. Eli is already abed and snoring. He and the men visited the wood shed once more and imbibed some of Grandpa O'Reilly's whiskey. I do not understand why they need to do this, but as Emily reminded me yet again, they are men and must have their fun.

My Lydia and her Edgar are husband and wife. May God protect them and keep them as they begin their life together. And may they be safe in these perilous times.

Eli and I are giving them the *Gazette* as a honeymoon for a few days. They deserve at least a bit of privacy and peace before... I know not how to conclude this. Before returning to day-to-day life? Before war comes? Only God knows, but God is silent.

As for Frankie, every day she reveals the Holy Ghost through her words and deeds. Is she called to preach, I wonder? If so, what church would have her? Oh, how I wish that women were not perceived as weak creatures in need of protection, but as children of God, capable of doing whatever it is they are called to do! I wish that kind freedom for my daughter – but with freedom also comes danger. What would the novelty of a woman preaching the Word of God bring to her? Scandal and criticism, to be sure, but perhaps also praise and flattery. Did too much of the latter change Jeremiah Madison? Did all the kind words and the adulation warp him in some way and pull him away from Christ? I do not know. I can only guess, and that perhaps is the problem for us all. We can never know. And so I pray that the Spirit will strengthen and guide Frankie, and that she will not be led into temptation.

I also wonder what the future has for Eli and me. I am no longer young, I shall be forty years old soon, but then again that is not yet too old to have children. But if we do have children, what then? What if we go to war with the South? How will we protect our family if war comes to our town?

Oh, Journal! I have had more excitement in a short time than one should have in an entire life! And I have more than enough thoughts to fill the heads of several women! We do not need a war, and we do not need the upheaval and publicity of a trial and execution. I dearly wish for things to settle down in my house. I wish for peace – even for boredom. I wish again to count the small things – a successful day of washing, the joy of my family round about me – as big events.

O, good and loving Savior, bring us peace and stability, please, but – although I tremble to add this, I must – not my will, but Yours be done.

CHAPTER NINE

The members of Blaineton Methodist Episcopal Church had gathered round the pastor after the conclusion of Sunday worship. It was December 23, the day before Christmas Eve. Mr. Wesley McGregor, the retired minister chosen to serve in the interim until a new pastor could be appointed, faced a full assault of congregational wrath. Beleaguered, his eyes shifted from person to person as they surrounded him near the kneeling rail. He had backed up as far as he could until his heels had hit the rail's foundation. Unable to retreat further, he clearly was at a loss as to how he could restore peace.

Maggie, standing at the back of the group, was appalled at what she was hearing.

"We will not allow this blot to remain on our church's record," Mr. Opdyke was rumbling.

Tryphena Moore nodded in agreement. "His name must be struck!"

"Such a scandal," Mrs. Kendall chimed. "And in our church!"

Mr. Kendall stood with arms crossed and eyes steely. "This must be done, and you must demand that the Newark Conference remove his name from their records as well."

Although it was getting chilly in the sanctuary – the pot belly stove was by now unattended – Mr. McGregor mopped his face with a worn handkerchief. "Ladies and gentlemen, please. I have never heard of such a thing being done."

"And I have never heard of a minister doing such a thing as he did here!" Tryphena snapped.

"He must disappear from the record," Mr. Opdyke demanded. "As surely as he will be hanged, we must make sure that his name vanishes with him."

"But we cannot do that," Mr. McGregor countered. "Simply because he is accused of murder, we cannot erase his name as if he never existed. I understand that he has a brother over near Phillipsburg. How would he feel?"

Tryphena sniffed. "Relieved, no doubt!"

Maggie could hold her tongue no longer. "I cannot believe that. One cannot stop loving someone because he has done wrong."

Tryphena glared over her shoulder at her. "Oh, what do you know? You're making a fool of yourself by visiting him! The papers are saying that you and the others have been taken in by the man."

"The *Gazette* does not say that."

"Only because it is owned by your husband."

"Neither has the *Easton Express-Times* criticized us."

"Well, all the other papers say so." Tryphena leveled her glare at Mr. McGregor once again. "We cannot afford to have the world think of us as naïve bumpkins, sir. We must take a stand!"

The minister mopped his face once again. "Brothers and sisters, please. Have you forgotten mercy?"

"The man deserves no mercy!" Mr. Kendall snapped.

At this Frankie elbowed her way past her mother. Maggie watched, open mouthed, as the girl blurted, "*Everyone* deserves mercy! And forgiveness! Is it right to pick and choose whom we will forgive? How is that being like Jesus?"

Tryphena glowered at Maggie. "Oh, do make that child be quiet. You're her mother, for pity's sake."

Stunned, Maggie paused only for the briefest of moments, and then straightened her back as she said, "You're absolutely right. I *am* her mother, and as such I believe that she is absolutely correct. You all may do as you wish, but as for me and my house, we choose the path of compassion and mercy. Good day." With that, Maggie took her daughter by the arm and steered her down the aisle and out the door.

****

From Maggie's Journal, 23 December 1860

I walked out of my church today. I do not know if or when I shall return. But I could take no more. The strongest voices there clamor to remove Mr. Madison's name from the church record and from the records of the Newark Conference. Those of us who visit him are called fools. The anger and hatred is palpable and shocking – and all of it is happening near the anniversary of our Savior's birth. Shame on us!

I have always been faithful. My church is dear to me. I love singing with the congregation and joining in prayer. I have experienced sweet times when our hearts are united and when we live and breathe as one Spirit, together in Christ – but not so now. Now they snarl and snap after Mr. Madison like so many mad dogs. Even though the trial is set for January 7th, they have already found him guilty and condemned him. He is beyond the pale to them, and so are those who dare to offer him any comfort.

Oh, my Lord, how is it that I no longer wish to be among my own people? They are so full of vitriol and many cry out for vengeance. I am drifting and the only succor I find is with my family and my boarders. But You, Lord, where are You? I used to find such comfort in Your presence. But I wait and I wait, and now there is nothing.

****

Usually, Maggie took a great deal of pleasure in preparing Christmas gifts for each member of her family. But, truth be told, she felt little joy this year. Despite this, the week before the holy day, she had dutifully gone forth to the shops to purchase gifts and at home had made small presents in secret. By Monday, Christmas Eve day, she only had Eli's gift left. She knew that he needed a pocket watch and, as she hurried out into the crisp air and down Main Street, she was afraid that the clock smith's shop would have nothing left. But to her delight, there in the display case lay a gold watch with a simple design on the cover, and it was perfect. Maggie closed her eyes to say a brief prayer. If the price was too high, she would have to wait to buy it until a later time. She asked for God's grace so that she might accept whatever needed to be done. When she opened her eyes, she inquired about the price. To her further delight, Mr. Sipperly, the clock smith, quoted an amount that came to a bit less than that which she had put aside for the watch. Maggie happily made the purchase, thinking that Eli would be very surprised and pleased.

As she stepped out into the street to go home, she nearly collided with the Moore sisters. Tryphena stepped directly into her path, looking her squarely in the face and saying in tones of ice, "I am sorry that you walked out of church yesterday. I hope you were not ill."

Maggie clutched Eli's gift and met Tryphena's gaze. "No. I was quite well, thank you."

"It was unlike you to leave in that way," said Tryphosa.

"I agree. It is not like me at all. Good day." Maggie moved to step around them, but Tryphena blocked her progress.

"Do not be a fool," the older woman hissed. "Would you cut yourself off from the church over a murderer?"

Maggie drew herself up, eyes flashing. "Mr. Madison is *accused* of murder. The trial has not yet begun and therefore he has neither been found guilty nor has he been sentenced to death. As for cutting myself off from your fine fellowship, I find that I need time to think and pray. The air in our church these days feels most unhealthy."

"Well!" both ladies said in unison.

"No, it is most unwell, if you ask me! I have suffered great losses. My niece is dead, my brother and his family distraught. I became ill and lost my baby. I discovered that my dear pastor and friend is accused of murder and attempted murder. I know this crime all too well. *You* may wish to wallow in anger and hatred, but I no longer can afford that luxury. I cannot – nay, *will* not – allow such emotions to eat me alive, to darken my soul! The only thing that keeps me from sinking into that black mire is God's grace. The only thing that moves me to visit Mr. Madison is Christ's command, 'I was in prison, and ye came unto me.' I have not healed yet, I have not rid myself of my own demons, but, dear ladies, I am hoping for a miracle in my soul, as should we all! Good evening!" And with that, Maggie swept around the two gape-mouthed sisters and strode off toward the square.

In her mind, she could hear Eli's predictable, whimsical response: "Good ol' Saint Maggie, offending the populace with the truth again."

It would be a joke, of course, but truth often lurks within a joke. And Eli's assessment would be absolutely correct. Her little tirade had no doubt offended the Moore sisters. Perhaps, she thought, it would have been better to have said nothing, and then angrily wondered when she would learn to tame her tongue. There was a time for everything, including a time for truth-telling, and sometimes it was wiser simply to remain silent. The trouble was, Maggie just was not sure whether this was a time for silence or truth.

On the walk back to the boarding house, she suddenly noticed how many people were refusing to meet her gaze. She smiled grimly. So, not only were her words offending people, but her mere presence as well. After all, there was more than one way to speak the truth. Am

I doing wrong, she wondered. Should I *not* be visiting my niece's murderer? Should I *not* forgive Jeremiah and should I *not* do acts of mercy? Would people find me more acceptable if I drowned in my own hatred? Is acting with compassion such a terrible thing, such a wrong thing?

Shaking her head, Maggie tried to wrestle her way free of the questions. And then she remembered the afternoon at the camp meeting, the time that she had gone for solace to the little stream in the farmer's field. It had happened a scant four months ago, but it seemed like another time and place. In the midst of her misery, God had spoken to her in the words of a hymn. It was then that Maggie remembered what she had vowed to do.

The simple truth was that it didn't matter what people said or how they treated her. God had called her to follow the law of love. The right thing was to act out of love. Jeremiah needed comfort. He needed God's grace. And if that grace came through her, or Frankie, or the Johnsons, or even Eli – for God had worked with less likely candidates – then it was worth all the snubs and cool looks in the world. God didn't promise that the world would like her, after all. In fact, God had promised just the opposite.

So Maggie stiffened her upper lip, grew a tougher skin, and went home to wrap Eli's gift and await his return. And she waited, and waited. And then waited some more. It was late Christmas Eve, after everyone else was abed, before he finally burst into the room. "Sorry I'm so late, sweetheart. I lost track of time."

She thought of his gift and smiled. "It is easy to do."

He briskly rubbed his hands together. "I got to tell you, I'm about as cold as a block of ice. The *Gazette* was freezing."

"You let the fire go out again, didn't you?"

"Guilty as charged. But it's freezing outside, too!" He pulled his shoes off. "And, frankly, it's not much better in here. Brr!" He tossed off his coat, leaving it where it fell, and dove directly onto the bed.

"Elijah Smith!" she cried, as she bounced on the mattress like a ship on a stormy sea and feared the imminent collapse of the bed frame. "What are you doing? You're still dressed!"

"Believe me, I've got to warm up before I can take anything else off." He happily wrapped his arms about her and pulled her close, sighing, "Ah, warmth, at long last."

He was, indeed, utterly freezing. Maggie immediately began to shiver. "This isn't going to work. You're making *me* cold."

Eli only laughed and rolled onto his back, pulling her atop him. "I don't think so. We're far too good at warming up." He gave her a very hungry kiss. "Hooray! It's working. God bless you, woman!"

"Shh!" she hissed. "Not so loud. You'll wake everyone."

"Maggie, they all know what married people do."

"Not Frankie."

"Then tell her, for goodness sake. Her room is directly above ours." He kissed her again.

Something sharp jabbed Maggie in the side. "Ow! Eli, what on earth is that?"

"I think you ought to know what that is by now."

"Not *that*," she said. "That." She patted the pointy-edged object in his waistcoat pocket.

His eyes twinkled playfully. "Oh, *that*." Maggie sat up, rubbing her bruised side, as he fished the thing out of his pocket. Eli held up a small box wrapped in tissue paper and tied with a rather crumpled red bow. "Why, I do believe that this is a Christmas gift."

She was speechless.

"Would you like to open it, Mrs. Smith?"

"Shouldn't we wait 'til tomorrow?"

"Nope." He looked very much like a small boy on Christmas morning. "I'm too excited! Open it now."

She took the little box. Her hands were trembling a bit with anticipation as she carefully untied the ribbon, folded back the paper, and lifted the lid. Inside was a silver locket and chain. "Oh," her voice tightened with emotion, "you didn't need to do this."

"Oh, yes, I did. I love you."

She lifted the necklace and watched it sparkle in the lamplight. It was lovely.

"Merry Christmas," he said. "Want to put it on?"

She nodded. She couldn't really wear it until the mourning period was over, but she just wanted to put it for a few minutes that night. Eli sat up, placed the chain round her neck and fastened it. "Let's see." She turned and he smiled. "Looks beautiful on you. I knew it would."

She giggled like a schoolgirl. There she was, dressed in her nightgown with a delicate silver locket round her neck. But none of that seemed to matter to Eli. He only saw that his gift had surprised her and made her happy – and so she was beautiful to him. Maggie thanked her husband with a kiss, and then reached into the night stand, found his present, and passed it to him.

Eli's face lit up. When he saw the watch in the box, he was uncharacteristically speechless. "Oh, no, Maggie," he finally stammered. "This is too much."

"No, it isn't. To quote *you*, 'I love you.'"

He recovered himself enough to joke, "Gee, now I actually have something to go in my watch fob."

They both chuckled and exchanged another kiss. Eli got up and, still complaining about the cold, changed into his nightshirt. When her shivering husband dove back under the covers, Maggie snuggled close. After a short time, she said, "I am afraid that the Moore sisters and others in town do not care for the way I conduct myself."

Eli toyed with the braid into which she had woven her hair.

"People have let me know that they don't appreciate my visits to Mr. Madison."

"Ah," he said lightly. "Well, that's because those people are idiots."

"Eli, do try to be charitable."

"I am. Be glad I didn't say what I really thought."

Maggie shut her eyes, comforted by the way he was gently stroking her hair. "Am I wrong? Do you think that I shouldn't be making visits to the jail?"

He gave her a reassuring hug. "If you're doing what your conscience says to do, and I know that you are, then it's between you and God. Never mind the tongue-waggers."

She smiled. Good, old, reliable Eli. Relieved, she pressed her face against the linen of his nightshirt. "Why were you so late getting home?"

He hesitated. "It's not important."

"It must be if it made you late."

"I'm not so sure you want to hear it."

"Tell me."

"Some very bad news came over the wire today. A few days ago, December 20th to be exact, South Carolina voted to secede from the Union."

She became very quiet.

"I don't know," he said with a heavy sigh. "This war's going to tear the Union to shreds. And I'm willing to bet that we'll never completely recover from it."

She swallowed hard. "Will you go, when the war starts?"

"Maggie, you know I'm not going to sign up to fight."

"No, but you'll go off to report on the war, won't you?"

There was a long pause. At long last, he said, "I don't know."

She hugged him tightly. "What if I don't want you to go?"

"It's just that sometimes you have to do what conscience dictates."

"What conscience dictates," she repeated, and suddenly became very angry. "Why is doing what conscience dictates so painful? Why is it so difficult?"

"Because it's right, I guess and because the easy way is the lazy way."

"Damn it!" she growled, shocking both Eli and herself. "Will we never have peace?"

He sighed, and then hugged her more tightly. "Yes, but I have come to believe that peace is not a state of affairs, but a state of heart, mind, and soul."

Maggie wanted to cry. "Then may God give me that peace."

"The peace that passeth all understanding," he added, and kissed the top of her head.

****

The morning of Christmas Day was usually spent in worship. This year presented a problem, for Maggie had lost heart for her old church. Without Jeremiah and with the strained, angry and confused atmosphere, the Methodist Episcopal congregation was no longer a warm place to be. She dreaded sitting in her pew and suffering the stare of disapproving eyes aimed at the back of her head. She knew that she was feeling unwelcome even in her own congregation. But Christmas Day was supposed to be a time joy and hope, and she desperately needed both of those things, as did her daughters and – although he wouldn't admit it – Eli. When Maggie had confessed her feelings to Emily, her friend immediately invited the family to the African Methodist Episcopal Church – and Maggie accepted.

As they got ready to leave, Eli had teased her, saying, "If you think people are talking about us now, wait 'til this afternoon."

But she no longer cared. And so she, Eli, Lydia, Edgar, Frankie, and Patrick walked with the Johnsons over to the little church on Water Street.

Surprisingly, church was held in the harness shop. Surrounded by bridles, harnesses, bits, and the smell of leather, Maggie found church in the people, rather than the building. The singing, fervent prayers, and pointed preaching was just the tonic they all needed. Maggie had been concerned that they would stand out – six white faces among the darker ones – but that was not the case. They were welcomed and loved. The Spirit's uniting power was tangible, and it convicted her heart. She realized that the people of her congregation would never welcome Nate and Emily into their church. There would be no such warmth if the tables had been turned.

****

From Maggie's Journal, 25 December 1860

We in the North are so critical of the Southern institution of slavery, yet I fear that our critique is merely lip-service and that true affection between the races is a fiction. We white Northerners may not keep colored folk in chains, but we hold them at a distance. We make them live apart from us, and deny them access to education and worship. Perhaps some of us even wish that they would go away, move to Africa. So do we really have any cause to boast? Morally, we are on the same level, for we do not recognize the colored man or woman as a child of God.

And, yet, despite this, a mood of joy did descend upon me today. All of us returned home refreshed and inclined to return to the A.M.E. church for regular services. Journal, how scandalous it would be if we gave up our family pew at the Methodist Episcopal Church! Oh, there would be a flurry of talk then! White town people here would call us any number of names and whisper dreadful things about us. But I no longer care. When we heal from our trauma, I would like to stay with the A.M.E. church and care for others in it and outside it.

Filled with the joy of the day, my rooming house family gathered round the small tree in the parlor and presented one another with gifts. This was followed by a long, jolly dinner. I do so wonder how Jeremiah is faring at the jail. It is cold and cheerless there. We shall visit him tomorrow.

After dinner, as is our usual custom, we took clothes, small gifts, and food to the orphanage on Fourth Street. Many people undertake these acts of charity at Christmastime, for it is simple logic. Christ had been born in a poor stable and had proclaimed that the poor were blessed by God. It is only fitting therefore to be thankful for our prosperity and to help those less fortunate, especially on this most special of days.

The expression on the children's faces was beautiful to see. We spent some hours playing with all the youngsters. Frankie initiated a particularly uproarious game of blind man's buff. Patrick joined in, and I am coming to believe that he fancies my youngest daughter. I am not sure, however, how she feels about him. Later Lydia played carols on the piano, while we all sang along. I couldn't help but notice how good Eli was with even the smallest inmates of the orphanage. They all loved to be picked up and swung in a circle by him, to leap upon him and try to pin him to the floor, and to be given rides upon his shoulders and back. This vision of him as a father to small children makes my heart ache for little ones of our own. I try not to mourn our lost baby but it is so difficult, especially when I see him with children. And, in all truth, Journal, I do miss having a young child about.

****

After saying goodbye to the children and caretakers at the orphanage, the rooming house family tumbled out onto the street and started the long walk home. It was dark by then. A light blanket of newly-fallen snow coated the ground. The air had a clean bite to it, and the stars stood out bright and hard against a perfectly black sky. Despite all the talk of war, the world seemed strangely at peace that night. A profound stillness blanketed the town, and all was love, beauty, and calm.

"That was fun," Eli commented as he walked arm in arm with Maggie. "That little Bob fellow sure can eat, can't he? If I didn't know any better, I'd say he was my son."

She chuckled. "He does take after you in that respect. Anyway, if you ask me, you *should* be someone's father."

"Hey, I already *am* a father – to Lydia and Frankie."

"Oh, you know what I mean: one of our own. I wonder why I haven't conceived again."

"I don't know. But we could just go ahead and adopt one of those little ones we saw tonight."

"I suppose we could. I never thought of that."

"Or," he suggested with a sly grin, "we could work at it every night 'til you *do* conceive."

She chuckled. "*Every* night? I'm not sure I'd have the energy."

He chuckled back. "Oh, I'm sure you *would*, because I've noticed something about you, Mrs. Smith." He abruptly stopped walking, slid an arm around her and pulled her close. "I've noticed that you *like* it!"

"Oh, yes," she sighed and kissed him on the mouth. "I do, indeed."

Frankie suddenly loomed up beside them. "What do you mean?"

Eli broke their embrace and cleared his throat. "I think I'll go have that chat with Carson." And he hurried away, leaving Maggie to answer her inquisitive daughter's question.

She had avoided this discussion entirely too long. Christmas was hardly the time for it. Or was it? "We were talking about having a baby," she said.

"Oh. That."

"Yes. That. You've seen animals -- the bulls with the cows, the stallions with the mares."

"The dogs," she giggled.

Maggie laughed. "Yes, well, they're rather rude, aren't they? Right in the middle of the road. Well, thank goodness humans are a bit more restrained. But physically we behave in about the same way."

Frankie wrinkled her nose. "I was afraid of that. How humiliating. Having to bend over and –"

"No, no," Maggie interrupted, keeping her voice low. "It's not *exactly* the same. We can choose how we would like to, um, perform the act. Generally, people prefer face to face, but there *are* – variations. Also, for animals the act is the result of their instinct to reproduce. The female goes into heat and that signals the male. But with humans it's more complex. The physical activity is actually an act of love and, unlike animals, we can choose when and how to express that love."

"Love?" she protested, wiping her nose on a mitten. "How can *that* be love?"

"It *is*, Frankie. You hug and kiss Lydia and me. Well, when a man and a woman love each other, it's similar, only much stronger. They want to share everything with the other person – even their bodies. It's the deepest, most intimate form of affection. It's why husbands and wives share a bed."

An appalled look crossed her face. "Mama! Do you mean that you and Eli –?"

"Yes."

"And Lydia and Edgar? And Nate and Emily?"

"Yes."

There was a pause. "Well," Frankie sighed, "at least that explains all the noises from the bedrooms."

Maggie was glad it was dark and Frankie couldn't see how beet red her face was. "Do you have any questions?"

"No. It just doesn't sound like something I'd be interested in."

Her mother stifled a chuckle. "You might change your mind later."

"And I might not. At least *now* I know why there are so many old maids around! I just might join them." Scooping a handful of snow from the ground, Frankie patted it between her mittens. "Whom shall I hit?"

"Eli," her mother suggested.

She nodded. "Well, he does deserve it, considering." But then she grinned impishly. "No. I think I shall hit Patrick!" With that she heaved the missile in the boy's direction.

One well-aimed snowball at Patrick's back erupted into a full-fledged fight among the group that lasted a good block or two. As everyone dusted themselves off and caught their breath from their exertions, Maggie caught up to her husband.

"Did you tell her?" he asked.

She nodded.

"How did she take it?"

"She wants to be an old maid."

He threw his head back and laughed at the sky.

****

The next morning at breakfast, the talk was of visiting Jeremiah Madison. As Emily and Maggie brought platters of steaming scrambled eggs, ham steak, and biscuits to the table, Edgar was lamenting the fact that the defense, represented by his firm, had so little to work with. After all, Jeremiah had readily confessed to the crime.

Eli acknowledged this with a nod. "The prosecution will easily sew it up. But I just keep thinking that there's something odd about his case. I mean, where is the real proof that Madison is the one who poisoned Leah? There are no eyewitnesses. We only have Madison's word that he did it. And yet the jury will probably find him guilty."

"Do *you* think he did it?" Frankie asked.

Eli stared into space. "I used to think so. Now I'm not so sure. People confess to crimes for any number of reasons."

"Why would he lie?" Lydia asked.

"I don't know." He scooped a pile of eggs onto his plate and passed the platter to Nate.

Edgar took a sip of coffee and thought for a moment, holding the cup between both his hands. "If we had some evidence . . . and I don't mean that vial they found in his room. If we just had some real, hard evidence things might change."

Nate nodded. "Pass the ham, please. You know, I'd hate to think Mr. Madison was convicted on his confession alone."

"Well," Maggie said, as she buttered a biscuit, "what about that bottle of arsenic? He had to buy it, didn't he? Where did he get it from? And could we talk to the proprietor of the store?"

Eli paused, fork halfway to his mouth. "Mrs. Smith!" he cried and put the fork firmly back down onto his plate, "I do believe you're on to something."

"I am?"

Edgar's eyes brightened. "Yes, indeed! In our interview, Mr. Madison said that he had purchased the arsenic at a shop called Quinton's Pharmacy in Easton, Pennsylvania."

Eli was looking quite pleased. "When the shops open up, how'd you like to take little a trip to Easton, Maggie?"

"That would be most invigorating and enlightening, Mr. Smith."

But Edgar raised a hand in caution. "This of course may tell us who purchased the arsenic, and more than likely the buyer *will* be Mr. Madison."

Frankie's eyes had grown wider and wider throughout the conversation. "Yes, but we need evidence, especially if we do not want him to be convicted on his confession alone."

"And," Emily added, looking from one person to another, "especially if we do not want a guilty man to be released for lack of evidence."

****

Maggie and Eli took an early train to Easton and, after asking directions, found their way to Quinton's. The interior of the shop was small, dark, and full of shelves containing bottles and tins. A red-haired pimply boy, no older than sixteen, stood behind the counter. Eli asked if they could speak with the owner of the store. The boy nodded and disappeared through a door into the back of the building. In a few minutes, the proprietor emerged. He turned out to be a short, bald fellow whose tiny head supported an enormous mustache. He listened intently as Eli inquired whether a tall man with chestnut-colored hair had purchased arsenic during October. At this, the proprietor frowned and shook his head. "No, sir, no one answering that description has ever come into our establishment. And I should know. I almost always dispense the dangerous materials – for safety's sake, you know. But let's check with my assistant, just to be sure. Perhaps he'll recognize the man. It just may be that I had been out of the shop when the fellow you're looking for came through."

Within a few minutes, the acne-plagued boy returned to the front; but when questioned he also had no recollection of anyone fitting Jeremiah Madison's description. No one even vaguely resembling him had purchased arsenic or indeed had ever come into the shop, he reported.

"Huh," Eli muttered as he and Maggie went out into the frosty air. "Don't that beat all? They never heard of him."

"That is most strange," she agreed. "Why would Jeremiah say that he bought the arsenic at Quinton's when he had never set foot in the place?"

The town was crowded. People brushed by the couple on their way to the shops and businesses. The streets were clogged with horses and carts and carriages, and the tang of wood smoke, coal, horse flesh, dung, and people filled the air.

Maggie frowned as they pushed along. "Why would Jeremiah want everyone to think that he bought the poison?"

Eli pursed his lips. "I don't know." He reached inside his coat, produced his new pocket watch and checked the time. "But I'll tell you this much, we'd better get to that train station quickly or we'll be stuck here 'til tomorrow."

Snow was sifting from the sky by the time they got off the train in Blaineton. The two huddled close together, walking arm in arm, as they hurried up Second Street. Suddenly Eli became unaccountably happy. Maggie wondered at his mood until he said, "You know I always feel like a boy when it snows. The stuff just makes everything look magical."

Maggie lifted her face to the sky. "Like a fairy land."

"Hey, ever catch snowflakes with your tongue?"

She laughed. "I haven't done that since I was a girl."

"Well, it's high time to do it again." Eli stopped, tipped back his head and stuck out his tongue. Maggie followed suit, and they both fell to laughing as the cold flakes hit their tongues.

When they resumed their walk, he asked, "What about snow angels? Ever make them?"

"I did when I was a child."

"Well, when all this trial business is settled, Maggie, let's you and I go out in the back and make some. But, I warn you, my imprint looks more like a snow bear these days than an angel."

She hugged his arm. "You'll make a wonderful father."

He chuckled. "I'll be the type children can jump all over and bounce right back off."

Laughing, they turned into the walk that led to the rooming house. They had very nearly forgotten the reason they had gone to Easton as they paused on the porch to stomp and shake off the heavy snow.

That evening, after dinner the family gathered in the back parlor. Eli and Maggie reported their news to the group. Edgar took it in and sighed tiredly. "I fear the trial's outcome will be as expected."

"But couldn't the judge also move to dismiss the trial due to lack of evidence?" Mr. Carson asked.

"He could if Mr. Madison had not supplied us with so many details. For instance, he was quite clear that he put the arsenic in the sugar bowl intended for Mrs. Madison's use. He told us how long it took to poison her, which matched the results of the Marsh Test."

Patrick flashed a smile at Frankie, proud of his accomplishment.

The girl gave him a wondering glance, and then smiled back.

"Then a guilty verdict is certain," Carrie said.

Maggie frowned, "But neither the proprietor nor his assistant remembers anyone matching Jeremiah's description. Doesn't that mean anything?"

"It means maybe Madison did not purchase the arsenic at Quinton's," Eli offered.

Emily considered this. "It also may mean that the proprietor and his assistant have bad memories."

Edgar wrinkled his forehead in thought. "But what if Mr. Madison weren't the one who bought the poison at Quinton's? The question then becomes: who did?"

"That's hardly likely," Carrie said quickly. "That means someone else would be involved."

"What about Leah?" Eli suggested.

Maggie took a surprised breath. "Leah? Eli, then you're suggesting –"

"Suicide, yes."

Edgar sat straight up in his chair. "We must go back to Quinton's first thing tomorrow. If they didn't recognize Madison's description, then they just might recognize Leah's."

Indeed, that was precisely what the proprietor of the pharmacy and his assistant did. Yes, they both replied, a young woman with blond hair had purchased arsenic toward the end of October. She was new to both their eyes and therefore stood out in their minds. Furthermore, the fact that she was quite pretty helped impress her image in their memories. They added one more thing: she had not returned to the shop since that time.

The trio rushed back to Blaineton in their hired carriage. But when they presented the information to Edgar's senior colleague, who was the lawyer for the defense, he shook his head. "This is no doubt a mystery. Mr. Madison insists upon proclaiming his guilt, and yet here we have witnesses who say that a woman matching Mrs. Madison's description purchased the arsenic. I suppose we can build a case for suicide, but Mr. Madison insists that he poisoned his wife. We would then have to disagree with our own client."

"Let me talk to him," Maggie offered. "Perhaps he'll confide in me and maybe he will want to change his plea."

A few minutes later, Eli and Maggie were in Jeremiah's tiny, drafty cell. There was nothing for it but to be blunt. "We know that you didn't buy the arsenic," she told him.

He grew a bit pale. "Oh, yes?"

"The proprietor at Quinton's didn't recognize your description. However, he did say that a pretty, young girl with blond hair made the purchase."

Jeremiah stood up and paced across his cell.

"You need to be honest with us, Madison," Eli said. "Did Leah commit suicide?"

He turned. "Leah?"

"Do not try to deny it, Jeremiah," Maggie said. "She's the one who bought the arsenic. The people at Quinton's recognized her description. You might as well tell us the truth. *You* didn't kill Leah, did you? She took her own life with the poison."

The young man looked away for a moment. He appeared to be composing his thoughts. "I think she *meant* to kill herself," he finally said, back still toward them. "But she didn't have the nerve. She hid the arsenic in a drawer where she thought I wouldn't find it. But I did find it. And I was the one who poisoned her. I'm guilty."

Eli frowned. "Oh, come on, Madison. That's nonsensical. Why are you covering for her?"

He turned around. "I am not covering for her." Striding over to his cot, he sat down on it and stared at his hands. "I'm telling the truth. Why would Leah mix arsenic with the sugar and then leave it in the kitchen where someone else – namely your wife – might accidently take it? Wouldn't she immediately carry the bowl upstairs? And would she not plan to take enough arsenic to kill herself straight off? Why would she poison herself over the course of weeks?"

"Madison!" the other man sputtered in frustration. "Do you *want* to die? Because that's what's going to happen, you know."

Jeremiah smiled faintly. "I don't wish to die, Mr. Smith. But I've committed a crime and I must pay the penalty."

"But you should not die if Leah took her *own* life." Maggie blurted. She was did not understand. Jeremiah made sense, but what he said also seemed somehow wrong. "Please don't commit suicide by claiming that you killed Leah, when it was she who took her life."

"Let me go, Maggie," he said softly. "Please."

The couple returned home, confused and frustrated.

****

While the scandal of a minister arrested on charges of murder continued to torment Blaineton, an impending conflict between North and South was creeping ever closer. Eli, completely immersed in the latest news, was constantly getting information from the telegraph office and the New York papers, and turning that information into article after article for the *Gazette*. Federal troops had occupied Fort Sumter in South Carolina immediately after Christmas, and the South Carolina militia had responded by taking over Charleston and Fort Moultrie. President Buchanan declared that Fort Sumter would be defended if attacked. Things would grow worse in January: Florida, Louisiana, Georgia, Alabama and Mississippi would secede from the Union, and state militias in the South would occupy federal forts and arsenals.

But that was in the future. In the meantime, all of Blaineton was focused on the murder trial. On January 7, the first day of the proceedings, Lydia, Carrie, and Maggie located themselves in the balcony, where they were crushed among a sea of crinolines. The *Gazette*, of course, was covering the trial. From her vantage point, Maggie could see Eli scribbling into a notebook on the main floor. She knew that he was still puzzled by Jeremiah's insistence that he was guilty. Eli would be absorbing every nuance, hoping to discover the "why" behind the discrepancy in the minister's confession. Also among the crowd downstairs was Mr. Carson. At the end of the day, he and Eli would meet, compare notes, and eventually write the weekly *Gazette* copy regarding the trial. Once the stories were written, Maggie was to comment on them and proof-read the copy.

But Eli also had hired her to write a short piece on the woman's view. He had watched her record in her journal, read her letters, and had come to the conclusion that he wanted her to begin contributing to the *Gazette*. Maggie was flattered, but somewhat daunted by the responsibility that he was bestowing upon her. After all, Eli was a man with many years' experience in journalism, while she ran a rooming house. And, as society would never let her forget, she was a woman. Her sphere was the repetitious drudgery of the home. Many believed that she had no right to venture into male territory. Maggie knew that was not true. Her brain functioned as well as any man's and so she was determined to do her very best. Besides, she wanted to make Eli proud. And more importantly, Maggie wanted to prove to the world (and to herself) that she could write.

The courthouse balcony, the only place where women were permitted to sit, was crowded with curiosity-seekers, so Maggie was privy to much talk. Mr. Madison was such a handsome man, the female voices were commenting, not to mention a man of God. What would cause him to kill his wife? It was all too horrible to think about, they whispered. And yet, they were obviously still thinking and talking about it. There was a strange tension beneath their commentary. Many of the women knew Jeremiah. Some had even gone to him for counsel. To be plain, the scandal was giving them a thrill. They had allowed themselves to be in the same room with and had bared their souls to someone who had committed an act of utter evil. The knowledge that danger lived in the midst of their mundane routines – and indeed had touched their very lives – was terribly exciting. Although shocked, these women also were all a-tingle. We human beings are a curious lot, Maggie reflected.

And so, they sat waiting for the judge to emerge. Carrie stirred at length and asked, "Do you really think they'll find him guilty?"

Maggie paused before answering, "Well, Mr. Madison has *confessed* to the crime."

"But is there any real proof?"

"I'm not sure." She was curious about the girl's question. Did Carrie still care for him? Did she feel remorse at reporting their affair? "Certainly no one saw him poison Leah. The only evidence we have is the arsenic discovered in his chambers. And, Carrie, you're going to be on the witness stand. When they question you, you'll be asked about your relationship with him. That very relationship amounts to a motive."

"Yes, I know," she replied, face unreadable.

"Moreover, the prosecution's strongest argument is built on the fact that Mr. Madison has confessed. And it's precisely because of that confession that I don't really hold out much hope for him. If he admits to the murder, what more can be said?"

"Couldn't he change his story?"

An unusual question, Maggie thought. "Yes, I suppose he could. He also could plead insanity. Or he could say that Leah took her own life."

The girl considered this, but then said rather quickly. "No. I don't believe he would do that."

"Why do you say that?"

Carrie's face was framed by a drab, brown bonnet, which hid her shiny blond hair. Still, Maggie thought, she is a striking young woman. No wonder Jeremiah turned to her when Leah proved to be so difficult.

"I don't know," the girl replied, almond-shaped eyes so green and innocent that Maggie couldn't tell what she was really feeling. There was something about her, though, that was beyond simple privacy – something that was self-contained and almost hidden. "It's just the way I feel."

Maggie realized that Eli was rubbing off on her, for suddenly she sensed that there was more – much, much more. "Carrie, is there something that you haven't told us? Is there something that we need to know?"

Lydia nudged her. "Mama! Don't be rude." Smiling, she whispered, "Do consider Carrie's feelings. She was, after all, good friends with Mr. Madison."

Maggie knew that only too well. But the chance that the little maid might have seen something was raising her curiosity. "I am only questioning her because Carrie could be either helpful or detrimental to Mr. Madison's case. For instance," she turned and addressed the girl once more, "you helped him care for Leah when she took ill. Did you notice anything unusual about his demeanor, or see anything unusual in the room that might lead you to believe that he poisoned his wife?"

"Oh, no, ma'am. If anything, he seemed most upset at her illness. And I saw no bottle or package that was not there before Mrs. Madison became ill." She dropped her eyes demurely. "I know that he was unhappy with her, but I find it hard to believe that he poisoned her. He was always such a kind and gentle man. But if he says he killed her, then it must be so." She raised her eyes and looked down at the judge's bench rather than returning Maggie's gaze. As Carrie watched the activity on the floor below, she added, "After all, why would a man of God lie about a thing like that?"

****

The trial was messy. The details of Jeremiah Madison's courtship with Leah Beatty were laid bare for all to see. Letters that had been exchanged in private by the couple were now read aloud in public. Jeremiah's initial warmth, then coldness toward Leah, and Leah's begging and threatening, and her pregnancy before the wedding, all became a matter of public record. Their equally unhappy marriage was also lifted up through the voices of those who had witnessed the couple's tiffs and those who had been subject to Leah's never-ending complaints and tantrums.

And, of course, everyone all had their turn on the witness stand. Samuel described Leah's emotions of misery, anger, and melancholy during her short marriage. Dr. Lightner testified that the cause of Leah's death had been changed from gastric fever to poisoning upon the discovery of arsenic in the contents of the deceased's stomach. Maggie described her own brush with death, which occurred after drinking tea laced with poison. She told of the night that she had witnessed the couple's argument and of the day that Leah and Frankie had nearly came to blows, as well as the fact that she had been Jeremiah's confidante with regard to his marriage troubles. Sheriff Miller took the stand to report that a vial of arsenic had been discovered in the minister's escritoire on the same day that he had disappeared. Carrie, with blushes and humility, admitted that she had a dalliance with Jeremiah, but that he also appeared to care for his wife.

As she had done with Maggie, she told the jury that she had seen nothing suspicious in the Madisons' chamber, even though he had told her that he would "fix things" so that they could be together. Her green eyes filled with tears as she said, "But Mr. Madison is incapable of such a foul act as murder. It is so outside his character."

The most compelling testimony of all came from Jeremiah Madison himself. He plainly, and without apology, stated that he had poisoned Leah over the course of three weeks by putting arsenic in the sugar for her tea. When the prosecutor asked him where he had purchased the arsenic, Jeremiah readily replied that it was at Quinton's Pharmacy in Easton, Pennsylvania. He had told the proprietor of the shop that he was purchasing the poison to kill an infestation of rats in a woodpile. "I do not know why they do not remember me. As for the blond-haired woman well, many people buy arsenic as rat poison," here his voice softened, "but I did not intend to use it that way. I truly believed that there was no future for either Leah or myself. I intended to take my own life, too, but when Leah died, I am ashamed to say that I lost my nerve."

A week later, the prosecution and defense made their summations – hours-long exercises of dazzling oratory designed to sway the jury. The defense reminded his listeners that, despite Jeremiah's confession, all the evidence was circumstantial. He suggested that Jeremiah was unstable. Indeed, the minister had admitted to wanting to take his own life. Furthermore, Leah had also been mired in a state of melancholy and thus it was still possible that she may have committed suicide. "Do not condemn this poor boy," the defense warned, "unless there is no reasonable doubt in your mind that he is guilty. Otherwise, you will be committing a grave miscarriage of justice."

The prosecution, however, went straight for the throat, saying that Jeremiah was not a "poor boy," but a stranger and an interloper in the Blaineton community. The evidence all added up: a forced and unhappy marriage, an illicit affair, poisoned sugar, a vial of arsenic, Leah's autopsy, Jeremiah's disappearance, and finally Jeremiah's own admission of guilt. "This is not a poor boy," the prosecution boomed, "but a monster of the worst sort, a wolf among the lambs, a beast of no discernable conscience or sensibility, who pretended to be a man of the cloth. Gentlemen of the jury, can you afford *not* to bring back a verdict of guilty?"

And thus on January 14 the trial came to an end.

CHAPTER TEN

From Maggie's Journal, 15 January 1861

The jury deliberated for a mere hour before returning today and finding Jeremiah guilty. Judge Talbot then sentenced him to be executed by hanging on Monday, March 25th. I do not know what to think or how to feel anymore. There is a flatness to my senses, as if I have felt and thought too much by far.

Eli's treatment of the trial and sentencing has been moderated by his new understanding of and by his familiarity (I dare not call it "friendship") with Jeremiah. However, other papers like the *New-York Times* are not nearly so kind, and even the *Easton Express* has joined the crowd. To them, Jeremiah is a monster, plain and simple. They invariably portray him as a smooth-talking confidence man who managed to dupe an entire congregation, a whole town, and the Newark Conference of the Methodist Episcopal Church. The fact that a few people dare visit this vile excuse for a human being to offer him comfort is roundly ridiculed as religious sentimentalism. And woe to those, such as myself, who are intimately connected to the murder victim and yet dare to offer the prisoner succor! My activities, and the activities of those in the rooming house, are viewed with disbelief and suspicion. A very dark, powerful magic is afoot, the papers imply. To follow their logic, Jeremiah Madison is able to work his monstrous wizardry even behind bars. Personally, I feel neither stupid, nor duped, nor bewitched – and the newspaper articles irk me to no end. Eli reminds me that the comments are merely opinions and that their writers have a right to voice them. "Of course," he adds "those writers are complete asses." And this makes me laugh.

****

The one bright spot for Maggie was February 10 when Emily Johnson went into labor late that evening. Eli stayed with Nate in the back parlor while Sister Brady, the midwife from the Water Street community, attended Emily. Lydia and Maggie also helped out. Around six on the morning of February 11, Maggie hurried downstairs to fetch hot water. Hearing her footsteps, Eli sleepily emerged from the back parlor and followed his wife into the kitchen. "How is she?"

"Pushing," Maggie replied as she wrapped a towel around the hot handle of the kettle so she could lift it from the stove. "Not much longer, I should think."

Eli exhaled tiredly. "Nate's a wreck."

"Tell him that she's handling it very well." She gave her husband a smile. "Emily is a strong woman."

He nodded, but didn't look convinced.

Maggie gently laid a hand on his arm. "Eli, we both know childbirth is painful and dangerous, but most women make it through. Things are progressing normally. Don't worry."

"All right, if you say so." He reached for the kettle. "Here, let me take that for you. It's heavy."

The two climbed the stairs to the second story of the new wing. As they drew near they could hear Emily crying out as she pushed. Eli winced, passed the kettle to Maggie, and hurried away.

Men, she thought. They talk eagerly of war, but cannot stand the thought of childbirth.

As she entered, she saw that Sister Brady had Emily squatting over layers of towels laid on the middle of the floor. Lydia was behind Emily giving her both physical and emotional support. Maggie paused in surprise but Lydia explained, "Sister Brady says it's supposed to help. Gravity pulls the baby out."

The midwife was right. Within a few pushes, a squalling newborn slid into the world and Emily collapsed back against Lydia. Sister Brady passed the slippery, howling infant to Emily, who scooped the baby up and wailed in gratitude. As soon as the umbilical cord was cut, Maggie helped Emily back to the bed, while Sister Brady took care of cleaning the baby and Lydia found a clean nightgown for the new mother.

It was a boy, sturdy and healthy, and as the midwife laid the swaddled infant in Emily's arms, the other women finally gave into relieved smiles and joyful tears.

Looking into Emily's glowing face and touching the baby's silky skin moved Maggie. She always had despised the notion of war – and could not comprehend why people had to resort to violence in order to solve disputes. But as she looked upon the small, hiccupping bundle in Emily's arms, every part of her mind and heart knew that he had indeed been born a free human being. And Maggie knew without question that she would struggle to preserve his rights. If she had to, she would even *fight* for it. To her amazement, she also realized that when the time came she would find a way to help with the war effort, because the Johnson baby needed all the advocates he could get.

"Oh, he's so beautiful," she said, brushing the tears from her cheeks.

Emily's face was beatific. "He *is* beautiful, isn't he? Maggie, I'd like you to meet Nathaniel Elijah Johnson."

The baby began to fuss and Emily cuddled him. When he quieted down, she whispered, "He's named after two good men. He can't go wrong."

Maggie nodded, kissed her friend on the cheek, and went to fetch Nate.

****

From Maggie's Journal, 20 March 1861

It seems as if the End of Time inches toward us. God remains silent – except in the gurgles and coos of little Natey. Otherwise, though, all is upheaval. We have a new President, Mr. Abraham Lincoln. Scant weeks after he took office the Southern states, which now call themselves the Confederate States of America, adopted a constitution of their own. This constitution sends ice through my veins, for it forbids the passage of any law that would weaken the institution of slavery.

I had had hopes that the Peace Convention in Washington, D.C. would bring the nation back together again, but it failed miserably. And so we have President Abraham Lincoln here in the North, and President Jefferson Davis who represents the C.S.A. Our country has been completely rent in two.

All that remains is to commence the shooting. Oh, Journal, when that happens, we cannot fail! We cannot! The insidious plague of slavery must be ended. When I look into little Natey's eyes, I see God's child, perfect and equal to me and to every other human being. I know the C.S.A. claims that their grievance is over the right of states to determine their own policy – but slavery rises about states' rights. It is about living, breathing, feeling human beings – God's children, all. And so I tremble at the idea that we might not prevail.

The lamp of my soul grows darker still as we approach Jeremiah Madison's execution. Today, when Frankie and I visited, he asked if we would pray with him just before they took him from his cell. He begged us not to watch the execution, for it is not something that ladies should see, he explained and then added that he had caused us enough distress and did not wish to bring us any more.

I do not know if I can bear the next few days. I do not have the strength to withstand the grief and fear. Oh, my God, where are you? Why do you not speak to me? Why do you not comfort me? My soul suffers so. Sweet Jesus, you know what it is like to suffer anguish. Will you not intercede for me? Hear my prayer. I beg of you.

****

The hanging would be in the jail yard. Public executions were illegal in New Jersey. Some members of Blaineton actually had offered to pay the fine involved so that the public could watch, but the judge held firm and issued tickets to only 50 observers. Eli had one of those tickets, as did Mr. Carson. Nonetheless, there were large numbers of people pining to watch Jeremiah Madison receive justice. The competition was fierce and rumor had it that some tickets – which had been distributed free of charge – were now being sold to the curious for obscenely high prices.

A few days before the hanging, people began to come into Blaineton. Maggie watched from the front parlor windows of the rooming house as waves of folks walked in from the train station, drove in carriages, and rode on horseback. Carrie was busy all day answering the door. Those desperate for accommodation went from house to house begging for a room or even a modest pallet on a parlor floor – and were willing to pay handsomely for the privilege.

A few weeks earlier, Eli had been contacted by two acquaintances of his from the *Times*. At first he resisted, protective of the rooming house family but also, Maggie suspected, protective of the story that he planned to write. In the end, though, journalistic brotherhood carried the day. After some discussion with Maggie, Eli told the duo that they could occupy Jeremiah Madison's former room. The reporters were thrilled to be in the very chamber that the murderer had used. Having them in that location meant Eli could keep an eye on them from the room he shared with Maggie across the hall. However, before his colleagues moved in, Jeremiah's belongings needed to be safeguarded – reporters after all were an inquisitive lot and, according to Eli, had no qualms about ransacking a room to flesh out their story. He also wanted to avoid any other unfortunate occurrences, such as having Jeremiah's personal effects suddenly become souvenir items for sale on the Blainteon green. So before the visitors arrived, Eli, Maggie, and Nate packed up all of Jeremiah's things and hid them for the duration on the second floor of the new wing behind the storage room's locked door.

The morning before his fellow reporters arrived, Eli gave his family a final piece of advice. "I'm a newspaperman, and I know from whence I speak. We'll stop at nothing for a story. So be careful what you say to whom. If my friends want to talk to you – and they will – don't do it unless I'm around." Maggie knew the advice was for their protection, but part of her also wondered if Eli was ensuring that if any paper got a scoop, it was going to the *Gazette*.

A few hours later, she, Eli, and Frankie threaded their way through the throng in the square and presented themselves at the entrance to the jail. By now, the jailer was nearly on first-name terms with them and readily let them in, much to the disgust of the strangers milling around the courthouse and hoping to get a peek at the murdering minister.

The visit this day was awkward. It had grown more so as the execution grew near. But Maggie did her best to appear upbeat. Not surprisingly, Jeremiah wanted to spend most of their time in prayer, and they all complied.

But as they were preparing to leave, a visitor unexpectedly appeared at the door to the cell.

Jeremiah staggered to his feet. "Miss Hillsborough! How good of you to visit."

"I've come to say goodbye, Mr. Madison."

****

From Maggie's Journal, 22 March 1861

Journal, her voice was so stiff, so icy and dismissive that it was stunning. I had seen their passionate embrace in the kitchen. I had heard her tell of her affection for him. One would expect her at least to show a bit of melancholy or distress – after all she was saying farewell to a lover. But she was neither of those things.

I am not a sentimental fool. I know what Jeremiah had done to her. He had betrayed her as surely as he had betrayed us all. Anger and confusion were appropriate three months ago, but not now. And so I wonder if Carrie still mired in those feelings. I had truly believed that she had forgiven him. During our evening prayers, she has given every indication that this is so.

However, perhaps all do not act the same when presented with sorrow. Perhaps it is easier for Carrie to remove herself from the event that will soon happen, rather than experience deep sympathy and grief.

Eli, Frankie, and I rose and excused ourselves from their presence. As we left, I looked back at them. Jeremiah was standing rather awkwardly before Carrie, whose face had gone hard and cold. It was such a very strange tableau, one that simply did not look right.

****

On their walk back, they found that some curiosity-seekers had gathered near the boarding house. As Maggie, Eli, and Frankie passed by, the strangers pointed and began to make comments that could easily be overheard.

"That's the house. That's where he lived, and those are the ones who lived with him."

"Do you suppose that's Mrs. Smith, the one whom he poisoned first?"

"I understand that they have left the Methodist Episcopal Church here."

"No! Whatever would possess them to do that?"

"Well, they *are* strange folk. Mr. Smith is a free-thinker. And Mrs. Smith, well, let me tell you that there are stories about *her*."

"Do you know the youngest daughter actually preached at a camp meeting last summer?"

Maggie had just started to climb the porch steps when a man suddenly called, "Can we come in and look at Madison's room? We'll pay!"

That was more than Frankie could bear. Wheeling about, she faced the crowd with surprising ferocity. "Of course not! This is our *home*! Why don't you rude people just go back to your *own* homes, where you belong?"

Eli immediately took her arm, steered her up the steps, and pulled her onto the porch. "I think it's time for *you* to go home, my dear."

"They've been doing this for two days," she grumbled. "I don't like rude people."

"Oh, so you're rude back to them. Good thinking. You know, if you weren't so doggone big, I'd turn you over my knee." With that, he propelled her through the front door.

"But Papa . . ." she whined.

Eli stopped cold in his tracks. "Papa?"

Maggie smiled at him and shrugged.

"Don't that beat all," he mused, and grinning like a fool, he turned to the onlookers. "Hey! My step-daughter just called me Papa!" After a bit of thought, he added, "You know what? My step-daughter is right. You *are* rude. You're no better than vultures. Get out of here! And leave my family alone!"

Of course, they did no such thing. Near evening, Maggie found herself wading through the ever-growing mob once more. Edgar Lape had arrived a few minutes earlier with a message from Jeremiah Madison that simply said, "I must see you at once." As Eli was busy with his *Times* friends, Maggie threw on a cloak and went out.

The sun had not yet set, but the air was quite chill, as it could be in March. She ignored the nattering voices around her and pushed her way to the door of the jail. The jailer greeted her like the old friend she was becoming and in a few minutes she sat across from Jeremiah at the small table in his cell.

"I have some letters here for you and the others," he said and passed four small packets to her. Then he leaned in toward her and, as if he were afraid that others would hear, whispered, "Maggie, I cannot die without you understanding the truth of my situation."

She forced herself to look calm.

"You're convinced that Leah took her own life, are you not?"

"Yes. She bought the arsenic. It is clear to me that she wished to kill herself."

"That simply is not true."

Maggie opened her mouth, ready to ask a thousand questions, but he held up his hand. "What I have said all along is God's truth. I murdered her. But there is more, and that is why I wrote the letters." He laid his hand over hers. Maggie noted that it was cold, as if he already were dead. "Do not open these 'til after my death. I do not want you trying to forestall the execution. I have sinned and deserve the punishment determined by my peers. I am not afraid. I've asked forgiveness of God and he has granted it. Of that I am sure."

She grasped his hand tightly in hers. "Jeremiah, please, if there's something we can do, then we ought to take action."

He shook his head. "There is nothing, dear friend. My letter will explain all." Before she could stop him, the young man turned to the cell door and called, "Guard! Mrs. Smith is ready to leave."

****

Maggie fretted all through dinner and scarcely slept that night. Should she do as Jeremiah said and withhold the letters until after his death, or should she give everyone the letters now, when perhaps something else might be done? She was obviously distracted the next morning, and fumbled plates and cups one time too many for Emily's taste, who suddenly shoved a basket into her arms and told her to take it to their new visitors in the secret room. "Make sure they get their breakfast and these new things to wear."

Maggie was glad for the distraction. Clutching the basket, she hurried across the yard to the *Gazette*. The escaped slaves were called Matilda and Chloe, a mother and daughter respectively. In the confusion that dominated the run-up to the war, they had somehow managed to find their way North. Maggie listened to their story as they ate, but her mind was still on the letters. Finally, she made a decision. Her friends and family would each decide what to do with the letter addressed to him or her.

And so she returned to the boarding house and gathered Nate, Emily, Lydia, Edgar, Frankie, and Eli in the back parlor. The letters had been safely stowed in the pocket of her apron. Maggie took them out, briefly glanced at the packets clutched in her hands, and then cleared her throat. "I brought you here because you must decide something. Yesterday Jeremiah gave me these to give to you." She handed them out: one for Frankie, one for Lydia and Edgar, one for Nate and Emily, and one for her. "However, he said we should not open them until after the execution."

Eli frowned. "Why?"

"He indicated that the contents would reveal extra information."

Edgar sat up. "Indeed?"

"Well, let's open them!" were Eli's next words.

Maggie was torn. "The trouble is that Jeremiah said not to. This is his last request. We cannot deny him that, can we?"

All eyes turned to Edgar. "Well, it was only a verbal request, nothing in writing and if there is something pertinent to the trial in them, then – "

"They may be opened!" Eli finished.

"Yes, yes, I believe that they may."

Maggie took a deep breath. "Then each of us may choose to open or hold our letter."

Frankie, who was seated on a sofa next to Eli, immediately broke the seal on hers and began to read, but her eyes quickly teared up. Eli put a protective arm round her shoulders and murmured, "It's all right. Tell us what the letter's about."

She sniffed, messily wiping her face and nose with a hand. "He – he left me all his books on theology."

Eli kissed the side of her head.

Lydia looked up from her note. "He gave us the pictures from his room."

"Did he hear us discussing how we wanted paintings for our chamber?" Edgar asked.

Lydia shrugged, and smiled. But when she looked back down at the letter, she frowned. "There is no other information here, aside from a prayer and a blessing."

Nate broke the wax seal on his packet and opened it. As he read, a stunned expression came over his face. "He had a little money. He says what's left after his burial is ours to do with as we please."

"I think it should go to our church," Emily immediately said.

"None of these letters have to do with the case," Edgar observed. "These are bequests. Why would he want to wait 'til after his death?"

"There is one more letter, remember." With that, Eli glanced at Maggie.

She sighed. "All right, I'll open it." She broke the seal, and as she did so, it seemed to make a deafening crack, much like a rifle shot. Even the crackle as she unfolded the paper filled the room. After a moment, she began to read:

My dear Maggie,

Although I am now gone from this earth, I must make one final confession. As you know, my marriage to Leah was difficult. There was little in it in the way of comfort or cheer. However, that is barely an excuse. I sinned against my poor wife – I sought out and found solace in the arms of a paramour, Carrie Hillsborough.

After a particularly alarming argument with Leah, in which she sprang at me and began striking me, I shared my heartbreak over our failing marriage with Carrie, and unknowingly lifted the lid to a Pandora's Box. I told her that I feared I would be living in misery forever, as divorce would likely cause me to lose my ordination, but I could no longer bear being married to Leah. I was in deep despair at this time.

Carrie asked me if I wished to be free again. I said I did. She then confided that Leah was dreadfully unhappy too. In fact, my wife had said that she wished to die. Carrie informed me that a day earlier she had caught Leah with a knife and, after she had taken it from her, Leah burst into tears, sobbing that she had intended to use it to slit her wrists. Leah does not wish to live, Carrie assured me. Her life is a misery.

Maggie, what she suggested next appalled me. Carrie said that there were ways of handling such a sad situation. If done over time, she said, arsenic poisoning is rather gentle and would give my poor wife the peace she so deeply desired.

Maggie shuddered.

"Oh, my God," said Eli. "Carrie?"
"Read on!" Edgar urged.
Maggie, hands cold, looked back down at the page.

I told Carrie that those were wicked thoughts. She was adamant that they were not; claiming that if a person truly wishes to die, to be out of her misery, then why not help her? "Do you wish to be free and happy once more?" she asked. "I know that Leah wishes to be free. You would be doing no wrong, believe me. It is only a matter of time before your wife will try to take her life once more. Should she succeed, the scandal would be terrible. To allow Leah to slip quietly from this world would be best for all concerned."

I do not know why I agreed. I knew that it was wrong; but Carrie made it sound so reasonable, even kind. I knew that Leah was disturbed and sinking ever deeper into melancholy and irrational behavior. If she no longer had a desire to live, then she would indeed eventually take her own life.

And so Carrie was the one who went to Quinton's and bought the arsenic.

Maggie stopped reading and looked up. "She was the girl with blonde hair."

"Why didn't we think of that?" Eli muttered.

"Carrie was always so helpful, that's why," Emily said. "She seemed like such a nice girl."

Nate shook his head. "Looks like 'seemed' is a long way from 'was.'"

Maggie returned to the letter:

And so we began to put arsenic in the sugar, which Leah liked to take with her tea. But as my wife gradually began to sicken, I came to my senses. The arsenic was giving her pain and making her vomit. It was not gentle at all. Of course, I knew nothing of the effects of arsenic and thus was shocked. I told Carrie that we must stop, and that we must allow Leah to become well. Carrie was all sweetness, saying that she would do as I requested. But that very day, she put a large dose of arsenic in the sugar, and that was the day that you became ill, my dear Maggie.

When I learned of your illness, I confronted Carrie and warned her to stop. When we learned that you had seen us embracing in the kitchen, I became quite fearful, lest the doctor discover the true cause of your illness. But Carrie was ready for my fears, telling me that we must finish what we had started. If Leah received a final, strong dose of arsenic, the doctor would suspect that she had caught gastric fever, too, and all would be well. I was so frightened and confused that I agreed. For this may the Lord have mercy on my miserable soul!

When you discovered poison had made you ill, Maggie, and when I learned that Leah's body would be exhumed, I did not know what to do. By the time the truth came out about Leah, I was beside myself. That is why I ran away. I knew I would be arrested and wished to escape the hangman's noose. Carrie originally had possession of the vial of arsenic, but as soon as I left, she must have placed the vial in my writing desk for Sheriff Miller to find.

But thanks be to God, even as I wandered confused and fearful, my Lord would not let me escape but sent me home to confess my sin, receive the consequences for it, and be forgiven.

After I was arrested, Carrie came to me, apologized, and pleaded with me not to tell anyone of her involvement in the crime. She admitted that she was terrified of hanging, and that she was deeply sorry for what she had done. And then she told me something else. She said she was going to have a child, my child. That sealed my decision. An innocent life was involved now. I would take the punishment and leave her out of it. Carrie could repent and begin a new life.

But earlier today, when she came to me, something shocking happened. "You would not be here now if you had not tried to stop our progress," she told me. I explained that Leah was in pain and it frightened me. Her next words dripped of cruelty, "You are such a coward! I'm glad you are going to hang." I murmured that I too was glad I was going to the scaffold, for then I would be out of this world and with my Lord. My only regret was that I would not live to see our child born. At this, Carrie threw her head back and laughed. "Oh, you really are a fool! There is no child. There never was." I cannot adequately put into words the condition of the smile on her face, save to say that it was purely of the Devil. "Instead, I shall sell my sad tale to a book publisher and earn a little money. Perhaps I shall even undertake a speaking tour – how I was seduced by the murdering minister. Everyone will want to hear that. And then I shall be rich!'

I was stunned, and asked if she felt no remorse whatsoever for Leah's death or for your illness, Maggie. Carrie laughed again at me. "If you think that you're atoning for your sins and justifying yourself with God, then you are even a bigger fool than I thought. God pays no attention at all to what we do. We're on our own. The only difference

between you and me, Jeremiah, is that I know the truth."
And then, with a perfectly wicked smile, she bid me
farewell and left.

The pit of Maggie's stomach was cold and roiling, but
she forced herself to read the final sentences.

Carrie must be brought to justice, dear Maggie. You will
find, hidden in my Bible, a note from her written shortly after
she proposed poisoning Leah. In it, she once again assures me
that killing Leah would be a kind thing to do. Between that and
this letter, you should have enough evidence to convict her.
God bless you and Eli. I hope your lives henceforth
will be happy and trouble free.

Yours in Christ,
Jeremiah Madison.

A moment's silence fell upon the room.
And then suddenly everyone leapt up, charged into the new wing,
and trampled upstairs. Nate got to the door of the store room first.
"Key, key!" he shouted.
Maggie searched her apron pocket, found what he needed, and
slapped it into his waiting hand.
The door was open in the wink of an eye. Nate, Eli, and Edgar
pressed into the little room, squeezing themselves among crates, old
furniture, and sundries.
"Found it!" Eli cried. In the next second, he was passing the
wooden box that held Jeremiah's books to Nate and Edgar. The two
brought the box into the hall, set it down and literally pulled every
tome out of it. The Bible, of course, was on the very bottom. Edgar
handed the book to Eli who, in an act made Maggie gasp, held the
sacred text up by the spine and gave it a shake. A loose page fell out
and fluttered to the floor. Nate was the first one on the paper. He
squinted at it for a second, and then whistled. "*Dang*. This thing is
detailed! She even tells him where they can buy the arsenic!"
Eli took the letter from him and scanned it. "Why, the stinking,
lying little bi –"
"Elijah!" Maggie warned.

"*Witch*," he corrected. "I was going to say, stinking, lying little *witch*. She pretended to be helpful, but was really a cold-blooded killer, a reptile!"

He passed the letter to Maggie, who read it next and blanched. "She speaks of killing Leah as if she were going to put down an old horse."

Frankie shivered. "I don't believe I've been sharing a bed with her."

"Don't worry," Eli assured her. "That's over."

At this point, Nate cleared his throat. "Folks, I know we're all shocked, but don't you think we ought to go find this girl?" They stared blankly at him until he added, "*Now?*"

With that, they scattered and began to search the new wing. Carrie was nowhere to be found there. As one, they charged into the kitchen and down into the cellar, but no luck. As the whole tribe pounded back upstairs and down the hall toward the parlors they nearly collided with Patrick McCoy.

"What's going on?" the boy asked. "Why's everyone running? I mean, Carrie just tore out the door like the devil was after her."

Not bothering to answer, Eli plowed past the boy, all but knocking him over, and slammed out the front door. The rest of the group caught up with him on the porch, and together strained their eyes as they tried to spot Carrie among the throngs of people in the green. But it was no use.

Maggie threw up her hands. "She's gone."

"Damn, damn, damn, and *damn!*"

She turned to her husband. "Eli, please watch your language. I'll put up with it when we're alone, but I won't have you swearing in public."

He gestured irritably at the noisy crowd. "Maggie, how're we supposed to find her in all *that?*"

"We aren't. That's why she ran out here."

Nate put his hands on his hips as he stared at the mass of humanity. "Guess we'd better report this to Sheriff Miller."

"I'll go with you," Frankie offered. "I sure don't want her back in my room anytime soon – or ever."

The two jogged into the green, forgetting even to take their coats, despite the chill day. The remaining rooming house family heaved a communal sigh and returned inside where they met up with a very confused Patrick. "What's going on?" he was asking. "Why are you getting the sheriff? Has Carrie done something wrong?"

"Maybe," Eli snorted. "Does murder count as 'something wrong'?'"

Patrick's naturally pale skin went several shades paler.

"Mr. Madison was not the only one who poisoned Leah," Maggie explained. "It was Carrie's idea, and she administered the final, lethal dose."

"Oh, my," the boy gasped. "How – I mean, why – I mean, what –"

Lydia took Patrick by the arm. "It's a very long story. I'll tell it to you over tea."

Edgar said, "I'd best get to the office. May I have the letter and the note? We will need this as evidence, once we find Carrie."

Maggie passed both items to Edgar, who gave Lydia a quick kiss and walked toward the door.

"Wait!"Lydia called. "Your coat! You'll catch cold."

"I'll be all right," he replied over his shoulder and was gone.

Emily sighed and shifted Natey onto her shoulder. "Guess we still got some pots to scrub."

Lydia moaned. "How I hate porridge! It leaves such a mess."

As they started down the hall toward the kitchen, Patrick followed them, saying, "I'm coming with you. If there's a murderess on the loose, you'll need a man to protect you."

"Good," Emily replied, "you can help with that porridge pot."

That left Eli and Maggie alone in the hall. Outside the crowd was talking and laughing. Both of them were numbed and tired.

Eli finally removed his glasses and rubbed his eyes. "I don't believe this." Replacing his spectacles, he heaved a sigh. "Maggie, this is the most God-awful mess I've ever heard of."

She nodded wearily.

"But it's positively, and without a doubt, the best *story* I've ever heard of."

Her mouth fell open.

"I've got to get something written and printed before the rest of the reporters around here get wind of this."

Maggie's was still speechless.

Eli frowned defensively at her. "Hey, I *am* a newspaperman, you know! A good story's a good story. And this is one heck of a scoop." He took her hand. "Come on. I'll need your help."

She barely had a chance to grab a shawl on the way out the kitchen door. Eli pulled her down the back porch steps and dragged her through the backyard. "Are you mad?" she gasped. "Jeremiah will be executed tomorrow at noon. Carrie's at large somewhere. And you want to get your silly paper out?"

Her words made him stop dead in his tracks. "Margaret Ann Beatty Blaine Smith, it's not a silly paper. It's a very respectable penny weekly. And that's precisely the trouble. It's *respectable*. I seldom get to write a story with any real drama. I've covered I don't know how many church fairs, weddings, funerals, and minor trials. I've even written about livestock sales 'til I thought I'd puke. But *this* – *this*, my dear woman, is journalism. And if I let this story slip through my fingers, I might as well retire to the back parlor and start darning socks 'cause I sure as hell won't be a newspaperman any longer."

"Oh," she said.

"So here's what we're going to do. We're going to write down everything we know. If they find Carrie today, we can add it in. If they don't find her today, then we'll go with the story as is and print a special edition later. But whatever happens, we're going set the type tonight. Understand?"

She nodded.

"Good." And he hauled her through the rest of the yard and up the three steps to his kitchen door.

But what they saw when they entered brought them come to a dead halt.

Carrie was standing between the kitchen and the work room. One arm was wrapped around the neck of Chloe, the slave girl, while her other hand was pointing a small revolver at the child's head. Matilda, her mother, was on her knees pleading for her baby's life.

"What the –" Eli sputtered and then said, "Carrie!"

The young woman looked at the two newcomers and smiled. "Welcome. I found your little secret."

Matilda turned pleadingly toward Eli. "Please, mister! Please! My baby! Help my girl!"

"Shut up!" Carrie snarled.

Eli looked from the woman to the child and then to Carrie. "Let her go."

"Why? Slave hunters are looking for her. I might get some money out of this."

"There are no slave hunters up here anymore, so that little girl is no use to you."

"You're right." With that, Carrie released Chloe, who scrambled away and into her sobbing mother's arms. The maid now aimed the pistol at Eli. "This is much better."

While her husband tried to reason with Carrie, Maggie noticed that the escaped slaves had backed their way to the kitchen door. She quickly whispered to Matilda, "You must leave now. Never mind us. Go hide!"

The woman looked at her in bewilderment.

"We'll be all right," Maggie insisted. "Go. *Now.*"

"Yes'm, yes'm," the woman replied and, clutching her daughter, slipped away.

"So," Carrie was saying, "abolitionists, part of the – what is it called? The railroad?"

"The *Underground* Railroad," Eli corrected. He nodded at the gun. "Where'd you get that thing?"

"A gentleman friend gave it to me for protection."

Maggie mutely stood by, watching as her husband calmly said, "Look, Carrie, I don't have any weapons on me. Neither does Maggie. You don't need to use that."

"Yes, I do need to use it. And don't think I won't. I've done it before." She leveled the weapon at his heart. "I was born in the Five Points. I don't remember my father, and my mother and two brothers died of the cholera when I was eleven years old, so I had to make my own way. It's surprising how many men like eleven year old girls, but I learned it paid well. And when the men got troublesome – and they always do – I learned how to use arsenic, as well as a pistol."

Eli kept his voice level and reasonable. "Come on, Carrie. This isn't the Five Points. Put the gun down."

She corrected her aim. "I'm not about to go to prison and hang like Jeremiah. I thought my chance had finally arrived when I met him. I struggled to get ahead all my life, but I was always beaten out by rich girls. That's the way it always is, isn't it? The rich get their way, and the poor get poorer. Well, this time I wanted to change the ending of the story. Too bad you got in the way." She glared at Maggie. "Think it was an accident I left that bowl full of poisoned sugar in the kitchen? I knew you saw us. It might have worked nicely, but you didn't have enough sense to die. And then you had to ask questions about what you saw, and you had to check with Quinton's. If you'd just minded your own business, things would have been fine."

Eli took a step toward the girl. "Carrie, it's over. The sheriff knows what you did. Nate's telling him now. Please put the revolver down. I know you don't want to shoot anyone."

She raised her eyebrows, "Oh, no?" and pulled the trigger. The report rattled through the house.

Eli flinched and looked at his right arm. Blood was oozing out of his shoulder. Dumbfounded, he touched the wound and stared at the blood on his fingers. "My God –" he said. "Carrie, what are you –"

In rapid succession, she fired two more times, hitting him in the right side of the chest and in the left leg. Maggie heard the impact as the bullets tore into him. When he fell heavily to the floor, she immediately became unglued from her spot. Everything was swept from her mind – especially the fact that Carrie had a gun. She dropped down beside Eli. It took all her strength to wrestle him onto his back, but she managed it. Cradling his head on her lap, she whispered, "Eli?"

He blinked up at her. "Damn," he breathed. "She shot me . . . Maggie . . ." Then his eyes rolled back and he was quiet.

"No!" she cried. "Eli!" She shook him. "No! Don't you die! You can't die!" He was bleeding profusely. Horrified, Maggie tried to stop the flow of blood from his chest with one hand and the blood from his arm with the other. Dear God, she prayed, he can't die. Don't let him die. Suddenly she feared that he was already dead. Quickly putting a hand over his heart, she held her breath and felt for a beat. Some of the cold terror went away as she detected a rhythm against her palm. She exhaled in relief, but knew that she had to get help or he would be dead, and very soon. And then reality rushed in upon her – she could get no help until Carrie put the pistol down.

After gently easing Eli onto the floor, Maggie slowly stood up, her husband's blood wet and cooling on her dress and sticky on her hands.

Carrie had the revolver aimed at her.

"Where's your God, Mrs. Smith?" she taunted. "Go ahead. Ask him to save you."

"He's already saved me," Maggie heard herself say.

"And are you ready to die?"

"If I must."

Carrie glanced at Eli. "Is he dead?"

"Not yet."

"He will be soon. He's bleeding to death."

Maggie wanted to shriek and throw herself at the maid, tear her eyes out, rip her throat open. But she did none of that. All she said was, "I know."

Carrie frowned. "I *am* going to shoot you, you know. Just because you were kind to me doesn't mean I can't do what needs to be done."

"Is killing what needs to be done?"

She hesitated. "It's not because I don't like you. You're actually rather nice. But I couldn't have Jeremiah because of you. You know what really happened to Leah."

"More than a few folks know that, Carrie." Maggie was surprised at the words coming from her mouth.

"I know. I overheard you reading the letter."

"So tell me, how many other people do you intend to kill, then? First it was Leah. Then Eli. I'll be next. And after me, who else? The whole rooming house knows. You could shoot them. That's what? Ten people? And the sheriff knows, too. You can go to the courthouse and shoot him and Jeremiah's lawyer, too. So how many, Carrie? How many more?"

"Look, I don't *want* to kill anyone," the girl protested. "Not really. But it *has* to be done. It's the only way."

"The only way for what?"

The revolver began to tremble in Carrie's hand. She bit on her lip as tears filled her almond-shaped eyes, causing them to look nearly emerald in color.

"The only way for you to escape?" Maggie suggested.

"Yes." Her voice had a quaver to it.

"You don't need to escape. You need to give yourself up."

"I can't." Tears were flowing down her cheeks. "I don't want to hang. I won't *let* them hang me."

"How do you intend to stop them? Will you kill everyone who comes after you?"

"I don't know. If I have to."

Maggie could not believe that she was so calm. "Go ahead, then," she said. "Shoot me. My husband's bleeding to death on the floor. My heart's gone out of me. I no longer care if you shoot. I'm at peace with my Lord. But are you? Because eventually they'll find you and you'll still have to pay the price. You'll hang no matter what. You need forgiveness, not escape."

Carrie laughed amid her tears. "Oh, and who is going to forgive *me*?"

Maggie's next words surprised even herself. "I will."

The girl shook her head.

"I will. And if you ask, God will, too."

"God," she said among her sobs. "There is no God. And if there were, he wouldn't want *me*. I'm lost."

"No one's ever lost unless they want to be. There's someone who knows *exactly* where you are. God really does care what happens to you, Carrie. He loves you. He wants you to come home to him because you're his beloved child. He wants to hold you close. Let him, Carrie. Let him do this one thing. Stop the killing. Please. No more killing."

The girl shook her head. "No."

"Oh, please. There is peace and real life waiting for you. Don't kill anymore."

"I'm sorry," she whispered and put the revolver to her head. "One more."

Maggie suddenly became herself again. "Carrie! Don't!"

The kitchen door banged open the same moment Carrie pulled the trigger. Maggie saw the bullet tear through the girl's skull and spatter blood, bone, and flesh onto the wall. Stunned, she fell to her knees as Carrie's body collapsed.

"There they are!" The voice belonged to Matilda. When the woman saw what had happened, she immediately covered her little girl's face with her apron and wailed, "Oh, Lord! Oh, Lord! Look!"

People were tumbling into the room. Maggie couldn't move. It was as if she were watching all the excitement but had no stake in the scene at all.

Lydia and Emily immediately took the situation in and knelt beside Eli. His face had gone ashen and he was lying terribly, terribly still. Lydia felt for a pulse, and heaved a sigh. "He's alive."

"Oh, thank you, Jesus," Emily prayed. "Thank you!"

Lydia ripped open Eli's shirt – and tore it into pieces. She wadded some of the material up and pressed it onto the chest wound. Emily reached for another piece and applied it to his shoulder. "We've got to stop this bleeding," Lydia was saying, as she looked up at the others. "Someone needs to come over here and help staunch his leg. And for pity's sake, someone go get Dr. Lightner!"

"Yes, ma'am!" Patrick blurted and sprinted out of the room.

Matilda whirled her daughter around and sent her toward the door. "Go out there and sit on the steps," she ordered. "I'll tell you when you can come back in." In the next instant, she was kneeling beside Lydia and Emily. "I'll take his leg." She tore a piece from her new skirt and pressed the wadded blue calico over the wound.

Meanwhile Frankie had just raced into the room. The girl took one look at her mother and gasped. "Lydia, Mama's covered in blood!"

"Have you been shot, too, Mama?" Lydia asked, as she pressed on Eli's chest.

"No," Maggie managed to say. "Eli's blood."

Edgar, who had been outside frantically working the pump, stumbled through the door with a bucket of water. Frankie scrambled to the dry sink, searched the drawers, and returned with a dish rag. She dipped it into the bucket left by Edgar, took Maggie's icy hands, and began to clean them. All the while, tears were rolling down her cheeks. Maggie, however, was unable to do anything but stare at her daughter in wonderment.

Nate and Sheriff Miller had entered by now and were standing over Carrie's body. "Can you tell me what happened, Maggie?" the sheriff asked.

"She shot Eli three times," she answered, feeling completely detached. "Then she shot herself. Carrie said she was afraid to hang. She didn't understand." Without warning, Maggie began to shiver fiercely.

Grandpa O'Reilly led her to a chair, sat her down, and then sat on a chair beside her. He wrapped a blanket round her shoulders. "We've got to get her warm, Frankie. She's shocked. Go get the bottle in the wood shed, and a glass." While the girl was gone, he hugged Maggie tightly. "It'll be all right, my daughter. We're with you now."

Maggie was amazed at the fuss he was making. I'm not upset in the least, she thought. I'm just cold.

When she looked up again, she saw Frankie pouring amber liquid into a glass. Grandpa took the glass from her and pushed the cold rim to Maggie's lips.

The smell of what was within made her recoil. "No. No whiskey!"

"*Drink it,*" Grandpa ordered and tipped the glass.

The whiskey tasted dreadful – it burned all the way down her throat and the fumes made her cough, but in the very next second, warmth began to seep from her stomach into her icy limbs.

Grandpa gave her another sip and smiled as she coughed. "There, there, my daughter. That's better," he cooed. He wrapped his bony arms about her. "There now, you'll come round soon."

Edgar and Mr. Carson were fashioning a stretcher out of a blanket and two poles. When it was done, Lydia, Matilda, and Emily stepped back and let the men shift Eli onto it and then carry him to the boarding house. Maggie followed the little procession as it hastened carefully along the backyard. She felt as if she were seeing everything in slow motion. The whole parade seemed to take forever. Finally they trundled Eli up the back steps, through the door and the kitchen and into his room, where they transferred him onto the bed.

Seconds later, Dr. Lightner hurried into the room. He put his medical case down on the chair beside the bed. With Lydia as his guide, he carefully observed Eli's wounds. He heaved a sigh, looked up, and said, "I'm going to need to dig those bullets out." He glanced at Lydia and Patrick. "I'd like you two to assist. Lydia, if you'll get some hot water so I may wash, I would be most grateful. Patrick, I'll need you to help me lay my instruments out, and I'd like you to administer the ether if Eli comes round. Don't worry, I'll tell you how to do it."

Maggie meanwhile had made her way to the bed and taken Eli's hand in hers. He moaned softly and opened his eyes a crack. "Oh, Eli, thank God," she whispered.

He took an unsteady breath and winced.

"Do you know where you are?"

"Our room?"

"Do you know what happened to you?"

"I was . . . shot."

"Three times."

"Shot three times," he repeated, as if he were trying to comprehend the situation. His lips were as pale as his face, his breathing a bit labored. He swallowed dryly. "Everything hurts."

"You took a bullet in the arm, the leg, and the chest," she told him. "Dr. Lightner is here. He is going to remove the bullets."

"Carrie." Eli turned his head ever so slightly in Maggie's direction. "She shoot you?"

"No."

"They get her?"

Maggie hesitated, and then told the truth. "She turned the gun on herself. She's dead."

"Dead." Suddenly, he seemed to rally. "The execution's tomorrow."

"Yes." Maggie lifted his hand and kissed it. "But please don't think about any of that right now."

He frowned. "But the story . . ."

"Forget being a newspaperman. You're injured. You need to rest."

He pretended that he didn't hear her. "Carson needs to interview you. Help him write the story about Carrie, set the type, do the printing."

"Elijah . . ."

"It's a *scoop*." She could tell that he was beginning to weaken. "A big one. Best I ever had. Got to beat those snobs at the *Times*." His voice grew faint. "Take my ticket, Maggie. Go to the execution with Carson. Write that story. Special edition."

The execution – she doubted if she could stand watching it, but the expression on Eli's face melted her heart. "All right," she said, and wondered where she would find the strength.

With that, Eli sighed and fell back into unconsciousness.

"We're about ready to begin," Dr. Lightner gently told her. "Why don't you wait in the kitchen?"

"Will he be all right?"

"I'll do my best," he replied. "We all will."

Emily took Maggie's arm and led her away, with Maggie looking back over her shoulder until she was well out of the room.

The operation seemed to take forever. As Emily plied Maggie with cup after cup of tea, Grandpa O'Reilly resumed his seat beside her and held her hand. Nate paced aimlessly, while Mr. Carson calmly smoked his pipe, Edgar stood quietly by the range, Matilda hugged her daughter on her lap, and Frankie sat, eyes closed and hands folded, at the table.

Finally they heard the sound of the bedroom door opening in the new wing. Maggie was instantly on her feet, meeting Dr. Lightner in the corridor before he had taken two steps into it.

"I got all the bullets out," he told her as he dried his hands with a towel. "That one in his leg was mighty deep."

"How will he be?" she asked. Her heart was beating against her rib cage.

"He's lost a lot of blood, so we'll have to wait and see if he will be able to recover his strength. Build him up. Give him fluids and beef tea. A little at a time at first, though. Ether can make people nauseated. The arm was a flesh wound and, as far as I can tell, the bullet to the chest was rather shallow and did not touch his lung. But as for that leg," he shook his head, "I'm just not sure, Maggie."

She swallowed and screwed up her courage. "Please be plain with me."

"All right." Dr. Lightner was a man only in his 50s, but somehow looked much older at that moment. "If the wound festers, I fear he may lose the leg. It is difficult for me to tell what damage has been done, but my guess is that the best we can hope is for him to walk with a cane."

"Thank you," she whispered as she searched her heart for even a scrap of extra strength.

A tired smile lifted the corners of his salt and pepper mustache. "You should be very proud of your daughter, Maggie. She is quite a nurse. And that Patrick – he has a natural gift. When things settle down, I am thinking of asking both of them to apprentice with me. The town is growing. I need help."

"They would like that very much, I'm sure, doctor."

He placed a hand on her shoulder then nodded toward the door. "Why don't you go in and see him now?"

As Maggie entered the room, Lydia and Patrick were just finishing cleaning up and gathering the items used for the surgery. On her way out the door, Lydia gave her mother a tender kiss on the cheek.

Once the door shut behind them, Maggie was alone with Eli, with her love. She pulled a chair to the bedside and sat down so she could look at him. She was relieved to see that he was breathing softly, but his skin was extremely pale.

Without warning, tears flooded her eyes. Exhausted, grieving, and bewildered, Maggie slumped and buried her face into the quilt, where finally, she began to weep long and hard.

Nothing made sense: poor, frightened, angry Carrie; poor deluded Jeremiah; lust, violence, murder, poison, hatred, and bullets; Eli injured and fighting for his life.

The pervasive presence of sin and evil gnawed at her heart, mocking her faith and hope. It whispered that love was a fraud –

something that she turned to so she wouldn't recoil in horror at the coldness of the world and the wickedness of people's hearts.

Not true, her better self argued. Love is real, it is powerful, and it will survive when nothing else does. Love will never die.

Once she had cried her heart out, Maggie sat up. As she looked down at her husband, she took a handkerchief from her sleeve, wiped her tears, and blew her nose. She sniffed once, twice, and then she took a huge breath.

She had a job to do.

With one last look at Eli, she stood and left the bedroom for the kitchen. She and Mr. Carson needed to write an article.

****

The next day, at around 10:30 in the morning, Frankie, Patrick, Mr. Carson, and Maggie set out for the jail for the last time. Blaineton's square was crammed with people. Some of the more agile among them had climbed into the trees in the green and were perched on the sturdier branches. Others had scrambled up onto the roof tops. The four from the rooming house passed a vendor selling booklets describing Jeremiah Madison's crimes. Another vendor was selling food. A few steps further and they found a man hawking photographs of Jeremiah. Someone else claimed that he had the murderer's autograph for sale.

It was a carnival. People were selling thrills at every turn. The scene nearly made Maggie sick. A man was about to be executed, and people were earning a profit from his name and story. She wanted to shut her eyes and ears, but that, of course, was impossible. And so they pushed their way past all types and conditions of people – farmers, women of questionable repute who apparently were doing brisk business that day, old ladies in old-fashioned dress, fashionable young women and men, and small boys sucking on gingerbread and rock candy. Knots of men sharing a bottle or a jug clustered here and there. It was a great rowdy party – everyone laughing, jostling, shouting, eating, drinking – all punctuated by occasional scuffles.

This was not the death of a neighbor gone wrong, but an event, an occasion. Maggie's heart pounded wildly with anxiety and disgust. She thought that she had understood the depth of sin after being exposed to Leah's poisoning and Carrie's suicide, but now she realized that she had only brushed the surface. Sin entered into all people at each and every opportunity. Even good folk, like most of those in the Blaineton Square, could turn ugly given the right opportunity. And this was one of those opportunities.

Representatives of the county militia were stationed at each entrance to the courthouse and jail. No one could get in without the proper documentation. Mr. Carson took charge at this point, showing the passes for Frankie, Maggie, and Patrick, and displaying his own ticket. Once they were inside, the comparative quiet came as a blessed relief. Mr. Carson escorted Maggie to the jail, while Patrick shyly did the same for Frankie, who appeared baffled at this display of chivalry. The group paused one last time before entering the cell block.

"I will wait down the hall," Mr. Carson said softly. He patted Maggie's arm and then with a slight bow, left.

Now it was Patrick's turn. He looked Frankie in the face. "I'll sit with you while your mother goes outside. I don't want you to be alone."

She blinked her hazel eyes. "Thank you."

"It's just – you know – you shouldn't be alone and – I want to be here."

Maggie could see that Frankie suddenly understood his meaning. "That will be a great comfort," she said.

The three then sat with Jeremiah for two hours. During that time they sang hymns, prayed, and shared stories. As the hour drew near, Jeremiah asked Frankie to pray one last time with him.

The girl bowed her head. "Our Father, we commend the soul of Jeremiah Madison to Thy eternal care. We ask that he may have peace, courage, and strength in his last minutes. May he be surrounded by the peace that passeth all understanding, and be assured that he has been forgiven in the name of Thy Son, Jesus. Amen."

And, then to Maggie's surprise, Jeremiah prayed for them. "Heavenly Father, I beseech Thee that these people here before me and those in the rooming house will continue to walk in Christ's way and to live with love, courage, and honor. I give them into the care of Thy Holy Ghost and Thy dear Son. Amen."

When they looked up, the jailer and the Reverend Mr. Arthur were standing at the door. With a smile, Jeremiah rose. He kissed the two women on the cheek and shook Patrick's hand. "Goodbye," was all he said. The procession then left the cell: a praying Mr. Arthur walking first, Jeremiah following, and the jailer behind.

Trembling, Maggie rose and took a step toward the cell door. "I must go." Without warning, she fell into tears and covered her face with her hands. "How can I? How can I do this?"

Frankie immediately flew to her mother's side and put her arms round her. "You must do it. For Eli. I'll be fine, Mama." She glanced over her shoulder at the blushing boy who sat on one of the rough wooden chairs. "Patrick will stay with me. Mr. Carson will stand with you."

Nodding, Maggie took her handkerchief from her sleeve and mopped her face. Then, straightening her shoulders, she walked out of the cell.

A few seconds later, she found herself standing beside Mr. Carson. A light wind was moving through the bare branches. It whisked almost tenderly across Maggie's face, but left a chill echo behind. As it moved, the breeze caressed the noose on the gallows, causing it to swing gently for a moment.

Within a few minutes, Jeremiah was led out. The crowd fell silent, but muffled noise from the mob outside the courthouse walls seeped in. The young minister held his head up as he climbed the stairs and stepped to the trap door. Then he stood, head bowed, as Mr. Arthur prayed over him one last time. When the prayer was over, the jailer asked, "Have you any last words?"

Jeremiah looked out over the people who would witness his death and said in a clear, strong voice, "I have done wrong, grievous wrong and for this I am happy to take my punishment. But I also know that my Lord has forgiven me and that my soul, praise God, has been cleansed. May this God, who has dealt so kindly with me, keep you safe from sin this day and for ever more."

The jailer passed a white handkerchief to him. "When you are ready, you may drop this."

Jeremiah nodded. With that, the hangman placed the hood over his head, followed by the noose over his neck.

Mr. Carson slipped his arm reassuringly through Maggie's, but a great dread fell upon her. She had never witnessed a hanging. She whispered quickly, "You must watch, for I cannot."

The older gentleman patted her arm in agreement. As Maggie squeezed her eyes shut, she could hear Jeremiah praying softly under the hood – and then he fell silent.

In the next second there was the sound of a lever being pulled and a body falling with a dull thud. Maggie grimaced, pressing her face further into Mr. Carson's shoulder, and she waited tensely.

"Mr. Madison is still," the old writer murmured. "I believe his neck broke straightaway. Dr. Lightner is walking over to the body. Now he is putting a stethoscope to Jeremiah's heart and listening. Ah, he is looking up now and nodding to the jailer. The jailer has signaled one of the guards, who will fire his rifle to announce that Mr. Madison has expired."

The crack of the rifle triggered a great roar from the crowd beyond the jailhouse walls.

Mr. Carson patted Maggie's arm once more. "Let us go. We will fetch your daughter and Patrick."

As they passed the gallows, Maggie steeled herself and dared to take a peek. Jeremiah's hooded body hung motionless and slack. She could barely comprehend what she was seeing. Just the same, her heart fell to her feet. Oh, Lord, she prayed desperately, please welcome him, do not shun him.

Upon returning to the cell, she found her daughter sitting next to Patrick. The girl's face was drawn and tear-stained. Impulsively, Maggie rushed over and scooped her into her arms. Frankie hugged back fiercely. Her body was blessedly warm and alive. Maggie pressed her cheek against her daughter's head. "It is all right," she whispered. "He is with Jesus." She no longer was sure she believed what she was saying, but she knew that her daughter needed to hear the words. Oh, please, she prayed in the midst of her darkness, let the light return. Please, dear Lord.

They could hear "Madison is dead!" shouted over and over as if it were something to celebrate. Upon stepping into the street, the four discovered a madhouse of people cheering and hooting and shouting. Men and women were drinking out of bottles and jugs. Near the Presbyterian Church, people were dancing a reel as if they were at a wedding. Some of men, in broad daylight and in the midst of the crowd, were doing things with women best left private. The gathering had become a macabre party, but the host – the one who called the party – was dead and so all were celebrating.

Somber in the midst of the revelry, the quartet did not go unnoticed.

"There they are!" a man cried. "The ones he lived with. Why are they so sad? Madison's dead."

"That woman must be mad. Her niece is dead of poison and she mourns the poisoner!"

"Cheer up, madam, the devil is dead!"

"Perhaps she had a part in it!"

"Yeah, did you poison the girl, as well?"

Their voices were chilling. Maggie, fearing for their safety, was relieved to see that they were only steps from the rooming house. Carson, who was sheltering her from the mob, began to quicken his pace. In seconds, the lunacy of the streets had been left behind.

They walked silently down the hall, their footsteps sounding unbearably loud. But once they entered the kitchen, they were welcomed into warmth and light. Maggie accepted the mug of hot, strong tea that Lydia pressed into her hands. Edgar, Grandpa O'Reilly, Nate and Emily joined them at the table. And so they all sat – sipping, but not speaking – for quite some time.

Finally, Maggie caught Mr. Carson's eye. He nodded silently, and the two of them rose and walked to the parlor, where they would write the details of the execution.

****

From Maggie's Journal, 3 April 1861

It has been a long time since I picked up a pen, Journal. I simply have not had the strength.

Last night I dreamt about John Blaine. This time, he simply smiled at me as if to say, "All will be well."

But I do not see how all will be well, for all is still chaos. It is as if I have been transported to the world before Creation. I struggle vainly to swim in a dark, roiling sea. I feel as if my soul is gone and the shell of my body and my mind are left to go about their daily tasks.

As Eli requested, Mr. Carson and I wrote the articles about Carrie and Mr. Madison. The others helped us lay the type and leading and together we printed the special issue of the *Gazette*. I could scarcely stand to be in the paper's office. My mind kept seeing the horror that had happened there, despite the fact that the blood had been washed away and the room put to rights. Whether our communal effort "scooped" the other papers, I do not know, nor do I care. I only know that this was Eli's wish and that I had to make it so.

I sit writing in Jeremiah's old chamber, as my husband is resting. He has passed the crisis and is recovering his strength daily. His leg wound has not festered. For this I am grateful, but so much is still unknown.

How odd it is to be in this room and not have Jeremiah around! When I look back on the recent events, I see that he was not an evil man, nor was Carrie an evil girl. Just the same, through them, my town, my family, and I have felt the touch of Satan: lust, jealousy, anger, hatred, violence. And I, I walked into the Valley of the Shadow of Death, believing that my Lord would be with me each step – but now I am trapped in that Valley, alone and in the dark. I see Leah's pale, dead face; Jeremiah's body at the end of a rope; Carrie shattering her head with a cold, relentless bullet. My husband lies in bed, his body wounded. My baby was aborted by the madness of arsenic. Brothers and sisters in my church, for whom I once had great affection and whose behaviors I believed to be merely quirks, became mad dogs, snarling after Jeremiah's blood.

Like Jesus, I cry out, "*Eli, Eli, lama sabachthani?*" Where are you, my God? Will you leave me in the dark forever? And if you do, how will I be able to live without your presence?

****

Maggie sighed, laid her pen aside, and blotted the ink on the page. She heard Emily's footsteps in the hall. She was coming to check on Eli. The door to the bedroom opened and Maggie heard her friend enter.

Suddenly a loud ruckus commenced.

"No!" Emily was shouting. "Oh, no, no, no!!" Footsteps flew to Jeremiah's room before Maggie had a chance to get out of her chair. "Come quick, Maggie! Now! Hurry!"

Alarmed, she rose and as she did she heard a great clumping and thumping. Dashing into the hall, she was met by the sight of Eli, dressing gown thrown over his night shirt and perched on two homemade crutches. Standing in the doorway to their bedroom, he gave her a crooked grin.

"What on earth –" she gasped.

"Got tired of lying in that bed," he replied as he thumped toward her.

Maggie's hands flew to her mouth.

"As soon as Patrick made the crutches, I practiced in our room when no one was around," and he thudded past her and into the kitchen.

Eyes glistening with tears, Maggie turned to Emily. The two women laughed, cried, and then fell into each other's arms.

Finally, Emily turned her friend around and pointed her toward the kitchen. "Go on," she whispered. "Make sure he doesn't fall."

Maggie caught up to her husband in time to hear him saying, "It's a beautiful day out there. It's a shame to waste it inside."

Hovering over him like a nervous mother hen, Maggie followed Eli through the kitchen and out onto to the back porch. She watched as he maneuvered the crutches and, with some effort, lowered himself onto a chair. He heaved a sigh, and then indicated the chair beside him.

As she sat down, Maggie finally found the voice to say, "Are you sure you ought to be doing this?"

"A man can only lie around so long."

"But how does your leg feel?"

"Hurts like hell." He waited for her to chastise him. When she didn't, he said, "Yesterday I read the articles you and Carson wrote last week. You're an excellent writer, you know."

She blushed. "You say that because I'm your wife."

Eli pushed his spectacles up his nose. "My dear woman, I'm not saying that you write well because you're my wife. I'm saying it because, as an editor, I know good writing when I see it. I want a *good reporter* as a reporter, not a woman, not a man. You have the talent and the instincts." A few second passed. "You know," he added, attempting to sound casual, "I've been thinking. I believe we can build the *Gazette* into a fine regional paper. We could even go from a weekly to a daily publication. Of course, when I say 'easily,' I mean with a whole lot of work. But we could do it."

Maggie was stunned. "Do you mean you, Mr. Carson, *and me?*"

He nodded.

"But I must run the boarding house. I can't–"

"Ah, that, well, I've been thinking about that, too. Lying around all day does that to you, you know. Anyway, it seems to me that Emily and Lydia are more than adept at running Second Street. In fact, they make an excellent team. And now that Matilda's here, they have an extra set of hands. Trust me. Things will run smooth as silk without you."

"Without me? But—"

He laughed. "You know, Maggie, I think you treat the house and the people in it like your child. You gave birth to it and you nurtured it. But a time comes when you have to let it grow up."

"And so I become unnecessary?"

"No, you're very necessary – to me. The *Gazette* needs you." His voice softened. "And *I* need you, Maggie."

She fell silent and stared out at the yard and at Eli's little shop beyond. Even though the shattering violence had passed, she could still feel the chaos of its echoes, even from the back porch. A kind of exhaustion permeated the *Gazette* building, the yard, and even the boarding house.

But now Eli was offering her growth and change and life.

"I need you, too," she finally whispered, blinking a tear from her eye. As she shifted her gaze to the chicken coop, she saw that the old oak nearby had begun to sprout small red buds on its branches. "Eli, the oak…" A frown creased her forehead. "It's budding."

The air had a warm promise to it, even though it was early April. And, as she took in the yard, Maggie was taken aback to discover a yellow blush creeping along the forsythia bushes. And when she saw the garden, she couldn't believe her eyes. "Are those daffodils?" she asked.

He looked in the direction of the garden. "I believe so."

"So soon?" She got up, walked down the steps, and approached the flower bed. "Oh, they are daffodils!" Bending over, she gently touched one of the bright yellow cups. The bloom was soft as velvet. "I shall have to clean the bed of all the winter debris."

Inside the house, little Natey began to cry. Maggie heard Emily gently shush him and then start singing softly in her rich alto voice. Chloe's voice chimed in too as she talked to the baby.

Straightening up, Maggie glanced back at the house. As she did, Frankie and Patrick came out the kitchen door. They saw Eli and stopped to speak with him for a moment. Then they spotted her.

"Mama," Frankie called. "We're going to walk round the square, if that is all right."

When she nodded, the two proceeded down the steps, into the yard, and turned toward the street. Patrick reached for Frankie's hand. And she gave it to him.

A slight smile touched Maggie's lips. "Why, I do believe they're courting."

"Spring," was all Eli said.

Spring.

After the dark and cold of winter, the warmth and beauty of spring was emerging. It was such a blessed, blessed relief.

And with that thought, her smile broadened, because now it all made sense.

She had never been abandoned to the dark. Not ever. God had been there, quietly working to bring forth the spring. And now winter was over, and new life had begun.

For the first time in what seemed like ages, Maggie felt at peace. More than that, she felt genuinely loved. She remembered the Apostle Paul's words, "And now abideth faith, hope, charity, these three, but the greatest of these is charity."

The greatest is love.

She was loved by Eli, by her daughters, by her rooming house family – and by God, always by God.

A warmth kindled in her heart and began to spread. Maggie smiled once again, and then walked back to the porch where Eli was waiting.

EPILOGUE

From Maggie's Journal, 16 April 1861

Yesterday, President Lincoln declared the situation with the South to be an insurrection, after the bombardment and surrender of Fort Sumter. He has requested that 75,000 volunteers join up to serve the military for a period of three months. Patrick and Edgar say that they will volunteer. Lydia and Frankie, of course, are at once proud of them and frightened for them. Nate also wished to join up but, I am sad to say, colored men are not wanted by our Army. This tells me that the North is little better than the South, and we do not consider colored people as equals. I cannot understand how we refuse to recognize the humanity of the very people we endeavor to free. All of which makes me wonder what kind of status they will have, should the North prevail.

The changes over the past year for my country and my family have been great. In the spring of 1860, I would not have been able nor would have dared to imagine that which has transpired.

Escaped slaves now live under our roof, rather than hide underground. Matilda and her daughter, Chloe, have taken up residence in Mr. Madison's old room and are a happy addition to our home. We say that Matilda is Emily's widowed cousin, should slave hunters dare enter our little town. Of course that is unlikely, as the newly-declared state of war will make null the Fugitive Slave Act. Just the same, there is talk among the town folk, since our household on the Square now has *two* colored families in it. Their presence shocks the less enlightened, who would like to keep those of a darker hue contained to Water Street. Frankly, I care not for what *they* may think. I only do what our Lord would have me do, which is to love others. Matilda risked her freedom and her daughter's freedom to bring the help that saved Eli's life. I owe her more than I can repay. Am I then to say, "Well done, now go live in a shack"? If I could, I would bring everyone from Water Street to the Square! Of course, I would promptly be pilloried – but it would be well worth it.

My brother, Samuel, comes to visit me more and more. He and I are becoming brother and sister once again, and I could sing for joy. He would like me to return to the M.E.C., and says that those who railed so unmercifully against Jeremiah Madison are a few. I know most at the church are good-hearted people who endeavor to follow our Lord – but, Journal, I am happy worshiping God in the harness shop with the A.M.E. congregation. My spiritual home is with them.

And good news! This day we learned that we shall have yet another addition to our home: Eli and I have been approved to adopt little Bob from the orphanage. Now that Eli is up and about, we are ready to make at least one child's life better. Perhaps we will adopt more children as time goes by. I should like that.

Life is not static. It ebbs and flows, like the tide – always changing, always moving. Eli must use a cane these days to get around. I fear that his injuries will leave him with a slight disability; but that is a trifle when compared to the fact that he has his life and his leg. The good news is that he does not need his legs to write and edit! So far, his injury has not diminished his enthusiasm for his beloved *Gazette* or for the ones he loves.

I am quite pleased and more than a bit delighted at my new title: reporter. I shall be doing what I always had thought was impossible! My daily routine has been exploded, and a future I cannot predict lies before me. It is both unnerving and deliciously exciting.

I am not naïve, though. All will not be rosy. It never is. Difficult times lie ahead. I do not know how war will touch our small community and our family. Just the same, I cling stubbornly to hope and love – because I know without a doubt that light vanquishes darkness, and that the promise of spring lives even in the deepest of winter.

I know this because we have already lived through a terrible thing, something that has shaken the very core of our souls. I was made privy to things that I did not wish to learn: Acclaim and praise, as welcoming as they are, easily warp a man's understanding of himself; the visages of beauty, talent, and power will seduce; jealousy, abandonment, greed, and anger inevitably lead people to do fearful things; and good, Christian folk will turn their backs on Christ in favor of hatred, anger, and vengeance – willfully stopping up their ears to our Lord's message of mercy, compassion, and love.

Thus, what I have seen and experienced should cause me to curl up and tremble.

But I refuse to do this, for my soul also knows that there is something greater, stronger, and more powerful than that which I can perceive. As the Apostle Paul said, "For now we see through a glass, darkly; but then face to face: now I know in part; but then shall I know even as also I am known." Thus, I am content knowing that I simply cannot see the entire picture. I cannot even perceive how near God is to my every breath! I am mortal, and so I rest easy in the knowledge that all will be revealed when I leave this world and go to the next.

The truth is that tragedy and sorrow strikes us all. Death will come without warning. Like a starving wolf, war will consume soldiers, civilians, property, and perhaps friends and family. And yet there is a greater Truth, so these things no longer have the power to frighten me. I have learned that three things abide when all else crumbles: faith, hope, and charity. And, as the Apostle says, "the greatest of these is charity."

When I saw John Blaine, I caught a glimpse of heaven and God's love. When I was mired in melancholy and despair, I found that love in the new life of spring, a baby's cry, a mother's lullaby, and a boy and a girl holding hands. I found God's love also in the scrubbing of pots and pans, and in the sacrifice made by a slave woman. And I find that love in my dear husband's eyes and smile.

So I hold fast to God's love. But it is not sentimental love. It is stubborn love – a ferocious love – a love that refuses to let go – the kind of love that God has for us even when we can't feel His presence and even when we are so entranced by ourselves and our world that we cannot hear Him calling to us. It is the kind of love that sent a beloved Son to live among us and allowed him to be mercilessly killed – but a love that also refused to let murder be the last word and responded with the glory of the Resurrection. Yes, God's love is among us, ever abiding, and will not let go.

God's love never fails.

ACKNOWLEDGEMENTS

I would like to thank Dr. Leigh Eric Schmidt for shepherding me through the process of researching and writing the original paper while I was at Drew University. He along with my advisor, Dr. Kenneth E. Rowe, taught me invaluable lessons about the discipline and joy of scholarship. I cannot thank either one of them enough.

Thanks go to friends and family who offered support, criticism and proof reading: Elaine Hudson, Joanna Sasso, Dr. Paula Cameron, Dr. Brid Nicholson, Rev. David Lehmkuhl, my pile of crazy cousins, my sister Diane Stafford and her partner Sarah Grey Thompson, and my step-daughter Kristina Shebchuk. Thanks also to all the many other people who knew I was doing this and cheered me on.

Finally, I want to thank my love, Charles G. "Dan" Bush. (Don't ask why he's called Dan when his given name is Charles Gordon, it's a long story.) He pushed me to pull out my old manuscript, do several more drafts, and get it published. Dan, you really have been the Eli to my Maggie. I love you, dude!

NOTES

This novel has its roots in a paper I wrote around 1995 while in graduate school at Drew University, Madison, NJ. The class was a tutorial with Dr. Leigh Eric Schmidt, who is now at Harvard University. Our topic was ministry and scandal, and in my research I found a story about the Rev. Jacob Harden, a young pastor in Warren County, NJ. Harden apparently was a gifted preacher, charismatic, good looking – and a ladies' man, to boot. A few un-chaperoned moments with young parishioner Louisa Dorland led to the inevitable shotgun marriage. Louisa and Harden had a rocky relationship and – this should come as no surprise since you have read the novel – in 1859 he murdered her.

Despite Harden's miserable home life, why he resorted to murder haunted me. A nagging wife and a shotgun marriage are difficult to content with, but why would this young minister resort to sprinkling arsenic on the apples he gave Louisa to eat? It is clear that his career as a clergyman was taking off, and most likely a bad marriage would hold him back. Without a doubt, a divorce would have had dire results for his career. But didn't he know that murder would not only end his career, but his own life, as well? Apparently not, for in an autobiographical pamphlet entitled *Life, Confession, and Letters of Courtship of Rev. Jacob S. Harden, of the M.E. Church, Mount Lebanon, Hunterdon Co., N.J.* (Hackettstown, N.J.: E. Winton, Printer, 1860), Harden incredibly states that he did not know poisoning was a capital offense and he did not know arsenic was detectable. So when I wrote my story, I wanted Madison's reasons for poisoning Leah to be equally vague, confusing, and unsatisfying.

My original research paper focused on how Harden was portrayed by the media of his time. I discovered that the further a newspaper was from Warren County, the more likely it was that Harden would be portrayed as evil. For example, *The Warren Journal* was nearly sympathetic, portraying him as a poor boy gone wrong. *The Easton Evening Express* (Easton, Pennsylvania) saw Harden as a moral monster, but had sympathy for his family. *The New-York Times*, meanwhile, took the hardest line, painting Harden as a devilish confidence man, portraying the parishioners who visited him as fools, and lambasting the carnivalesque crowd that gathered outside the Belvidere jail on the day of his execution.

It is from these sources that I built the environment surrounding Madison's arrest, trial, and execution. Harden's execution – and in turn Madison's – was very much like a rock festival, a carnival-like party. Tickets were actually distributed to control who witnessed the murderer's death – and some tickets apparently were scalped. And people were actually selling souvenirs to the crowd that invaded the town.

The attitudes expressed in the news articles also helped me understand the ambiguity that often surrounds those who commit murder, as did Karen Halttunen's essay, "Early American Murder Narratives: The Birth of Horror" (*The Power of Culture: Critical Essays in American History.* Ed. Richard Wightman Fox and T. J. Jackson Lears. Chicago: The University of Chicago Press, 1993). It seems we have been struggling to understand why people commit murder for as long as humans have been around. How often do we hear of a heinous crime committed by a person whom neighbors inevitably describe as quiet, polite, friendly, and private? We want to label the murderer as a soulless monster, but frequently cannot rectify his or her violent actions with other more benign aspects of his or her personhood. For instance, the murderer may be charming, friendly, or even caring. And so we are left to decide that he/she must be a hypocrite, a liar, mentally ill, or perhaps even possessed. Regardless, our explanations and diagnoses are usually unsatisfying. Perhaps our Puritan forebears were correct. Their public executions usually included a sermon to remind the crowd that any of them could commit a similar crime. There but for the grace of God go us.

While Harden lived in a rooming house, there are no details about his landlord/landlady. And certainly I do not believe there was anyone around like Maggie Blaine Smith. When I first thought about writing a story based on Harden's case, I decided that it would be interesting to tell my story through the eyes of the woman who ran a boarding house. Somehow she became the unconventional Maggie.

Truthfully, her attitudes regarding the full humanity of African-Americans would have been advanced for her time – but I like to think that her long friendship with Emily and Nate shaped her beliefs. Also, it is important to note that Emily and Nate were the ones who drew

Maggie and Eli into helping with the Underground Railroad. Most white Northerners were not involved in this act of civil disobedience, although it has often been portrayed that way. There is also some scholarly controversy regarding the numbers of slaves who passed through the Underground Railroad. But, as it was designed to be secret, I doubt that we will ever know how many escaped in this way. So, to those who feel that too many slaves visited the rooming house, I apologize. This is, after all, fiction.

The Water Street community in Blaineton is small. That is because race relations in New Jersey were poor and, as a document in the Digital Collections of the New Jersey State Library indicates, the African-American population declined dramatically in the state, from 8.0 at the time of the 1800 census to 3.8 by the 1860 census (author unknown, "Afro-Americans in New Jersey," p.16; http://www.njstatelib.org/NJ_Information/Digital_Collections/Afro-Americans/AFAMB.pdf). Given those facts, I decided that the Water Street community was comprised of about 5-6 families. The white population probably would have been content to have them remain there – and certainly would not want African Americans living in a house prominently located on the town square!

Maggie's forays into women's rights would have been rare for a woman of her time, but not improbable. If a female in her situation had been given Margaret Fuller's book, it very well might have stimulated her to think about other possibilities and pushed her to want more opportunities for her daughters.

Within the overall movement for women's rights, females of the time also argued that they too could be called into ministry as preachers and church leaders. Religious and secular goals often overlapped in the nineteenth century and, in my opinion, the compartmentalization of the religious and secular does not fully overtake American culture until the mid-to-late twentieth century. Thus, a budding feminist such as Frankie may very well have dreamed of going to Oberlin and of entering some kind of ministry. Early in the nineteenth century, the experiences of the Second Great Awakening gave permission for women to preach, the argument being that the God calls and gifts the soul, not the sex. Even though many opposed it, there were a number of women preachers circulating in the nineteenth century, among them Sojourner Truth, Phoebe Palmer, Antoinette Brown Blackwell, Jarena Lee, Anna Howard Shaw, and Amanda Berry Smith.

I am not certain that a good, nineteenth-century evangelical like Maggie would have walked out of her church and into an African-American congregation. However, her response does fit in with the spiritual struggle she has during her "dark night of the soul." She also obviously was influenced by Eli's lapsed-Quaker, emerging progressive perspectives.

The bad behavior by the Moore sisters and a few others in the Blaineton Methodist congregation come from my own experiences, having served in six congregations (to date) and witnessed first-hand how a few people are more at home with a belief system emphasizing legalism and punishment. Sadly, this sometimes leads them to behave in a destructive and un-Christian manner. But let me make one thing very clear: Congregations are not comprised of saints, but recovering sinners. Those who complain that churches are full of hypocrites and un-Jesus-like types are correct – but that is because on any given day someone is having a bad moment or a struggle. Holiness is not 24/7 purity and goodness, but rather a journey and a process.

Finally, this novel is not really about scholarship and historical studies. It is a *story*. I told it because it was worth telling. We live in a world that is every bit as uncertain as Maggie's. We choose how we will respond to that world and the journey that we call life. Like Maggie, I believe the journey is about faith, hope, and love – but primarily about love. So we have a choice. We may cave in to the forces of darkness and violence – or we may vanquish them with the power of love.

DEFINITIONS AND BIBLE REFERENCES

Definitions

Call: the sense that God wants one to enter the ministry.

Camp Meeting: an event usually held in the woods or a field provided by a farmer. Participants camped out for one to three weeks, listened to preaching and exhortations, sang hymns, and took part in prayer meetings. Some camp meeting grounds still exist and some are still in operation, such as the Ocean Grove Camp Meeting Association in Ocean Grove, NJ.

Corsage: bodice

Eli, Eli, lama sabachthani: Translates as "My God, my God, why hast thou forsaken me?" Jesus' prayer on the cross found in Matthew 27:46. Jesus is praying from Psalm 22:1.

Five Points: a notorious slum in New York City

Holy of holies: the name given to the most holy place in the Jerusalem Temple. It was believed to house the Presence of God and held the Ark of the Covenant, upon which a yearly sacrifice took place to cleanse the Jewish people from their sin.

Lord's Supper: a ritual that involves eating a small piece of bread and drinking a little wine and serves as a reminder of Jesus Christ's presence with the congregation. In 1864 the General Conference of the Methodist Episcopal Church recommended that Methodists use grape juice, rather than wine in the sacrament; eventually this led to Methodist organizations using only grape juice. In Maggie's day, however, it is possible that her congregation may have imbibed wine.

Parable of the Prodigal Son: See Luke 15

Pinkerton: someone who works for the Pinkerton Detective Agency, which was founded in 1850 by Allen Pinkerton

Presiding Elder: a minister charged with oversight of a district (an administrative unit made up of Methodist churches in a particular geographic location).

BIBLE

All quotes are from the King James Version

And now abideth faith, hope, charity, these three, but the greatest of these is charity.

1 Corinthians 13:13

And this is his commandment, that we should believe on the name of his Son Jesus Christ, and love one another, as he gave us commandment.

1 John 3:23

Behold, I send you forth as sheep in the midst of wolves: be ye therefore wise as serpents, and harmless as doves.

Matthew 10:16

For now we see through a glass, darkly; but then face to face: now I know in part; but then shall I know even as also I am known.

1 Corinthians 13:12

He that saith he is in the light, and hateth his brother, is in darkness even until now. He that loveth his brother abideth in the light, and there is none occasion of stumbling in him.

1 John 2:9—10

He told Jesus that he had spoken the truth, 'for there is one God; and there is none other but he: And to love him with all the heart, and with all the understanding, and with all the soul, and with all the strength, and to love his neighbor as himself, is more than all whole burnt offerings and sacrifices.' And to that Jesus responded, 'Thou art not far from the kingdom of God.'

Mark 12:32-34

Hear, O Israel; The Lord our God is one Lord: And thou shalt love the Lord thy God with all thy heart, and with all thy soul, and with all thy mind, and with all thy strength: this is the first commandment. And the second is like, namely this, Thou shalt love thy neighbor as thyself. There is none other commandment greater than these.

Mark 12:29-31

I was in prison, and ye came unto me.

Matthew 25:36

If they cannot contain, let them marry; for it is better to marry than to burn.

1 Corinthians 7:9

Judge not, and ye shall not be judged; condemn not, and ye shall not be condemned: forgive, and ye shall be forgiven.

Luke 6:37

Love your enemies, bless them that curse you, do good to them that hate you, and pray for them which despitefully use you, and persecute you.

Matthew 5:39-6:1

My little children, let us not love in word, neither in tongue; but in deed and in truth.'

1 John 3:18

Stand fast therefore in the liberty wherewith Christ hath made us free, and *be not entangled again* with the yoke of bondage.

Galatians 5:1

There is neither Jew nor Greek, there is neither bond nor free, there is neither male nor female.

1 Galatians 3:28

Though I speak with the tongues of men and of angels, and *have not charity*, I am become as sounding brass, or a tinkling cymbal.

1 Corinthians 13:1

What doth the Lord require of thee, but to do justly, and to love mercy, and to walk humbly with thy God?

Micah 6:8

HYMNS

The two hymns in the book are "O For a Thousand Tongues to Sing" and "And Can It Be that I Should Gain," both by Charles Wesley. The hymns' texts come from *Hymns for the Use of The Methodist Episcopal Church with Tunes for Congregational Worship* (New York: Carlton & Porter, 1857).

LaVergne, TN USA
15 March 2011
220251LV00001B/4/P